By Stone
By Blade
By Fire

A Barbara Holloway Mystery

ALSO BY KATE WILHELM

A Flush Of Shadows
All For One
And The Angels Sing
A Sense Of Shadow
A Wrongful Death
Abyss
Better Than One
(with Damon Knight)
By Stone, By Blade, By Fire
Cambio Bay
Casebook Of Charlie and Constance
(Volumes 1&2)
Children Of The Wind
City Of Cain
Clear And Convincing Proof
Cold Case
Crazy Time
Death Of An Artist
Death Qualified, A Mystery Of
Chaos
Defense For The Devil
Desperate Measures
Fault Lines
For The Defense
(aka Malice Prepense)
Heaven Is High
Huysman's Pets
Juniper Time
Justice For Some
Let The Fire Fall
Listen, Listen
Margaret And I
More Bitter Than Death
Naming The Flowers
No Defense
Oh, Susannah!
Seven Kinds Of Death
Sister Angel
Skeletons
Sleight Of Hand
Smart House
Somerset Dreams And Other Fictions
Storyteller
Sweet, Sweet Poison
The Best Defense
The Clewiston Test
The Clone (with Theodore Thomas)
The Dark Door
The Deepest Water
The Downstairs Room
The Fullness Of Time
The Good Children
The Gorgon Field
The Hamlet Trap
The Hills Are Dancing
(with Richard Wilhelm)
The Infinity Box
The Killer Thing
The Mile-Long Spaceship
The Nevermore Affair
The Price Of Silence
The Unbidden Truth
The Winter Beach
Torch Song
Welcome, Chaos
Where Late The Sweet Birds Sang
Whisper Her Name
With Thimbles, With Forks, And Hope
Year Of The Cloud
(with Theodore Thomas)

A complete bibliography may be found at katewilhelm.com.
Ebooks are available at infinityboxpress.com.

By Stone By Blade By Fire

A Barbara Holloway Mystery

Kate Wilhelm

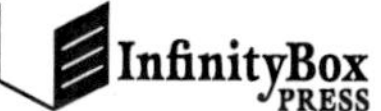

ISBN-13: 978-1-62205-012-3

By Stone, By Blade, By Fire
Kate Wilhelm

First edition

For more information, write to:
InfinityBox Press LLC
7060 North Borthwick Ave.
Portland, OR 97217
www.infinityboxpress.com

Designed by: Richard Wilhelm

CHAPTER 1

FRANK KNEW VERY well the office rule chiselled in stone: *No books are to be removed from the law library.* He had cut those words himself, decades before, when he first began stocking the shelves, but the two books he had just deposited on his desk were going home with him, his weekend reading, in his own good comfortable chair, with his own good reading lamp. He had a busy weekend lined up. Reading to do, and potatoes to plant before St. Patrick's Day. He glanced around in annoyance when there was a tap on his door, and, too quickly for him to say go away, the door opened.

"Frank—" Patsy started, and was stopped by a man pushing past her, leaning heavily on the door frame.

He was ash gray, breathing rapidly, and looked ready to sink into the floor. Frank hurried across his office and supported the man with his arm about his waist. "Come on, let's get you to the sofa. "Patsy, 911, *now*."

She nodded and scurried away as Frank led the stranger into his office and toward the sofa, but the man twisted around and lurched toward the desk and clients' chairs.

"Attorney agreement," he said in a strangled voice as he sank into one of the chairs. He was clutching a briefcase close to his body and kept it on his lap. A violent tremor shook him and he ducked his head, as if to suppress a moan. It was a futile effort. "Agreement… " he repeated in a whisper, not looking up.

Moving quickly Frank went to his desk and found a client-attorney agreement in the drawer. He put it down before the man and put a pen by it, but the new client, groping in his briefcase, appeared not to notice. He withdrew a manila envelope and with a visibly painful effort put it on the desk.

"Don't let them have it," he rasped in barely audible words. He tried to pick up the pen, his hand shaking so violently he couldn't grasp it.

"That can wait," Frank said. "You need medical attention."

"Now," the man said and attempted again to pick up the pen.

Leaning across the desk, Frank put the pen in his hand.

The man had just started to write when his body spasmed and he pitched forward, hit the desk with his shoulder and crashed to the floor, knocking over the chair as he fell. Frank ran around his desk to see the man crumpled, the chair partly on him, and papers from the briefcase scattered. He pulled the chair away, leaned over and felt for a pulse in the man's throat.

"Dear God!" Patsy cried, entering the office. "They're on the way. Is he dead?"

"I don't think so," Frank said, straightening, regarding the fallen man with a frown. "Who is he?"

"I don't know. Should we do something?"

Frank looked at her then. She was pale, staring wide-eyed at the man on the floor, and looked to be in shock. Patsy had been with him from the first day he had been able to afford a secretary, and until now he had never seen anything faze her. Annoy her, yes. Make her furious, absolutely. But put her in a state of shock, never. He touched her arm. "Go sit down. He doesn't need anything we can give him or do for him. The medics should be here any second now." When Patsy continued to stare at the man without moving, Frank took her by the arm, turned her around and pointed to the sofa across the office. "Go. Sit."

Walking stiffly, she crossed the office and sat on the edge of an easy chair.

Frank shook his head, then studied the man on the floor. He didn't think he was dead, but as close to death as a fellow could be and not yet crossed over. About five feet ten, sandy thin hair, no visible scars, medium weight, worn, faded jeans and a plaid flannel shirt, running shoes. Forty, forty-five years old? Hard to tell, he decided. That gray color, the shaking and moaning, made age a guess.

"Mr. Holloway, they said—" Elsie, the receptionist, gasped and moved out of the way as medics rushed in with a stretcher.

"What happened?" one of them said as he knelt by the man on the floor.

"He just collapsed and fell," Frank said. He went around his desk to sit as the medics went to work. It didn't take them long to get their patient hooked up to an IV, on the stretcher, and out the door. Only when they were gone did Frank rise and cross the room to where Patsy was still sitting like a statue.

"I'll get us some coffee," Frank said, touching her arm.

"You?" She looked up at him, then jumped to her feet. "No! I'll do it. I'll make coffee." She never let him make coffee, and he took in a breath of relief that his own Patsy was rejoining the land of the living.

"In a minute," he said. "First tell me what just happened here."

"Elsie called me and said a man wanted to see Mr. Bixby or you. She said maybe he was sick or drunk or something and I went out to see for myself. He was leaning on the front desk. I said I'd tell you, but he followed me, leaning against the wall most of the way. I asked him to wait a minute, but he kept coming." She was talking too fast, running words together.

"No name? Did he give his name to Elsie?"

"She said he didn't."

"He asked for Sam or me? In that order?"

"I don't know. That's what Elsie told me. Mr. Bixby is in Los Angeles, so she called me. I should go make coffee, shouldn't I?"

"No," Frank said. He went to the bookcase and opened the bar concealed behind it. "We both could use something a bit more potent than coffee."

He brought out brandy and two glasses. Patsy accepted the brandy without hesitation and drank it down as if it were medicine, as it probably was for her, Frank thought as he sipped his own. Spots of color flared on her cheeks and she looked just like she always had, a tubular woman with eternally black hair, determined to keep him from waiting on himself or anyone else. "If you're up to it, you could help me gather up that stuff," he said after a moment, eyeing the scattered papers.

"I'll do it," Patsy said quickly and put her glass on the coffee table.

"We'll both do it."

Lists of names, he realized a minute later as he picked up a folder and papers, examined some and stuffed them into the man's briefcase. Probably they had been in some kind of order originally, but that order was lost now. Just lists of names. Donors to a cause? Membership names? Voters? Not that, he thought, studying a sheet in his hand. *Medford.* Under this label, Mabel and Don Crusick, followed by numeral three. A family? He shook his head and added that last sheet to the ones in the briefcase.

"I guess if they revive that fellow, he'll come back for them," he said. "And if they don't, someone else will come by."

Patsy rose and automatically straightened her skirt, looking around as if searching for something else she should be doing.

"Go on home," Frank said, walking to the coffee table to retrieve his brandy and deposit the briefcase. "I'm going to sit at my desk and finish my drink. Then I'll be off. On your way out tell Elsie I'll have a word with her before she leaves." Going to the door with her, he said, "You heard him say he wanted an attorney-client agreement?"

"I thought that's what he was saying," she said. "I wasn't sure. Should I open a file for him?"

"Afraid not. He didn't get that far." Frank opened the door. "Go on home now."

A minute later, sitting at his desk, he brooded about the man who had collapsed, the agreement with an ink line running off the bottom, and about the envelope the man had thrust onto the desk. He felt certain that Patsy had not heard the fellow tell him not to "let them have it." Who? Not let *them* have it? Police? Someone else? Who?

Finally he drew the envelope closer and opened it, pulled out several papers, and blew out a sigh of exasperation. Lists of names, apparently like the others in the briefcase. Southern Oregon towns and cities followed by names. After glancing at several more papers, he replaced them all and closed the clasp envelope.

Frowning, he regarded the unsigned client agreement. That ragged line that had run off the paper made up his mind for him. He was a client, damn it. And he had charged Frank with not letting *them* have it, whoever they were. He picked up the envelope, crossed to his safe concealed in a paneled wall, opened the safe and placed the envelope inside.

Done, he put the brandy away, shoved his two books inside his briefcase, glanced about, and left his office to have a word with Elsie.

✦

Monday morning he was at a library table with a pile of books, his notebook, a legal pad, and several pens. He was not at all surprised when Patsy came to his side and said in a low voice that that man wanted to see him.

"Lieutenant Hogarth?"

She nodded. To her the lieutenant would always be *that man.*

"Well, let him cool his heels for a minute or two while I wash my hands," Frank said, rising. "Oh, Patsy, please bring us some coffee if you're not busy. Coffee first, then the lieutenant."

The coffee service was in place on the table by the sofa and easy chairs when Patsy showed Hogarth in. Frank motioned for Patsy to come in.

"Morning, Milt," Frank said, crossing to the comfortable seating arrangement. "So it was a homicide. Why don't you grill Patsy while I make like a host."

Milton Hogarth was a heavyset man with scant fading red hair and a pink scalp, sharp blue eyes, and a scowl that seemed permanent. He nodded and seated himself in the chair he always chose. "So what happened here on Friday?" he asked brusquely, turning his scowl onto Patsy.

Frank poured coffee, moved the cream and sugar across the table toward Hogarth, and listened to Patsy recount almost word for word what she had told him on Friday.

"What did he say to you?" Hogarth snapped.

"Nothing." She didn't quite snap back, but came close.

"Tell him what you heard the fellow say to me," Frank said.

"Something about an agreement, a client agreement. I couldn't hear it all. I was on my way to call 911."

"You just let a guy you didn't know walk in here without giving a name or—"

"Now, Milt," Frank said. "You asked her what happened and she told you. Good coffee, Patsy. Thank you." He nodded toward the door and she turned and walked out.

"My turn," Frank said after the door had closed. He told it succinctly, leaving out only the part about the envelope in his safe and the one thing the dying man had said to him. *Don't let them have it.* Police? Maybe, he thought. Maybe not.

Hogarth added cream and sugar to his coffee as Frank talked.

"Unknown fellow wanted either Sam or me, in that order," Frank said when he finished. "Suggests he wanted a senior partner, doesn't it? Who was he? What killed him?"

Hogarth hesitated, added more sugar to his already sweetened coffee, then said, "He was a nobody. A gofer. Robert Daggart. He did odd jobs for a Portland church. Came down from Portland with membership lists and was heading to California. The church bookkeeper said he stopped in just long enough to pick up another list to take down to Medford on his way and left. An hour, hour and a half later he shows up here beaten to a pulp. Died at four in the morning yesterday. Never regained consciousness." He drank coffee in big gulps.

"Not a visible mark on him," Frank said after a moment.

"They worked his body over. Internal bleeding. Both kidneys pretty much smashed, broken ribs, esophagus—" He stopped and drank more coffee. "You get the picture. The doctor said it was a miracle that he made it to your office. Not your usual blunt instrument," he added. "Loaded fists. A professional job." He helped himself to more coffee. "Jesus, Frank, it's ugly. The world just gets uglier."

Frank could only agree that this was ugly. A man with a roll of quarters in his fist, maybe both fists, beating a man to death. He didn't bother to ask about fingerprints, not with a professional job done by professionals.

He gave Hogarth a copy of the agreement with the line that ran off the paper, and the briefcase with church membership lists. There wasn't much more to be said and Hogarth summed it up tersely. The attackers must have left him for dead, but he had managed to drag himself to his car and drive it to the parking space reserved for Sam Bixby, then get to the office. The car had been towed and recovered by the police. The church would claim the body since Daggart had not listed any family in his personnel information. Finally, the coffee carafe empty, Hogarth heaved himself to his feet.

"I'm getting too old for this crap," he said on his way to the door. He paused there and muttered, "What the fuck was important enough for him to go through hell to get up here?"

Frank shook his head, deeply troubled. "I wish to God I knew."

✦

CHAPTER 2

BARBARA STOOD GAZING out her office window, seeing little or nothing on the street below. She glanced at her watch and cursed under her breath. Six minutes after four. The last time she looked, it had been five minutes past, and before that three minutes past four. It was a beautiful warm day, September at its best, a perfect day for a long walk, but she already put in overtime walking, until her thighs had become fire-hot and throbbing. No more walking, but neither could she stay in her office and watch the minutes drag by.

Todd and a couple of pals would be at the house working on advanced calculus and eating everything in sight; they would be talking and joking, one minute four-year-olds, the next adolescent boys who had not quite gotten used to being on the cusp of manhood.

"Dad's it is," she said under her breath. He could still be at his office and that would be fine. She and Darren were due there for dinner later anyway, and she'd show up early. She was not fit company for a snake and he might try to cheer her up, which she couldn't stand. Shelley had tried, Maria had tried, and all they had gained from their efforts was her silence and withdrawal. Either that or a scream, she admitted to herself. Silence was better.

She crossed her office to the door to the reception room where Maria, working on her computer, looked up with a too-cheerful smile when Barbara entered. Before Barbara could tell her to knock off and go home, the outer door opened and a woman walked in.

She was wearing a raw silk pantsuit, the exact shade of blue of her eyes. Nicely tanned, with a few freckles, thick short curly hair that probably had been blond but had darkened to a ripe wheat color, forty-something, she was handsome rather than pretty. There was nothing ostentatious about her, nothing that signaled big money, but neither was she one of the impoverished clients who believed it was okay to walk in without an appointment.

What she shared with those clients was fear. A palpable sense of fear made her lips tremble and her voice tremulous when she spoke.

"Ms. Holloway? I'm so glad I caught you. May I have a few minutes of your time?"

Barbara couldn't stop her involuntary glance at her watch. A few minutes, she decided, and pushed her door open. "Of course. Come in."

As the woman went to one of the clients' chairs, Barbara walked around her desk to sit down and regard her visitor. The nice tan didn't altogether disguise her pallor, or the shadows under her eyes that were shiny with unshed tears. "What can I do for you?"

"I'm Ashley Loven, and my son is charged with murder. He didn't do it, Ms. Holloway. He didn't have a gun, and he had no reason to kill Joseph Peel, but they say he did. Two people said they witnessed it. But he didn't do it!"

Barbara had a vague memory of reading about it. Usually an avid follower of criminal cases reported in the local newspaper, she had paid scant attention to this one. Her impression was that it was an open-and-shut case, complete with eyewitnesses.

"You want me to defend your son?" she asked when Ashley Loven ducked her head and became silent.

"Yes. Will you talk to him, get his side of the story, help him?"

"Ms. Loven, according to the newspaper account your son is an adult. Why hasn't he asked for me to represent him? Why you?"

"He thinks it's hopeless!" she cried. "He's given up already. They told him that with a former police officer testifying that he saw it happen, there was no chance of anything but a guilty verdict if it goes to trial. They said it would be better for him if he confessed up front, save everyone the trouble and expense of a court trial. I don't know what all they told him! He's only twenty-three and they terrified him. He needs professional help. Your help."

Barbara couldn't suppress a ripple of anger that stiffened her. They had him in jail and were still hounding him with questions and threats. How long had they been holding him on suspicion of murder? They could keep hammering him with questions, stoke his fear with suggestions until he had an attorney.

"Ms. Loven," she said, "please understand what I'm about to tell you. Your son is an adult. Unless he's incompetent, he is the one who must decide on counsel. Has he asked for anyone to represent him?"

Ashley Loven shook her head. "I don't think so. He was hit in the head, knocked out, and had stitches, and I think he's still suffering from his injury. A concussion, they said. He was released from the hospital today, and they took him straight to jail. He isn't thinking clearly, but I know he needs an attorney."

"He needs someone. But it has to be his choice." She paused, thinking, then said, "Will you see him again today, this evening?" At a nod from Ashley Loven, she continued. "Tell him to say nothing until he has talked to an attorney. That's his right, to remain silent. I'll go around in the morning and have a talk with him and we'll go on from there. I can't guarantee that I'll take his case but I can give him advice in any event."

"You can't see him today, this afternoon?" She leaned forward, clutching the arms of her chair.

"I'm sorry, but it has to be in the morning. Meanwhile, he's to remain silent. Tell him it's important that he remain silent until he talks with an attorney. Where can I reach you after I see your son?"

Ashley bit her lip and tensed even more, as if ready to spring up in protest. After a moment she slumped in her chair. "I'm at the Hilton, room 312. I'll wait for your call. I can pay you, Ms. Holloway. Travis doesn't have a cent, but I can pay your fee."

"Tomorrow," Barbara said, rising. "Travis Loven? Is that his name?"

"No. He's Travis Morgan. I divorced his father years ago and remarried."

After seeing Ashley out Barbara returned to her desk and cursed under her breath again. If it turned out to be a plea bargain case, Shelley could handle it, she decided. If it turned out that a trial was in order, Shelley couldn't do it alone—and considering the months of preparation, delays, intense concentration—none of that was on her schedule.

It depended on what happened at the board meeting that evening. Darren, her lover, had handed in his resignation at the clinic, but now, weeks later, it still had not been accepted. At the meeting the decision would be forthcoming, and the board members believed they had little choice but to accept his resignation. The alternative was to have their tax-exempt status questioned, probably lose it. Go from a non-profit charitable clinic to a for-profit corporation or something.

Acknowledged as one of the best physical therapy clinics in the country, many of its patients were unable to pay for extensive therapy. Without donations, the clinic would have to severely limit the number of non-paying patients. Darren was unwilling to let that happen, even if it meant leaving, and that meant a move. For both of them.

"Don't borrow trouble!" Barbara told herself sharply. "Maybe they'll kick the can down the road again." And maybe tomorrow the sun won't rise, she added, standing, ready to go to Frank's house.

She walked through the house to the kitchen where Frank was washing something in a colander. He turned to grin at her, wiped his hands, and picked up a tomato.

"Ah, Bobby, look at this!" Frank said. A broad smile activated every muscle in his face. The tomato was so dark red it looked black and was the size of a softball. "Isn't that a beauty!"

"It's a beauty," she agreed.

"Help yourself to wine. I'll get a quick shower and some decent clothes. Won't take more than a couple of minutes. Cheese in the fridge." He drew close enough to give her a peck on the cheek, and continued toward the hall to his bathroom, but paused.

"I can't figure out Sam," he said. "He's turning into an ambulance chaser or something. Swept a promising client right out from under my nose today. Maybe he's getting senile, or sees that I have more fun than he does. Or something." He shook his head.

"Okay, Dad. Let's have it. What's the rest of the story?"

"Well, Annie McIvey came by to ask about that major who threatened the clinic. It happened that Sam was in my office, and he began asking her questions. I was right there, but he was doing the asking, not me. She told him about those two incompetents the major wanted to put in the VA system as physical therapists, and she told him that Darren had flunked them both, and so on. Anyway, next thing I know he's talking about his pal Senator Treadmore and his subcommittee looking into the use of contractors in the VA, and for some reason Sam was getting redder and redder, ranting about mercenaries, until he finally said maybe he could help Annie, since I was so busy with the new book and all that. He whisked her right off to his own office. Ambulance chaser. I don't know. Maybe at a certain age we should all retire."

Shaking his head, he turned to go on to his bathroom.

"Dad, is Pete still in Afghanistan?" Peter Bixby was an army lieutenant, and she knew very well that he was. Sam talked about him at every opportunity.

Frank glanced back over his shoulder. "I believe he might still be over there. See you in a few minutes. Oh, I believe Sam told Annie to tear up that resignation." He vanished into his room at the end of the hall.

Barbara sank into the nearest chair. Of course Sam would have been in Frank's office when Annie arrived. Of course they would have talked about the major who had threatened to pull strings at the IRS if Darren refused to give accreditation to two contractor guys, who, Darren said, weren't qualified to empty bedpans without supervision. Of course Frank knew that Pete was in Afghanistan, in harm's way, that the day could come when he might need physical therapy. And of course Frank knew about Sam's many friends and acquaintances in the government.

Frank had manipulated Sam every inch of the way and Sam would never suspect that he had done exactly what Frank had planned. She could almost pity the major who had made his outrageous demand to the clinic while Darren was on vacation. Sam would be relentless in his pursuit of that guy. How many other incompetents had the major succeeded in placing, satisfying some big contractor, making money on each deal?

Smiling, she lifted her glass in a silent salute to her father. Then she began to think about the recycle box in the hall. It would have this week's newspapers. Ten minutes later when Frank rejoined her in the kitchen, she was at the table reading about the murder of Joseph Peel and his killer, Travis Morgan, who had been subdued at the scene of the crime.

CHAPTER 3

BARBARA WAS SEATED at the table in the conference room waiting for a guard to bring in Travis Morgan. The room was tiny and windowless; the table, bolted to the floor, was ugly grey metal with years of grime ingrained in molding that edged the top. Two chairs opposite each other, also metal, were very uncomfortable. The room was not designed to lift the spirits of an already dispirited prisoner.

She watched in silence as the door opened and Travis Morgan walked the few feet from the door to slouch into a chair without a word or a glance toward her. The guard nodded in her direction and left, closing the door hard behind him. Travis sprawled in his chair, his legs out to the side and, keeping his head turned slightly, his face averted, studied the tabletop as if it contained a secret map. He looked much like Ashley. The little she could see of his hair appeared thick, darkening blond, and from the brief glimpse she had seen of his face, his eyes were just as blue. He still had a bandage on his head. He appeared to be well built, muscular, and she assumed the rigid line of his jaw was not permanent but rather a visible effort to keep control.

"You know who I am?" she asked. "Why I'm here?"

"Sure. Holloway. My mother hired you." He didn't glance her way as he spaced the words in the manner of a bored middle school student.

"Let's get a few ground rules established. First, I don't answer to Holloway. It's either Ms. Holloway or Barbara. Your decision. Second, your mother did not hire me. Neither did she retain me. Again, that's your decision. And third, if you want me to defend you, you'll have to face me. I don't speak to the side of anyone's head longer than it takes to say 'so long'."

In an exaggerated act of compliance, he straightened and folded his hands on the table, then looked at her. It was a mocking gaze.

She met his gaze steadily. "Let me tell you what I know about you," she said. "You're tough. You've had to be to get by on your own since you ran away at sixteen. You have all the street smarts a guy needs to get by, and then some. You think you understand the system you're up against, and you don't know squat. You walked into a house and according to two eyewitnesses you shot and killed a man in cold blood. You cooperate with me, or with someone like me, or you'll spend the rest of your sorry life in prison. And if it's with me, you'll cooperate or I'll walk out. You need me a hell of lot more than I need you. If it's me, I'm going to be in your face a lot. I'll know you as if you were my blood brother before this is over, and you'll answer every question I ask, fully, in detail, and truthfully."

She continued to gaze into his blue eyes until he turned away.

"I didn't shoot Peel."

"Do you want me to defend you?"

"Yeah. My mother said you were good. Not that it matters." He added with a touch of the earlier sarcasm, "My ass is grass."

"What happened Friday night?"

"I rang the doorbell and a guy opened the door and said they were expecting me. He took me down a hall to a door, reached around me and shoved it open. He gave me a push and I took a step into the room. Peel was starting to stand up. Then I got hit in the head and woke up in the hospital."

"Who hit you? The man who opened the door?"

"It couldn't have been," he said after a moment. "He was behind me, pushing. Someone else. I never saw him."

"Okay, that's the outline. Let's fill in some details. You rang the bell and a man opened the door. What did you say to him? What did he say?"

"I told you. I said my name and he said they were expecting me."

"That's all you said? Just your name?"

"Jesus! I said my name and I had an appointment. And he said they were expecting me."

"Walking down the hall, did he say anything?"

"No. And neither did I."

"So you reached the door. Then exactly what happened? You said he reached around you to open it. Why?"

Travis glanced toward the door as if measuring his chances, then turned his gaze to her. He looked as if he wanted to reach across the ugly table and throttle her, but he said, "He was walking behind me. He reached around me for the doorknob. He opened the door and gave it a shove. Then he gave me a push."

"Where was Joseph Peel? Did you know him? Were you surprised to see him instead of your father?"

"Yeah, I knew him and, sure. I was surprised. I didn't know the guy was taking me to him. Peel was behind a desk… He looked surprised… Yeah," he added as if he had just thought of this. "He was surprised. He sort of jumped to his feet. Like, *what the fuck*? Then *blooie*. Out."

"Good," Barbara said. "Why did you go to see your father that night? Had you kept in touch after running away?"

He tightened again, and the ridge of his jaw became hard and sharp. "No. I hadn't seen or heard from him for seven years. I had to tell him something."

"So tell me what were you planning to tell him."

For a moment she thought he wouldn't answer. He became even more tense, and both hands clenched on the tabletop. He looked directly at her, then past her at the wall.

"My mother and I had a court order to exhume the body of my

sister, and if she had a mark on her, a scar or bruise, anything to indicate abuse, we'd see him prosecuted for kidnapping and abusing her." He drew in a long breath, then said in a rush, "I wanted to tell him myself, face to face, watch his expression, watch him sweat and squirm."

She leaned back in her chair, and thought, Dear God, he wanted to kill his father. His act of arrogance, sarcasm, indifference, impatience had vanished in a flash, leaving hatred, a passionate hatred clearly visible, the undeniable hatred of a young man for his father.

She watched without speaking as his hands unclenched, and he regarded them curiously as they trembled. With an abrupt jerk he moved both hands from the table to his lap.

When he lifted his head again, she saw what his mother had seen—the face of a very frightened young man.

"Tell me about your sister, Travis," Barbara said.

"She was being held somewhere and they hurt her. She wanted me to come get her… "

As the words trailed off, he looked at Barbara and shook his head. "Never mind. It's too crazy. You won't believe me."

"What I've learned is that when people make up stories, they make them sound as rational as they can. Sometimes the craziest sounding ones are the truth. Try me."

He gave her a long searching look before speaking again. "I was hanging out with a g— with someone, using her computer. I was on a blog and signed myself Stinkbug, with a link to my email address. A week later June emailed me. She asked me to tell her what I gave her once when she caught me doing something I shouldn't do. It was a bag of marbles, agates. I asked her what I'd been doing. Then, after another week or a little longer this time she answered: smoking. She signed herself Junebug. It was her, my sister."

He told it haltingly, watching Barbara for a reaction. June had not owned the computer and had to sneak a minute or two when she could in order to use it. She was being held somewhere, but didn't know where. She had a tiny apartment in a big compound of some sort, a small garden area she could use, with a high fence around it. They had cut her. She had a guard who pretended to be a nurse, and another girl came in four times a week, a companion or something.

When he stopped, Barbara asked, "Did you go to the police? Tell anyone? Try to get help?"

"Yeah. I tried. They didn't believe me, said it was just a kid pulling a scam of some sort, having me on." He looked toward the door again, this time with a look of near desperation. "My mother has the emails, all of them. Printouts."

"I'll need the computer you used," Barbara said after a moment. "People can trace the sender, the recipient, everything. Didn't the police or anyone else try that?"

"No. The girl I was with ditched me. I used her laptop. I couldn't find her, and June stopped emailing. I began to use a library computer, checking every day to see if there was a new message, but there wasn't. I decided to come home and see if my mother would or could do anything. I found out that June had died."

He was very pale and a tic was jerking in his jaw. All that jaw clenching, Barbara thought, plus a head injury. He'd had enough, she decided. She opened the folder she had brought and withdrew two client agreements, slid them across the table to him. "Okay, Travis. We'll call it a day. If you want to retain me, you'll need to sign an agreement." She told him what to expect in the coming days, and that no one could question him again unless she was present. She explained that he could ask for a plea bargain at any time, and what it meant: possibly a reduced sentence.

He shook his head. "I didn't shoot him."

"So that's what we'll go with," she said and put a pen by the agreement.

Although he gazed at the paper, it was obvious that he was not reading it. Mumbling, he said, "I don't have any money."

"Your mother said she would pay for your defense."

When he picked up the pen and signed his name, his blue eyes were as shiny with unshed tears as Ashley's had been.

When Barbara got to her offices, she stopped just inside the door and said, "For heaven's sake." It was less in surprise than in resignation. A tall lovely blue vase on the floor between two chairs held blue and violet irises and several sprays of pink pampas grass. A glass vase on Maria's desk had an assortment of flowers. "Shelley?" she said, walking again.

"She said she had to do something," Maria said with a broad smile. "You know, to celebrate."

They had all been jubilant that morning when Barbara said no move was in sight, that Annie McIvey and Sam Bixby were prepared to fight the whole government if necessary. And, of course, Shelley would have to do something.

Going past Maria's desk, Barbara said, "I hope she's left room enough for me to walk." Maria laughed.

Pausing at her door Barbara said, "See if you can get Bailey, will you? Ms. Loven will come in this afternoon; and if Bailey calls back while she's here, just tell him I want him at about four thirty. And ask Shelley to hang around if she checks in after her stint at Martin's."

Maria nodded happily. "We're back in business!"

That summed it up, Barbara thought, opening her door. They were back in business. But her office suggested that it was a florist's business. A basket of flowers under a window, a large vase of flowers on the coffee table, a shimmering cut-glass vase with rosebuds on her desk. Once Shelley had said that when she was young she jumped up and down when excited, but as an adult such behavior was unseemly. She found other ways to express her excitement, and Shelley never did things by half measures. The office smelled like gardenias and roses.

Barbara was smiling when she went to her desk and put in a call to Ashley Loven.

"At a good time for you," she said, and Ashley said, "Now." Fifteen minutes later she was in the office.

"You'll defend him?" she asked anxiously as she entered the office.

"Yes. Let's sit by the table and talk." Barbara gestured toward the sofa and easy chairs.

If Ashley even noticed the flowers, she gave no sign. She sat stiffly in one of the comfortable chairs, and Barbara on the sofa. "Do you believe him?" Ashley asked. "You do, don't you?"

"I think he believes his story," Barbara said. "I don't know enough to believe or not believe. I need to know why he hates his father. Is that a good starting place?"

Ashley looked deflated by her words. It appeared that she had not slept much during the past few days, and it showed in the shadows under her eyes. She drew back in her chair and shook her head.

"We should start a few years earlier," she said. "Back when I was still married to Arlie. I was nineteen and he was twenty-nine when we married. Travis was born ten months after our wedding. It… it wasn't an easy pregnancy. Morning sickness that lasted six months, and hemorrhaging afterward that put me back in the hospital."

Although her gaze had become fixed on the flower arrangement, Barbara doubted it was what she was seeing as she continued in a dull voice.

"June was born five years later. Ms. Holloway, over a period of ten years I became pregnant seven times and had two live births. Miscarriage after miscarriage, and they became progressively worse. The last one occurred in a shopping mall, and my sister came from Denver to be a blood donor. I was so ill that she insisted on taking me home with her to recuperate. In Denver I saw her gynecologist. Another pregnancy could kill me, she said, and I believed her. I had a tubal ligation. My sister paid for it. That was in the tenth year of my marriage to Arlie. I didn't tell him what I had done and I thought, hoped, he never would find out. Nearly a year later he did."

She looked at Barbara then. "I couldn't leave him, or so I thought, because there were two young children. Over the years, he had changed and I had been too ill too much of the time to realize how much he had changed. I began to hear what he was saying, and he sounded like a madman. He's a preacher. His message had become one of condemnation of the sexual act for anything other than procreation. He was obsessed with it."

She paused a moment, shook her head, then continued. "He received a late bill from an anesthetist. Mistakenly it was sent to our house, not to my sister. He immediately moved out of our bedroom and didn't touch me, speak to me, or even look at me. I was glad, Ms. Holloway," she said with a touch of defiance. It didn't last long. "Then he denounced me in church. He told the story of Jesus and the fig tree and said the woman who rendered herself sterile was cursed also. She was an abomination in the eyes of God. He kept his eyes on me through it all. I got up and walked out."

"Good for you."

"Not so good, the way it turned out," she said dully.

"Take a break," Barbara said, standing. "Do you drink coffee? Tea? A Coke?"

"Coffee."

"Coming up." Barbara went to the door. When she opened it, the smell of brewing coffee overwhelmed the fragrance of flowers. She nodded her thanks to Maria, who held up two fingers. "It's already on," she said, returning to the table.

"I'll get an apartment here," Ashley said in a low voice. "I'll visit him every day, take him whatever they'll allow." Her unseeing gaze was fixed on the flowers again. "I lost June. Travis was lost to me for so many years. I can't lose him again, not like this."

Maria tapped lightly on the door, entered with the coffee tray, and put it on the table. Barbara thanked her and poured. She and Ashley sipped coffee silently for several minutes.

When Ashley continued her story, her voice was a monotone, as if she had repeated this history to herself so many times it had lost all meaning. She had seen a lawyer but so had Arlie; suit and countersuit for a divorce followed. There was a court hearing about custody, and he won. He charged her with multiple abortions, wanton behavior, denial of his conjugal rights, claimed she was unfit to be around children.

"He used Travis," she said in that curiously toneless voice. "Arlie's lawyer asked him a few questions, like who took him to after-school events. I never did because we had one car and Arlie kept the keys. I never drove. I had read to them a lot until Arlie banned any book that he didn't approve of, nothing with fantasy, magic, the things kids love. Not even Dr. Seuss. Then the kids didn't want me to read anymore. The attorney asked Travis if I read to his little sister. He had to say no. It was like that. Anyway, when it was over, Arlie had custody, and I had visitation rights only if he was present. Those visits were ugly. No one had anything to say, and he glared at me and kept a tape recorder on. June would get disturbed and cry, and Travis began biting his fingernails. I stopped going."

"You didn't see your children after that?"

"I was ordered to stay at least two thousand feet away from them unless he was there. The judge said it would be a criminal offense if I disobeyed his orders. Jail time. Arlie would have made them follow through. I used to go to the school and park half a block away just so I could see them."

Barbara drew in a long breath to quell her anger. "Then what happened?"

"The usual, I suppose. Depression, poverty, job hunting. If it hadn't been for my sister, I would have ended up on the street. I just didn't care. My doctor put me in touch with a singles support group, newly bereaved, newly divorced, single parents. I met Maurice Loven there. He had lost his wife and daughter in an accident. We had coffee, talked, and we helped each other, oddly enough. Sixteen months later I married him. He urged me to go back to school, finish my degree, go on to graduate school." Her eyes were downcast and she began to trace the pattern of inlay on the coffee table. "Maurice was killed in an arson fire at his cabin on the coast three months after we married."

Abruptly she rose, looked about the office, then walked to one of the windows and faced out. "He taught me so much, Ms. Holloway. It's possible to love someone without constantly judging them, without constant orders to do this, do that, stop doing something else." She ducked her head and stopped speaking.

After a short silence she returned to her chair, poured herself more coffee from the carafe, and continued without touching the newly poured coffee. She had kept watching her children from a distance. Then Travis stopped showing up after school and a detective had come to her apartment to search for him.

"He would have been sixteen in a week when he left," she said. "He had been gone for ten days when the police came. That's when I learned he had run away."

She became silent again, longer this time, and Barbara waited without speaking.

"Then two years ago June stopped coming out of school. She was attending a private girls' school. I waited three days and went to my attorney for advice. I was so afraid she had run away, too. A girl like that on the streets... We had a detective look into it, and his report said that Arlie had pulled her out of the school. A drug-crazed gang kid had tried to kill Arlie, and he had been afraid that June might become a target. He placed her where she would be safe. The detective hadn't been able to find out where she was, and Arlie wasn't required to divulge that information, not even to me, her mother."

She had sent both children cards, notes, gifts from time to time, Christmas presents and birthday presents, but nothing had ever been acknowledged. Travis had told her they never received anything from her.

This time when she became silent, Barbara didn't wait for her to resume with past history. "How did June die? When?"

"In June. Her death certificate listed the cause as pneumonia." Her voice broke and she bowed her head, held her face with both hands, convulsed with sobs that were almost inaudible, and more terrible because of their silent intensity.

Barbara rose and took the coffee carafe to the door and motioned to Maria, who came swiftly to take it from her. *"Five minutes,"* Maria mouthed. Barbara nodded and returned to the sofa to wait out Ashley's weeping.

After Ashley was composed again, her eyes red rimmed, her face puffy now, she told the rest of her story. She had been out of town for five days on a business trip for her company and learned on her return that June had died and had been buried. At the end of July Travis had shown up.

"At first he was so belligerent," she said. "I made him listen to me, hear my side of the story, and he told me the lies Arlie had fed to them over the years. We went together to the cemetery and we wept together there. We took the emails to my attorney, and he said pretty much what the police had said, that without one or the other computer, the emails had little legal standing."

Like Travis, she believed they were from June. No one had known about their secret names for each other except her. No one else could have known about the agates, smoking, any of it. Barbara asked if she had intervened when she overheard the children bargaining.

Ashley shook her head. "Children need their secrets. Arlie had renamed us all, good biblical names, and he insisted that we use them. June had to be called Ruth. Travis was Isaac, I was Sarah. He called himself Benjamin. The children rebelled, but never in his presence. I don't think any of us ever laughed in his presence."

Stymied, but determined to find out what had happened to June, Ashley had petitioned the court for the exhumation. Her attorney pleaded her case, that she had not been notified of her daughter's death in time to say goodbye. She had a necklace passed on from her own mother that she wanted to bury with June. No one had made any attempt to locate her although her company could have furnished the information if they had been asked.

"We were going to do it," she said. "That's why we came down to Eugene. I had to know if June had been mistreated. If he had abused her in any way."

"Was Travis abused before he ran away?"

"He said he hadn't been, but something happened that made him run away. He said it was a lot of little things. It was more than that, but he won't tell me what it was." She paused, then said forcefully, "He did not have a gun. When he arrived he had a backpack full of dirty clothes and books, nothing else. A few dollars. He didn't know anyone in Portland, and he hardly ever left my apartment. We bought him a bicycle or he used buses or the light-rail when he did go out. He never had a chance to buy a gun, steal one, or get one any other way. He never fired a gun in his life. He just wanted to tell Arlie that we were going to exhume June's body. He seemed to think that he had to tell him in person."

It was after four when Barbara stood and stretched. "You've been through enough for one day, more than enough. I'd like to photocopy those emails and the death certificate."

"You'll want a copy of the exhumation order," Ashley said. "I intend to go through with it myself."

"Of course," Barbara agreed. "I'll handle the details."

Chapter 4

"Now you know as much as I do," Barbara said to Shelley and Bailey. He was gazing morosely into a glass of melting ice without a trace of the bourbon he had started with. Shelley's eyes were wide and she had a slight frown on her face.

Bailey heaved himself upright from the deep chair and ambled to the bar, where he added bourbon to the dwindling ice. "Want to tell us something, Barbara?" he said, returning to his chair. "You act like you're going full bore ahead on this one. Why? Two witnesses, one an ex-cop. Why's it more than a plea bargain?"

"He said he didn't do it."

"Don't they all?" When she didn't respond, he said, "It looks from where I'm sitting like you're out to get the preacher for what he did to Loven, or what she said he did to her. He said, she said all over again. But what's that got to do with shooting Peel?"

Barbara shook her head impatiently. "For the time being we run with it. I don't know for how long. I have a list of names for you to start with. I'll find out what I can from homicide, have a look at the scene, and make arrangements for the exhumation."

He shrugged as she pushed the list across the table. Without a glance at it, he picked it up and put it in the old duffel bag that he called his junior detective kit. "Loven's dime. A job's a job. Anything else?"

"That's it for starters," she said. Some day he was going to question her once too often and she was going to punch him in the nose, she thought angrily, enjoying the image that rose in her mind. If it weren't for the fact that he was probably the best private detective on the West Coast, she would have done it long ago. When he stood and made his slouching way to the door, she followed, to take the glass from him when he finished draining it.

He upended the glass, handed it over, and opened the door. As soon as he started to go through the doorway, she gave him a push. Mindful of the fact that he was still favoring his arm, recovering from a bullet wound, she was careful not to push too hard, just enough to make him catch his balance before he continued the step.

"That's why we run with it," she said.

Bailey stopped, turned, and gave her a salute. "Gotcha," he said and walked on through the reception room and out.

"He drives me crazy," Barbara said, returning to the sofa.

"It looks bad, doesn't it?" Shelley said in a low voice. "I mean, two against one. That always looks like a loser."

"Bad," Barbara agreed. "What else is bugging you?"

"The exhumation. If that body shows signs of abuse, it seems it might give Travis a real motive for killing his father, not just something that happened seven or eight years ago. Won't they claim that he was so primed to shoot that he probably couldn't have stopped even if he wanted to when he saw Peel instead of his father?"

"Indeed they will. God, I need a drink of something. You want a glass of wine?" It was a formality. Shelley seldom drank anything alcoholic. At the bar, pouring pinot noir, Barbara said, "There's something I'd like for you to do. Morgan's church. His sermons. Is he crazy, a true believer in this procreation-only business? Changing names? How crazy is he?" She looked across the room at Shelley. "Bailey had a point. I guess he got to me. I really do want to take down that preacher if a word of what Ashley Loven said holds up. I'm so damn tired of this macho-male game. Every day little things." *Like the way Bailey questions me when he would never dare question Dad*, she added silently. "Then something really big and foul—"

"Maybe I will have a little wine," Shelley said, coming to her side.

✦

Dinner was over, cleanup done, Todd, Darren's teenage son, had gone to bed, and Barbara and Darren were in the living room, where he was reading a thick book on economics or something else she considered dreary, and she was going through emails yet again.

—Stinkbug, is that you? What did you give me when I caught you doing something you shouldn't do? Where were you then?—

—Marbles, a bag of agates. The side of the garage. What was I doing? Do you remember? Junebug, how are you? Where are you these days? Why did you stop emailing me?

—Smoking. I don't know where I am. He changed the passwords. Only minutes at a time now, sneaking the computer. Prisoner. Guard pretends to be nurse, another girl brings computer sometimes. Gotta go—

—What do you mean, you don't know where you are? Prisoner? Guard? Tell me where you are. I'll come get you. I'm in San Francisco but I'll come to wherever you are. Tell me something about it, what's around it, anything. Has anyone hurt you?—

—They cut me and I woke up here. Mountains north, hot summer, cold winter. Two room apartment, small garden, high fence. Airplanes, trucks, horses, shooting sometimes—

—Junebug, that's not enough. Who's keeping you? Why? Can't you tell me more? Whose computer are you using? Give me a name, anything!—

—R sneaks laptop in or they'll take it away. If she knows about you she'll stop bringing it, afraid of them. I don't know who they are. Don't know why. Desert around, then mountains. Guard says I'll be married soon. I'll kill myself—

—Tell me more about the weather. Maybe I can find you that way. What do you mean they cut you? You don't have to get married if you don't want to. Don't even think about killing yourself. Just give me some clues. I'll come for you. I promise.—

—Rain, hail, sleet today, cold, freezing wind from north, strong. Snowed yesterday. Guard Sandra. Rosita's laptop. I don't see anyone else. Don't know who they all are, men mostly. I hear them sometimes—

There followed an increasingly desperate series of emails from Travis, no more responses from June. Barbara turned the photocopies down and rubbed her eyes. The first email was dated March 2, her last one April 20. Five emails from her in seven weeks or a little longer, then nothing. She looked up to see Darren's gaze fixed on her.

"You should have them memorized by now," he commented.

"Engraved in my retinas. And worthless."

"Why worthless?"

"A girl is being held against her will somewhere. She doesn't know where she is and the only clues she can give are vague—desert, hot summer, cold winter, mountains to the north, snow in April, rain, sleet, and hail in April. Where's Waldo?"

"Maybe a meteorologist could help pinpoint it if you have the exact dates of snow, rain and hail, and if it's in the country, not Tibet or someplace like that."

Barbara caught in her breath. "Darren, you're wonderful! I hadn't thought of that, but it's possible. Maybe. Probably in the states, possibly Mexico. Then Google Earth or something like that to narrow it down. It's possible, isn't it?"

"Let's ask Todd. He's still flailing about for a project."

Todd had announced his intention to become a climatologist after he and Darren had gone on a glacier-viewing trip. He was taking classes in meteorology at the University of Oregon and more advanced math classes in high school than Barbara could fathom anyone tackling.

"I'll make a note of the dates, the times of the emails, and weather reports," Barbara said. "If not Todd, then maybe a professional meteorologist."

"Let's go celebrate again," he said, smiling. "Not fair to wake up the kid just to give him an assignment."

She was already on her feet, her hand outstretched to him. "Much more celebrating and I won't be able to walk."

"I'll carry you," he said.

Barbara had been to the police station where she got a report of the murder call and the follow-up and now she stood outside the Duval Funeral Parlor. Half a dozen cars were in the adjacent lot, and a weeping woman was on the porch of the building. People just keep dying, so they do a good business, she thought and mounted the few steps to the porch. She nodded to the weeping woman, who paid no attention. She entered a wide foyer with photographs of people she assumed were important, several large pots of ferns, a table with pamphlets, and a few people in conversations. Ignoring them all she walked to a somber-faced man in a black suit.

"May I help you?" he asked in a low, soothing voice.

"Yes. I called for an appointment with Mr. Duval. Barbara Holloway."

"Of course, Ms. Holloway. Please come this way. I'll tell Mr. Duval you're here."

His tone was sepulchral. He bowed slightly toward a corridor, then preceded her down it to a closed door. "Please make yourself comfortable," he said, opening the door and stepping aside.

The room had a long polished table, a deep pile carpet of a suitable gray hue, and many more ferns. There were a number of oversized bound books on the table. Six chairs at the table had high backs of dark wood, and thick padded cushion seats. She chose the head of the table, and nodded when she sank into the cushion. Foam.

She didn't have to wait long before the door opened and Clyde Duval entered. Dressed in a black suit with a dark tie, he approached her with both hands outstretched, and a sorrowful expression. A tall man, slightly stooped, mid-fifties, with finely chiseled bones and deep-set dark eyes, he smelled slightly of mint.

"My dear, Ms. Holloway," he said as he approached, "anything we can do for you, we are completely at your service." He looked a little surprised when she didn't meet his hands halfway, then pulled out a chair and seated himself.

"I'm not here to arrange a funeral," she said. "I'm an attorney, and I have a court order for the exhumation of June Morgan." She passed the court order to him and watched his expression change from one of sympathy to a cold frown of disapproval.

"I don't understand. This is outrageous, to desecrate the grave of the deceased is a sacrilege. There must be a mistake."

"I'm afraid not, Mr. Duval. All I want to know is when this can be done. As soon as possible, of course." He was biting his lip as he reread the court order. "When?" she prompted.

"Can you tell me why this order was issued? The purpose of this… this outrage?"

"All I want to know is when we can have the exhumation. The court order speaks for itself."

He jerked up from the chair and pushed the order back toward her. "I'll get in touch with you."

She stood and put the paper inside her briefcase. "Mr. Duval, surely this isn't the first time such a thing has happened here. When can we expect to have the exhumation? Give me a date and time now, not at some indeterminate future time."

He was biting his lip again and he looked about the room as if seeking an answer. "I have to contact Harrison, the manager at the cemetery. I can't order this on my own authority."

"Mr. Duval, when someone dies there usually is a funeral within the next few days. If you can bury them that fast, you can also dig them up without delay. Let's say Saturday. What time?"

"Dawn," he said after another beseeching look about the unresponsive room. "Before anyone starts visiting. Six thirty, Saturday morning."

"Thank you." He was already walking toward the door when she asked, "Mr. Duval, why so many ferns? Why just ferns?"

He gave her a bitter look. "They demand very little care," he said and walked out.

Two chores done, she thought, leaving the funeral home. Next was her father, and if he echoed Bailey's reservations about the case, she would scream. It would be unseemly for a grown woman to slug her old man, she thought derisively, a scream would do.

In the reception room of the law offices, she waved to Elsie. "I'll just go on back," she said. Patsy was already stepping out of her office when Barbara drew near her door.

"He's in there," she said, motioning toward the hall that led to the library. "If you can get him to leave those books for a while, that would be good. He's going to ruin his eyes, the way he's going. Will you be wanting coffee?"

"That would be great. Thanks." At the law library door Barbara paused to regard Frank for a few moments. He was seated at one of the long tables. Six or seven books were stacked on one side of him, and an open book in front of him, along with a legal pad, several pens, and a pad of Post-its. He looked contented, she thought. Probably he was humming, a deep almost inaudible rumble that was like a cat's purr. Finding a new way to deal with the law suited him remarkably well. He was gathering material for a new book, this one on opening and closing statements of famous and sometimes infamous trials. He loved doing it.

Knowing that if she remained in the doorway until he noticed her, she would have a long wait, she crossed the room to his table. "Hi, Dad. When you have a minute… "

"Bobby!" A big smile spread across his face. "Time I took a break. Let me gather this stuff first."

"I'll wait in the office. No rush."

Walking through the corridor to his office, she thought of the many times as a girl she had prowled those halls, dreaming of the day when she would have an office here, pretending this was her own door, or that one. For a time Frank had dreamed that she would occupy his spacious office. He had said casually that he was keeping it warm for her. They both had laughed.

Poor Sam Bixby never had a chance, she thought, entering Frank's office. If Frank hadn't been able to keep her in the law firm, he would move heaven and hell to keep her within reach, here in Eugene. Manipulating Sam would have been child's play for him.

When Frank walked into the office, he looked at her with amusement. She was sitting on the sofa with her feet on the coffee table, both hands behind her head, exactly the way he sat when he was puzzling out something. Sometimes he was startled by her mannerisms that reflected his own; other times, it just seemed the way to do things.

"Take a minute to wash my hands," he said, going on to the bathroom.

A few minutes later, after Patsy had brought in coffee, Barbara told him about the new case.

"Tell the DA about the exhumation," he said when she finished. "Of course, it could add to the boy's motive, but if that girl had been abused, it adds another dimension, doesn't it? At the moment I don't see any way you can tie that family's past history to Peel's murder, but it's good to keep all options open. Has Travis told you why he cut and ran when he did?"

"No. Not his mother, either. She doesn't think he was molested sexually, but that's still a possibility."

"It's a tough nut to crack when there are two eyewitnesses. I'm guessing you want me to walk him through the gauntlet."

"Would you mind?"

"Nope. Like they say, it's a dirty job but someone's got to do it. Let's go meet the young man. He knows bail is out of the question for him, doesn't he?"

"He knows. A runaway before sixteen, on his own in San Francisco for seven years, he knows."

"Reckon he does. After we see him, I'll look over that house with you. I'm curious about the happy coincidence of having a guy just happen to be in the right place with the right kind of object in his hand to open Travis's head to the point of needing stitches."

Barbara leaned over and kissed his cheek. "You're the greatest," she said. "And after all that, lunch. On me." She knew it wouldn't happen that way. He would end up with the check for lunch, but she would try.

When Travis was brought into the conference room, he looked startled and suspicious when he saw Frank. Barbara introduced them. "We often work together," she said.

"Actually I work for her now and then," Frank said. "And she's a hard taskmaster, let me tell you. How's the head?"

"It's okay," Travis said. Then he turned toward Barbara. "I didn't do it, and that means that those two guys in the room must have shot Peel. They're in it together."

"Why would they do that?" Frank asked. "Any theory about why?"

"Money. There's money coming in all the time, that theater they use in Portland, the church here, a driver and car, a bodyguard. It takes money and Peel was the bookkeeper, handled the money. He must have caught them stealing and they had to get rid of him." He leaned back in his chair as if to say case closed.

"Sounds like a pretty good theory," Frank said thoughtfully. "Something to keep in mind. How was the fellow dressed, the one who let you in?"

Travis looked confused again. "I don't know. Black pants, sport jacket, just like other guys. Nothing special. Why?"

"Did you know him before?"

"No."

"Did you think he was a servant, something like that?"

Travis shook his head. "I didn't think anything about him. Just a guy who let me in."

"Details," Frank said. "Sometimes they add up to something, sometimes they don't, but it pays to nail them down when you can. Exactly what did he say when he opened the door and you told him your name?"

"They were expecting me. I already told her," he said impatiently, motioning to Barbara.

"They? Is that the word he used?"

"Jesus! He said, and I quote, 'We were expecting you.'"

"See?" Frank said. "Details."

He had a few more explicit questions and Travis began to stop and think before he answered each one. There were slight variations from what he had already told Barbara. He described the walk down the hallway to the closed door.

"He was a little behind me most of the way. Then he was right behind me to open the door. That's when he gave me a push."

"Show me," Frank said, standing and turning his back to the table. "How hard a push was it? Pretend this is the doorway." He made a sweeping gesture with his hands to indicate the doorway.

Travis looked at Barbara helplessly and she nodded. With obvious reluctance he went to stand behind Frank.

"Okay, now you've opened the door and I start to take a step. Or do I?"

"Yeah. He opened the door and I was going in when he shoved me."

When Frank started to take a step, Travis put the flat of his hand on Frank's back and pushed, not enough to make Frank fall or even to stagger much, but enough to make him duck his head and stretch out his arms to steady himself.

Frank completed the step and turned to Travis. "Thank you. That was helpful. You must have stopped when you reached the door, long enough for him to open it. Is that how it was?"

"Yeah. I was just starting to go on walking and he pushed me."

Barbara asked her questions next. How was he dressed that night? How did he get to the house? Had he had anything to drink beforehand, any drugs? His answers were showing increasing impatience, taking on a sharper tone when she asked, "In San Francisco, did you have any encounters at all with the police? Picked up on any charges, questioned, stopped for any reason?"

"No," he snapped. "Nothing."

"Travis, this is very important," Barbara said. "If your name appears on any police blotter, it will come out, and it will be used against you. No matter how insignificant the incident might have been, it can be used against you. If you used a different name there won't matter if they have your fingerprints on file." As she spoke, the tic came back to his cheek, and the ridgeline of his jaw became hard and tight again.

"We'll let it go for now, but next time we talk I'll want to know what you were doing in San Francisco for seven years, how you lived, how you survived, everything. Be thinking hard about it." She drew back in her chair, nodded to Frank to take over, and continued to study Travis's changing expressions. He was relieved that she was done, visibly more relaxed than only a second ago. She had touched a nerve, she thought in satisfaction, and she knew that she had to probe that nerve hard in the next few days.

"Okay," Frank said. "Let's talk about arraignment, what happens. I'll be with you for it, by the way."

"You didn't bring up the question of why he ran away," Barbara said later in Frank's car as they headed for the house where Peel had been shot. "Why not?"

"Guy talk," Frank said. "I expect he'll tell me eventually."

On East Thirteenth Street he pulled up before a blue, two-story house with a deep porch and white shutters. It was one of the older houses, built in the thirties or even earlier, and well maintained through the years. The street was shaded by mature horse chestnut trees and a few massive old-growth fir trees. On down the street the Bijou Theater, a restaurant or two, an ice cream parlor, fast-food eateries had taken over, but a few very nice old structures remained, most of them set well back from the busy street. Some of them had been bought by commercial businesses, a real estate company, a bookstore, but a few remained residences.

When Frank pulled in at the curb a young man left a bicycle chained to a porch newel to hurry to the side door. "Ms. Holloway? Jefferson Obie, from the district attorney's office. I'll unlock the door for you."

God, Frank thought, they get younger every year. Obie looked to be thirty at the most, and probably was even younger. His cheeks were flushed, his hair ruffled from his ride.

They shook hands all around, went to the porch and Obie rang the doorbell. "There's a housekeeper," he said. "The crime-scene room is padlocked, of course."

"Of course," Barbara murmured. "Is the housekeeper a resident?"

"I really don't know," Obie said. "She's here every day."

Just a gofer, Frank decided, one who might know something, but not likely to. The door opened and a pleasant-faced, middle-aged woman surveyed them with a noncommittal expression. "It's back down that hall," she said, moving aside as they entered. She was dressed in khaki pants and a yellow T-shirt and was wearing green and gold running shoes.

"Hello," Barbara said. "Ms.— ?"

"Pleasance, Abigail Pleasance. The room you'll want to see is down the hall."

"All this must be very trying for you," Barbara said sympathetically. "People in and out at all hours. Were you here that night when it all happened?"

"No, thank God. They wanted dinner early, and I made it and left before that man got here. Thank God!"

"Down this way," Obie said, as if only then had he realized that Barbara fully intended to quiz the housekeeper if allowed to do so.

"Lead the way," Barbara said.

He led them down the hall. It was wide, with a staircase on one side and an open door to a living room on the other. Barbara paused long enough to glance into the living room. Ten feet or so in, a sofa faced two easy chairs with a fireplace on the wall beyond them. An end table by the sofa held a lamp, a couple of chairs were by windows in the front of the room, all dark and dismal looking. The walls, like the walls in the hall, were a neutral beige color without ornamentation of any kind, the floor was carpeted in low-pile beige, with a similar carpet in the hall and on a runner on the stairs. Barbara and Frank walked side by side with Obie in front. He reached the door, unlocked it, and moved aside for them to enter.

The room was sparsely furnished, about fourteen-by-fourteen feet, with a desk facing the door, several straight chairs along one wall, a sofa on the opposite wall, and two file cases on the wall opposite the door. More beige carpeting made Barbara suspect that someone had hit a closeout sale of the stuff. Slowly she examined the uninviting room, carefully stepping around bloodstains on the floor. A bookshelf on the wall to the left of the door held a few bound books, with one bookend made of brass, possibly. It was an eagle with partly spread wings. She looked over the books—a Bible, something about myths in the Bible, bookkeeping theory… Then she picked up the brass eagle. Holding it, she turned to Obie, who was trying to watch both her and Frank at the same time. Frank was at the desk.

"Was it something like this that the guy slugged Morgan with?" she asked.

"Just like that. It's a pair," he said. "The officers bagged it."

"It's a wonder he survived," she murmured, replacing the eagle. It was very heavy.

Frank stood at the desk with his hands in his pockets. A calculator, computer, ledgers, pens, file folder… He caught Barbara's eye and made a slight sidewards motion with his head.

"How are those windows fastened?" Barbara asked Obie and motioned for him to come as she walked to the windows. There were two of them, heavily draped with a beige fabric.

"They're sash windows," Obie said. He pulled back a drape to show her the fastener. "Nothing was broken, no sign of a break-in, nothing like that. In fact, there's a security system that would have sounded an alarm if there had been an attempt to open the windows. Satisfied?"

Looking past him she saw Frank once again, with his hands in his pockets, regarding the desk. He nodded slightly. "Yes, satisfied. I just wanted to check it out." She walked to the desk, again skirting bloodstains on the floor, and helped Frank examine it for a short time, then said, "Dad, why don't you sit in Peel's chair. Let me go over to the door and see how things line up."

He pulled out the chair and sat down and she went to the door, out into the hall, closing the door after her, then opened it again and stepped into the room. Frank was sitting directly in front of her, about eight or nine feet away. As she entered, he started to jump up, then slumped forward, and would have fallen over to the floor, if he had not stopped his movements. He straightened, left the desk and joined her in the center of the room.

Barbara said, "I guess we're done here. Thank you, Mr. Obie. This has been helpful."

"Right," he said with a slight shrug.

✦

In the car with Frank driving again, Barbara said, "God, I want to see those crime-scene photographs."

Frank agreed. So did he.

"What did you find?" she asked. "Did you open the drawer?"

"No. I wanted a peek inside that file folder. Lists of names."

Several pages of names and southern Oregon towns, exactly like the one that fellow had brought him months before. *Don't let them have it.* He had put that envelope in his safe and it was still there, and he still didn't know who *they* were. He had not thought of that envelope for a long time, one of those incidents over and done with, no consequences, no follow-up. He glanced at Barbara, started to tell her about it, then clamped his mouth tight. After lunch, he decided. Lunch first, then back to the office.

"Dad, were are we going?" she asked minutes later as he drove out into the countryside.

"King Estates for lunch. I had Patsy make a reservation. Out under the awning where we can see the vines."

"Dad! That's not what I had in mind," she said indignantly. "I have work to do."

"I know you do. And I know you've been under a hell of a lot of tension for weeks now. What you need is a very good wine, a very good meal, and a beautiful vista to feast your eyes."

Later, under the awning, having had a scrumptious lunch of crab salad, she breathed a sigh of contentment. The vines stretched out with an abundant harvest, gently rolling waves of grapevines as far as they eye could see, with birds wheeling overhead, a breeze, the awning softening sunlight, murmuring voices, distant music, all framed by towering dark fir trees. It was a scene of perfection.

"Thanks, Dad," she said. "Knots have come untied that I didn't even know had been tied in the first place."

"You're welcome."

"Tell me something," she said. "When I told you about Travis, eyewitnesses, all of it, you didn't bat an eye and point out what a hopeless case it was. Why not?"

He regarded her thoughtfully for a short time, then said, "Honey, intuition is a power ally if you learn to trust it. I trust yours absolutely. With cause," he added. "That boy didn't shoot Peel any more than I did."

✦

Back at the office building, they rode the elevator up and walked through the reception room without another word from him. Barbara waved to Elsie as they passed her desk, and Frank paused long enough at Patsy's door to tell her to hold any calls until further notice.

Inside his office, he motioned Barbara toward the sofa, then went to his concealed safe, opened it, and brought out a manila envelope. He put it down on the coffee table and seated himself in an easy chair.

"Last March," he said, and proceeded to tell her about the man who had come into the office only to collapse before stating his business. "That's what he said," Frank told her. "'Don't let them have it.'"

He opened the envelope and handed her the lists of names. "That's what he was talking about."

She looked through the papers, then to him. "What does it mean? Why bring it up now? Did you find out anything about him or the names?"

"One at a time," he grumbled. "I don't know what it means. I don't know who shouldn't be allowed to have the lists. I don't know a damn thing about the fellow beyond a name, Robert Daggart. Milt came by a couple of days later to ask a few questions. Daggart died without recovering consciousness. He was beaten to death. It was a professional job, done by professionals. As far as Milt could learn, Daggart was a nobody, an errand boy, on his way to California. He was to deliver lists of names to a preacher in Medford, church membership records. His church claimed his body since he had no known relatives. And after that, nothing. Only mention in the newspaper was that a handyman had been beaten to death."

He paused and eyed her narrowly. "As for why now, today in Peel's office, in that file folder I saw lists of names just like those names. Names and towns. Joseph Peel claimed the body and retrieved the papers. I don't like professional hit jobs, professional beatings, and I especially don't like coincidences."

Barbara put the lists down and stood to walk to his desk, back, then again. "Why does a preacher need a bodyguard? Why a driver? Where does the money come from?" She walked to the desk another time, turned, and said, "I feel as if I opened a door expecting to see nothing more than a small closet, maybe uncover a few skeletons, and instead the door opened to a whole edifice that's entirely dark. But big."

Frank nodded. That summed it up. Big and dark.

CHAPTER 5

WAITING FOR SHELLEY and Ashley to show up, Barbara searched for Arlie Morgan's name on the Internet. Many references turned up. Many more appeared when she used the name Benjamin Morgan. By the time Shelley arrived, Barbara had a page of notes to follow through on.

She told Shelley about her father's encounter with Robert Daggart. "We don't know that it's connected," she said, "but if it is, we have to be careful. You especially, since you'll be doing background on the church. Not a word to Ashley about any of this, the lists, Daggart, any of it."

At Shelley's nod she went on. "I'd like for you to pick up Ashley on Saturday. It's a godawful hour, but that creep at the funeral home doesn't want visitors getting upset at seeing anyone dug up again after being properly planted. Ashley knows more about Arlie Morgan than anyone else, no doubt, and I want you to wring her dry in the weeks to come."

"I'll find out if he wears his socks to bed," Shelley said.

Barbara laughed. "You got it. Now, what's still hanging from Martin's?"

They were talking about Shelley's cases when Maria buzzed. Ashley had arrived. She was as pale as before, but the hollows under her eyes were not deeper or blacker, which Barbara regarded as a good sign. After introducing Shelley, Barbara said. "The exhumation is set for six thirty on Saturday morning. I want Shelley to pick you up for that."

"That isn't necessary," Ashley said. "I can drive myself to the cemetery."

"I know you can, but I don't want you to drive afterward. Shelley will take you back to your hotel. Dad's coming over to meet you in a few minutes. Tell me something about your situation, housing, your job."

"I'm looking for an apartment," Ashley said. "As for my job, I work for an architect firm, Dorrance and Merritt. After Maurice died, I went back to school and got a master's in urban planning, and I landed a good job. About six years ago the company created a department to research new energy-efficient materials. I work in that department." She stopped for a moment, then continued. "I asked for time off, a leave of absence without pay, or I would have to quit. They made a counter offer. There's a lot I can do with a computer and telephone calls, so I'm on part-time. It's a good arrangement, giving me something to do when— It gives me something to do."

"It also suggests that they don't want to lose you," Barbara said. "And it suggests that you don't have to work, that financially you're in good shape."

Ashley hesitated a moment, then, with downcast eyes, she said, "Maurice left me a lot of money. Arlie told Travis that I married Maurice for his money. He said the fire that killed Maurice was so suspicious, it surprised him that there wasn't an investigation. Actually there was, but nothing came of it, and I was never a suspect."

Frank arrived soon after that and Barbara watched in amusement and admiration as he charmed Ashley Morgan. As a kindly, sympathetic and understanding uncle, he won her over within minutes. He held her hand and patted it when he said, "After it's over tomorrow I'll take you to a very nice coffee shop where they have award-winning pastries. And I'll challenge you to resist having something."

It was dark Saturday morning when she left the house to pick up Frank, dark and cold, she thought grumpily. The days were still warm and sunny, but as soon as the sun took its dive, the temperature went with it and stayed down until the sun was high again, and her car heater was slow to cooperate. Frank was just as grumpy when he got in the car and they headed for Roosevelt Avenue.

She turned onto Bertelsen and south to the cemetery, where Shelley's car was already in the parking area with Shelley and Ashley inside. Faint ambient light made the manicured grounds surreal, with tombstones, headstones, monuments, trees, and shrubs shadowy and somehow menacing. They looked like humped-over figures, frozen into stillness when observed, ready to move when not seen. Ashley led the way to a distant section, where there loomed a shadowy domelike shape with its own glow. The cemetery manager had put a lighted tent over the gravesite.

Several others were already under the tent when they arrived, among them Clyde Duval. He looked miserable, huddled in an overcoat, wearing a black hat. She nodded to him, then turned her attention to the casket that had already been raised and cleaned. Another man came to their small group.

"John Kirkpatrick," he said, extending his hand to Barbara. "From the district attorney's office." He shook hands with Frank, then with Ashley, and he stood nearby as Clyde Duval approached.

"Ms. Holloway, there is no need to remove the casket in order to open it."

"No one can examine the body out here," Barbara protested.

"Of course not. I have already spoken to the manager and he agrees with me. We'll open the casket here."

As he spoke, a thin man approached the casket and lifted the top. Everyone moved in close. The casket was empty.

Ashley made a deep-throated moaning sound, and Frank took her by the arm.

"Shelley, take her back to the hotel," Barbara said sharply. Ashley's face was ashen. "Stay with her. I'll join you as soon as I get to the bottom of this. Go now."

"I'll walk to your car with you," Frank said, keeping a firm grip on Ashley's arm. She was shaking.

"Where can we talk?" Barbara demanded as Shelley and Frank took Ashley away.

"There's an office," Duval said. "Mr. Harrison has made it available. This way." He motioned toward the right, and held open the tent for Barbara to leave.

In silence she and John Kirkpatrick followed Duval through the forest of tombstones to a white building. When they entered, Duval opened a door off the foyer and they went inside a small office.

Barbara's feet were cold after tramping through dew-wet grass, but inwardly she was hot with fury. "What the hell is going on here?" she demanded. "You knew that damned coffin was empty. What's the meaning of this charade? Why didn't you say so when we spoke?"

He was biting his lip again. She hoped he would bite through it.

"I couldn't tell you," he said abjectly. "He, the reverend, made me sign a nondisclosure agreement, a confidentiality agreement. He said he'd ruin me if I told anyone, if I broke the terms of the contract. My grandfather, my father, and now I have had an honorable business, a necessary business for many decades, in the third generation. I couldn't risk losing it all."

"Wrong beginning," Kirkpatrick snapped. "Where's the body?"

"Cremated," Duval said in a low voice. "It was his wish to have her cremated, and that's what we did. He said the public, his parishioners wouldn't understand, and he wanted us to go through the regular funeral proceedings, with a closed casket."

"Crap," Kirkpatrick said. He pulled his coat closed, looked at Barbara, shrugged, and said, "I'm going home and back to bed." He stamped out.

"There's nothing more to say," Duval said, tentatively looking at the door.

"Oh, sit down," Barbara snapped. "We're waiting for my father, and when he gets here, you're going to tell us exactly what happened, when that decision was made, and why."

"I've already told you," he said, not quite whining.

"You'll tell us more, or I'll haul you into court and you'll tell the world how you put on a show for the masses."

Duval sank into one of the chairs and took off his hat.

Barbara went to the door to watch for Frank. Leaning against the door frame, she studied Duval briefly. Craven, terrified of ruin if word got out that he had held a mock funeral, that people had wept over an empty coffin, ready to take the money and follow orders.

Frank arrived, his cheeks flushed with the morning chill and a brisk walk, and with anger that narrowed his eyes and hardened his features. She gestured and stepped back into the office. "Clyde Duval," she said in way of an introduction. Frank nodded and closed the door.

"All right, Mr. Duval," Barbara said, "start at the beginning, when you first learned that you had a new customer."

He rose and stood fingering his hat, looking first at her, then at Frank. "It was routine," he started in a firm voice. Quickly his voice lost its firmness and he was whining. "I had no reason to treat it as anything other than routine. A grieving parent, a friend assisting in wrenching decisions about funeral arrangements. Mr. Peel was with Reverend Morgan. He said the young woman had died of pneumonia and cardiac arrest. She died at home, with Dr. Edward Knowland in attendance. He filled out the death certificate."

He cleared his throat. "He, Mr. Peel, picked out the casket, a lovely white-and-gold casket. He said to spare no expense. White flowers only, nothing garish, nothing colorful, just white, orchids, lilies, roses… " He was twisting his hat as he spoke fast, his gaze shifting back and forth between Barbara and Frank.

"All right," Barbara snapped. "They were picking out flowers. Then what?"

"Reverend Morgan was very upset, agitated. It was only natural, of course. His daughter, his child, gone so fast, so young. He said he wanted to see her, he had to see her one last time. I tried to dissuade him. She had not yet been prepared for viewing. He insisted. He had to see her and I took him to the workroom, the preparation room, where Bill and Lenore Mitchum were waiting for orders. He didn't want me to go in with him, and he sent them both out so he could be alone with his child. I imagine he was praying, being a minister, you know, but it was uncomfortable. Awkward. Not how we usually do things." He was biting his lip again, and gave up trying to read their expressions. He looked away from them and his voice dropped lower. "When he came out, he was very much more upset than before, beside himself, almost incoherent. He said he had changed his mind. People couldn't gawk at her. No one could look down on her. He kept saying gawk. He couldn't have people gawk at her. Back in the office he changed the plan. Go ahead with a funeral as usual, he said, but with a closed casket and a memorial service in his church. And he said he wanted her cremated. He would spread her ashes in a very special place away from prying eyes, those who would gawk at her. He said it that way. He told Mr. Peel to make arrangements to carry out his wishes, to write the check, whatever it took. He warned me that if I told anyone he would destroy me and the funeral home. He would have his attorney draw up an agreement, a confidentiality agreement, a nondisclosure agreement. And he said Mr. Peel would collect her ashes when he was notified it was time. And he left. Just like that. Mr. Peel was as surprised as I was. He followed him out and came back in a few minutes and confirmed what Reverend Morgan had told me to do. And he said he would return with the confidentiality agreement."

Duval stopped speaking and faced them again with a helpless expression. "What else could I do? It wasn't illegal. People order cremations all the time. Sometimes the bereaved appear irrational. They want strange things placed in the caskets—a toy, a favorite book, a special pillow. We get that kind of thing often. His demand was unusual, but not illegal. He had a right to order whatever he chose."

"You called him after I left, didn't you?" Barbara said. "What did he say?"

"He said, 'Let her dig up the grave.'" His voice dropped even lower and he said unhappily, "He said he wanted her to have the casket raised, he wanted her to look inside."

CHAPTER 6

"WHERE DO YOU want me to drop you?" Barbara asked in the car.

Frank glanced at her grim face and said, "The Hilton. I'll tell Ashley. After you tackle the Mitchums, join us."

She gave him a swift look and nodded. He knew what she was going to do without a word of explanation necessary: get to the Mitchums before Duval had a chance to order them not to discuss the cremation of June Morgan's body.

She drove to the Hilton and then on to the Duval Funeral Parlor, this time driving around the guest parking area to the rear of the building. No other cars were in sight in the parking area. She pulled in, turned off her engine, and settled down to wait.

Ten minutes later a Honda Civic pulled in, and before the couple in the car unstrapped the seat belts, Barbara was at the window of the driver's side. She tapped on the window and he rolled it down a few inches.

"Mr. Mitchum?"

"Yes?"

"My name is Barbara Holloway. May I have a few minutes of your time? It's about a cremation your company performed."

Mitchum turned to his wife, who was leaning forward to listen. She said, "You probably should talk to Mr. Duval, not us."

"I've already spoken with him. He said you two are the ones who prepare the bodies."

They exchanged glances, then Mitchum said, "We do. But if there's a problem, it's really not our place to handle it."

"No problem. I just need some information. Is there a place where we can talk in private for a few minutes?"

Mrs. Mitchum said hesitantly, "We could go in the lounge. No one's here this early most days, especially on Saturdays."

Barbara nodded. "That's good. It won't take long, I promise."

They got out of the car and led the way to a back door that Mitchum unlocked. Here the flooring was tan industrial vinyl, and there were no ferns. A chemical smell was strong. The lounge they entered had a few upholstered chairs, two small tables with straight chairs, a vending machine, and a closed door to what Barbara assumed was a restroom.

"What did you want to know?" Mitchum asked, taking off a jacket. He and his wife looked to be in their fifties, and both were wearing jeans, T-shirts and old sneakers. He was about five feet five and she was several inches taller.

"It's about the cremation of a young woman last summer," Barbara said. "Her name was June Morgan, or perhaps Ruth Morgan. Do you recall her? They buried an empty casket and she was cremated."

Mrs. Mitchum nodded. "That was strange, real strange. But people get crazy sometimes when they lose someone. They can get real crazy, what with grief and all."

"What I need to know is how closely you examined her body, how much preparation was necessary, how far along with it you were when you learned that she was to be cremated."

"We didn't hardly get started," Mitchum said. "We didn't know what they wanted yet. It's one thing if it's a cremation, something else if there's embalming involved. And what the family wants the deceased to wear. You know, for the viewing. Things like that."

"Of course," Barbara said. "Did you have a chance to examine her body? Clean her up or anything?"

"Well, the remains were delivered a couple of hours before anyone came to tell us. Lenore washed her. We always do that, no matter what else."

Barbara looked at Mrs. Mitchum, who was regarding her with an intent expression. "Did you see any signs of physical abuse on the body? Old scars or bruises?" Barbara asked as dispassionately as she could manage.

Mrs. Mitchum drew in a sharp breath. "No! If there had been

anything like that we would have told Mr. Duval right away. That's our duty, to report something like that."

Back to square one, Barbara thought. She believed Lenore Mitchum was telling the truth, and clearly she was indignant that anyone would even ask such a question.

"That young woman died of pneumonia," Mitchum said in a thoughtful way. "And I guess she'd been sick a long time, but she didn't have a mark on her."

"What makes you think she'd been sick a long time?"

"Weight loss," he said, spreading his hands. "You can always tell if there's been a recent big weight loss. Lose skin, wrinkles. It shows. She'd lost a lot of weight. Twenty pounds or more. And her hair. Dry and brittle. That shows if someone's been sick very long."

"That was the dye," his wife told him in a sharp tone, as if she had said this before. "Those girls," she said, turning to Barbara, "they think they can just bleach out the color, add some dye, and look like those models they see on TV. Her hair was bleached and dyed a bad yellow. That's what happens when you dye black hair and go for blond, unless you get a professional to do it for you. I told Reverend Morgan I could lighten it, brighten it up, but he wasn't listening to a thing I said. I could have made her look real nice, with good color and all, and nice hair, but he didn't pay any attention. Of course, I would have wanted a picture. You know, for the hair."

Barbara nodded. "So she was a brunette. How tall would you say she was?"

Mrs. Mitchum was starting to back off, Barbara realized as the woman stiffened slightly.

"I'm just trying to fill in some blanks," she said. "There was a suggestion that possibly it was a mistake, misnaming her or something. I'm sure there's nothing to it, but we have to check when there's a suggestion of a mistake. The death certificate, her father's visit here, it will be cleared up quickly."

"Well, a father knows his child," Mrs. Mitchum said, with a satisfied nod. "And he was that torn up, just torn up when he saw her. He said a closed casket, no viewing, nothing like that. He just didn't want anyone else to see her with yellow hair. A quiet cremation, that's all he could think of. Poor man, he was really torn up."

Barbara looked at Mitchum and repeated her previous question in a more roundabout way. "I suppose you have to know the body weight, height, things like that in order to embalm the deceased. And you guessed that she had lost a great deal of weight. Still, her height wouldn't have changed, would it?"

"No way," he said. "Yeah, I have to know a lot. Lenore here does the cosmetic stuff, skin and hair, fingernails, but I do the embalming. She was about five seven. It makes a difference, you know. But if they go straight to the incinerator, without a viewing or anything like that, then it don't make any difference. Still I noticed, just out of habit, doing the usual routine until we got told otherwise."

Barbara didn't stay much longer, and when Mitchum walked to the back door with her, she thanked him sincerely. "You've been very helpful. I appreciate it," she said.

At the Hilton, Ashley opened the door at Barbara's knock, and before she was even inside the room, Ashley asked, "Did you find out any more?" She was pale and no longer shaking, but she was too rigid, too tight.

"Yes," Barbara said. "I talked to the two people who work at the mortuary. They're the ones who prepare the deceased, and they both will swear that there was no sign of abuse, no scars, no bruises, none of the signs of mistreatment. I believed them, Ashley. They are simply doing a job with nothing at stake, and no reason to lie about it."

Ashley drew back and crossed the room to sink down onto a sofa. A coffee table in front of it had several printouts of photographs of a girl. Staring at them, Ashley said, "I took her picture so many times over the years. She was so beautiful." She fell silent.

Barbara moved close enough to see the pictures of a teenaged girl, as blond as Shelley, with long hair in a ponytail, dressed in a blue skirt, white knee-high socks, a cardigan sweater that matched the skirt. She was with several other girls about her age, all in identical clothes, all laughing. Only one was in sharp focus, June. She was slightly built, and if she was five feet seven inches tall, then two of the girls with her would have been close to six feet tall.

"I used my camera with a long distance lens, a telescopic lens," Ashley said. "I didn't dare get closer… " She trailed off and ducked her head. "We'll never know what he did to her. I'll never know."

Frank had examined Barbara's expression closely, and now turned his gaze to Shelley. "Shelley, you know the Beacham sisters? Margaret and Harriet? Over on Ninth."

"Yes, of course." They all knew the sisters and their nice old house. They often placed witnesses there awaiting their day in court, or for safekeeping from time to time.

"Why don't you give them a call, see if that apartment is available. I think it would suit Ashley just fine, good location, nicely furnished. With antiques," he said in an aside to Ashley. "There's only one problem with it. The sisters, widows, in their sixties, no doubt will leave cookies on your doorstep from time to time. They can't control their urge to make cookies and feed them to their guests."

"I have to go see Travis," Ashley said faintly.

"Well, of course," Frank agreed. "Shelley can make the call, you visit Travis, maybe have a bite of something more substantial than a piece of toast, and then go see the apartment."

"I can't tell them apart," Shelley said. "But they don't seem to mind. Miss Margaret or Miss Harriet, they just laugh if you get the name wrong. Twins. They have amazing life stories, the way twins so often do: got married on the same day to men with the same given names, lost them at the same time… "

"I'll keep in touch," Barbara told Ashley, who was looking from her, to Frank, on to Shelley as if bewildered by this sudden U-turn. "You and Shelley make your plans for the day, and with any luck you'll be out of this hotel by evening." She glanced at Frank. "Ready?"

In the lobby Frank grasped Barbara's arm. "What else did you learn?"

"I don't know who they cremated, but it wasn't June Morgan." In a low voice she told him what the Mitchums had said. "A brunette with badly dyed hair, one who had lost a significant amount of weight, but a young woman who obviously couldn't have passed inspection by anyone who had known June. They would have wanted a picture in order to do her hair. So Morgan had her cremated. End of problem."

"You did right," Frank said. "No point in telling Ashley, at least not at this time. They could say June dyed her hair black, then bleached it, that she had gained a lot of weight and lost it again."

"It's a given that the cops won't take an interest," Barbara said. "Not when there's an official death certificate, a grieving father who happens to be a minister, a licensed physician's cause of death. That asshole from the DA swallowed it whole. But, damn it, there is something I can do," she said emphatically. "Whoever that girl was, she was taken to the residence when Ashley was out of town. She conveniently died and got herself incinerated. I don't like coincidences any more than you do. And that's just too damned convenient. Also," she said more slowly, "if she was a patient in his house, why did Morgan wait until he saw her in the funeral home to decide on cremation? He would have seen her before that day. Her appearance shouldn't have been a shock. Bailey work."

She saw Travis late that afternoon and found him as hostile and distant as he had been at their first meeting. He refused to meet her gaze, stared at the wall off to the side, and his jawline was as hard as it had ever been.

"They lied," he said flatly. "June said they cut her and she woke up in a prison or something."

"I don't think they were lying," Barbara said. "June's notes were cryptic, incomplete. We don't know what she meant about several things."

"Just whose side are you on?" he demanded. "What the fuck are you up to, siding with the cops?" He jumped up from the table. "I want to go back to my cell. Get out of here! Leave me alone!"

"For now," Barbara said, rising, "you need time alone, and I need time to sort things out. I'll see you on Monday."

And that was it, she thought that night, watching Darren's son bolt his dinner. Todd was about the same age that Travis had been when he ran away. Could Todd manage on his own in a city like San Francisco? Would he even survive on his own? A loving father and mother, even though no longer together, they both cared deeply about him and wanted only a good life for him. Todd would get to where he wanted to be, but he was still the boy/man who bolted his dinner because there was a high school football game that night.

What had happened to Travis? What terrible things had happened to him that made him jump ship and run away before he turned sixteen? She might never find out, she knew. If he decided to send her packing, there was nothing she could do about it. And she knew he would do that if he thought she was siding with the police.

She was jolted from her thoughts when Todd rose from the table, collected his plate and silverware and said on his way to the sink, "Remember, I promised to do all the KP tomorrow night. See you later." He left his things on the counter and ran from the room. A minute later the front door closed hard.

"He does stay busy, doesn't he?" Barbara said. "Were you ever that carefree?"

"You know the answer to that one. Were you?"

"Yes, and I didn't appreciate it one bit. I just took it for granted. But kids who get in trouble sometimes straighten out. You certainly did."

"Sometimes they turn out okay," he said after a moment. "I think more often than not scars gathered along the way tend to burn like fire sometimes and seldom completely heal."

She nodded. "Sometimes the scars that are invisible tend to take the longest time to heal, if they ever do. Travis is scarred, deeply scarred."

If June had been cut enough to mention it in an email, there should have been a visible scar, and Travis knew it.

CHAPTER 7

BARBARA HAD FILLED Bailey in on everything, exactly as she always did. She leaned back on the sofa and said, "Double down on all of Morgan's crew, that doctor Knowland, the driver, and the bodyguard. I want to know about the fire that killed Ashley's husband. Where was June being held? When did that other woman get taken to the residence? Officially June Morgan is dead, but someone else was cremated in her name. Peel, the widow, kids, the works. And the names with bullet points on those lists." She looked at the lists she had photocopied and shook her head. Single male names set off with a bullet point. No clue about what it meant, if it meant anything. She glanced from the lists to Bailey and waited while he made a note.

"The original lists are in an envelope in Dad's office," she said. "As far as I know he's the only one who touched that envelope. I didn't. His fingerprints, Daggart's and someone else's are on it. I want to know whose. And whose prints are on the lists in the envelope? You'll find mine and Dad's, and who else's? Is there any way you can get Daggart's fingerprints? And Peel's prints. Can you get them?"

Bailey had grown more and more unhappy as she went down her

want list, and his scowl became more and more pronounced. "Jeez, Barbara, give me a break. You said call in help. I'll need an army."

"Then get it." He had done the background check on Ashley, probably the first thing he had done, she thought, and Ashley Loven was loaded, he had reported. She had inherited four million from Maurice Loven. Bailey liked to know in advance if there would be money in the till to cover his expenses and fees.

"There's going to be one more name, at least," she said. "Travis has to tell me the name of the woman who owned the computer he used when he was emailing June. I'll want her, and that computer."

Bailey groaned and snapped his notebook closed. "And she might be in any one of the fifty states. Or Paris or Istanbul." He was stuffing things into his duffel bag, and added, "That's a lot of digging, and it's going to take time. Don't ride my back about it. Okay?"

"I'll try not to nag. The trial's set for January, but there are a lot of holidays between now and then and that always slows things down. Just gather your troops and get them moving."

He pulled himself upright, drained his coffee cup, and took his time going to the door.

"Bailey," Barbara said, "remember what Dad said about Daggart. He was beaten to death, a professional job done by professionals. Watch your step."

He turned to give her a salute. "And both of you. Especially you, if you start attending that church," he added to Shelley. "Some churches that let you in don't want to let you out again. Be seeing you."

As soon as the door closed behind him, Barbara said, "He has a point, Shelley. You don't need to go to the church again. We'll get his DVDs."

"He wasn't even there," Shelley said. "It seems that he spends as much time in Portland as down here, and when he's up there, they have a closed-circuit television sermon here. I had my hair in a scarf, old clothes, nothing flashy. No one paid any attention to me." She shuddered. "Ashley had it exactly right. He thundered about the sin of lust, the sin of sexual intercourse with no intention of making a baby, the joy of abstinence and so on. It's spooky to hear someone rant about sex like that. He makes it sound filthy."

"Don't go back," Barbara said. "I don't like it that people near him seem to get hurt one way or another." She looked at her watch and stood. "Well, I'm off to see Travis and shake some sense into him, if it's possible."

That day when Travis was brought into the miserable conference room, he was sullen and withdrawn. Barbara watched him sit down and put his hands on the table, not folded in that mocking manner as before, but rather as if he didn't care about her and her questions. Humoring her, she thought. He was going through the motions without hope of anything coming of it.

"Listen to me, Travis, and listen good," she said crisply. "You're a pretty smart guy, I'm betting. You know that if there were three men in that room when Peel got shot, one of them did it. And if those guys don't back up each other, one could get a murder charge and the other an accessory charge. They aren't likely to fess up and risk a thing. So you're on the spot. Maybe, as you suggested, it's a simple case of robbing the collection box. Maybe not. In any case it's going to be a tough call to turn the spotlight onto them. Anonymous donors, a charitable organization, they aren't required to divulge donors who want to remain anonymous. And they don't have to reveal the amounts of donations they receive from individuals, just the aggregate amount. We may never learn how much is involved."

"So I'm dead meat," Travis said hopelessly. "A perfect setup, and a schmuck of a fall guy on hand. Count your blessings."

"I'm working on it," Barbara said, keeping her tone sharp. "I happen to believe you didn't shoot Peel. That's my starting position. I'm putting an army of investigators on your case. There's no point in trying to get the police interested in anything concerning June. You know how you were given the brush-off in San Francisco when you tried. And more importantly, we don't want them to hear that you're convinced that she was injured, or that your father might have been responsible. That's a good motive for murder in their eyes."

She was a little surprised to see that he was listening intently. Whether it was her tone, her manner, or hearing her say she believed him didn't matter. He was listening.

"We're trying to find out where June was being held against her will," she continued in the same crisp voice, "and we need a name. The name of the woman you were with. Don't give me any bullshit about it, just give me her name."

"What difference does it make if June's dead? You can't prove anything without her body, her scars. There's been plenty of time to clean up the place, get rid of any evidence there could have been." He wasn't arguing, just stating the obvious.

"The woman's name. What's her name?"

"I told you she disappeared. Left with a guy. I couldn't find her. No one I knew had a clue."

"You're not a trained investigator. Of course you couldn't find her. I don't know if anyone can, but we can try."

"Judy Margolis," he said with a shrug. "Twenty-six years old, works at whatever she can get. Manicurist, receptionist, maybe prostitution. The guy she dumped me for is a creep, maybe a pimp."

"Description."

"Pretty. Dark brown hair, brown eyes, five five, one-twenty. Tattoo on thigh, flower. One on her back, abstract something. Just a design. Pierced lip, sometimes a ring in it, sometimes not."

"What's the name of the guy?"

"I don't know. She called him Baby. Told me to beat it because she was with Baby."

"What does he look like?"

"Tall and skinny. Pale, too pale. Blond hair. That's all I saw of him coming out of her place once."

Bitterness and resignation were written all over him, Barbara thought with a stab of sympathy. He must have thought Judy was his girl, and losing contact with his sister, out of touch with his mother, it had been a lot for him to deal with.

"Travis," she said in a softer tone, "I don't know where it will go with trying to find out where June was being held, and I don't know if it has anything to do with the charge against you. My first and primary objective is to defend you against the charge of murder. Have you told anyone here about June, what you intended to tell your father, the exhumation, the reason for it, anything? Think, Travis. It's important for me to know if you did."

He shook his head. "The only thing I told them is that I didn't do it, that I didn't have a gun, and never shot a gun in my life."

"Good. Tell me how you survived in San Francisco on your own when you were still a kid."

"I wouldn't have if it hadn't been for Sheila Barrington," he said after a moment. "She got on the bus at Medford, around midnight. It was cold and raining. She was cold and dead tired. She had a little pillow you could blow up. I changed seats with her so she could lean against the window and try to rest. She'd been with her family in Cave Junction and had to get back to the city to go to work on Monday morning. She was so cold she couldn't stop shivering and I put my jacket over her sometime during the night. I couldn't sleep," he added. "I was scared. I had twenty-two dollars, didn't know anyone in San Francisco, and I didn't know where I'd go when I got there. Sheila helped. She said I reminded her of her little brother and she did for me what she hoped someone would do for him if he ever needed help."

He talked about Sheila freely. Her boyfriend had been in Iraq and would be home in seven months. During those months Travis stayed with Sheila in her apartment. She made a deal with him. He had to go to the library every day she worked, and he had to stay there for at least four hours and read. She didn't want him on the streets all day. She had a friend who cooked in a restaurant on the wharf and got Travis a part-time job washing dishes. She told him that if he ever used drugs she would kick him out instantly, and she meant it. Living with her, he kept the place more or less clean, and he did most of the cooking. She showed him around the city, the museums, the parks, the places she and Paul liked, and she introduced him to a lot of people. He became a reader again and liked spending hours in the library and never stopped spending time there.

"They emailed each other every day," he said, "and she talked about Paul a lot. They were going to get married as soon as he got home. But he was wounded, lost a leg, and got sent to Germany, then to Walter Reed. When he got to San Francisco, I moved out. That was the plan from the start," he added quickly. "I went over now and then, just to visit. Paul was pretty messed up in the head, and San Francisco was too much for him. They went back to Cave Junction for him to recuperate. They're still there. They raise sheep."

"Did you ever visit them in Cave Junction?"

Instantly he became tense and distant. "No."

"Why not?"

"He would have found out. I was still underage, under eighteen. He has church members in that area. One of them would have told him."

Barbara could almost feel his hatred, and more than that, fear. He had been and still was afraid of Arlie Morgan, afraid of his father.

She forced herself not to ask the question that needed to be asked and answered: What happened to him that made him run away, that made him afraid of his father? Guy talk, she reminded herself. Frank would get an answer to that question, and she might get only a new surge of distrust and hostility. She changed the subject.

He became much more vague when he talked about the next few years. He had worked on the wharf part-time, then full-time, had been beaten up twice and learned to avoid gangs and their turf. When he seemed to be skipping too much, Barbara called a halt.

"Enough for this time," she said. "It's been helpful, filling in a picture. Thanks, Travis."

He regarded her soberly for a moment, then said, "You remind me of Sheila. She wouldn't take any crap from me, either."

Sheila had been his big sister, Barbara thought, walking by the river half an hour later. He had met people who treated him decently, and even after he no longer lived in Sheila's apartment, some of those people continued on friendly terms with him. He had not gotten into trouble, that was the important point, she told herself. He had stayed clean. The police had reported that no drugs or alcohol had been found when they did their routine examination while he was in the hospital. And that was important.

Those Brownie points could be irrelevant, she knew, if she could not find a way to implicate the other two guys in the room that night. She had already decided that she could not put Travis on the stand to undergo the kind of cross-examination she knew he would be given. His hatred of his father was too near the surface not to bubble out if he was pressed. And the jury must never be allowed to see that he feared his father.

She sat on a bench to gaze at the murmuring river, still summer clear and sparkling without a hint of the changing season, not yet quickened with the run-off of fall rain and snow in the mountains. The sunshine was warm but it wasn't like the heat—pure August sunshine; the air had a different smell, an early autumnal smell, and the warmth of the sun was moderated by a coolness rarely felt in earlier months. Also, juncos had arrived. Dozens of the little gray birds with their neat black heads were busily pecking in the grass. That meant snow in the mountains, change of seasons.

Signs and portents, she thought then. The color and speed of the river, juncos, the freshening air, even the light from the sun heading south was different, diluted, and it was all connected, a moving, living tapestry of nature, all of a piece.

And Travis's case, she realized, had the same kind of connectedness, like a Catherine Wheel, throwing arms out in many directions, but connected at the center, and that connection point was Arlie Morgan, the man who called himself Benjamin.

CHAPTER 8

"WHAT MORE DO you want from me?" Travis asked that day when Frank sat opposite him at the metal table. "You guys have milked me dry." He grinned as he said this.

Frank laughed. "We've barely started. But actually I don't want anything in particular. I brought you something. Since I'm a member of your defense team, I get a few privileges, such as getting in when I ask nicely, and bringing you enlightening material to help your intellectual growth. And that's what I've done. Here, it's for you." He passed a book across the table and watched Travis pick it up and open it to the title page.

Travis looked up quickly. "You wrote this? You're a writer?"

"No claims to being a writer, but yes, I wrote it. I thought you might find it interesting. Cross-examinations of criminal cases. Actually, to say I wrote it is likely a mistake. Rather, I lifted page after page from trial transcripts, added a bit of commentary, and found a publisher."

Travis appeared to be impressed. He opened the book at random and read a few lines, then laughed. "You call that commentary? I call it dissection. You're ripping that yahoo to pieces, aren't you?"

"Well, sometimes it seemed to me that one attorney or another was missing something," Frank said. "Were you always such a good reader? You zipped through that little bit in seconds."

"Yeah, I guess. Now and then, anyway. It got me in trouble in school, though. I don't know how they did it in your day, but in grade school they handed out reading books, and I read mine the day I got it. The next day the teacher said we should read from page three or something to page something else. Four or five pages. I'd already read the whole thing, so I didn't bother, and she sent a note home saying I needed to learn to follow instructions. Trouble."

"Did you get a whipping? Get sent to bed without dinner?"

Travis shook his head. "I had to read a chapter from the Bible out loud every day for two weeks."

"Cruel and unusual punishment," Frank said gravely. "Eighth amendment. Travis, tell me something, how did you tackle a whole library? Did you have a reading list? A guide?"

"I wish. I was amazed at how many books there were," Travis said. "It was overwhelming. I decided that I had to have a method or I'd never get anywhere. I started with A, one fiction, one nonfiction. I'd get hung up on something now and then," he added after a moment. "I couldn't seem to get enough of Egyptology."

Frank leaned back in his chair, nodding now and then as Travis talked about the books he had read, what had fascinated him, what he had found boring. Economics, boring; philosophy, exciting. Dostoevsky, big-time exciting. "I cheated and read three in a row," he said with a quick glance at Frank, who nodded and said, "Me too."

"Psychology... I got hung up on that," Travis said with a faraway look. "I kept reading more and more, and one day I realized that I was looking for something to explain me, him, all of us. It was when I found Skinner. You know, stimulus and response, like we all have on and off buttons, and if you know the right button, you get the response you want. Pavlov's dogs," he said in a low voice. "We can all become Pavlov's dogs if the right person finds the right button to push. Mom was reading *Alice in Wonderland*," he said in an even lower voice. "He came in and took the book away from her. After that, she could only read books he brought home, and... Well, we stopped family reading." He was gazing past Frank with a distant look, as if that past was playing out before his eyes and he was unable to stop watching.

"What else did he do to you, Travis?" Frank asked softly. "Stimulus, response. What else happened?"

"He said if I had wet dreams, I had to tell him and he'd talk about it with me, that I wasn't responsible. If I touched myself, that was different. I had to tell him, and he would have to punish me, make me become responsible, to accept that I was sinning, and sinning had to be punished." As he spoke, his expression changed from a distant preoccupied look to one of hatred and contempt.

Abruptly he turned his gaze to Frank and said vehemently, "He turns everything human into something evil, something to be punished. If I'd stayed, he would have turned sex into something to be ashamed of, evil, demonic. He's crazy, Mr. Holloway! He's insane! That's why I ran away. I was afraid of him because he's crazy!"

"What was his punishment for masturbation?" Frank asked mildly.

"I don't know," Travis said, looking away. "I lied to him," he said, as color flared on his cheeks. "But I knew he'd find out."

Frank reached across the table and patted Travis's arm. "You saved yourself, son. That's the important thing. You saved yourself. Just a kid, you realized at that young age that you had to get away from him, his philosophy, and you did. Not understanding the rationale of the need to run, you ran, trusting your instincts, and you did the right thing. If there had been someone to talk to, it might have worked out differently. But you don't talk about those things with just anyone."

"If Derek had stayed around I could have talked to him," Travis mumbled. "He tried to warn me, but I was too young. I didn't know what he was talking about."

"Who is Derek?"

"Derek Peel. I overheard him talking with his mom and dad. He said he wouldn't stay in that house. He was going to go to college, Oregon State in Corvallis, and *he* wanted him to go to the U of O and live at that house. I didn't hear much of it, but I asked Derek why he wouldn't stay in our house. He said I should get out the minute my… the minute he started to talk to me about sex. Just take off, he said." His face twisted, and he looked down at the table. "He probably thinks I killed his father."

Frank stayed a while longer. Travis talked about the household, about Peel and his wife, about Derek, about several things, but not about his father. When Frank was ready to leave, Travis said awkwardly, "Thanks, Mr. Holloway." Belatedly he held up Frank's book. "For the book, I mean."

"I know. You're welcome, Travis. I'll drop by in few days and we can talk over some of those cases if you'd like. Pretty interesting stuff in there."

Thoughtful and troubled, Frank headed for Barbara's office.

"How did it go?" she asked when he walked in.

"Interesting," Frank said, taking one of the easy chairs. "I have that answer that's been missing these past few weeks."

"Why am I not surprised," she murmured. "What is it?"

He told her about his long conversation with Travis and watched her face flush as her anger mounted.

"That bastard! That goddamn bastard!"

"Hold on a minute," Frank said. "I'm starting to wonder if first Ashley and now Travis are right. Is the man insane?"

"I don't care if he's as nutty as peanut brittle. I want his scalp."

"I know you do, and that alarms me," Frank said quietly. "Bobby, if he's as irrational as the signs indicate, if he truly is insane, he's dangerous in a way that your usual suspect isn't. He's unpredictable. You can't penetrate the psyche of a madman and anticipate his next actions unless he's caught himself in a loop. You can't predict, and you can't get through to him if he's delusional. Reason can't win against irrationality grounded in a belief system. The good old Faith v. Reason no-win situation." Knowing her anger was not subsiding, he continued. "Tell you a story. Faith and Reason were invited to the same swank dinner party. Reason declined the fish entree, saying it was not fresh, had a bad color, and the odor was not good. Faith said they were in the best restaurant in town, with the best chef, and he helped himself to the fish. He got sick as a dog, and would have died if Reason had not gotten him to the hospital. Heroic measures were applied and Faith was saved. Triumphantly he shouted, 'See, God decided it isn't my time yet!'"

Barbara nodded. "And the kid who doesn't get the antibiotics dies in spite of the prayers and the laying on of hands because God said it was his time. Right."

"The parents mourn the loss of their child, but their faith is not shaken," Frank said soberly. "And that's the whole point. Getting between a zealot and his faith is like getting between a dog and his supper dish. You might get your hand bitten off." He stood and glanced at her desk that had many piles of papers. "Making any headway?"

She shook her head. "I'm making folders for all the different aspects of this mess, starting with Daggart, who chose your office to start dying in. Ashley's stack, Travis's, the arson fire that killed Ashley's husband, June's stack, COPAR's—" She stopped when Frank held up his hand. "The Church of Purity and Redemption," she explained.

She walked to her desk and held up several disks. "His sermons," she said. "I've been putting off playing them, in no mood for sermons, I guess. Maybe it's time to have a look."

"I'll provide the popcorn," Frank said. "When, where? If you make it my place I can duck out now and then when I start to feel the spirit moving me."

"Good. No point in punishing Darren and Todd. Tomorrow evening? I'll see if Shelley can join us, compare the disks to what she saw at the church."

"Right. Now I'm off to pick beans before the rain moves in."

"And I'm waiting for Bailey to deliver his next package of useless and endless information," she said with a sigh.

After he left, she sat at her desk again and regarded her many piles of papers with disgust. It was early in the case, she acknowledged, but she could not find a straight line to any decent defense against two eyewitnesses. And she had yet to find a way to put Arlie Morgan in the picture. He, his driver, and his bodyguard had all given statements that he had been in his upstairs study with Dr. Knowland when Travis arrived. He had directed Boris Rostov to take Travis to Peel, who then was to escort him up to Morgan's study.

It was close to five when Bailey showed up. Barbara was still sorting material, separating and cursing the various threads of her spider web of a case. She left it all to sit at the table for Bailey's report. He fixed himself a bourbon with a hint of water before joining her.

"My guy found her," he said glumly. "Judy Margolis in San Mateo, shacked up with Stephen Myerson, who happens to be a computer geek with a software company, and who she calls Baby. It's a wash, Barbara. Judy's computer got a virus and Baby couldn't get rid of it and ended up reformatting the thing."

"No trace of those emails left?"

"You got it. Wiped clean." He drank, put his glass down, and brought out a folder from the duffel bag. "The latest on Boris Rostov, the bodyguard, and Tony DiPalma, the driver."

"Good. I have a tidbit for you. Dad had a long talk with Travis today." She watched Bailey grow more and more uncomfortable as she related what all Frank had told her. Bailey was more prudish than almost anyone she knew, and talk about sex was on his taboo list of subjects for discussion between males and females. Today, however, his discomfort was accompanied with a growing indignation, even outrage.

"That stinks," he said when she was finished. "Why'd he want to mess up his own kid that way?"

"Because he's a nutcase," she snapped. "We're going to watch a couple of his sermons on disk to see if we can get a glimpse of the man behind the curtain."

"When?"

"You want to see him in action?"

"Yeah," Bailey said. He drained his glass and stood. He started toward the door in his shambling gait, paused, and said, "Barbara, I talked to one of the guys who knew about Daggart, and he was impressed by the pulping that poor guy took and still managed to get to your old man. An arson murder fire out at the coast, the wrong body at the mortuary, a missing daughter, an attack on Morgan's life up in Portland a couple of years ago. Yeah, I want a peek at the center of the hurricane."

Back at her desk after Bailey's departure, she quickly scanned his report about Judy Margolis and her friend Baby. Wearily she labeled a new folder Dead End, and placed the report in it.

She paid more attention to his report about the bodyguard, Boris Rostov, the dates of his military service, the years with the police department in Dallas, then with the security firm, and the question arose: Why leave such a lucrative job to become the bodyguard of an obscure preacher? The final paragraph of this report said little more than Rostov had been the one to shoot and kill the intruder who had made an attempt on the life of the Reverend Morgan.

She started to place the report in its own folder, then withdrew it again and reread the final paragraph. She looked over her desk until she found the folder marked Morgan. In it she found the items about the attack that ended up with a dead teenager.

The event had happened at Morgan's condominium in Portland in April two years ago. The boy, John Varagosa, had gotten in and fired several shots, yelling incoherently that he wanted Morgan, who had not been home. Rostov had ordered him to drop his gun, and when Varagosa instead turned his weapon on Rostov, he was shot and killed. Two witnesses, no one else injured. No reason was given for the attack. John Varagosa, it was reported in a follow-up story, had been a gang member, had been in a gang fight ten days before the fatal encounter, and had been in the hospital briefly following the fight.

Barbara closed her eyes trying to visualize the scene where a wild-eyed boy burst into a private apartment shooting a gun, only to get shot dead. A boy who several days earlier had been beaten severely enough to put him in the hospital. Following which he had sought out Morgan.

"And," she muttered under her breath, "Rostov was already on hand to take care of him."

The newspaper stories were too sparse, she knew, too unreliable to be taken seriously, but there were those in Portland who would know the whole story, or as much as could be learned, at any rate. And she knew some of those people, some of those people were friends. She found her address book in her desk drawer and looked up Wanda Haviland's phone number, glanced at her watch, and dialed anyway, hoping Wanda was still in her office. It was twenty minutes before six, but Wanda, like Barbara, was a defense attorney, and as far as Barbara could tell, they all kept irregular hours.

Wanda answered her phone in a disgruntled, snappish sort of a way, "It's after office hours."

"Before you tell me to get lost, listen. Barbara Holloway, and I need your brain."

"Sorry. I thought it was someone else. What's up?"

"I need to talk to someone who knows the inside story of an incident that happened two years ago. A kid named John Varagosa was shot dead when he attempted to murder Arlie Morgan. I need some details. Who might be the someone who knows something?"

There was a long silence on the line and when Wanda spoke again it was in a carefully measured voice, her attorney voice. "Can you tell me a little about why you want that someone? What it's about?"

Barbara felt her pulse quicken. She recognized that nuanced demand for information before committing herself to anything. "Indeed," she said in her own attorney voice. "You may have read that I'm the defense attorney for Travis Morgan, accused of murdering Joseph Peel, Arlie Morgan's bookkeeper. Travis didn't do it, so I'm digging. It may be that the incident in Portland will help my case."

There was another long silence, then a distinct sigh. "Not on the phone," Wanda said. "Yeah, I know something about it, but it's complicated. Can you come up here and talk?"

"You bet I can. When?"

"Not until the weekend. I'm swamped, that's why I'm hanging out after hours. Saturday, twoish. Not at the office, at my place. Barbara, if you promise to tie the knot, I'll furnish the rope to hang that son of a bitch."

"Good," Barbara said in satisfaction. "You know it's Morgan I'm really after?"

"Who else? You called him Arlie. His followers call him Benjamin. Got a pencil handy? I'll give you my address."

CHAPTER 9

ARLIE MORGAN LOOKED like a middle school history teacher, Barbara thought as the first of three videos started to play. He was middle everything: average height, weight, average appearance with brown hair and pale blue eyes, no distinguishing features. Just an average guy you might see in a supermarket out of his depth before a hundred kinds of cereal, taking his kid to a ball game, apologizing for getting in the way of someone in a hurry.

Morgan was being the good father, telling his congregation, his children, a story. "So the three good fairies gave the baby girl beauty and good health, a cheerful disposition, obedience, and so on. Then the evil fairy gave her a gift, and that gift was a curse. Sleeping Beauty was cursed. She slept the pure sleep of innocence until her prince came and woke her up with a kiss. Yes, he woke her up with a kiss and her innocence was gone."

He looked into the camera and his voice dropped; his words came more slowly and sounded ominous. "That fairy tale was never meant for children. It is a tale for grown-ups to think about, to ponder its meaning. Wise men figured out the human condition, and they chose fairy tales to try to express what could not be said because the kings and princes, the highest church, the Catholic Church, threatened their deaths if the truth be told. That fairy tale is the story of the creation of mankind itself."

His voice rose and he stared into the camera with intensity. "God created man in his image, and God is pure good. He created man to be good, to be pure. God does not lust! And the mankind he created did not lust. Then Lucifer, the fallen angel, the evil one we call the Devil, Satan, bestowed his gift, his curse on all mankind. It was not knowledge that damned mankind. It was lust! Lust of man for woman, of woman for man, lust of man for man, woman for woman, lust of adults for children, lust forever in all hearts in all seasons."

He began to pace on the stage, stopping to stare into the camera again and again, speaking directly to his audience. "God said there is a season to sow and a season to reap. The gentle cow does not lust for the bull when it isn't her season. The bird on the wing has a season to build a nest, to create life. The fish that return home know their season. But Satan said let there be no season for lust. Only man knows no season and is consumed by lust. And that is Satan's curse on mankind."

His voice was rising again and he thundered, "Let the man or woman who succumbs to that everlasting lust, yield to it, deny God's purpose, defy his command, let that damned soul burn in everlasting hellfire for all eternity!"

Thing One leaped from Barbara's lap and stalked from the room with his tail bristling and as rigid as a bottlebrush. Barbara could not blame him.

"You fornicators, you adulterers, you men who lie with men, women with women, you who take pleasure in your own bodies, you who murder the growing life within your bodies, you who render your bodies infertile, you who use chemicals or other devices to thwart God's will, you who lure the young and innocent into your sinful ways, all of you will suffer the hellfire of eternity. Your flesh will writhe and fall from your bones, your burning eyes from their sockets, your stomach will explode with agonizing pain, your bowels will run blood, and you will not be released from your torment. Again and again and again will your flesh writhe and fall from your bones, your burning eyes from their sockets. There will be no release, no mercy, no escape. Hellfire is forever!"

Thing Two decided to follow his brother.

Morgan was red-faced and sweating, the middle school teacher gone, a fanatic in his place. Barbara felt a chill watching him. He believed what he was saying, she thought distantly. He was his own true believer.

He was telling his audience how to save their souls. "God created man in his image and he bestowed on him this beautiful, bountiful world, and he said, 'Go forth and multiply.' He didn't say go forth and have your momentary pleasure of the flesh. He gave mankind the gift of procreation, the gift to create new life, to multiply. Sexual intercourse is God's gift, not for the fleeting pleasure of the moment, but to bring forth life. Live together as brother and sister, as loving friends, and know that when you have sexual intercourse, it is to create new life, as God intended. This is the way to purity, to redemption, to your salvation. It is the only way."

He talked about abstinence. About creating new life. About hellfire again, and then suddenly he was talking about government, about the world of advertising, about the welfare state, how they were Satan's tools, how they dimmed the sight of the righteous and tempted them to the flesh, away from God.

Barbara wasn't certain when God was dropped from the sermon, which had become nothing more than a rant against the state and those who ruled. It was a message of sound bites berating big government, she thought, and glanced at Frank. He was frowning, his fingers drumming on the arm of his chair. Morgan was back to God, she realized and paid attention again.

"Those who have heard the word of God will rise up in the end times. They will scour the halls of government, scourge the tempters, purify the temple. And they shall know their God is with them in their wrath. His presence will give them strength and courage. The end times draw near. The sign will come, and they shall rise up and the righteous will rejoice knowing the kingdom of heaven and earth is theirs."

Barbara turned the sound down when a choir began to sing. "Whew. You win, Dad. Nutty as they come."

"I'm going to put dinner on the table in five minutes," Frank said. "Just a casserole and salad."

He walked out and Barbara turned to Shelley. "Was that pretty much how it was in the church?"

Shelley nodded. "I kept watching others, how entranced some of them seemed, especially in the first part. More fidgeting when he began to rant about big government, but not a sound or movement when he was talking about sinners, hellfire, burning eyeballs. He gives me the creeps."

"Me too," Bailey said. "He would have fitted right in when they burned witches to save their souls. He'd toast marshmallows in the fires." He helped himself to another drink from the tray Frank had provided.

Barbara poured more wine and sipped it, agreeing with Bailey. Morgan would be in the front row of any burning of witches. Or fornicators, adulterers, masturbators. "I'll see if Dad can use a hand," she said and left Shelley and Bailey in the living room.

Frank was removing the casserole from the oven. "It's all taken care of," he said when Barbara asked if she could do anything. He put the casserole down, removed the lid, then said, "After Shelley and Bailey leave, hang around a minute or two. Something we should talk about."

"The disks are labeled one, two, three," Barbara said at the dinner table. "His introduction to the true religion. Says so on the labels."

"If it's all the same to you guys, I'll pass on number two and three," Bailey said as he spooned out a second helping of chicken and rice. "I wanted to see him in action. Did that, and done with that."

Barbara looked at Shelley. "You don't have to sit through any more of it. You've done more than enough, the church and now this. I really just wanted to know if he's the same before his congregation as when he's making a DVD and the camera's rolling. I guess the answer is yes. Turn him on and watch him rant."

"Good," Shelley said. "I feel as if I've had enough religion for one day. Maybe Bailey and I can clean up in the kitchen while you and your father play the next disk."

Bailey gave her a baleful look. "Sure. We'll do KP. If he drops a bomb or something, give us a call."

He didn't drop a bomb, but he went on at length about the temptations Satan used to lure the unwary: naked women, painted women, playthings for the men, new cars, trucks, electronic marvels… "Lust in your heart makes you the tempter, makes you reveal your body, flaunt your powerful toys. Just as the peacock spreads his beautiful feathers to lure a mate, you use Satan's toys to lure your prey. And it never ends; there is always another woman, another man, another child. But you can resist Satan's beckoning finger. The act of sexual intercourse to procreate only is your most powerful weapon against evil. Rejoice in your hearts when you lie with your mate, know that you are fulfilling God's plan, know that the seed that is planted in fertile ground is God's gift."

Barbara felt her finger twitching over the fast-forward button, and resisted. Hear it out, she told herself. Know your enemy. One of the cats joined her, left, the other one tried it and left. As before, after a lengthy harangue about sex, Morgan went on to the evils of government, those who governed, the teachers who corrupted youth with misguided lessons, the evil perpetrated by science in alliance with Satan…

When the DVD ended, she looked around to see Shelley in the doorway. "I thought you were gone," Barbara said.

"Bailey left. I wanted to see if he's like that again and again. He is. One-message Morgan. Why do people go back? What's in it for them? I guess I just don't get it."

"He's putting a name on their insecurities," Frank said. "Aimless anxiety is self-devouring. He's giving them something to fear, to focus on, and he's damn good at what he's doing." He stood and went to Shelley. "Go on home. No more punishment for this evening." Glancing at Barbara, he added, "I don't need another lesson. I'll be in my study when you're done in here." He took Shelley by the arm and walked to the door with her. "As you drive home, replay in your mind the best day of your life, complete with minute details."

Barbara refilled her coffee cup and put in the third disk. This time she didn't still her twitching finger over the fast-forward button. She was about to hit the button again, when Morgan began to talk about punishment for the transgressors in our midst.

"Let them know the stone and the blade, let them know the purifying flame, let them suffer the bitter cold of winter without shelter, the pain of hunger in their empty bellies, let them see their children dig for scraps in the garbage, their parents beg for deliverance from thirst and pestilence. Show no pity toward those who would defile you, corrupt you, lead you on the path to hell… " She hit the button.

When it ended, she sat for several minutes before the dark television. Watching three in a row was psychological torture, mind bending, mind breaking, soul numbing. She thought about what Travis had told Frank. He had run away because he was afraid of his father. Damn right, she thought.

Finally she stood and went to the study where she found Frank in his favorite chair under his favorite lamp on a large end table almost hidden by books. She knew he would keep that chair until it collapsed under him and she no longer bothered to remonstrate about it. He put down a book when she entered. Thing One grunted and rearranged himself when Frank moved.

"Done," she said, sinking into another chair. "Done in is more appropriate. What's on your mind?"

"A lot of things," Frank said. "I like Travis Morgan, for starters. But, Barbara, try as hard as I can, I don't see how you're going to rope Arlie Morgan into the murder of Joseph Peel." He held up his hand as she started to speak. "Let me have my say first. If those three stick to their stories, and they will, I just don't see a good defense shaping up. The two in the room will stick to their stories because they're professionals, and Morgan's a professional, too. A professional zealot with a mission. You know the story of Isaac, don't you? A father willing to sacrifice his son to prove his loyalty and love for his god. That's what you're dealing with here."

"I can discredit those two in the room," she said hotly. "Bailey's finding more all the time to show them for what they are."

"You can't discredit them enough," Frank said. "They'll play the mea culpa ploy. Yes, I made mistakes when I was young, but now I've found religion. Reverend Morgan restored my faith, or introduced me to faith. You know that script. It's one that plays well with juries, especially when the prosecution paints the accused as a runaway who lived on the streets of San Francisco for seven years, and we all know what those young people are up to. It's not enough, Barbara."

"What are you suggesting?" she asked carefully.

"Possibly not what you think," Frank said. "I said it alarms me that you're focusing so much on Morgan. What he did to Ashley. What he would have done to Travis. What happened to his daughter June. Who he incinerated in place of his daughter. He's the target in your gun sight, and I agree that he should be taken down, but not in this context, maybe not by you. There's too much to try to introduce at the trial. Too many directions, too many stories. You'd need a bevy of witnesses to try to fit them all in, but you'd be brought to heel over each and every one of them. No judge will let you drag him through the mud in defense of your client. The prosecution will accuse you of trying him instead of defending your client. The jury will automatically assume that he's a man of God and if you go for him, it could backfire and make it worse for your client. Meanwhile, in the next few weeks, I suggest that you ask Minnick to have a few talks with Travis."

"You want him to go for an insanity plea?" She couldn't mask her incredulity. "That never works, and you know it. The state would have to have their own panel of experts—" She stopped when Frank held up his hand.

"I do know that," he said. "And no, I don't want him to plead insanity. But the prosecution will think that's the way you're heading and that might be good. I want Minnick to crack open a wall Travis has erected. There's still something behind that wall that needs airing." He regarded her soberly, then said, "Barbara, if nothing breaks, you might have to go with a plea bargain. You have to keep that in mind. And you have to shift your focus from Morgan to the task at hand, how to save Travis Morgan's life. You can't expend your resources on a hopeless massive project when they're needed for your main purpose, to save that young man's life."

"I talked to Ashley about the expenses," she said hotly. "If she's not worried about that, and she's not, then neither am I."

"I'm not talking about financial resources. I'm talking about the priceless resource of your brain."

Slowly Barbara rose and started to walk to the door. "You think I'm wasting my time, Ashley's money, but I know that Morgan's at the bottom of this trial. I'll give a lot of thought to what you've said. Now I should go home. I have reading to do tonight."

Frank heaved himself upright and followed her. He doubted that she realized the coolness of her response, but he felt a pang, and expecting her rejection of his arguments did not lessen that pang. He went to the front door with her, where she thanked him politely for the use of his television and the lovely dinner. She sounded like a well-mannered acquaintance.

"Bobby," he said at the door, "I could have overstepped, and if I did, I'm sorry."

She gave him a curious look and shook her head. "What I was thinking of was when you said it pays to trust your intuition. That's what I'm doing, Dad. Good night."

He watched her car back out of the driveway, watched the taillight diminish, vanish, and only then stepped back inside, cursing under his breath. She would do exactly what she planned, what she needed to do, and it could lead her and Travis to disaster. In the living room Thing One had found the cheese on the coffee table and Frank's silent curses became audible.

Driving home, Barbara replayed Frank's words in her head. He didn't think she could make a case for the defense, and since there was no case to be made, he did have a point. She knew the judge would not allow her to rake Morgan over the coals when all she had to offer was history and suspicion without a shred of proof of wrongdoing on his part. But having Dr. Minnick talk to Travis was a fine idea, she decided. It would keep the prosecution guessing about her intentions, but more, it would be good for Travis to talk to him.

Dr. Minnick was a world-renowned psychiatrist who had specialized in adolescent schizophrenia before his retirement. He had written a number of highly regarded books, published papers in the most prestigious journals, taught at Columbia... His list of accomplishments was awe inspiring. Very likely he had saved the life of Shelley's husband, Alex. Dr. Minnick, Shelley, and Alex lived together in the foothills of the Coast Range.

The prosecution would be sure to think they planned an insanity plea. They would have long conferences, the expert witnesses who would have to be called, the added expense and confusion when two sides presented conflicting expert testimony, and they might be relieved and ready to deal if it came down to a plea bargain.

She hit the brake pedal suddenly and muttered a curse. He had done it to her, she realized. He had manipulated her ever so skillfully. "There is not going to be a plea bargain!" she said aloud. A horn sounded behind her, and she began to drive again.

CHAPTER 10

EVER SINCE BARBARA had known her, Wanda Haviland was going on a diet, just finished with the latest diet or midway through one. She had the most beautiful hair Barbara had ever seen, lustrous black, halfway down her back, and abundant enough for two women. It was in a thick braid that day with a red satin ribbon braided in. She was wearing tight black pants, a red shirt and house slippers. She greeted Barbara with a quick hug.

"Come on in to the pigsty," she said, gesturing to the room.

There were stacks of newspapers and magazines on the end tables, more on chairs, empty Diet Pepsi cans here and there, books in stacks at the side of a chair, and many papers and folders on a coffee table.

"Sit wherever you can find a space," Wanda said, looking around with a frown. She went to one of the chairs and picked up newspapers, then, after another glance around, deposited them on the floor by the chair. "So you jumped in on the Peel murder case. A no-win case, if the newspapers are within shouting distance of the truth. Eyewitnesses, prints on the gun, the works for a quickie of a trial."

"Except," Barbara said, "he didn't do it." She sat on the newly cleared chair.

"Right." Wanda positioned herself warily on the sofa, which had many more folders scattered about on the cushions. "It would be a shame to send him up for getting the wrong guy. Going up for Morgan might be worth it. John Varagosa thought it would be worth the price."

"That's what I want to know about. Were the news accounts within shouting distance of the truth?"

"No way. I know what the newspapers said, and it was bullshit from start to finish." She leaned forward on the sofa. "I was on the inside from the get-go. I knew the Varagosa family from years back and they came to me when John showed up butchered. His father has an automobile repair shop and has kept my car up and running forever. John worked with him after school and on weekends. He was a good kid, almost too handsome, with a great smile. Good grades in school, never in trouble. What happened, straight from John's own account to me, was that he stayed late at school with a few others to work on a play they were putting together. Building stage props, scenery. He was the last one to leave. He was walking to the bus stop when he was slugged on the head and dragged into a van, hit again, this time knocking him all the way out. He didn't see a face or what kind of van it was. When he woke up he was naked, gagged, and blindfolded, strapped to a hard surface with plastic under him."

Wanda paused, picked up a Pepsi can and took a sip. "That's when they went to work on him. Someone cut a big letter F on his cheek. And they castrated him."

Barbara gasped.

"They waited until he was awake," Wanda said. "They could

have done it while he was out, but they waited. He passed out again, and the next thing he knew he was bundled up in the plastic, in a car or van. They stopped and rolled him out onto the ground and took off. It was raining hard, he was bleeding heavily and too groggy to do anything. Two women, just off a late shift at their office heard his moans and found him. It was two in the morning. They called 911 and he was taken to the hospital. If they hadn't come along, he probably would have bled to death in the rain."

Abruptly she jumped up, slammed the Pepsi can to the table and said, "Let's go out to the kitchen, get something real to drink. You look like you're going to pass out on me."

Barbara felt that was a fair assessment. She was nauseated.

The kitchen was spotless and very neat. "The trick to living with chaos," Wanda said, going to a cabinet, "is to keep it contained. What will you have? Vodka, rum, bourbon, even a little cognac. I'll settle for vodka and bitter lemon."

Barbara nodded when Wanda glanced her way, and they both remained silent until Wanda mixed the drinks and brought them to a table, motioned for Barbara to sit down.

"They found opiates in his system," Wanda said after taking a long drink. "He had been missing for thirty hours, with no memory of any of it until he woke up and they butchered him. They had kept him drugged apparently, but the cops decided he was a dopehead. Once they decided that, it was open and shut for them: gang war, revenge, et cetera and all that crap. They never believed a word the kid said."

"There wasn't anything about castration in the accounts I read," Barbara said after a moment.

"No. They were afraid of copycat incidents. Hospital personnel agreed to keep it quiet, and the family wasn't going to say a word about it, either. Roberto was devastated, fell into a deep depression that he's still struggling with, and his wife wasn't much better. She came to me for help and told me the truth about the matter. John wouldn't leave the house, wouldn't see anyone, just kept to his room, crying. Ten days after he was grabbed, he broke into his father's gun cabinet, took out a revolver and left. He went to Morgan's condo and forced his way in. He was screaming that he wanted Morgan, and even fired off a couple of shots. A man named Boris Rostov, Morgan's bodyguard, shot and killed him. End of that."

"Jesus!" Barbara said. "Where was Morgan?"

"He left minutes before John arrived. The night they grabbed John, Morgan was at a meeting early, then on his way down to Eugene. He's always somewhere else."

"Why was his bodyguard still at the condo if he was going out?"

"Morgan said he felt safe in a public place like a restaurant. He told Rostov to stay in the condo that night."

"Now the big question," Barbara said. "Why did John Varagosa want to kill Morgan? Did they have a history? Did he go to Morgan's church?"

"He never met him," Wanda said. She finished her drink and regarded the glass for a moment, then stood. "I'm not supposed to touch booze with this crazy diet, but screw the diet. Do you want to top off yours?"

"Thanks, but no. I'm good." Her glass was almost full.

"I'll put on coffee for you if you're not going to drink that."

Barbara watched Wanda start the coffee and refill her glass. "What did the family want you to do? What could you do?" she asked when Wanda returned to the table.

"Make it right. See that justice got done. Clear John's name. Prove that Morgan had done that to him and see to it that he got sent to prison for life, or that he was executed, something." She took a very long drink. "And there wasn't a goddamn thing I could do," she said bitterly. "The police had their story: a dopehead went on a rampage after a vicious gang attack."

"Why did Morgan have a bodyguard? The account I read implied it was because of the attack, but Rostov was on hand before that. Why?"

Wanda nodded. "I asked the same question. Answer: there had been anonymous threats that Morgan took seriously." She held up her hand, as if to forestall Barbara's next question. "Morgan said he doesn't believe people should turn to the government for all their needs. Some things you should take care of yourself, like protecting yourself. So he hired a bodyguard and never reported the earlier threats. Another period."

Barbara couldn't quell the sick feeling in her stomach, the fury the story had engendered, the rage that the police had not done more than accept the easiest scenario and let it go at that. Dope, teenager, violence. Wrap it up, hide it away and get on with things.

"After your call I went to see the family," Wanda said. "I told them you were going after Morgan. I asked permission to confide in you, to release their statements, to assist you in any way I can. They agreed. They're done maintaining silence if there's a chance you can do what I couldn't do. And, Barbara, I mean this very sincerely, I'm hoping and praying the same thing." She stood and went to the door. "I have copies for you, statements, notes, hospital records, police records, the works. For now, I'll just summarize and let you read everything later." She walked into the living room, returned with the folder and put it on the table. It was quite thick.

"Julietta, John's sister, fifteen years old at the time, was a student at the Kenmore Academy for Girls," Wanda said after sitting down at the table again. "It's a private school for girls. Ruth Morgan was also a student."

Barbara felt an adrenaline surge. Ruth Morgan, June!

"They were friends, in the same classes, same age. When it was raining hard, or if it was really cold, John used his father's car to pick up his sister and a couple of her friends, including Ruth, at school. He was a senior, had shorter days, fewer classes to finish up, and he had the time. Usually he took the girls home and went back to the garage until about six, when he and Roberto went home together. After the Christmas holiday, he asked Ruth to sit up front with him. He liked her. She was pretty and smart and she understood his jokes and laughed at them. After that, he always took her home last. One evening he was nearly an hour late in getting back to the garage. They'd been talking, he said. They stopped for a Coke and were talking and he lost track of time.

"John's senior class was rehearsing a play, working on props, the music, all that. They were going to stage it just before Easter. He asked Ruth for a date, to attend the play and the party afterward. She said her father wouldn't let her date. That was just a week before they kidnapped John. She said she'd ask."

Wanda took a long drink and set the glass down hard. "Most of the rest of it comes from Julietta. She said that Ruth didn't turn up at school for a couple of days. She called her at home and a man answered and said she had the flu and couldn't come to the phone. A few days later their teacher said that Ruth had been withdrawn from school to recuperate from the flu and that she was in a private nursing facility. Julietta never saw her again. She never called or wrote or anything. And four days after she stopped going to school, John was kidnapped."

Barbara understood why the police had paid little attention to the story. A couple of kids had a Coke and got home a little late. Big deal.

"Julietta talked a lot about what she had learned about Ruth's home life," Wanda said then. "She was afraid to ask her father about the party, but she finally did. He didn't let her have a cell phone. She couldn't go to the movies with other girls. She didn't have her own television. Or her own computer. They used them in school and she was really good at it, but she wasn't allowed one at home. After her brother ran away she used to email him, but when her father found out, he stopped her and put a password on his computer so she had to ask permission to use it, and use it under his supervision. He treated her like a prisoner to be kept under control. And then she wanted to go out with a boy. He probably saw that as threat to his control, and the boy had to be punished. Maybe he saw them kissing or something."

She shook her head. "Even if either of them wanted to, they didn't have a chance to go beyond a little necking, a kiss. John was always back at the garage before six."

"Did John ever mention Morgan?"

"A couple of times. He said he sounded like an eighteenth-century tyrant, or as if he was a throwback to one of the Puritan colonies. Or he believed in Sharia law. I don't know what she told him to make him say those things. One thing is clear: John went to that condo to kill Arlie Morgan. That's the only true statement in that goddamn police report."

CHAPTER 11

ON MONDAY MORNING Bailey dragged out his folder from the duffel bag, saying, "My guy came through with prints, Peel's and Daggart's. Peel's prints are all through the lists, and Daggart's are on the envelope."

"There's something in there that we're missing," Barbara said. "A duplicate set of members' names. What difference would it have made if someone else had it? Anything else?"

"One little thing. Morgan's driver, DiPalma, has a pilot's license. I'm still digging to find out who he flies and where."

"Okay. Anything on those names with the bullet points?"

"Single guys, farm hands, farmers, a forest worker, a dockworker in Coos Bay. Several have girlfriends living with them, nothing permanent. And it seems that several of them get together and go on a religious retreat now and then. They all go to the Church of Purity and Redemption, but not regularly. Maybe that's why they're singled out, to focus on them, make them better churchgoers, or make them ditch the girlfriends," he said gloomily. "It's a tough one, Barbara. City guy starts asking questions and the iron walls bang down. Neighbors aren't likely to tell an outsider diddly."

She nodded. "I was in Portland Saturday, getting the lowdown on that attack on Morgan two years ago." As she told them what she had learned, she watched Bailey's face contort and then freeze in a scowl deeper than she had ever seen. Shelley paled and looked as sick as Barbara had felt in Wanda's apartment.

There was a lengthy silence when she finished.

Bailey was staring at the folder he had placed on the table. Abruptly he rose and picked up his duffel bag. "You got anything else for me?" His voice was hoarse and he had a murderous expression.

"Just keep digging," Barbara said. "I'm groping, Bailey. Nothing's going anywhere, except in circles."

Bailey started for the door, stopped just short of it and turned. "That girl he incinerated was taken to the residence at ten after three in the morning. That could be a starting place to find out where she was taken from, and maybe where June Morgan is still being held. How tight is that rein on me?"

"No rein," Barbara said.

He saluted, walked on to the door and out.

"Dad suggested that it might be helpful if Dr. Minnick talks to Travis a few times. Want to bring it up with him?" Barbara asked Shelley.

"Why? An insanity plea isn't likely, is it?"

"No. But Travis has a terrible guilt hanging over him. He thinks he betrayed his mother at the time of the divorce. He was a kid, cornered into saying what Morgan wanted him to say and no more. I think it bothers Travis more than he realizes. And a guilty conscience betrays itself, not for the crime he didn't commit but for what he thinks he did to his mother. An observer just sees the guilt. Also, he has a deep and terrible fear of his father. I want to know why."

"I'll bring it up tonight," Shelley said. "And I can make the arrangements at the jail."

"Thanks. For now, I want to find out what's important about those lists of names if I possibly can. May have to shake Dad's memory box hard about it, but he's the likeliest one to come up with an answer. Possibly the only one who saw both lists, with the exception of Peel himself."

Frank shook his head. "As far as I could tell they were the same. The name of a town followed by names."

"There has to be something," Barbara said. "You said you and Patsy picked up the papers and put them in the briefcase. Why two of you? There are only five sheets."

"No, more like fifteen or possibly eighteen," he said. "I didn't count. Each town had its list on a separate sheet, as if it had been intended for a leader in that particular community to have his own list, but not the others. I remember seeing Ashland, with no more than four couples' name, but on a sheet of paper by itself."

"That's a difference," Barbara said. "They must have been scanned or inserted. At the bottom of one list the next one was added. Peel must have done that. His prints and yours are all over the papers. But why?" She spread out the five sheets of paper with the names in a single column. "And why bullet point some singles and not others?" She pointed. "Woody Styvesant, bullet point, and Herbert Myers, no bullet point. Both single men."

Frank was gazing at the lists with a thoughtful expression. He looked from them to Barbara and said slowly, "I don't recall seeing any bullet points on the spilled papers. They could have been there and I failed to notice, or maybe not. Who would know is Patsy. She spots a misplaced comma in a five-hundred page manuscript as if it's in blinking neon." He turned the papers face down, went to his desk and buzzed for Patsy.

"Do you want coffee?" Patsy asked when she entered Frank's office.

"Not this time," Frank said. "Do you remember that fellow who came in last spring and collapsed on my floor?"

"Of course, I certainly do. I was afraid he would die there. He gave me some brandy," she said to Barbara, nodding toward Frank. "I needed it."

"Patsy, think a moment about the papers the fellow dropped and we picked up. I'm sure your memory is better than mine. What do you recall about those papers?"

She looked puzzled, but closed her eyes for a second or two, then said. "Lists of names. Towns in fourteen-point font, bold, two double-line spaces, then names and addresses. A single column of names, numbers by them, and addresses. You want any particular name? I don't think I made a mental note of individual names."

"No names. You're doing fine," Frank said. "Anything else?"

She thought another moment then shook her head. "Just names and towns. And the numbers, like John and Jane Doe, followed by a number, two or three or something."

"Were there any bullet points? Any other marks?"

"No. Bullet points stand out. I would have noticed, but I didn't see any."

"That's what we wanted to know," Frank said. "Thank you."

Patsy gave Barbara a suspicious look. "That's all?"

"That's it. You're a marvel, Patsy. Thanks."

Patsy shook her head, turned and left the office.

"So, Peel must have wanted Daggart to have those particular names," Barbara murmured, once again looking over the lists. "Why? As far as Bailey's been able to find out, those guys are just ordinary workers, a farmer or two, just men getting along. Why them? Was Peel colluding with someone not in the inner circle? Exposing something? Brings it back to the opening gate, doesn't it, Dad? Who was Daggart and what was he after? Why didn't the official investigation find out a thing about him?"

"The last one is fairly easy," Frank said. "He was a nobody, no known family to scream for an investigation, and he was carrying worthless papers, not cash or gems or dope. Just church membership lists, obviously not their target. He was. They probably ran his fingerprints through the FBI as a matter of routine business, but I doubt they put more effort than that into an investigation."

"Dad," she said, "something else occurred to me. You said each community, each town and its list was on its own separate page or pages. Didn't you also say that the packet was to have been delivered to someone in Medford? That person in Medford could have been instructed to distribute the lists to the various pooh-bahs in each separate place. It suggests a whole hierarchy in place to get the lists to the proper locations. Why?"

"Search me. Barbara, you're making a lot of leaps with very little to go on."

"I know," she admitted. "I tend to do that, don't I? I have to talk to the widow Peel, or at least to her son, Derek Peel."

"You do that and you open yourself to a charge of witness tampering."

"I know that too," she said. "But those lists, what was going on between Peel and Daggart, Daggart's murder, and finally Peel's murder, that's at the heart of this matter. Until I know something about all that, I'm just chasing shadows in circles." She gathered up the lists, returned them to her briefcase and stood. "Well, I'm off. Thanks, Dad. Why is it that clearing up one thing just leads to three more questions? Strange way to run a world."

Frank sat at the round table for several minutes after Barbara left. That scene with Daggart ran again in his head, and Barbara's summation connecting that with the lists with Peel's murder. He nodded to himself, accepting her reasoning. It was all connected, and it spelled trouble, real trouble. A professional beating, done by professionals still at large, he was thinking, when he got to his feet and went to his desk where he dialed Bailey's number.

That afternoon Barbara was at her desk reviewing what little she knew about Margaret Peel and her son Derek. Not much because, as Bailey had said, there wasn't much to find out about them. Derek was twenty-nine years old, had a master's degree in political science and did not have a job. He had been staying with his mother since Peel's death. He worked on the family farm that produced organic raspberries and grapes, primarily, sold to local outlets and at a farmers' market. Margaret was fifty-eight and had been married to Joseph Peel for thirty-four years. They were members of a Methodist church in Harrisburg. She volunteered at an elementary school cafeteria five days a week during the school year.

Barbara closed the unhelpful folder, trying to think of a way to make Derek Peel consider her as anything other than an antagonist, the defender of his father's murderer. The son wouldn't be on the witness list, she reasoned, and he might be amenable, she hoped.

How to make him agree to see her was the problem. Nothing came to mind. *So go in cold*, she ordered herself and dialed the number for Derek Peel.

The call was answered by a girl. "Derek? Sure, he's around. Hold on. I'll call him."

Barbara could hear her yell, "Derek, it's for you." Then his voice came on, "Derek Peel speaking."

"I'm Barbara Holloway," she said, "and I represent Travis Morgan. He told me that you gave him good advice many years ago when he was too young to understand what you were talking about. Mr. Peel, I would like very much to talk to you. May I come out to your place for a brief conversation?"

"No. I don't think we have anything to discuss."

"I think we do. I have reason to believe that your father was not on good terms with Arlie Morgan, and that their relationship has a bearing on my case."

He was silent for what seemed a long time. She could hear him breathing. "I'll meet with you," he said finally. "Don't come out here. I'll meet you somewhere. Not at your office. I'll be in town tomorrow and I'll be in work clothes, driving a farm truck. In a park or something like that, and just for a few minutes."

"I meet with clients at a small restaurant," she said quickly. "Working people for the most part. It's called Martin's Restaurant. Would you meet me there?"

She waited out another long pause. "I read about that place, that you and your partner do pro bono work out of there. I'll be there between three and four." He hung up.

That night, helping Todd with KP after dinner prepared by Darren, Barbara asked how the project of locating a particular place through weather reports was going.

Todd paused in scouring a skillet. "It's great," he said. "Dr. Chu is pretty excited by the idea, but we have to keep adding new parameters to the program we're writing. I mean, sometimes even here it can rain in one place, snow in another part of town, and have freezing rain somewhere else. The official report might be that it snowed, or maybe just rained, depending on where the weather station is. We decided we had to include the weather conditions that could make any of them possible, no matter what the official record is so the program keeps getting longer. Dr. Chu said that's okay. Gradually we're circling in on it."

He had just turned from an adolescent into a man of science, Barbara thought, watching and listening to him. His instructor's acceptance of and then excitement about his project had him floating. His name might be on an important paper, his résumé certainly enhanced, his self-esteem possibly raised a bit too high, if they could bring it off. A big if, she understood, but a possible if. Todd was so enthusiastic about it all that he was spending hours studying weather maps, topographical maps, researching weather and climate patterns on the computer.

They talked about it a few more minutes. Then, dishes done and put away, she went to the living room where Darren was reading a book. He closed it and patted the sofa next to him in an invitation. When she sat by him, he put his arm about her shoulders.

"Something came up today at the clinic," he said. "Senator Treadmore sent an aide out to talk to Annie and me about those contractor trainees and the major. We gave him a statement, and he said that they might want us to attend a subcommittee meeting next month. How about that?"

She drew back and examined his face. "Do you want to go testify? Some of those senators can be brutal in the way they treat witnesses."

"I think I can handle it," he said with a faint smile. "I didn't have anything to do with the deal the major forced on the board. I just tried to train two monkeys that proved to be untrainable. But I hate to leave when you're on a case. You work too hard and forget to eat and sleep sometimes. You need a keeper twenty-four/seven."

"Oh, knock it off!" she said indignantly. "I've managed to keep body and soul together for quite a few years. Next month? Before Thanksgiving? After? Any clue about when they'd want you?"

"Not yet. Actually, I thought that if the timing works out for him, I might take Todd. Let him see his Congress in action, and see something of Washington. He's never been back east."

"And not leave him on my hands," she said. It was a consideration, she knew. She didn't cook worth a darn, and she would be an unreliable surrogate parent in Darren's absence, as likely as not to forget to pick him up after school, or fail to have edibles in abundance in the house. "Anyway," she added quickly, "he's so wrapped up in that hide-and-seek project, he doesn't need to have to look after me as well."

She was startled to see a swift look of agreement cross Darren's face and vanish. He laughed and drew her close again. Good God, she thought. That was it. He would have instructed his teenage son to look out for her, probably make sure that she ate dinner, that her car was operable, whatever.

CHAPTER 12

BARBARA ARRIVED AT the restaurant a few minutes before three. When Martin opened the door, he glanced out at the curb. "No car?"

"I walked over," she said. "I don't want the locals to know I'm here. How's everything?" She waved to Binnie, who had stepped out from the kitchen, both hands covered with flour. She looked too small, like a child caught playing with dough, to be a great pastry chef, which she was. Binnie blew her a kiss and retreated to the kitchen.

"Things are good," Martin said. "Quiet, just the way I like it. I guess you don't want your sign up?"

"You got it," she said. "Just one guy today, maybe. Derek Peel. Anyone else gets the bum's rush. Any time between now and four. I'll hang out and wait."

Martin was the biggest, blackest man she had ever seen, she thought as she took off her jacket and draped it over a chair at the table she considered hers. When Shelley protested her meeting Derek Peel alone, Barbara had laughed. "At Martin's place? You've got to be kidding."

The restaurant had six booths and six tables. That afternoon each table had a small jack-o'-lantern centerpiece. Candles inside the pumpkins were not lighted yet. Later when they were burning, the light would be golden in the restaurant, and the smell of pumpkin and spices would fill the air.

"You're busy," Barbara said. "Go on and do your thing. I brought reading material." She pulled Shelley's report about the Church of Purity and Redemption from her briefcase.

"Work," Martin said with a laugh. "For a minute there I thought you might have some light reading. I'll get the door when he rings," he added, and walked back to the kitchen. A minute or two later he returned with the coffee carafe and a cup and saucer. "To keep up your strength."

It was fifteen minutes before four when the doorbell sounded. She remained seated as Martin admitted Derek Peel and the two men sized each other up the way men always did. Peel drew in a long breath and closed his eyes for a moment. He was almost as tall as Martin, and in comparison looked thin. Long legs and arms, a craggy face, Lincolnesque came to mind. He was wearing faded jeans, a faded Oregon State sweatshirt and well-worn boots. He held up his hand and said, "I'm filthy or I'd really like to shake your hand, Mr. Owens. It's a pleasure to meet you."

A fan, Barbara thought. Martin had been a star linebacker in the NFL before settling down to be a master chef in his own restaurant. Quite a few people remembered and respected him from his days in football.

"Restroom's over there," Martin said, pointing. "Will you be wanting coffee, a soda, maybe a beer?"

"A beer would be terrific. Thanks," Derek said. He turned toward Barbara. "Ms. Holloway, I won't be long." He held up his hands, then walked swiftly to the restroom door.

Martin never offered her clients beer, Barbara was musing as Martin vanished into the kitchen. Did he have a sincerity sensor or something? What had he seen in Derek Peel that she had not yet had time to glimpse? She filed it away under Interesting.

Derek returned and pulled out a chair opposite hers. She could smell the soap from the restrooms, but his hands still appeared to be dirty. Grape juice stains, she realized.

"Sorry about that," he said. "I've been working all day and I accumulate a layer of grime. What do you know about the relationship my father had with Morgan?"

"Well, you do get down to it, don't you?" she said.

"Look, I've been up since five thirty, spent hours bagging grapes, then hours delivering them. I'm tired. You represent the man who allegedly shot and killed my father. What did you expect from me?"

His eyes were deep blue, nearly black, and he was sunburned nut brown, his hair was sun-bleached in front, giving him a bicolor head of hair, dark brown on the sides and in back, much paler in front.

"I'm not sure what I expect," Barbara said slowly. "I hoped you could be helpful, not about the night of the death of your father, but about the relationship. I have good reason to believe that there had been a falling out, that your father might have been considering leaving Morgan's employ. I can't tell you why I believe that, not at this time anyway, but if you will agree to fill in some blanks, when this case is concluded I'll be more than happy to fill you in on what I have learned."

She felt a bit of a surprise to hear herself say that Peel would have been thinking of leaving Morgan, but there it was. He had betrayed him, gone behind his back doing something with Daggart that apparently no one else knew anything about. Doing something, she added, that might have gotten Daggart killed. Possibly got Peel himself killed.

Derek had not yet responded when the swinging kitchen door opened and Martin brought out a tray with a bottle of beer, a glass, and a sandwich.

"I didn't order anything," Derek said quickly when Martin put it down in front of him.

"Not in words," Martin said with a big grin. "You sure were trying to eat air onions when you got here."

Good food smells had been building up all afternoon, Barbara realized. She had grown used to them, but for Derek, coming in from the cool air, having worked all day, it must have been overwhelming.

When he looked at her questioningly, she shrugged. "He does that. Hungry people make him ache. Enjoy." Martin was already back in the kitchen.

Derek took a large bite, drank some beer, used the napkin, and finally said, "Look, Ms. Holloway, I don't know what went down in that room that night. I've gone back and forth believing Travis did it without a reason, or that he thought it would be Morgan sitting there and had a good reason. I understand your position. You're out to defend him and no doubt you'll do whatever you have to do to get him off. But that was my father and if Travis killed him, I want him to go to the penitentiary for the rest of his life."

"I don't want to talk about that night," she said. "Just about the relationship your father had with Arlie Morgan. Am I right that your father had become disillusioned, that he wanted to leave that position?"

"Yes. He did." He took another bite. Then, eating as he talked, he said, "For the past couple of years, Dad was getting more and more ready to hand in his resignation. It was the mortgage on the farm that kept him working. They, he and my mother, knew that if he held on for two or three more years, they'd be in the clear and he'd walk out. Dad didn't like working for Morgan, and he sure as hell didn't like his sermons. A few months ago it seemed as if he couldn't last much longer. He was getting more and more antsy. He almost quit then, but he ended up saying he would stick it out through the summer, but when the grapes were ready to be harvested, he intended to be on the farm."

As he talked, he looked at her with a direct gaze, and chose his words with precision, without pauses. He majored in political science, she thought distantly, and no doubt he had a career in politics before him. He would make a good politician with that direct approach, a man speaking to one person at a time, capturing the attention of that one person, presenting himself as a self-confident man who knew what he wanted, knew what he meant, knew how to get it across and win the trust of that audience of one.

"Do you recall when your father almost quit?" Barbara asked.

"I was finishing my thesis, living in my own apartment, not in the house. In the spring, that's all I can say. My mother told me later, early summer, after I was done with school for now. The point is, they talked it over and Dad agreed to stay until the end of summer."

Not the point at all, Barbara was thinking. In the spring, about the time that Peel and Daggart were conniving at something? About the time that Daggart was murdered? She didn't press the issue. He said he didn't know when. Instead, she changed direction. "Travis is grateful that you tried to give him good advice, and he's sorry he was too young to understand. He said he heard you and your parents talking about the possibility of having you live in the church residence here in Eugene and you wouldn't agree. The living arrangements of that house have baffled me. Who lived there, who didn't? Will you tell me about that?"

He thought about it for a moment, then said, "Sure. After Morgan began to get those donations, everything changed. Morgan and his family had a small house in north Eugene before, then he bought the church residence here. There was the divorce, and he and the kids lived in the big house for a while. A theater in Portland was leased, renovated, used as a church, and Morgan got a condo up there. After that, he and the kids lived in Portland during the school year, down here for the summer up until Travis ran away and it was just Morgan and June. She was in a summer camp every year for a couple of months, in the condo, I guess, the rest of the time. He came down now and then for a weekend, to preach here. Morgan suggested that I could live in the residence during the week, go to the university here, and be at the farm for weekends. I said no. After he squirreled June away somewhere, he was down here more often, I think. I guess he still is here a lot, but I don't know. We never talked about him much. My parents never lived in the church residence here. Dad commuted. He had minimum contact with Morgan since he was at the farm when Morgan was in town for the weekend. He went to Portland only once a month, on his way to Seattle to pick up the donation."

"He went to Seattle monthly? To pick up donations?"

"Dad said that's what the donor demanded. He left it in a hotel safe. Dad drove to Portland, took the train to Seattle, checked in at the hotel and collected the envelope, took the train back down the next day. Morgan met him at the train station and Dad handed over the envelope, got his car, and drove home."

"Did he inspect the money, count it or anything?"

"Never. The envelope was sealed. He didn't mess with it." He shrugged. "Okay, weird. I give you that. Dad thought it was weird, but he followed instructions."

Weird was the word, Barbara agreed. It sounded as if Morgan had not trusted his bookkeeper. Obviously Derek had told her what he knew about that and she left it alone to think about later.

"I wonder why Morgan suggested that you should live at the residence to attend the university. Did he tell you why?"

Derek finished his beer and set the glass down hard. "He wanted to counsel me," he said sarcastically. "He wanted to save my soul."

"And you warned Travis, told him in effect that when Morgan tried to talk about sex with him, he should take off," she said. "Good for you. Good for him that he did so."

Derek nodded. "I think we've covered enough," he said. "You wanted some background and I furnished it. No harm done. Now I'm out of here. Nice meeting you, Ms. Holloway. I'll hold you to your word to tell me what made you call in the first place. I understand that it's unusual for the defense attorney to call the victim's family for help with their case." He stood and regarded her for a moment, then held out his hand. "Good luck," he said.

She rose to shake his hand, and stood at the table when he went to the door. "Thank you, Mr. Peel," she said.

He hesitated with his hand on the doorknob. “Is it important to know when my father wanted to quit last spring?”

She nodded. “It’s important.”

“I’ll be in touch,” he said and he left.

Walking back to the office Barbara made a detour to the rose garden and the river trail beyond. She had some thinking to do, new doors had been opened and the darkness of the edifice beyond them had expanded once again.

There had not been a killing frost yet, and the roses were in full bloom, exuberant in their last wild fling before the rains set in. The fragrance was almost overwhelming, and the beds of yellow roses, red roses, bicolor peach and pink, whites, the hum of bees, the order and serenity were otherworldly. The breeze was cool, the sun, low in the sky now, was warming. She reached the mammoth cherry tree and came to a stop.

The ancient tree was a giant, many of its massive branches propped up with sturdy supports, and yet, come spring it would bloom again and produce an abundance of cherries that a multitude of birds would welcome. A girl was sitting cross-legged in the grass under the tree. She was dwarfed by it.

Barbara sat on a bench and gazed at the tree still in full leaf, marveling at its size, its resilience, its tenacity, endurance. She imagined that the girl sitting under it was confiding something of importance. Barbara had done that in the past, knowing her secrets were safe with the tree, knowing she needed to tell it something, tell someone something, when there was no one she possibly could have told. Girls’ desperate secrets, she thought with a sigh, lost in the fog of time. The girl rose, bowed her head slightly, and walked away.

Barbara wasn’t certain when she began to talk to the tree. Not in spoken words—she never had uttered a sound to it—but in a silent voice in her head, feeling that it was enough. It would listen.

“I don’t know how to defend him,” she said silently. “I’ve come across a big three-dimensional puzzle, extending in time and space, ever expanding, and I don’t even know the shape of the puzzle. Am I distracting myself chasing shadows because I can’t find a way to build a defense? What does any of that extraneous stuff have to do with the murder of Joseph Peel? Even if I knew what it was that Peel and Daggart were doing, how could I introduce it when they’re both dead? How does the cremation of the wrong girl intersect with the murder?

Where is June, and does that have a bearing on the murder? The mutilation of John Varagosa, how does that fit in? I don't know how Daggart and Joseph Peel got together in the first place, or why they were conspiring, if they were. I keep getting more and more tidbits that I can't explain or even know how to pursue... "I don't want Travis to spend the rest of his life in prison," she whispered, then shook herself and quickly looked about to see if anyone was nearby, listening. She was alone with the tree, the faint rustle of its leaves the only sound.

"If I can't connect any of those other incidents to the murder," she said silently to the tree, "I have to stop opening so many doors, confronting too many unsolvable mysteries about the murky past. It's not fair to Travis if I let myself become distracted to the extent I fail him."

That was it, she thought then. That was what needed saying: Was she losing Travis and his case in the bigger mystery that Morgan presented? It chilled her to think of the weeks gone by already, with no progress in his defense case.

Then, as if part of her brain was trying to be reasonable, another part resisting, she thought again of the strange way Morgan's benefactor made his anonymous donations to the Church of Purity and Redemption. Why not just transfer funds electronically? Or use a cashier's check? Registered mail? Or drop a package in the collection plate? Why make Peel go in person to collect money, and then hand it to Morgan at the train station? Why not have him take it straight to a bank and make a deposit? He had been the bookkeeper, after all.

Because that envelope contained more than just money. She was startled by the answer that swam into her awareness.

Seattle could have been where Daggart and Peel had gotten together. No one had thought to check Seattle for a missing Robert Daggart.

Earlier she had been aware of the rustling of leaves, but suddenly she realized that the rustling had grown loud, that the sound had enveloped her, and her entire field of vision was an immensity of green leaves. She shook her head. The tree was just a tree again, the rustling just a murmur of leaves in a light breeze. The sunshine was gone and deep shadows lay across the gardens. She could not have said how long she had been sitting there. Shakily, she rose from the bench and bowed her head.

"Thank you," she whispered.

✦

CHAPTER 13

"YOU LOOK A bit frazzled," Frank said that Sunday evening when he admitted Barbara. Thing One and Thing Two crowded around, vying at which one had priority at sniffing her legs. They always acted as if they had never smelled another cat presence on her, although Todd's cat, Nappy, had been around for more than a year. They seemed to take offense and regard Barbara as a possible traitor when she first appeared, and forgot the whole thing minutes later.

"I have a right to be frazzled," she said, taking off her jacket. "I spent hours last night and again today poring over Seattle newspapers. Do you have any idea how many there are in that area?"

"No. And why?" He looked past her before closing the door. "Where are the fellows?"

"A patient at the clinic had a breakthrough or something and Darren's over there. He'll swing by the house to pick up Todd and bring him along later. As for newspapers, there are a lot. As for why, Peel and Daggart are the key. What they were up to, when and how they met, where Daggart came from. Are you cooking or something?"

"Come on to the kitchen and tell me while I bone a chicken."

"Bone a—? Never mind. I don't want to know about it." She followed him to the kitchen where he poured her a glass of wine and went back to the counter to pick up a slim knife and go back to doing whatever he had been doing to a chicken. She didn't watch.

"See, yesterday I met with Derek Peel," she said, and proceeded to tell him all that she had learned. "Bear with me," she said. "I'm going to make a lot of assumptions and pretend to believe each and every one of them is a fact. First, Daggart was from Seattle and met Peel up there. Next, one way or another they got chummy enough for Peel to agree to help Daggart uncover something, reveal something, or do whatever it is they were up to. Next, the envelope with money had something else, some other document or something like that, something that the unknown benefactor wanted hand delivered to Morgan. So, in March, Daggart got himself killed, and Peel decided to hand in his resignation, but didn't actually quit. Maybe Daggart's death frightened Peel enough that he didn't make an issue of resigning, but nothing else happened. No one made a stink about the second list, and he decided to hang in there through the summer as if he had nothing to fear, as if he didn't have a clue about Daggart's being anything other than the handyman gofer."

"So you spent hours reading Seattle area newspapers, looking for him. No missing-person report that could have been a match?"

"No. But there's another way to track him down. Daggart had a car. It must have been registered in his name, and he bought it from someone. What if Seattle Sue, aka Robert Daggart, sold it to him? He could have bought an old Honda Civic for cash and resold it to himself under the pseudonym. The sale would have been in Oregon, not Washington State, making him a bona fide Oregon resident with Oregon license plates. He wouldn't have wanted to call attention to his Seattle roots. That means his real name is on one of those registrations. Bailey work," she concluded.

Frank had finished boning the chicken apparently. She stood and walked past him on her way to refill her wineglass, eyeing the chicken along the way. It looked deflated, sprawled out like roadkill. He was rubbing it with a brown gooey paste. "That's disgusting," she said.

"Not so bad," Frank said. "One of my better boning jobs, actually. Ginger, garlic, soy sauce, scallions, sesame oil, a bit of cayenne, touch of honey. Smells pretty good already."

He had a ball of string at hand and began to tie the chicken back together, which seemed even more disgusting to her. "You could be right about all that," he said. "And it's a good idea to check back through registrations. But."

"I know. What's it got to do with the defense of Travis Morgan? I just think it's the key. What do they call the top of the arch that holds the whole thing together? Keystone? It's the keystone, Dad. I'm sure it is."

"Any guess what else might have been in the envelopes Peel collected?"

"Not yet. But another question is who is hand delivering them now? We'll find out."

"Could be that a more important question concerns the benefactor who seems to be underwriting Morgan, his church, the closed-circuit television, the whole works. A lot of folks up in Seattle have made a fortune in the world of dot-com, and Boeing's made a lot of folks super rich. A lot of those businessmen would not want anyone to pry too closely into their relationship with Morgan, and they have the resources to keep that from happening, in addition to the ruthlessness to use those resources."

He finished creating what looked like a Frankenchicken and rubbed it all over with sesame oil, then set it on a rack. "We'll let it rest awhile," he said and washed his hands. "Now I'll have a bit of that wine." He poured a small amount of wine, then joined her at the table.

He swirled his wine in the glass before looking at her. He was dead serious then. "Barbara, whoever is bankrolling Morgan has spent a fortune over the past years, and it's ongoing. He could be as crazy as Morgan is and believe he's doing the Lord's work, price tag be damned. Or he could be getting something out of it that's worth the price. Either way, he could be a very dangerous man, and he will learn how expansive your investigation is. You can keep it undercover only so long before someone notices how far astray you've gone asking questions, possibly getting answers."

"Dad, I don't have a choice," she said in a low voice. "You know as well as I do that I don't have a defense case. If I can't tie all this together, Travis is going down, either through a plea bargain that he says he won't participate in, or by being found guilty through a trial. I have to do this."

"I know you do. I know I can't talk you out of it. That's why I told Bailey to get in touch with Herbert. I want him here. On me," he added. "Nothing to do with Ashley or Travis. He'll be here next week."

Barbara felt a surge of anger cause muscles to go rigid. She met Frank's steady, implacable, and very grave gaze, and bit back a response, knowing that with or without her acceptance, he would do it. She moistened her lips with a sip of wine and nodded.

"Okay. He can use the apartment over the garage. I hardly ever work up there."

"Good enough. Bailey approves, too. It appears that your last meeting left him edgier than I've seen him in quite a long time."

He was still holding her gaze with his own. He could do that, she thought, turn himself into a stranger, remote and immovable. She drew in a long breath and said in a low voice, "He told you about Varagosa?"

"Did you tell him not to?"

"No."

"He seemed to assume that I was still part of a team."

"Dad, I'm sorry. I was afraid it would alarm you... or something."

"Bailey assumed I wanted Herbert because of Varagosa. He was wrong. I didn't know about that when I called him. Barbara, I need to hear you say that you will let Herbert do his job without interference. And I need to hear you say that you won't deal me out again for my own good."

"My word, Dad, on both counts. I apologize."

He continued to regard her soberly for a time, then lifted his glass and drank the wine in it. Standing, he said, "I never want to butt heads with you more seriously than this, because so help me God, I don't know which one of us would walk away. I have to put that chicken in the oven."

She watched as he took care of his ravaged chicken and then began to take vegetables from the refrigerator. He stopped and turned toward her with a smile on his face. "You remember that big shaggy mutt that Herbert travels with?"

"The wonder dog? Sure."

"Remember his name?"

"Not Wonderdog?"

"Morgan. The dog's name is Morgan."

"Oh, my God!" She burst out laughing, and at the sink Frank chuckled and put down a package of something green. It was over, Barbara thought with relief, and neither of them would ever refer back to that bit of serious business again. And she would never cut him out again, she promised herself. Never. She had to glance down at her fingers to make certain she had not unconsciously crossed them.

Dinner was a great success, as it always was. Frank looked pleased as his guests marveled at the succulent chicken slices with both dark and white meat and Todd pronounced it neat. "How did you do it?" he asked.

"Tell you what, one afternoon when you have time, we'll bone a duck. Same principle as with chicken, but we'll end up with pressed duck, and that's good eating. Let me know ahead of time so I can thaw it properly."

The grandson he never had before, Barbara thought, listening. He was teaching Todd how to cook when Todd had time, which wasn't often those days. And it was obvious that Todd thought Frank was, in his word, neat.

"Barbara tells me you had a patient who made a breakthrough," Frank said, turning to Darren.

Darren gave Barbara a rueful look and shook his head. "Breakdown is more like it," he said. "The poor guy decided nothing was going to work, he'd be in a wheelchair the rest of his life, and he wanted to get out of there. I showed him a video of what he was like when he was admitted, and put him through his routine to demonstrate the difference. It took a while," he added.

He looked tired and Barbara felt her guilt needle jump higher. She should have paid more attention, really listened. "Sorry," she said. "I guess I heard what I wanted to hear."

"It's a human trait," Frank said. "We see what we're inclined to see, hear what we're inclined to hear. Pretty people are believed more than homely folks. Whites more than blacks, depending on the listeners, of course. Caucasians more than Hispanics, in this society. That's why eyewitnesses are so unreliable."

"I thought they were the best," Todd said. "I mean, you see a guy hold up a store, you identify him. He's found guilty."

"That's how it works eventually," Frank said. "But you'd be surprised at the variety of descriptions you get from eyewitnesses right up until there's an arrest. By the time they get to court you couldn't shake them with a thunderbolt. The fellow was five feet six, weighed about one forty. Or he was six feet, weighed one eighty or more. Thin hair, full head of hair. Dark brown, blond... Then they point and swear, yes, he's the one. Most defense attorneys hate it when the decision relies on eyewitnesses."

He shook himself and said, "Well, enough of that. Let's clear the table and make room for some peach cobbler."

It was over dessert that Frank said casually to Darren, "Would you be willing to rent out that apartment over your garage? Bobby says she rarely uses it. It seems that Bailey wants some help brought in. You remember Herbert and his dog? He needs a job and Bailey needs help."

Darren stiffened and gave Barbara a swift look of alarm.

"It's between Bailey and Dad," she said. "I had nothing to do with it."

"He's bringing Morgan?" Todd asked eagerly. "He said he'd teach me some of his signals if he ever got up this way again."

"He'll have the dog with him," Frank said, and looked at Darren for an answer.

"Bailey work?" Darren asked.

"Yes indeed," Frank said. "Sometimes he gets too much on his plate, and he wants someone few around here are likely to recognize."

"It's okay with you?" Darren asked Barbara, studying her intently.

"It's fine with me," she said.

"Okay," he said.

She could hear the reluctance in his voice, almost feel the fear that had flowed through him. Herbert was primarily a bodyguard and had safeguarded a former client lodged in that same apartment. She had not told him an untruth, she argued silently with herself. She'd really had nothing to do with bringing in Herbert, but still it was implied that he was not to work on her case this time. When Darren learned otherwise, would he be angry, feel betrayed, lied to? Tomorrow's worry. First her father, next her lover, betrayed, misled.

Todd began to talk about the rope tricks that Herbert knew. He was clearly pleased that Herbert would be back and be in their apartment.

Darren and Todd prepared to leave almost as soon as the dishes were stashed in the dishwasher, and the pots and pans washed and put away.

"I won't be long," Barbara said, seeing them out.

Darren laughed and shook his head. "I intend to take a bath and hit the bed. I earned a good night's sleep today."

"I'll be quiet," she said.

When she closed the door and picked up her jacket, Frank said, "Level with him as soon as you can. He deserves to know the truth, but I didn't want to say more in front of Todd. He doesn't need to know more than what's been said."

"It will worry Darren. He thinks he'll be asked to go to Washington to testify before that subcommittee. He might even put if off."

"Of course it will worry him. He fell in love with a defense attorney. He knows damn well how involved you get, and he's prouder of you than he'll ever be able to express. Also, he's not a fool. He'll go to Washington. He knows how important that is. That's one reason I wanted Herbert here."

"Sam told you about the Washington trip?"

He nodded. "Remember that Annie is his client, and I'm the sap he stole a client from. He told me."

"You're the greatest, Dad. Did I ever mention that before? Just the greatest. Wonderful dinner, good advice, and now I want to go home and do some reading and thinking."

Frank watched her back out of the driveway, and then her taillights until he no longer could see them. He stepped back inside and walked to his study to do the Times crossword puzzle, a Sunday-night routine that he seldom missed. She wanted to get home and tell Darren before he went to sleep, Frank suspected. He had seen the expression on her face when he brought up Herbert, and he could well imagine the inner struggle she'd had over what was little less than an outright lie. He wondered if she had struggled when she decided not to tell him about Varagosa, then he put that aside. It didn't matter since it was cleared up. She had a propensity to protect people—her clients, her father, Shelley, Darren, everyone she came across, it sometimes seemed. Of course, he mused, opening the newspaper to the puzzle, she had known he would object to all the side trails she was following; and she had indeed been sidestepping an argument about the distraction of pursuing Morgan. He recalled what he had said, that he didn't want to butt heads with her over a more serious matter. He truly didn't know which one of them would walk away from such a confrontation, but he did know that irreparable damage would be done to them both.

When Darren emerged from the bathroom that night, Barbara was sitting cross-legged on the bed.

"Can we talk just a few minutes before you go to sleep?"

"As many minutes as it takes," he said, taking off his robe. He sat on the side of the bed.

"About Herbert," she said. "I learned tonight, before you got there, that Dad had told Bailey to bring him in. I really didn't know about it before. Dad thinks there's someone very powerful behind Morgan, and that he could try to stop my prying."

Darren shifted and reached for her, drew her close, and murmured into her hair.

"God, I'm glad you told me. I think I knew, and didn't want to know. Frank had it dead right. We hear what we want to hear. We don't let Todd in on it? Is that the idea?"

"That's the idea," she said. "We can't very well hide Herbert, but Todd isn't to know why he's here. I didn't know how I was going to tell you. I'm glad it came up the way it did. And it goes without saying that I'll use caution."

"It bears saying, and repeating many times." He moved her back far enough to see her face. "I don't have to go to sleep instantly, you know."

She stroked his cheek lightly. "You're so tired."

"I was. Now I'm not."

When he kissed her, she had to agree. Now he wasn't too tired at all.

CHAPTER 14

BARBARA WAS SITTING across the table from Travis again. "How are you feeling?"

He shrugged. "Okay. I work out, meditate a little, read. I'm learning a new way to do math. Dr. Minnick turned me on to it. He's pretty cool, Dr. Minnick. I thought he'd try to analyze me on the sly, but he's not like that. We talk about math and stuff, science, even philosophy. He's been explaining some of it to me. Sometimes we argue about stuff."

He gave her an appraising look. "He taught me a cool trick. He said to think of it as Displacement in Time and Space, a Star Trek way to deal with things. You know, a holodeck where you can replay things, or make up new things. You just close your eyes and visualize one of the worst things you've ever done, you know, like stealing candy from your sister when you were a kid. Or sneaking a cigarette. Or something."

He paused, then said, "It works. It really works. You have to see whatever it was that you did. And then you put out your hands like this." He held out his hands in a way that suggested he was holding an object. "It should be sort of like a box," he said. "That's where you put the thing you did. You move it from your head to the box and after that you can turn it around, be like a movie director and examine it from all angles."

"You remove it from your emotional response," Barbara said. "You have to do that to get any objectivity."

"That's it," Travis said, letting his hands drop to the table. "After he taught me that trick, I was able to see some things with some objectivity, I think. Including my own case. We can't win, can we?"

Blindsided, Barbara thought. He had blindsided her. Before she could think of a reassuring comment, Travis waved his hand as if to dismiss his own question.

"Your father brought me his book of cross-examinations," he said. "We've talked about those cases, and in every one of them the cross-examination had real facts to work with. In yours, for example, you did some homework, found out about fog, the distance the murderer had to be able to see, and you proved that he couldn't have seen what he claimed. Step by step you destroyed him. But you had real facts to work with. In my case you don't. A dead man, two witnesses, a guy unconscious on the floor with a gun by his hand, his fingerprints on the gun. Where do you find real facts to refute the goons? You don't. No matter what you bring up that they might have done in the past, like you say, discredit them, that's not enough. I know that. You can't put him in that room, and even if you could nothing would be changed. He gets others to do his dirty work, and there's no way you can even prove that much. We, Mother and I, know you're really going after him, and I hope to God you get him, but that won't change a thing in my case. It is what it is."

He still couldn't bring himself to say "Father" or to use his father's name. Always it was either he or him, knowing exactly who he meant, expecting her to know, or not even considering that she might not. How his expressions changed, she thought. One minute open and seemingly even younger than his twenty-three years, then the face she saw across from her. Bleak, cold and aware the way an animal might be aware of the futility of trying to escape a trap it was caught in, accepting its fate, beyond thought about good and evil, simply existing with awareness of its impending death.

"Travis, listen up," she said quietly. "You're right about your father. He's the one I'm after, but more than that, I think there's something bigger than just him at stake here. I intend to bring down that something, and when the dust settles, I intend to extract you, whole and exonerated. What I came for today is to learn more about your friend Sheila Barrington and the man she married, Paul O'Reilly. You said they live in Cave Junction. There are members of your father's congregation down there, and I want to find out whatever I can about them. Is Paul O'Reilly likely to be of help?"

Travis looked as surprised by her change of direction as she had been about his. He blinked a few times, as if to bring himself back from the trap, then nodded. "If he can, I'm sure he'll help," he said. "He lost a leg in Iraq, and he was pretty messed up psychologically when he came home. I haven't seen him since they moved to Cave Junction, but I've talked to Sheila a few times. She said he's okay now and they're happy. They raise sheep. But he's a local and if there's anything going on, he probably knows about it."

"Is there a chance that he might be a follower of your father's church doctrine?"

Travis shook his head. "Not unless he's changed since I knew him. He might have been pretty messed up, but not about sex or a screwball conspiracy theory or any of that stuff. It was about war, his injury, others he had seen hurt or killed. What he had to do. I think Sheila would have hinted at something like that, or she might even have left him over it. She just wouldn't put up with any bullshit."

"How sure are you about him?"

He gave her a searching look, then said, "I'd trust him all the way. We see eye to eye on most things."

"Thanks," she said. "After I see them, I'll tell you all about raising sheep maybe. Meanwhile, keep exercising, meditating, corralling hurtful incidents in that magic box you make with your hands. In short, hang in there, Travis. I'm working on it."

Although he nodded, the trapped animal look had returned to his face.

On Tuesday Barbara, Frank and Shelley were in her office listening to Bailey's latest report.

"The guy who sold Daggart the car is Edward Atkinson," Bailey said. "He's from Seattle, and he's dropped out of sight. He did a story about fraud in a car dealership outfit up there about eight years ago. Not a regular journalist, he went freelance and sold the story to a TV station and a newspaper. There's a sister, Nina Atkinson. She's an executive secretary for a dot-com outfit, Beam One. They make software. Games." He closed his notebook with a snap. "It's going to take legwork in Seattle to get much more than that."

"I have to talk to the sister," Barbara said. "Do you have a number for her?"

"It's in there," Bailey said, pointing to the folder he had put on the table. "How will you identify him?"

"I'll identify him," Frank said. "If he called himself Daggart here, I'm the only one who can identify him, unless it's one of Morgan's crew."

Barbara gave him a sharp look but didn't protest. The sister no doubt would have a picture and Frank had stated a fact. He had met Daggart. "As soon as possible, if she'll talk to us," she said. "We'll have to work out details. I don't think Herbert will have to go to Seattle with us."

"He'll tag along," Bailey said. "Probably Peel had it right. Drive up to Portland, take the train."

"You and Dad work out the details," she said impatiently. "You said you had something about DiPalma, Morgan's driver. What?"

"He's still a flyboy," Bailey said. "There's a twenty-passenger Learjet parked in the Portland terminal and now and then DiPalma hauls people around. The jet is owned by the Epsilon Group. Who's behind Epsilon will take a hundred accountants with a hundred calculators and databases, and a hundred years to unravel. Not my thing," he added.

A hundred attorneys, Frank thought, was what it would take to untangle the connections. He had known about the Epsilon Group for a long time, and as Bailey had said, they had their fingers in a lot of things, including legislation that threatened the status quo, specifically their status quo.

Back burner for now, Frank decided. If someone in one of Epsilon's shadow corporations was funding Morgan on his own, it was one thing. If it was Epsilon, that was something else. That something else was too big for Barbara to get entangled in. Besides, he told himself, it might be just another dead end, DiPalma out to make a little extra income taking whatever flying jobs he could get.

"Can you keep track of when and where DiPalma flies?" he asked Bailey.

Bailey nodded. "I'll get someone in there who knows something about flying."

Barbara picked up the folder Bailey had brought and found Nina Atkinson's number. She went to her desk. "Here goes," she said, punching in the numbers.

When the phone was picked up, there was a lot of noise, music, laughter, many voices in the background. Barbara asked for Nina Atkinson and the voice on the phone yelled, "Nina, it's for you." There was an answer that was drowned out by noise, then the one on the phone said, "She'll take it in her office. Just a minute."

A woman's voice came on. "This is Nina. Joey, hang up the

phone. I'm on." The line became quieter. "Sorry about that," Nina said. "Can I help you?"

Barbara introduced herself. "I'm working on a case here in Eugene, and I believe your brother Edward Atkinson can be of assistance. Do you know how I can reach him?"

"No. I haven't seen him for almost a year. Have you seen him? What do you mean he can be of assistance?"

"I haven't seen him, Ms. Atkinson, but I have someone here who possibly saw him in March. If we come up there, could we have a little of your time. If you have a picture, he might be able to identify your brother."

"You don't have to come up here for a picture. I'll scan one right now and email it," Nina said. "Would that work for you? Has something happened to Eddie? Why do you need to identify him?"

"A picture would work, I'm sure. Why don't you do that, and afterward, if he's the man we're looking for, we can talk."

She gave her email address and they hung up. "Now we wait," she said. "Shelley, will you see what time the train leaves Portland, and get seats."

"For today?" Shelley asked.

"For today. If that's Daggart, we can't leave her hanging until next week, and I can't tell her on the telephone that her brother's dead. If a false alarm we'll cancel."

Fifteen minutes later the email came. Barbara opened it and moved aside in order to let Frank see.

"That's him," Frank said.

The man in the picture had a big smile and his arm was around a smiling woman's shoulders. There was enough similarity to assume that she was Nina Atkinson.

Barbara turned to Shelley. "Reservations for hotel rooms for us. One night."

"Herbert will make his own hotel reservation," Bailey said. "I'll get the SUV and drive you up to Portland, meet your train when you get back." He looked at his watch. "One hour. At your houses."

"I don't see why Herbert has to go," Barbara said. "I never even see him."

"That's the way I want it," Bailey said. "Just so he sees you. And, Barbara, tell me something. What do you know about Nina Atkinson? Who does she play ball with?"

She had no answer.

"That's why Herbert will trail along," Bailey said and went to the door, turned to salute and said, "One hour."

One ride in Bailey's SUV, another on a train, a sedan with Herbert at the wheel, and now they were standing in the foyer of a large apartment building, waiting for the elevator. The security man at the front desk never took his eyes off them, and in the elevator a red camera eye continued the watch. Neither Barbara nor Frank said a word as they were whisked up to the fourth floor.

The apartment door opened almost instantly when Frank knocked. The woman who admitted them was muscular and compact, with steel-gray hair in a chignon, tiny gold studs in her ears, and was wearing black slacks and a pale blue sweater that was the color of her eyes.

"I'm Nina Atkinson," she said. "I'd like to see some ID, if you don't mind."

"Barbara Holloway," Barbara said, taking her driver's license from her purse. "This is my father, Frank Holloway." They both handed Nina their driver's licenses. She studied them, compared the photographs to their faces, and returned them.

"Thank you," she said. "Please come in."

They entered a room that looked like a conservatory at first glance. A wide window area was filled with plants on stands, in pots on the floor, hanging in baskets and more pots. It smelled earthy and green.

Nina motioned to a seating arrangement made up of wicker furniture with fuchsia-colored cushions around a glass-topped table. "Just toss your coats anywhere," she said. "He's dead, isn't he? Eddie is dead. That's what you came to tell me, isn't it?"

"I'm afraid so," Frank said. "I can't confirm it from just that one photograph, but I think that's the man I met last March. I'm very sorry."

"Thank you," she said and bowed her head.

Barbara and Frank took off their coats and draped them over a chair.

"I knew he was dead," Nina said, almost tonelessly. She motioned for them to sit down as she sank into a chair. "I think I've known since May. When he didn't come home, or get in touch.... Why you, Mr. Holloway? Why not the police? Someone official?"

"I want to tell you how I came to meet him," Frank said. He told her about the collapse of Daggart in his office without mentioning the envelope with the lists of names. "No one knew who he was. His ID was in the name of Robert Daggart, a Portland resident. He never regained consciousness, and he was buried under the name of Robert Daggart. I have the client-attorney agreement he attempted to sign, and I regarded him as my client. I felt it was my duty to inform you of what I know about it." He took an envelope from his suit coat and removed a copy of the agreement. "That's as far as he got before he collapsed," he said, passing it to Nina.

Her hand was trembling when she took the paper and studied it. "Why now, six months later? How could he be connected with your case?" she asked Barbara. "I looked you up after we spoke on the phone. I read about the murder case, and I don't understand how Eddie could be connected."

"Of course not," Barbara said. "When the man called Daggart collapsed and died, Joseph Peel collected his things, identified him, and claimed his remains in the name of his church. Peel was the victim in the case I'm handling, and investigating his background we discovered that he made monthly trips to Seattle, and that he might have met with Robert Daggart here. Learning that your brother was an investigative journalist made me suspect that he was tracking down a story that either involved Peel, or that Peel knew something about."

Before Nina could ask another question or raise another objection, she asked, "Was your brother working on a story? Doing another freelance investigative report?"

Nina nodded. "I don't know what it was about. He was excited, though. He said it was big, really big. I never heard of a man named Peel, or your client, Travis Morgan, none of those people mentioned in the article I read."

"Will you tell us what you can about what your brother said? When he mentioned it?"

"It was Thanksgiving a year ago," Nina said. "I had a group in, including Eddie. He told me that all his payable accounts were electronic transfers through his bank and that he had paid his rent in advance through April. He said he would be out of touch, but I shouldn't worry. This would make national news, not just nail a few locals." She looked down at her hands and her voice dropped as she continued. "I never knew whether to believe him or not. Sometimes he had grandiose ideas, plans, and he was so excited. In May the property management people got in touch with me and said his rent was overdue. I waited a week, then I paid for a month and had his things packed up and put in storage. I wanted to go to the police, but he had said no matter what happened, I shouldn't report him missing, that if I did, it might put his life in danger." Her voice quavered as she said, "I should have gone to the police, no matter what he said."

"You couldn't have changed anything," Barbara said. "If Daggart was your brother, he died in the middle of March. If you had gone public, Ms. Atkinson, you might have put your own life in danger."

Nina's eyes widened. "What do you mean? Why?"

"You would have told them what you just told us," Barbara said. "The people who killed him might have reasoned that he had confided in you, that you were aware of the material he was working on. They might have believed that you were in possession of his notes, computer, camera, tape recorder, something incriminating to them. If they considered him a threat, they might have considered you a threat as well."

Nina moistened her lips and whispered, "I have his computer and boxes of papers. I didn't want to put them in storage."

Chapter 15

Nina Atkinson rose and gestured toward a door across the garden room, but after taking a step, she stopped walking. "I put things in the spare bedroom," she said. "I thought when he came back he would need his papers before anything else. And the computer. Personal things. Then I thought if he comes back… " She took another step and stopped again. "I'll have to settle his affairs, won't I? There are things I must do… " It was as if it was only then really registering with her that her brother was dead.

"Ms. Atkinson," Frank said kindly, "if we can look through things, I assure you we're not interested in his personal affairs, just a possible connection to Joseph Peel, a hint of the story he was pursuing. While Barbara is looking for that connection, perhaps we could put on coffee or tea and I can advise you on the best course of action for you to take. You don't have to do anything instantly, and until his death is confirmed beyond a doubt there really is nothing you can do."

"But the picture— You said it was Eddie."

"That is not enough to satisfy the law," Frank said. "We have his fingerprints on file. His personal items will have his fingerprints, and it would be much better if we can match them. Let's get started, if you're up to it."

"I'm fine," she said unconvincingly. This time when she started to walk she kept moving through a short hallway to a closed door. "In here," she said, opening the door and entering with Frank and Barbara close behind her.

This was a large bedroom with a king-sized bed, bureau, a desk and chair, another easy chair with a standing lamp. There was a laptop on the desk. Bedspread, drapes, carpeting all were in coordinated greens of varying shades with copper accessories. Handsome and expensive, Barbara thought, as was the entire apartment, or as much as she had seen so far. They had passed a living room with modern sleek furnishings and an ivory carpet, the garden room with its window wall of plants, now a guest room that would have been a showcase room in its own right. The apartment meant money.

"In the closet," Nina said, opening double doors to reveal four boxes. "I just put everything in boxes and I emptied his desk drawers… and his bathroom articles, hairbrush… "

"Those would be good for fingerprints," Frank said. "Now, coffee or tea or something and we'll talk about what you can do next."

Don't break down, Barbara thought furiously at the woman, who seemed to have a start and stop button that was out of control. She had stopped again, her gaze fixed on the boxes in the closet. Frank took her by the arm. "Want to show me the way to the kitchen?"

"Yes, of course. Coffee." She turned a stricken gaze to Barbara, and abruptly looked away, as if she feared that by revealing her distress, she was also revealing weakness. "Coffee," she said again. "That would be good."

As soon as they left the room Barbara pulled out the first box. The folders were neatly labeled but in no particular order: Automobile, Insurance, Taxes, Lease, Vacation… One by one she opened the folders, scanned the contents, and laid them aside. Nothing. She refilled the box and started on a second one. His first published story about the fraud he had uncovered. There were several three-by-five notebooks, most pages filled with neat writing. Good, she thought, that's what to look for. The box didn't take long to examine. She kept out one of the notebooks in order to get an idea of how he made notes, what method of shorthand he used.

In the third box there was a thick file folder labeled COPAR. She drew in a quick breath and took the folder to the desk.

When Frank and Nina Atkinson entered the kitchen, he nodded in approval. Stainless dishwasher, stove, refrigerator, bright-red canisters and small accessories, a blender, food processor, toaster. The counters were white, with black marble sections. He stood aside as Nina began to prepare coffee.

"Tell me something about your brother," he said.

She stopped spooning coffee into a basket. "He was… our father was an alcoholic. He died when Eddie was six. I was fourteen. Once Eddie said, who needs a father when you have a drill sergeant for a sister. I wonder, can you talk yourself into being ill, being a chronic semi-invalid? Mother was ill from then until she died six years ago. They never diagnosed anything, but she died anyway." She bowed her head and became silent for a time. Frank did not say a word or move. Abruptly Nina shook herself. "I forget how many scoops I already put in."

"Two," he said.

"One more. Do you take cream, sugar? Eddie liked both in his coffee. I was always afraid he'd develop diabetes. He liked sweets so much. He couldn't hold a job. Or wouldn't. A few months and he'd be off doing something else. He called Mother a hypochondriac and she cried. We used to play games together, Scrabble mostly. He usually won." She was speaking with many pauses between the statements, often between words, sometimes just a hesitation, then longer pauses. During one of the longer pauses, she stood with the coffee scoop in her hand and her gaze fixed on the coffee maker. After a moment she said faintly, "I forgot to turn it on." She pushed the On button.

"We weren't poor," she said. "Grandfather helped us out as long as I can remember. My father's father. He set up trusts for Eddie and me so we had our own money. That made Mother angry, that he had given it to us instead of her. He wanted me to put Mother in a nursing home or something, but I couldn't do that to her. I just stayed with her until she died. And then I got this apartment. It's pretty, isn't it?" She bowed her head again and said in a near whisper, "Eddie said I finally got the family I missed out on. My geeky boys, he said. That's what he called them, my geeky boys."

In the bedroom Barbara was examining the contents of the COPAR folder. It had a printout of one of Morgan's sermons, highlighted in places, and a photograph of the theater in Portland that had been turned into a church. There was a photograph of the residence in Eugene and another of the small Church of Purity and Redemption, also in Eugene. A map with a black cross on Portland and two circles well separated, as if he had used a compass to indicate distance from city center, a hundred miles from Portland? Two hundred? She didn't linger long enough to figure out the distances involved. A Seattle hotel room receipt for two nights dated the previous November. Another one dated February, same hotel. Dozens of papers, printouts, newspaper articles…

She put that folder on the bed and returned to the box. There was nothing more of interest.

The last box had the miscellaneous items from the desk drawers, paper clips, pens… and his personal things: an expensive-looking watch, hairbrush, toothbrush, eye drops, electric razor… There was a wallet and a BlackBerry, which could be the real treasure if it had his contacts. She didn't pick up the wallet or any of the other items. As Frank had said, they would have his fingerprints.

She replaced boxes in the closet, kept out the one with personal items, and eyed the laptop on the desk, hoping it would not have a password. She opened it, turned it on, and the demand for a password came up. She cursed under her breath and left it, to look over the rest of the closet. Men's clothes, a few suits, sport coats, a dinner jacket… In the third sport coat she searched, she found a three-by-five notebook with the same handwriting that was in the others she had seen. She started to put it with the other notebook she had tossed onto the bed, then she hesitated. The expensive furnishings, the expensive apartment, Nina herself an unknown factor. Bailey's words came to mind: *Who did she play ball with?* She put the little notebook in her pocket and went back to her search of the other clothes.

She eyed the computer again, then leafed through the small notebook, hoping to find a password. If it was embedded somewhere, she missed it. She looked through the folder labeled COPAR and didn't find it there, either. Finally, with the folder tucked under her arm, stymied by the security of the laptop, she left the bedroom and followed the aroma of coffee to a dining area off the living room, where Frank and Nina were at a table. Nina was talking in a low voice and became silent when Barbara entered.

"Any success?" Frank asked, rising as Barbara approached. "Coffee's hot and very good." He poured a cup and placed it on the table.

Barbara sat down and put the folder on the table. She took a sip of coffee, thanked him, and then said, "In that folder there are photographs of the church in Portland, the one in Eugene, the residence, other things. That's the link."

"It's true? That man in Eugene was really my brother under an assumed name," Nina said dully.

"I'm afraid so," Barbara said. "Of course, I haven't had time to read anything in the folder, but at first glance there didn't appear to be anything connecting him to Peel, just to the church."

"I don't understand," Nina cried. "Eddie never was interested in religion. Why an interest in a church now? Are you suggesting that the preacher got through to him, that he found a mentor or something?"

Barbara opened the folder and withdrew the printout of Morgan's sermon. It was the one where he used a fairy tale to explain Satan's curse of lust to mankind. She passed it across the table to Nina. "Read a paragraph or two," she said. "Then you tell me if that preacher got through to your brother."

Nina looked from her to Frank, back to Barbara, and finally down to the papers before her and started to read. At first she read it as she might read any article, but soon she was simply scanning it, and abruptly she pushed it away with a look of disbelief or disgust on her face. "Good Lord!" she said. "That's crazy! Can he really believe what he's saying?"

"I don't know," Barbara said, returning the sermon to the folder. "Ms. Atkinson, as I said, I didn't spot Joseph Peel's name in that folder, but there is one more place we should look. Is that your brother's laptop in the bedroom?"

Nina nodded. "I didn't want to leave it in storage."

"Do you know his password? He might have left more notes on

the computer than in that folder. If we can open his files, may we have a look there? The computer is password protected."

Nina shook her head. "That's too private, too personal. His correspondence, sites he might have visited, maybe games… "

"Ms. Atkinson," Frank said, "we could bring the laptop out here where you can watch exactly what files we try to read. We're not interested in his personal life, only certain files that contain notes or research about the church, Joseph Peel, Morgan, things that have a bearing on our case. Nothing else. Morgan's the preacher whose sermon you looked at. Your brother was researching something having to do with him or his church, and Peel could have been his inside informer. That's what we're interested in."

"I know the password," Nina said, keeping her gaze on Frank. "You think of the first pet you can remember and how old you were then. What he remembered was a dog named Dasher, when he was four. You substitute any two letters for two in the name. He chose a q and a v and ended up with dqS0He4V. You ignore the numbers to get to the real word, and there's enough to remind you of it easily. He added the zero to make it eight letters long." She looked down and added, "He liked puzzles, solving puzzles, making them."

"Great," Barbara said. "I'll bring the laptop out here," she said rising, as if Nina had agreed to open it for them.

Minutes later they arranged themselves at the table in a way that let each one see the screen and Nina opened the computer, found a folder titled Research and opened it. There were half a dozen subfolders: Churches, Citadel, COPAR, Epsilon, Morgan, and Peel.

Bingo! Barbara said under her breath. *Pay dirt*! Neither she nor Frank made a sound or moved as Nina opened the first folder, which had a number of subfolders of its own, apparently various religious groups Atkinson had researched. The folder had been created three years in the past.

"That could be when he first got interested in religious groups," Barbara said. "It would take a week of reading to get through those documents. Try COPAR. That's what Morgan calls his church."

Although the folder was smaller than the church folder, it still had too much to scan in a short time, including several more sermons. The folder had been created two years earlier.

Frank leaned back in his chair frowning. "Ms. Atkinson," he said, "obviously we can't read that material here and now—"

"You can't take his computer," Nina said forcefully. "I won't let you take the computer."

"No, no. Of course not. But it's getting late and there's a lot of reading to get through. What I would like to do, with your permission, is to transfer those files to disks and take them home to study. And I would suggest that we make two copies, and that you might be well advised to store your copies as well as the computer in a safe deposit box as soon as you can. Do you have blank disks here?"

"Yes, but… "

"Ms. Atkinson," Frank said firmly, "when your late brother came to my office and I put a client-attorney agreement down for him to sign, I made a commitment to look out for him. I'm honoring that commitment to the best of my ability, and now it extends to you. He told you he was after something big, and I believe that. Had he lived he would have written the story he was investigating, and I say to you now that when we learn what he was after, we will divulge it in its entirety to you, and you will have the option to complete his unfinished work. To write and publish the story that could have led to his murder. Until that time, however, you must not reveal to anyone that you are aware of what he was doing, that you have good reason to suspect that he was killed, or what our purpose here tonight was. Go on with your life exactly as you have been doing. And you must safeguard the material still in your hands."

"You think you can find out what the story really is?"

"With his help," Frank said, pointing to the computer, "and yours, I believe we'll get to the bottom of it. Will you cooperate?"

She moistened her lips. "Yes. I'll write the story myself. He'd want me to do it."

It was going on nine o'clock when Barbara and Frank walked out of the apartment building into a hard rain. He was carrying a plastic bag with some of Atkinson's belongings, including his BlackBerry, which Barbara had added without comment and without an objection from Nina. In Barbara's large handbag was the file folder labeled COPAR and two disks.

Swathed in a long black raincoat, Herbert rushed to put an umbrella over them. "Car's right up there. Coast is clear," he said cheerfully, "far as I can see, and I'm telling you that ain't very far, not in this rain. Here we go." He opened the back door of a black sedan and they climbed in. He hurried around to get behind the wheel. "Your hotel?"

"Absolutely our hotel," Frank said.

"I'm starving," Barbara said. "Dad, you all but kissed her on the cheek on our way out. What held you back?"

"A gentleman has to be solicitous around a lady in distress, but not to the point of a possible misunderstanding of his intentions."

"The point of your intentions better be to see that this lady in distress gets some dinner pretty damn quick."

Herbert chuckled.

"If you say I'm no lady, I'll hit you over the head with my shoe."

His chuckle turned into a belly laugh.

At the hotel Herbert surrendered his key to a valet parking attendant. He opened the door for Barbara and Frank, held the umbrella over them to the hotel entrance, and entered behind them. Anyone paying attention would have assumed he was a hired driver, Barbara thought as she and Frank crossed the lobby to the elevators. At the elevator, she glanced back, but there was no sign of Herbert.

"My room," Frank said. "After I get out of these wet shoes, we'll order dinner sent up and compare notes. Good enough?"

"You bet. But we don't touch the personal things, not even the BlackBerry until Bailey's had a crack at it."

In Frank's room a few minutes later, Barbara rummaged in the minibar while he changed into his slippers. "Why did you tell her you'd give her everything so she could write a book or something?"

He went to the bedside telephone before answering. "Do you object?"

"No. Just curious. We really don't know much about her, do we?"

"Enough. She rambled for over an hour, after all. Actually, I wanted her to trust me so we could walk out of there with as much as we did. People who ramble at you tend to trust you afterward for whatever peculiar reason there is. Wild salmon steak okay with you?"

"Sure. Whatever you're having. In her rambles, did she tell you anything real?"

He regarded her for a long moment, then said, "Promise me something?"

"Of course."

"Promise me that you'll put me in a home of some sort if I ever get past the point of taking care of myself. Your solemn promise."

"Dad! Stop that! What are you talking about? Are you hiding something from me?"

"No. I'm well. Just promise."

When she hesitated, he said very quietly, "Nina Atkinson threw away her own life to care for her mother, who probably didn't need looking after. She didn't have time to make friends, to pursue a career, make a family. Now she's found a new family of computer kids, but she needs something more than that. She needs something bigger than computer games and genius kids. I want to give her that something. When anyone, man or woman, feels the need to hold on so tight that he or she can't allow tears to flow, that person needs something big in life. Nina's been holding on for so long that when the dam gives, she could reveal much more than she intends to. I want that dam to continue to hold until this business is over. You did agree to salmon, didn't you?" He pressed the telephone dining room number. He placed the order, hung up, and regarded her once more with the same sober expression as before. "Your promise."

Barbara nodded. "I promise, Dad."

CHAPTER 16

FOR BARBARA THE next morning was little more than a blur, as if yesterday's events were playing in reverse: hotel, train, drifting into a light doze, jerked awake, drifting, awake…

In the Portland station, she scanned the crowded waiting room for Herbert.

"Over there," Frank said, nodding toward the entrance to the checked baggage area.

She saw him then, talking on a cell phone. "That's our signal." Together she and Frank walked to the exit doors and at that moment Bailey pulled in at the curb, also on a cell phone. He pocketed the phone and waved them in.

No one spoke until Bailey had navigated the streets leading to I-5 and was heading toward Eugene. "Atkinson met in person with Peel at least twice, maybe several more times," Barbara said then. "He had rented a place in Portland by late October and at Thanksgiving he told his sister that he'd be out of sight for the next six months. But in early November he went from Portland to Seattle, spent some time in his apartment, and checked into a hotel on Monday, Peel's hotel. He knew Peel would be in Seattle on Tuesday and he knew the only way they could talk was if he was already a registered guest and they could meet in Peel's room. Peel got in on the same train we took, and left the next morning. He didn't pick up the envelope until morning, and he suspected that he was watched getting it and going to the train station. It was the same system both times, once in November, once in February."

"What did they talk about? Isn't that the real question?" Bailey asked.

Barbara shrugged. "Don't know yet. Atkinson spent time in his own apartment on those two trips, and quite likely over his Thanksgiving trip to Seattle. Those could be the only times he spent there while he was undercover. He probably made notes on his laptop while he was there. He didn't include much in his notebook, just some key words that don't mean squat until we get to the disks."

"Interesting that Peel didn't pick up the envelope until he was practically out the door," Frank commented. "If those were his instructions it means they didn't give him time to open it. A crowded train, busybody neighbors in adjacent seats. So Peel probably didn't know what he carried besides money. If Peel didn't know, then Atkinson didn't, either."

Barbara leaned back in her seat. For a time no one spoke until Frank said, "I think we should keep all the items we brought back with us in my office safe. You have the combination," he said, twisting around to look at Barbara. "We both can get to that material whenever we want, and we have night security in our building. You still don't know when Darren and Todd will be gone for a week or longer. While they're away, I want you to stay at my house. You, Herbert, and the dog."

An almost reflexive protest formed and she stilled it. She wouldn't be able to play the disks at home, not with Todd and Darren around. She had stayed up until after two that morning, skimming through documents, puzzling out the notebook, trying to make sense of cryptic notes. The thought of sitting in her office long after Eugene shut down for the night was not appealing. She nodded, and Frank straightened around again.

✦

When they reached Frank's office he asked Patsy to order sandwiches and salads, and suggested that a pot of coffee would be appreciated.

"Okay," Barbara said, "now for our loot. In that bag are a lot of things that should have Atkinson's fingerprints, along with his BlackBerry. After you lift the prints, I want to listen to any messages on it, and I'll want a list of names from his address book. We'll start going through the papers and the CDs and more names could pop up. My first order of business is to make backups of the CDs and stash them away in the safe."

"It's going to take me a couple of hours," Bailey said. "I'll skip out and come back later, say around four or a little after, give you both a ride home."

The lunches arrived and no one talked as they ate. Almost immediately afterward, Bailey ambled out with the plastic bag.

"Do you have some blank CDs?" Barbara asked Frank. He buzzed Patsy and asked for two disks. She brought them in promptly and Barbara made the backups.

"Now let's have a look at what's on those CDs," Barbara said. She dragged a chair around Frank's desk, turned his monitor so that they could both see it, and put in the first CD as Frank joined her to sit in his desk chair.

"What the hell?" she muttered when she opened a file labeled Outline. It was a rough draft of a book outline, she realized. History of fringe religions. Rise and fall of crackpot theories. Prophets and prophecies…

"He was going to write a book," she muttered. "Look! His title page." In bold fourteen-point font was centered, "The Country With the Fringe On Top." A subtitle was: "How Fringe Religions Captured the Imagination of America and Transformed a Nation."

She drew back, regarding the screen with a frown. "Enough of this for now?" she asked.

"Right," Frank said. "Try the other one."

She replaced the CD with the other one and nodded in satisfaction. There were folders with the same labels she had seen on file folders: COPAR, EPSILON, CITADEL… She opened the COPAR folder and found four subfolders, selected one and opened it, then sent the cursor to the end. Ninety-one pages.

She returned to the text, searched for November tenth, and there were his notes from his meeting with Peel.

He's frightened, wants to back out. Refuses to even try to look inside the envelope. He thinks just papers and the wad of cash. Talked about the special members down south. He'll get me a list of their names. Not until March, when the next membership list is distributed. Waits until the last minute to get it from the desk. What's in those papers? Doesn't know anything about Epsilon or Citadel. Doesn't know anything! Getting crazier…

Abruptly Frank pushed his chair back and rubbed his eyes. "I can't read any more on the monitor," he said. "I want Patsy to print out everything. This one file is ninety pages. There must be five hundred pages to get through, maybe a thousand."

Reluctantly Barbara agreed, exited the program, and removed the disk. "Why no notes from his February meeting? Or did he put them in a different folder? I'll play with the disks after we get hard copies. At least, I can use the search function to skip around."

Bailey returned at four thirty. "Fingerprint matches," he said, tossing a folder down on the table by the sofa. "And the BlackBerry." He put it down next to the folder.

He eyed the bookshelves that concealed Frank's bar. Frank obliged by opening his bar and pouring a generous amount of bourbon, added a splash of water, and handed it to him. Barbara started the playback of messages. A dental appointment reminder. Solicitor for a charity. Invitation to lunch… Nothing.

"It was worth a try," she said with regret. "Did you find anything?" she asked Frank.

He had spent the last two hours reading material while she roamed through the files on disk.

Frank shook his head. "Bits and pieces of this and that. History of cults, unaffiliated churches, leaders and followers. Interesting reading, but not relevant, far as I can tell."

"I might have something," Barbara said. "Under Citadel, which seems to have been a primary concern of his. He was following Morgan quite a lot before he turned into a handyman. He followed him to that landing field in Portland, in April, two and a half years ago. I have to check my dates, but it seems it was at the time that June Morgan was pulled out of school and vanished, days before John Varagosa was mutilated. Anyway, Atkinson saw Morgan and a woman board the plane along with a stretcher bearing someone. DiPalma was the pilot. Atkinson hung around until the plane returned, six hours and ten minutes later. Morgan was alone when he got out, and he and DiPalma returned to the condo."

Bailey made a note. "That's something," he said. "How far can you get in three hours?"

"He thought of that," Barbara said. "There's a whole page of times the jet took off, how long it was gone, and who was on board. Often it was a group of men, twelve to fifteen at a time. The plane was gone five hours, give or take ten minutes or so, returned without them, and ten days to two weeks later repeated the trip, brought them back in roughly the same time frame. Somewhere two and a half hours away. He drew circles on his map to see where the plane could have gone, and he concluded that it was within four hundred miles of Portland. Maybe a smaller radius than that, though, since there's no way of knowing how long it was on the ground wherever it went. He wrote *Militia* and underlined it."

Silently Frank rose and went to the bar, where he poured two glasses of wine. He was visualizing the vast expanses of mountains and basin-and-mountain formations within four hundred miles. Cascades, Strawberry Mountains, Wallowas, Blue Mountains, Steens. Mountains with snow likely in April, the heat of summer high desert, barren and remote, isolated ranches, resorts, ghost towns... He handed a glass to Barbara and sat down heavily on the sofa.

She was thinking that digging deeper seemed only to result in distancing herself further and further away from her immediate case of preparing a defense for Travis Morgan. She had found no mention of June or Ruth Morgan, or the young woman who had been cremated in place of June. Atkinson's interest had been in Morgan and a possible connection with a militia, not his personal life.

"Bailey," she said, "find out if Morgan is picking up the package from Seattle himself, or sending someone else to get it. I have to get my hands on one of those packages, see what besides money is in it."

✦

CHAPTER 17

A DAY LATER Frank put down the last page of the manuscript he was reading and regarded Barbara for a moment. She was gazing into space. "Anything?" he asked.

She gave a start and shook herself. "Maybe, but not anything I can use." She stood and moved restlessly about the office. "Always up to the door, never going through it." She paused at the round table after making a tour of the office. "I can't use any of this," she said, waving her hand generally at the papers spread on his desk, at the ones she had spread on the sofa and table. "Even if I could tie it all together, that's not the issue. Peel's murder is, and I'm wasting time day after day with this nonsense."

When Frank made no comment, she said dully, "You were right months ago. This is all just a distraction from my case, my client. No way will they let me bring any of it up at the trial. And I don't have anything else to bring up."

"Did you tell Todd to focus his search to within four hundred miles of Portland?" Frank asked.

"Yes. He said they have narrowed it down to twenty-six possible sites. This will narrow it down more. And if they find it, what then? I go knock on the door and ask politely if this is the place where Morgan's been keeping his daughter for the past two and a half years and may I please speak with her." She sank down onto the sofa. "I'm giving myself this one last weekend with Atkinson and his files. That's it. I'll read the sermons tonight at home." Then she said, "If I have to talk Travis into a plea bargain, I have to start before long. He's dead set against it, and so is Ashley. I may have to persuade her first, then him."

"Wrong order," Frank said. "First you."

She gave him a long searching look, and finally nodded.

When she drove home she did not see a sign of Herbert, but his big shaggy black-and-white dog met her with his tail wagging. Morgan's stub of a tail wagged his whole body and made him look ridiculous, but it was a welcoming sight. She rubbed his head, and invited him in. He sat down and watched her. “Okay,” she said to the dog, “stay out here in the cold. See if I care.”

Twenty minutes later Herbert arrived carrying a sack of groceries. Morgan came inside with him. Herbert waved to Barbara, said, “Howdy,” and continued on to the kitchen with Morgan at his side. Herbert was a large man, overweight, with thinning dark hair, and a genial manner. Bailey had once said that he could shoot fleas off a dog at fifty yards, and Barbara knew he could tell tall stories with the best of them. Sometimes he was a painter, or an installer of security systems, or a handyman. Or a bodyguard. He had made himself their cook, explaining to Todd that since Bailey didn’t have that much for him to do, he might as well make himself useful, and he liked to cook.

That evening, waiting for Darren to come home, she started to read the sermons that Atkinson had printed. In spite of herself, she kept hearing Herbert and Todd’s conversation in the kitchen.

“Why do you take Morgan all around our yard every day?” Todd asked.

“Well, it’s this way,” Herbert said. “Down south, Arizona, a while back, see, I was playing poker with a bunch of Apaches and I kept winning. Didn’t plan to, just lucky that night, but they began to act like they thought I was cheating or something. I wasn’t cheating. I’d be scared to death I’d get caught, but that wasn’t a good place to be, a big white dude with a bunch of Indians not far removed from their scalping days, and I was getting just a mite uneasy when there was a commotion in the next room and they all got up to have a look-see and I skedaddled lickety-split. A few weeks later I got to thinking that Indians don’t forget, and they don’t forgive, and it bothered my sleep so I had a little talk with Morgan and told him he had to warn me if they ever got on my trail. I always show him the boundaries, sort of, and if any Apaches set foot across it, I’ll have time to skeddaddle again, just like before. Don’t want no trouble with them, and I sure don’t want my head to show up naked one morning.”

Todd laughed and in the living room Barbara smiled, then returned to the sermon she was trying to read.

Dinner was as good as Barbara had anticipated: lamb croquettes baked in tomato sauce, crisp on the outside, meltingly tender with pine nuts and golden raisins on the inside, and a dessert Herbert called a peach thingy.

"You just dump some peaches in the pie pan, add some heavy cream with a little sugar and cornstarch, maybe a touch of cinnamon and toss on some puff pastry on top. Bake a while, and there it is, my peach thingy."

Darren laughed and then said, "Todd and I have our date with Washington. Annie got the word today. The Tuesday after Thanksgiving."

"Wow!" Todd said. "Cool! I thought it wasn't going to happen. I already have one assignment. I have to go to the Space Museum and write a report on it."

They talked about sightseeing, the must-not-miss museums and monuments, a possible tour of the White House... Watching them, Barbara had an irrational desire to chuck everything and tag along. The thought was swiftly followed by disappointment verging on despair. There went her chance to find out where June Morgan was being held. Thanksgiving was one week away and Todd would be busy planning his trip, too busy and too excited by it to give much thought to the problem she had tasked him with.

Herbert shooed her out of the kitchen when she offered to do the dishes. "Reckon if you got that pile of reading to do, you don't need to be getting dishpan hands instead."

"I'm reading sermons," she said with a grimace. "Washing dishes sounds like a lot more fun."

"Soul food," Herbert said. "Can't get too much soul food. Go on, out with you."

"Sermons written by a nutcase," she said glumly and scowled when Herbert laughed his big belly laugh. She returned to the sermons while Darren went to his study to look up places to stay, restaurants, sights often overlooked... With Todd in the basement den doing homework,

Darren off in the study, the sounds of activity in the kitchen gradually fading to nothing, the house seemed so preternaturally quiet, she couldn't even claim that it was hard to work at home because of the distractions. Grimly she finished one more sermon and picked up the next one.

When Darren reappeared with a notebook in hand, she put down another sermon, midway through it.

"Finding anything useful?" he asked.

"A lot of things. Like birds falling dead from the sky, dead fish washing ashore, two-headed anythings being born are all God's way of telling us he hates gays. Or, try this one: volcanoes, blizzards, wind storms, floods are God's message that he will not tolerate sodomy. Or, abstinence, chastity, purity are the only road to salvation. Or, women who wear pants, who go out to work, who do not submit to their husbands, or who make more money than they do are steps to the feminization of our men, a step toward what they're really after, which is a new matriarchy. They're all like that, concepts taken to their extreme outcome, and all against God's plan for humankind. He knows he's right because he talks to God and God gives a seal of approval. A few even provide Bible references so you can check it for yourself. Matthew 4:28, or something like that. After their unique lead-ins, they seem to share the same clichés that are so familiar we can all recite them: big government, one world order, socialism, communism, fascism, mind control, and so on."

After Darren went up to bed, she finished reading the remaining sermons and added them to the two stacks she had been making, one with highlighted sections, one without. Atkinson had highlighted the biblical references every time, she realized and admitted to herself that he had been more thorough in his research than she intended to be. Or he just had more time on his hands than she did, she added. At least, until his time ran out.

When Barbara called a few days earlier, Sheila Barrington had expressed bewilderment over what she could do to help Travis, then quickly added that if there was anything, she would do it gladly. She had suggested that they meet halfway, not down in Cave Junction. She and her husband had to be in Roseburg to go to the VA clinic there, she had said, and directed Barbara to a restaurant next to a Comfort Inn Motel just off the highway. "Whoever gets there first can wait," she had said. "I hope we can make it by one, but I can't say for certain."

Bailey picked her up at ten that morning. When she protested the elaborate plan he had come up with, he had said, "My way or no way. Your old man's orders."

"My old man, as you so delicately phrase it, is getting paranoid, or senile."

"Maybe so. Or maybe he's thinking of one guy killed in an arson fire, one beaten to death, a kid mutilated and shot, and another guy shot dead. What we'll do… "

He drove to a gas station where Herbert's truck was parked. She left Bailey's SUV and climbed into the truck.

It was a white panel truck with a Quality Painting sign, and it was very dirty, mud spattered, with a dent in the front right side, the kind of truck that few paid any attention to.

"Buckled up?" Herbert asked. "Don't want no ticket today, and they are fierce in these parts about little things like seat belts, all lights working, right kind of license plates. Law abiding like I never seen anywhere else."

He drove at the speed limit on a side road that paralleled I-5 for a few miles before there was an entrance to the highway. Once on it, he set the speed control at seventy miles an hour. "You just set back and enjoy the scenery," he said. "We're clear, and this here's a real pretty drive." They were passing warehouses and he added cheerfully, "As soon as we get down a ways."

It was pretty, Barbara thought when the industrial section was behind them. Wide fields, heavily forested hills, a few well-separated clearings with houses, cattle grazing. "That's where you want your milk to come from," Herbert said. "Cows are supposed to be out eating grass and you sure can taste the difference in the milk. Steaks, too. Best steak I ever ate was in Denver… "

He told her about the best steak, and she let his words drift past along with the scenery, thinking about her coming talk with Sheila Barrington, who, according to Travis, wouldn't put up with any bullshit. She knew so little about Sheila, and less about her husband, who had lost a leg in Iraq. For all she knew they both came from families deeply devoted to Arlie Morgan and his cult. Church, she corrected herself. The Church of Purity and Redemption. COPAR.

Then she was thinking again about the sermons. Why highlight those particular sections? She tried and failed to remember what all Atkinson had highlighted. Turned off so completely by what she had already seen and heard, she had skimmed through them. A mistake, she told herself with a silent curse.

More wooded hills, fewer farms, fewer pastures, more hills, buttes in the distance in the east… A fine rain began to fall. By the time they reached the exit for Roseburg the rain had become a steady downpour. It was ten minutes after twelve.

"What we'll do is drive by a MacDonald's or something, and get me something to eat, then drop you at the restaurant to meet your people. I'll eat in the truck and tend to that rattle I keep hearing while you're inside."

She was in a booth with a cup of coffee and a book. It was Eliot's *Four Quartets*, which she had told Sheila she would display in order for them to recognize her. Sheila said she would have a book on the table if she got there first. Strangers in the night, Barbara thought, literature the tie that binds. She looked up when a couple approached.

The woman spotted the book, and said, "Ms. Holloway, Sheila Barrington, and this is Paul O'Reilly." She slid into the booth and he followed. She was a few pounds overweight, round-faced with long pale hair in a ponytail, little makeup beyond a trace of lipstick. She looked tired. Her brown eyes were deep set with shadows under them. Paul O'Reilly was tall and lean, deeply tanned, and blue-eyed. He was examining Barbara with a cool, steady gaze, and while not openly hostile, neither did he appear friendly.

The waitress came to the table and greeted them both as if she knew them. "Another visit to the docs? How's it going?"

"Fine," Sheila said. "We only had to wait an hour this time." She picked up her menu. "Give us a few minutes, will you?"

"Sure thing. Just wave when you're ready."

As soon as she left, Sheila lowered her menu. "How's Travis?"

"He's holding up," Barbara said. "He didn't shoot that man. Peel."

"I know he didn't."

"You don't know anything of the kind," Paul said sharply.

"Yes, I do. I know him."

"A guy can change a lot in few years. You don't know what he's capable of today. Let's order some food." His face had become set in hard lines, and he had tensed as he spoke. He picked up his menu and disappeared behind it.

"Have you decided?" Sheila asked Barbara, who nodded. She motioned the waitress back.

After they ordered, very quietly Sheila said, "I do know. That kid lived in my apartment for nearly eight months. I know him the way I know my own kid brother. He didn't do it. What can I do to help him?"

Before Barbara could respond, Paul leaned forward and said, "I don't know what you want from us. She wouldn't be a good character witness, if that's your plan. From the time a kid is in his teens to where he is today can turn him into a stranger. Sheila's expecting a baby in three months, and she's been sick. We can't get involved. I won't get involved and I'll do everything in my power to keep her out of it. That's it. We don't have anything for you."

Sheila put her hand on his arm. He ignored it, keeping his hard gaze on Barbara.

"I didn't come here to ask her to appear as a character witness," Barbara said. "I know even better than you do how futile that would be. Do either of you know Arlie Morgan? He's also known as Benjamin Morgan?"

Sheila shook her head and he said, "Never heard of him."

"Do you know Ralph Shivers?"

"Yes," Sheila said. "He has a farm over by Cave Junction. I know his son better. Why do you want to know?"

"We both know them," Paul said. "Why are you asking about them? What do they have to do with Travis or the charge against him?"

"That's what I'm trying to find out. His name came up in our investigation and I'm following through with everything I can."

Their food was brought and they all drew back until the waitress left again. Paul took a bite of his hamburger, then said, "I can't even imagine how Ralph could be implicated in any way in the case against Travis, but what do you want to know about him?" He had become much more relaxed since Barbara said that she did not want Sheila to testify in Travis's defense.

"Just about everything," Barbara said. "I don't know a thing about him or his son. Start with his age, how well you know him, general things like that to give me a picture."

Paul glanced at Sheila, and Barbara felt that a private communication passed between then, exactly the way it did with her and Darren sometimes.

"He's about sixty-two or -three," Paul said. "He's isolated on his farm with just a few hands, dayworkers, and his son Peter. He's thirty by now, I guess." He looked enquiringly at Sheila. She nodded. "They keep to themselves and don't bother anyone," Paul said. "They have cattle, a good farm. He goes off on a religious retreat sometimes, or at least that's what people believe. And he goes to a church in Medford sometimes, not regularly, but enough to say he's a churchgoer."

He was choosing his words with care, and when he stopped speaking, he began to eat again as if he had said all he intended to say.

Sheila put her fork down and leaned forward. "There's a little more," she said. Paul gave her a sharp look, which she ignored. "When we first came back home, he came to the house to talk to Paul." She looked at him then and said, "Do you tell about it or do I?"

With an exasperated expression Paul said, "You weren't even there."

"So it should come from you."

"Jesus! Okay. He came to talk about a survivalist group or something. I'd only been home a month or two and I wasn't in the mood, but he kept going on about how I had more reason than most to be suspicious about government, and to know about safeguarding my property, my loved ones. I thought he was a nut. He was talking about a militia more than a survivalist group. He seemed to believe the day would come when we'd have to take up arms to keep what we had, that the end days would come sooner than anyone realized and we had to be ready. He was loony. He said that because of my training, I had a lot to offer, that it was my duty to help others prepare. I ended up telling him to get the fuck out of my face. He hasn't spoken to me since." He turned his gaze to Sheila. "Satisfied? Now can we finish our lunch?"

"Yes, dear," she said demurely. Then she laughed, and his expression softened.

Barbara let out a long breath. "Thanks," she said before she took a bite of her salad.

As they ate their lunches, she asked a few more questions and now Paul readily answered them. Did he know Drake Wallenstein in Medford? His name had been set off by one of the bullet points on the lists Atkinson/Daggart was to have taken to Medford. Paul said yes, he knew him. He was the leader of the church Ralph Shivers and his son attended. The retreat they all went on was through their church, he believed without knowing definitely. He didn't know how often they went off on their retreat, several times a year probably. Sometimes they stayed for a couple of weeks, sometimes just a few days.

They had gone in October, he said. "Our mail carrier mentioned that they were gone again. He doesn't approve of leaving a big farm in the hands of dayworkers for a couple of weeks at a time. I'd hear that he was gone again, or someone would make a crack that he must be getting filled up with religion. I don't ask questions about him but you hear things when you live out like we do and you've known people all your life. Our mail carrier is the town crier."

"Have those retreats been happening over the years?"

"Ever since we got back home," Sheila said. "You know Paul was in Iraq? Two tours, and I spent several years in San Francisco while he was gone. I don't know about those years, but for the last six they get their guys together and off they go."

"How many? I was imagining just Shivers and his son. Were there more?"

"At least eight, ten, maybe more," Sheila said. "I've heard that different men go from one time to the next, except for Drake and either Ralph Shivers or his son Peter. Drake is the leader of the religious group, so I guess it makes sense that he's a regular. He's not really a preacher, and it's not exactly a church. They get together in his living room and hold services there. They've been doing that for a long time, since before we both left.

She looked at her watch then. "We really should be on our way," she said. "It's a long drive back, and it will be slow with such hard rain. For you, too," she added.

Barbara nodded and picked up the check. Paul reached for it and she shook her head. "You've both given me valuable information and I'm grateful. I'll pay."

"Ms. Holloway," he said in a low voice. "I don't know where you're going with your investigation but I do know this. You're asking questions about men who are considered to be rough, and who are extremely suspicious about anyone from outside who comes poking into their affairs. That girl who waited on this table knows people here in Roseburg and she's a talker. She knows why we come over here, and if she mentions that a city woman had a long talk with us, then paid for our lunch, word will get around. I assume you'd rather not have that happen. I say we pay for our lunches, you pay for yours, and we let it go at that."

At his side Sheila nodded. Barbara withdrew her hand. "It's all on one bill, so I'd better give you cash for my share."

When the waitress returned to collect Paul's credit card and Barbara's cash, Sheila said, "We're trying to figure out who owes how much. I think we have it right." She removed the dollars from the small tray and handed them to Paul. The waitress left. She returned almost instantly with the receipt and credit card.

Paul slid from the booth and reached out to help Sheila.

"Mr. O'Reilly," Barbara said, making no motion to get up yet.

"You said you don't ask questions, and I think that's very wise. Also, if anyone asks you about today I think it would be wise not to deny that you both talked to me, that I wanted Sheila to be a character witness and you both refused."

He gave her another, even longer searching look and then nodded. "We come in to Roseburg so I can see my doctors. Period. Take care driving home. That rain means business."

Barbara waited long enough for them to have reached their car and leave before she left the booth and stepped out into the downpour, then ran to the truck. Draped in a long raincoat and a rain hat that nearly hid his face, Herbert was gazing morosely at the open hood of his truck. He slammed it shut as she climbed into the passenger seat. He paused at the driver's side to take off the raincoat, tossed it in the back, and got behind the wheel.

"Now you say, 'Home, James,' and off we go."

"Did you fix the rattle?"

"You know how it is, the tooth stops hurting just about when you think it's time to call the dentist, or the car stops rattling as soon as you drive up to the mechanic's shop. Open the hood with a wrench in your hand and she purrs like a little kitty cat. Can't figure out how that always happens." He backed out of the parking space and headed for the highway as he spoke. "We'll take it nice and easy all the way. So you just relax."

She already had her notebook out making notes.

CHAPTER 18

HERBERT DROVE TO the gas station and once more Barbara made the transfer, this time from his truck to Bailey's car. It was ten minutes after five. "Dad's house," she said to Bailey.

He groaned. "Hannah's making chili," he said. "She'd like it fine if I got home at a decent hour, you know."

"I won't stay long," Barbara said. "Your idea, playing car tag."

He drove carefully through a cold steady rain. "It'll freeze by morning," he muttered.

She called Darren to say she'd be there around six thirty, and she called Frank to warn him that they were on their way. Then she returned to her thoughts and minutes later they were in Frank's driveway.

Frank met her at the door and helped her shed her raincoat as the two cats made their own inspection of her legs. "Any problems?" Frank asked.

"Nope. But I waded into enemy territory today and word could get out." Bailey made a grunting sound and they all headed to the living room, where logs were burning in the fireplace and Frank had a tray with bourbon, wine, and cheeses waiting.

She told them what Paul had said. "So Drake Wallenstein is some kind of leader and he takes a group somewhere to what they call a retreat, sometimes with Ralph Shivers or his son Peter, sometimes not. The retreats last a couple of weeks, but he makes other trips with several of his followers now and then, those trips take three or four days. The last full retreat that Paul knows about was in October." She turned to Bailey. "Check that schedule for the plane, see if it was used in October. And run a deeper check on both Ralph and Peter Shivers, and one on Drake Wallenstein. Dad, this confirms that they've organized a militia. And suddenly the Citadel makes sense. A fortress, a storehouse for arms, a sanctuary for times of war. We have to locate it."

"ATF work," Bailey said after a short silence. "Homeland Security."

"Not yet. We don't have enough, but eventually it's in their lap." The federal agencies would have to be brought in, she knew, as soon as they had hard intelligence that was credible enough for them to act on.

She looked at Frank and said slowly, "I keep wanting to get out of all this, and I keep getting pulled back in. But I simply can't see a second-rate fanatic like Morgan behind a movement that takes the kind of money and organization skills that something this big requires. I think he's a throwaway pawn. And maybe that's my route to him that lets me bring it all back to the murder of Joseph Peel."

"He may be the pawn, but he may also be valuable to the chess player," Frank said. "Keep that in mind, Barbara. Sometimes a single pawn determines the whole game."

"Well, I'm going home now. I want a hot shower and food. I think

I'll put in time at your office tomorrow, away from the madding crowd. I want another go at a lot of that stuff in your safe."

She pulled on her raincoat and left with Bailey. Frank watched until Bailey's car vanished. He suspected that she was right, that Morgan was a useful tool for the power behind the militia that seemed to be taking shape. And she was also right, he thought soberly, that today she had ventured into enemy territory. A talkative waitress could make all the difference.

Barbara returned to Morgan's sermons after dinner, and this time she read word for word, cursing afterward that it had been a waste of time. He was a one-note preacher and his word was anti-sex. She looked up another one of the biblical references in his sermon. Matthew 2:23: *And he came and dwelt in a city called Nazareth: that it might be fulfilled which was spoken by the prophets. He shall be called a Nazarene.*

She read it twice, then looked again at the place in the sermon where it had been referenced. His sermons were all similar in most respects, first his passionate rant about the evils of sex for anything other than procreation, followed by a rant about the government, various laws, poison in drinking water, illusory freedom, slavery in the name of democracy... She read again the part that included the highlighted reference. *You are slaves of the government, all of you, slaves! The government makes you submit your children to vaccines, poison injected into your innocent children. It makes you send your children to its handmaidens to be indoctrinated in its ways....*

At ten thirty Darren left to pick up Todd. Barbara continued to check out the references, becoming more frustrated with each one. She was pacing when Darren and Todd got home, bringing a pizza with them.

"Join us," Darren said, beckoning her to the dining room. "Mushrooms and Canadian bacon."

Barbara and Darren each had a sliver of pizza and kept Todd company while he devoured the rest of it. When they began to plan Todd's transportation to and from Dr. Chu's laboratory on Saturday and Sunday, Barbara went back to the sermons. She was still at it when Darren came into the living room.

"You're looking disgruntled," he said with a grin.

"Pissed off might be a better choice of words for how I look and feel. Darren, you're a reasonable man, well read, educated, with a great vocabulary, so tell me something. Elucidate for me. So, I'm ranting about how floods, earthquakes, tornadoes are all God's way of saying he doesn't like gays. Then I get into the whole hate big government thing, precious bodily fluids kind of talk, fluoride in water, mandatory school days. You get the gist. So I reference it with this passage from the Bible." She read: "*And at Gideon dwelt the father of Gideon; whose wife's name was Maachah.*" It goes on to name more people in the following lines. His firstborn son Abdon, and Zur, and Kish... More names, some begats, and so on. What the hell does that have to do with the wrath of God over gays, or with mandatory school days, or with anything else under the sun?"

"Beats me," he said. "But you're asking the wrong person. I thought preachers were supposed to explain things so that the congregation can understand the deeper meaning."

"Not this loony tune," she said, indicating the sermons on the coffee table. "He just tosses the reference to you as if it's a life jacket, and it's up to you to figure out how to use it or sink. I keep sinking."

Disgruntled was far too mild a word to use, Barbara thought on Saturday after studying the topographical map of Oregon with a circle she had drawn with a Magic Marker. The area enclosed was most of the state and Washington State. There seemed to be a thousand mountains and endless desert, and any spot with mountains to the north and desert around could describe the place where June Morgan's e-mail said she was being held.

She was poring over the map, trying to estimate the size of ranches, when Frank walked in. "People out there know something's going on," she said. "You can't fly a Learjet in and out without people noticing."

Frank took off his raincoat and hung it up. "Good morning," he said equably. "Have you had coffee? Want some?"

"Sorry. Good morning. Coffee's in the carafe and it's pretty cold by now."

He nodded, picked up the carafe, and walked out with it. She returned to her map.

Frank brought in fresh coffee, poured for them both, and for a short time neither spoke. "I've been thinking," she said finally, "that Shelley might as well start getting detailed county tax maps together, have them ready if Todd and Dr. Chu come up with the list of possible places. I think we can rule out a lot before that. Like Smith Rock. It's remote enough, but it also gets a lot of traffic—hikers, photographers, picnickers, tourists, and there are too many ranches and farms too close. I don't think any place within several miles of a highway would be a good bet."

Frank agreed. "You don't want to put in too much time with it until you get that list from Todd. No point in knocking yourself and Shelley out for nothing."

"Right. Just to have the maps on hand. And speaking of too much time, I have to see Ashley this afternoon, and then drop in on Travis. I haven't seen either of them this week. They might ask questions about our progress, and I just don't know how much to tell her. As little as possible, but where to draw the line is a problem."

"She knows you want Morgan's hide, and you said she was good with that. I'd guess it's where the line gets drawn. You wonder where all his money is coming from, for instance. Checking out everyone you can." He shrugged. "Change of subject. It's time for Herbert to put that truck in a garage, out of sight, and become your driver. If Morgan can have a personal driver, so can you."

"Dad, I can't operate in a cage with a personal guard at my elbow."

"Yes, you can. You know how the fellows in these offices come and go all hours, weekends, holidays, and you know they can get careless about locking doors. Someone got in a few years back, remember, and he had murder on his mind. It isn't going to happen again."

She remembered all too clearly. A security man had been killed that night, and one of the firm's attorneys had been bashed in the head. But to have Herbert at her side in the car… "I'll have to gag him," she said.

"Then gag him." Frank got to his feet. "I'll call Bailey and get him to send someone to drive that truck away, and Herbert will drive you to see Ashley and then to the jail."

Seething, Barbara drank her coffee. She knew he had a point, but still— But still, nothing, she told herself sharply. He had a point. That waitress could have heard Sheila say her name, the truck was memorable once it was noticed at all, and the meeting in the restaurant could very well be mentioned in a casual conversation with the wrong person.

The bigger point, she knew, was that she was looking into what could be a very big, very well financed operation, with ruthless people pulling the strings. In their eyes she could well be the throwaway pawn.

Barbara thought of all the people who had become involved one way or another and who might be at risk because of it. She added Sheila and her husband, Paul. All because she had become incensed at the way Arlie Morgan had treated his wife, the mother of his two children. So be it, she thought, her team would see this through, risk or no risk, and that was that. Being driven by Herbert was a minor nuisance to be tolerated, and if she had to tell him to cork it, she would tell him.

CHAPTER 19

YOU ADAPT OR die, Barbara thought. She had been surprised at how quickly she had adapted to having Herbert practically within reach throughout her wakeful hours, and more surprised to find that she welcomed his nearness when she walked by the river on the trail, which on many days was almost deserted.

"The hardest part, maybe, is not having anything to do," Travis had said on Saturday. "I work out, read, and then it's stare-at-the-wall time."

"Travis," she had said, "there may be something else you can do that would help. From the time your family moved to the condo until you took off, jot down the daily routine, who came in, visitors, business people, whatever. What kind of security they used then. I mean, how careful were they? Keep everything locked up tight, or leave papers around? It doesn't have to be suitable for an English teacher's eagle eye, just enough to give me a sense of what life was like. I'm assuming that routine things don't change a lot and I know kids don't pay much attention to their parents' business affairs, but whatever you recall would be helpful."

He gave her a curious look and quickly looked past her. "Kids see more than you know. They hear things all the time and keep their mouths shut. You learn that real young, just keep your mouth shut. But kids know what's going on."

"Okay," Barbara said. "Another homework assignment, life in the condo. Deal?"

"Sure. Deal."

She had to make him stop tensing every time Arlie Morgan's name came up, she had decided. Make him think of his father, write his schedule or whatever, remember he was just a man, one who had no power over him any longer. Travis was better than he had been months before, but it was still there, withdrawal, tension, fear.

That day the river was gray, swift, and high with snow melt and recent heavy rains. It seemed to be in the throes of a panic rush to the coast, rolling, tumbling over itself, creating waves with whitewater spray, urging itself onward in a low rumbling voice: faster, faster.

Shelley was busy collecting the county maps, and much happier than she had been in recent weeks when there had been little for her to do beyond the walk-ins at Martin's. And that left her, Barbara, and all she was doing was taking long walks. She had finished all the material Atkinson had left and she had come to a standstill. She had added nothing usable since talking to Sheila and Paul. Suspicions, tenuous threads, nebulous associations, lists of church members…

Abruptly she turned to retrace her steps to the car. Herbert gave no sign of recognition when she walked past him. Poor Herbert, she thought then. He was not as happy walking in the rain as she was. On Thursday, Thanksgiving, they would all go out to Shelley and Alex's house in the foothills of the Coast Range for dinner, and she would hike up the mountain behind their house, up into the rain forest. Deluge, snow, fog, hail, sleet, no matter, she would hike the mountain without Herbert dogging her footsteps. He had already said he maybe could help out in the kitchen. She smiled to herself as she thought of the three men in the kitchen: Frank, Dr. Minnick, and Herbert. A three-way competition? She doubted it. Dr. Minnick didn't play such games.

The days melted like snow in warm rain, a presence for a brief time, then gone. With nothing accomplished. Thanksgiving came and Barbara had her hike, along with Alex and Shelley, Darren and Todd. They returned wet, muddy and hungry, with time for hot showers and a change of clothes and little else.

They all agreed that dinner had been stupendous, enough for

three times as many as graced the table, and leftovers were carefully portioned out to be taken away by the guests. Herbert drove them in Bailey's SUV.

After dropping Frank off at his house, Herbert drove to Darren's.

Derisively Todd said, "Now you and Morgan will make a tour of the yard, make sure the Apaches didn't break down the fence. Right?"

"Dang right. They're crafty and they know I'm on to them. Can't be too careful when it's your hair at risk. When you ain't got as much as you used to, now don't you know how much more you value it?"

Todd laughed, and Barbara thought about what Travis had said: *Kids know what's going on.*

"Walls of Jericho still standing," Herbert had announced after one of his tours.

For Barbara that had been both nerve-wracking and reassuring.

Todd spent all day and into the night Friday with Dr. Chu at his laboratory, and came home clearly excited. "We'll have something for you tomorrow," he said. "Not pinpoint locations, but something."

"Have you packed yet?" Darren asked.

"I'll do it tomorrow afternoon," Todd said. "I have to wash some stuff."

"Put your stuff on the washer and I'll do it," Darren said. "You know we have to leave at four in the morning Sunday. Keep that in mind."

"Sure, Dad. I know. I'll be ready."

On Saturday, waiting for Todd and his map of possible locations, Barbara was too restless to sit still for more than a minute or two at a time. She paced endlessly, went up and down the stairs repeatedly, and had to take off her watch after she realized that she was watching the minute hand creep in slow motion when it moved at all. Todd called at three thirty and Darren hurried out to go pick him up, muttering something about Todd not even packed yet.

When they returned, Todd was carrying a rolled-up map, and he was grinning like a jack-o'-lantern. "See," he said, spreading the map on the dining table, "there are nine places where the weather matched. Dr. Chu circled them all. Some of them cover about ten miles, and one is at least fifty miles across. Latitude and longitude marked, and a scale there at the bottom, so you can see how big they are. We were working with a computer and blew up the image later."

The map was eighteen inches from top to bottom and two feet across. Barbara stared at it, then threw her arms around Todd and kissed his cheek. "You're a wonder! You actually did it!"

Embarrassed, he backed away and mumbled, "Dr. Chu did most of it, not me. We're not done with it, but it gives you the idea of where to look maybe."

"Now you pack," Darren said, trying hard to maintain a stern expression, and failing to erase his grin. "Good work, Todd. Really good work."

"Can we go out and get a memory card for my camera? And I have to Xerox a lot of pages from my books, or carry a ton of them with me."

Darren's expression turned murderous, and very softly he said, "You have to run errands now? Kinkos. A store for a memory card? Now? You can get the card in Washington." He drew in a breath and said, "Come on, we'll go to Kinkos."

Todd ran to the basement stairs. "Be right back with the books," he called and vanished to the den.

"That sums it up," Darren said ruefully. "We'll be right back."

Barbara had her cell phone out, and Darren shook his head. "Not tonight. Can't it wait until tomorrow?"

"That's what I was going to suggest to Dad," she said. "I'll see him tomorrow in his office."

She was dreaming when Darren stroked her cheek softly. She started to sit up and he pushed her back down. "Sleep," he said. "Annie's boyfriend is taking all of us to the airport. They'll be here in a minute and we'll be out the door. See you in a week or ten days. Be careful."

He kissed her and left. She rolled over and tried to recapture the fading dream. All that persisted was a single image of a mammoth gray building with slit windows and a flat roof where men stood with machine guns. "The citadel," she murmured, drifting back into sleep.

✦

CHAPTER 20

IN THE CONFERENCE room Barbara, Frank, Shelley, and Herbert studied the big map taped to the table. “I think we’ll have to mark up the county maps with those sites and work with them,” Barbara said. “You can get a lot of ranches in a fifty-mile-wide area.”

“I can do that,” Herbert said diffidently. “Back a time I did some surveying. Won’t be no trouble at all.”

“Go to it,” Barbara said, pointing to a marker and a ruler she had brought with her.

They watched as he expertly copied the circled areas to the county maps and the weather pattern became clear. A front had blown through, mixing Pacific-moist air with frigid air from the north, resulting in a swath of snow and freezing rain two days in a row. One of the bigger areas overlapped two county maps. Herbert taped them together and completed the long oval. All the marked areas were on the south side of mountains, sites with ranges warmed by the sun long before the north slopes melted.

“What we’re looking for are places big enough to accommodate a dozen or more outsiders at a time, a staff to serve them, and a runway big enough for a Learjet to use. Not too close to towns,” she said, eyeing Madras, which was included in one of the marked areas.

They settled into chairs at the conference table and began to examine the maps with their descriptions of improvements. From time to time someone murmured something.

“Not big enough.”

“Too visible from the road.”

“No runway.”

“That’s a writers’ retreat,” Shelley said when Barbara said she had a possible site. “I have a friend who goes there now and then. They stay for a week, up to six weeks, summer and winter.”

Barbara moved on.

“This might work,” Shelley said later. “There’s a guest house, a three-thousand-square-foot residence, a barn, another outbuilding. A road’s just a mile away. That could be used, I think, for the airplane.”

“Let’s circle possible sites with red and come back to them if nothing else works," Barbara said. She tossed a red pen across the table to Shelley, and continued to read about the ranches spread throughout the vast area from the Columbia River to the basin-and-range district.

They broke for lunch. "We'll leave all this and eat in the office," Frank said, standing and stretching. "I'll call for sandwiches and salads, and make coffee while we're waiting."

It was always eerie when the law officers were closed, Barbara thought a few minutes later, walking up and down the empty hallways. It was like a movie set waiting for action. She almost expected to see makeup people, props being moved, hear the rustling of actors getting ready to perform. There was only silence. Thick carpeting and closed doors smothered the echoes of pain that clients brought to law offices.

They ate lunch without much conversation and when done, they returned to the conference room and resumed their search. At two in the afternoon there were five areas circled in red, all questionable, all possible. There were many ranches with runways, Barbara had discovered, but they were too short, meant only for the small planes the ranchers used, not for Learjets. They could have been extended, she thought, poised with the red pen in her hand. Who would know if a rancher decided to lengthen his runway? They could even be camouflaged. She circled the ranch and moved on.

Then Shelley said, "I think I have it! This must be it!" Barbara moved to her side as Shelley went on: "It has a four-thousand-square-foot guest house, an indoor swimming pool, a three-thousand-square-foot main house, two barns, other outbuildings, and a two-mile-long improved road."

"Owner?" Frank asked from the other side of the table.

"Polson Corporation."

"Be back in a minute," he said, standing. In the library there were references to the various corporations with operations in the state, buildings they owned, ties to local businesses, ties to other corporations, management, personnel, a lot of information.

"The nearest city is Pendleton," Barbara said, studying the site. "And it must be fifty miles away by those crazy roads out there. That improved road dead ends at a gravel road, Old Cooley Road. The other end is even less promising. It joins what looks like a track, maybe a horse trail or something that leads to a private road to another ranch. Not one circled. Let's see if there's a mention of that place in any Pendleton papers. You go back from three years ago. I'll go forward."

She and Shelley both opened their laptops and began the search.

They were still at it when Frank returned, grim-faced. "You found it, all right," he said, taking his seat at the table again. He put down a legal pad and read his notes. "Owned by the Polson Corporation, CEO Charles Petrick, who serves on the board of Epsilon Group and half a dozen other corporations. Manager of the place is Edgar Fentwick. The guest house is called the Chateau and hosts executive retreats, hunting parties, skiing, and such."

Barbara felt a chill settle in her stomach as she listened. Piece by piece, she thought distantly. The Citadel, Epsilon, militias, retreats… She shook herself and looked again at her screen. "Well, we sort of knew it would go there," she said. "Now we definitely know. I expect the Chateau keeps various businesses happy in Pendleton and sooner or later there will be a mention of it."

"And you'll go nowhere near that place," Frank said. "No knocking on doors and enquiring about June Morgan. You'll have nothing to do with it."

"I get that. I have no intention of approaching it, but I'll see if there's a mention or two in local newspapers. No harm in that."

Frank began to gather up the various maps, folded them with exaggerated care, and aligned them neatly. Done, he leaned back in his chair, regarding Barbara with a sober expression. She had her foot poised over a hornet's nest, and God alone knew if she would put it down, or draw back.

There was an extended silence for a time, until Barbara looked up from her screen and said, "Listen to this. It's in the *Pendleton Herald*, dated April 18." She read: "'The body of a young woman was discovered on the side of Old Cooley Road on Thursday by a couple touring the state. Brenda and William Ellender, from Marin County, California, discovered the body and took it to the emergency room of Pendleton General Hospital where the victim was pronounced dead. The sheriff's office declared the death accidental from a fall from a cliff above the road. The victim was identified by her mother as Adelia Samos, an employee at the Chateau.'" She looked up from the computer. "That's about when June Morgan stopped emailing Travis. I have to talk to the Ellenders."

Frank knew she had lowered her foot on the hornet's nest.

It didn't take long for Barbara to locate Brenda and William Ellender. She placed the call. The phone was picked up by a woman.

"Mrs. Ellender?"

"Yes. I'm Brenda Ellender. Who's calling, please?"

"I'm an attorney, Barbara Holloway. Mrs. Ellender, I'm trying to learn about a possible misidentification of a young woman who died in April. I understand that you and your husband discovered her body."

"Oh my, yes! We did! It was terrible, a tragedy. When we saw her first, she was so beautiful, standing with the wind blowing her hair, making it look almost like a halo, gleaming in the sunlight, so pale and golden, and her in that long white dress, more like a Greek goddess, a statue or something. And then to see her all broken and smashed, bloody all over. It was terrible! Terrible."

"Mrs. Ellender, may I come talk to you about it?" Barbara said. "Will you tell me about it? I can be there tomorrow, or whenever it's convenient for you."

"Oh, tomorrow's fine. I'll be home all day, and probably William will be, too, but you never really know. He might take a notion to go play golf or something. But I'll be here. Where did you say you are?"

"I'm in Oregon. Will you give me directions about how to find you? Would you like for me to give you a call when I arrive in San Francisco, set up a definite time for a talk?"

"No, no. That's not necessary. I already planned to stay home tomorrow and prune my roses, so I'll be here. I'll see if I can find my camera before you get here. I have pictures of the poor girl, you know. She looked so beautiful, standing like a statue with the wind blowing her hair. I told William to stop driving so I could take her picture… "

Barbara had her eyes closed and was biting her lip to keep from telling the woman to stop prattling and give her the directions. When she finally hung up, with the directions written down, she let out a long breath.

"They saw June Morgan," she said, "before and after she died from a fall off a cliff. Mrs. Ellender has pictures. I have to make plane reservations."

"I'll do it," Shelley said quickly.

"For two," Frank said.

Both Barbara and Herbert nodded. For two.

"Will you tell Ashley?" Shelley asked. She looked to be near tears.

"No," Barbara said. "What's the point? As far as she and Travis are concerned, June died and was cremated already. She doesn't have to die again. If she was mutilated first, cut in any way, a fall from a cliff could make it hard to determine, and for all we know that second woman was cremated, too."

"Good," Shelley said, obviously relieved. "I'll get the reservations."

"I have to go home," Barbara said. "I'll pack a few things for the coming week at your house, Dad, and head over in a couple of hours. Tomorrow, we'll fly down, see the Ellenders and fly home again."

Traffic on the Golden Gate Bridge was moving briskly, and according to Herbert, they would be at the Ellender house within the hour. "Then some lunch?" he asked plaintively.

"Definitely lunch," Barbara said. "God, I hate flying anymore. Some choice, get groped or get exposed to X-rays. Bah and humbug."

"I told the guy I wouldn't mind the pat down if a pretty little lady did it and he threatened me," Herbert said in a hurt voice. "You're not supposed to joke about anything, seems like."

"Next time, keep your mouth shut and submit. The American way."

The directions were surprisingly precise: three miles, turn left; two and one half miles, turn right... Then they were watching for a front yard filled with rosebushes.

Herbert pulled into the driveway. "I can wait in the car," he said.

"Nonsense. You're my associate, Mr. Herbert. Just don't say anything. Let's do it."

The house was a lovely Tudor style, the yard a mass of rosebushes, and when the door was opened, Mrs. Ellender was the perfect homemaker. She was round faced with a round frame of tight, gray curls, a round little body dressed in a bright-red sweatshirt, and tight khaki pants.

"Mrs. Ellender, thanks for letting me talk to you. I'm Barbara Holloway and this is my associate Mr. Herbert."

"Well, come right in. Like I said, William might decide to play some golf or something. I was right about that. He doesn't want to talk about it, you see, and he practically told me, ordered me I might say, not to talk about it anymore. But, my goodness, it's not every day you come across something like that, you see, and I felt I had to talk about it." As she talked, she led them into a room that looked like a photographer's studio. Every level surface was covered with photographs, family pictures, two, possibly three generations. There were more on the walls.

"Please sit down," she said, motioning to chairs across a coffee table from a gold-colored leather sofa. The coffee table and end tables were covered with photographs.

"How did it all happen that day?" Barbara asked, seating herself.

"Well, after William retired, you see he worked for the same brokerage firm for nearly thirty years, and he decided to retire, and not a minute too soon, if you ask me, what with all the scandals and mismanaged money that was going on, and still is, if you ask me. And we decided we'd get a real nice camper and see some of our own country. One year it was Colorado, then up to New England, and that year, the year we saw that poor girl, it was Oregon. We got lost that day. I guess we missed a turn, or turned left when it should have been right, or something like that. People do that, I guess, and usually it didn't make any difference, what with the camper well stocked with food and water, an extra tank of gas. But we were on a really terrible road, all dirt with boulders, and steep drop-offs, deep ruts in places. William was looking for a place where he could turn around and go back the way we came when I saw her, just a glimpse of her, and William thought I was seeing things, or making it up or something. I told him to go slower and he said if he went any slower we'd be going backward, but we passed a few boulders and I saw her again and I told William to stop so I could get a picture or two. See, we were on a mountain road and there was a deep gorge on my side, then across it there was this flat place with a big mountain behind it. With trees on the mountain. There weren't any trees on our road, or on the flat place where she was standing. Just standing like a statue with the wind blowing her hair and her dress. Real blond, she was, long blond hair blowing in the wind, and a long white dress with long sleeves. I can still see her in my mind, how pretty she looked. She turned our way a little bit and I kept taking pictures until William began to drive again and we couldn't see her anymore."

Barbara felt almost breathless herself when Mrs. Ellender paused to take a deep breath.

"Did she see you? Did she wave or indicate that she saw you?"

Mrs. Ellender shook her head. "No. She didn't look over that way, she just turned a little bit, as if she was trying to see down the road, or maybe she was looking for a way down or something. There wasn't a way down, just a cliff, or back the way she must have come from."

"Was anyone else with her, or anywhere on the other side?"

"Oh no. It was a long stretch of flat ground. I would have seen anyone else. There wasn't anywhere to hide or stay out of sight."

"Then what happened? You kept driving on that mountain road."

"That's what William did. He gave up trying to find a turning place and just kept driving and we started downward, all terrible, every inch of it, terrible, scared me half to death, but we came to a gravel road and he turned onto it. I can tell you he was happy to get on a road that had been graded and leveled, even if it was gravel. So in about fifteen minutes or maybe longer, we saw this white thing on the side of the road, and at first we couldn't tell what it was, but we got closer and my heart just leaped up to my throat. It was her, the same girl I saw up there. She was dead."

It took her a long time to tell the rest of her story. Their cell phones didn't work, and they had no idea where they were, but figured out that the gravel road would go to a real road eventually, and then they could get up to Pendleton. They couldn't just leave her on the side of the road, they decided. Mrs. Ellender put a plastic tarp down in the camper, a sheet on it, and they moved the body to it, and Mrs. Ellender covered her with a sheet. An hour and a half later they drove into Pendleton and to the hospital there. Medics put the body on a gurney and took her inside, and Mr. and Mrs. Ellender were told they had to wait to talk to the sheriff.

"I was so nervous," she said, "and William was shaken up. Having her in the camper for so long, knowing she was dead, it was terrible, just terrible. We didn't even want to talk with her back there, dead. We just whispered. We left a marker so they could find where she died. There wasn't any wood to make a stake, so William piled up some stones and put a napkin down with more stones on top of it. You could see it just fine and they had to know, you see, for an investigation. So we told the sheriff about finding her, what we did, and who we were, showed him our identification, and for no reason at all, I started to cry. I still don't know why I did, nerves I guess, but I was crying and William was so shaken up he could hardly speak, and the sheriff told us to go to a motel and get some rest, we did what we had to do, and he appreciated that, and in the morning we should just start driving and finish our vacation. We signed a statement about it, but I think my signature was like a child's because of the way I was crying and couldn't stop."

"Did you tell the sheriff that you first saw her up on the cliff?"

Mrs. Ellender looked guilty and shook her head. "I forgot. I just wanted to get to a motel, take an aspirin or something, maybe have a little drink. We're not drinking people usually but sometimes that's what a person needs just to get through things. And I couldn't stop crying, choking on tears so much I couldn't hardly breathe. So I forgot and in the morning when I told William we should find that sheriff he said no, we were getting out of there and staying out of it. He said it didn't make any difference since she was dead, if she fell or if she jumped didn't make any difference and it might just bring more grief to her family to worry about it. I hadn't thought of it that way, that she might have jumped, and it upset me all over again, and William was impatient and just wanted to leave, so we did. And he never wanted to talk about it, just said to put it out of our minds, forget about it, as if a body could just forget."

"You said you had pictures. May we see them?"

"Yes. I had to find the camera. After we came home and I put the pictures on our computer, I just couldn't bring myself to use that same camera again so I bought a new one and that's why I had to search for the old one. I found it, of course. I always put pictures on the computer so I can send our vacation pictures to the children and grandchildren." She picked up a camera from the end table, and showed it to Barbara. "I'll find her pictures if you want me to. I never took them off the camera after I put them on the computer. It just didn't seem right somehow to erase them, so I didn't. There she is."

It was exactly the way Mrs. Ellender had described it: the side view of a slender girl in a long white dress at the edge of a cliff. She was facing west, into the sun. Her hair was streaming out behind her, the white dress tight against her legs, flowing backward. Barbara pushed the next command and the next until she came to the place where Mrs. Ellender said the girl had looked her way and now there was a three-quarters view. She was pretty, maybe beautiful, and her long hair was being whipped around her face, not enough to hide it but enough to make the picture iconic.

Choosing her words carefully, Barbara said, "Mrs. Ellender, as I told you when I requested this interview, we are investigating a case of a missing girl and the possible misidentification of a dead girl. This girl in your photograph fits the description of the one we're looking for, but a family member would have to make the identification official. Would you consider letting me buy the camera? You said you don't want to use it any longer, not since that tragedy touched you, and my client can possibly find closure in knowing that girl is her daughter, or even better in knowing that she isn't."

Mrs. Ellender looked hesitant. "It has our other vacation pictures."

"But you already downloaded them to your computer, so you know they're safe for your grandchildren, your family."

"That's true. I don't see why it would matter, and it might bring some relief for the poor woman searching for her daughter. I would want to know if any of mine disappeared." She looked around the room at the many photographs, then nodded. "You can have it. That mother needs to know if it's her child."

CHAPTER 21

WHEN BAILEY ARRIVED the next morning, Barbara told him what she had learned from Mrs. Ellender, and what Frank had learned about the Polson Corporation. His face tightened and froze in a scowl. "So we have the Citadel, now known as the Chateau, and we can place June Morgan there, and we know how she died. Whatever she had gone through, whatever she feared was to come, made her take the only way out she could see. She jumped."

"Any doubt about her being the Morgan girl?"

"I'll show you," she said, going to her desk for the camera and her photograph of June, made when she was not quite sixteen. She showed them to him. "No doubt. This week I have to go talk to the emergency room doctor in Pendleton, find out how that girl was passed off as a local's daughter, find out why the sheriff made his call of accidental death practically instantly, find out if June Morgan had been cut. The medical examiner is a city cop, and the sheriff claimed this case as his and closed it fast. So the emergency room doctor is my best bet."

"Jeez, Barbara, you'll be setting yourself up. They might all be in the pocket of the Polson group."

"I know. I won't call ahead, just drop in and test the water."

"I don't like it. Too risky. So far, you're just messing around with the murder of Peel, but you're getting too near the stove now."

"So plan me a plan," she said. "You and Herbert put your heads together and come up with a workable plan."

"You going to be at the old man's house tonight?"

She nodded. "And every night until Darren gets home, which might be a long time in coming. Washington's shut down by snow."

"I'll come by after dinner." He drained his cup and stood, scowling like a satyr. At the door he turned to say, "For all you know that Polson bunch owns Pendleton lock, stock, and barrel."

"So make it a good plan."

He saluted and left, and she finished her own coffee. Lock, stock, and barrel, she thought uneasily. The problem was he could be right.

They pulled up to the Pendleton General Hospital at two thirty in the afternoon on Thursday. Barbara was in a Lincoln with Bailey driving, and somewhere Herbert and Alan, Bailey's top operative, were in Bailey's SUV, which now had an Idaho license plate. The fact that she had not seen them or the SUV for hours didn't mean a thing, she knew. Bailey wanted it that way.

"Where did this come from?" she had asked, getting into the Lincoln that morning.

"I had a little business to discuss with Sylvia and happened to mention that I needed a good car for a little job coming up, and she insisted that I use one of hers."

Sylvia! Sylvia Fenton, married to one of the richest men in the state, itched to play cops and robbers with Bailey. She had been an actress in an off-Broadway show in Manhattan decades earlier, caught the eye of Joe Fenton and a few months later they were married, and it appeared that he was not only one of the richest men in Oregon, but also one of the happiest men in the world. Sylvia was flamboyant at times, played roles at other times, and was never predictable, except where Bailey was concerned. She wanted him to open a big detective agency and let her be a partner. He said she was the cross he had to bear.

"My God, Bailey! They'll trace this car to the Fentons!"

"Don't see how, not with those license plates we're using."

Barbara entered the emergency room of the hospital with Bailey at her side. No one except an admittance nurse was in sight. The nurse was engrossed with something on an iPod when Barbara drew near.

"Excuse me," Barbara said. "I need to find the emergency doctor who was on duty in the middle of April."

The nurse put her iPod down and examined Barbara. "Why?"

"I need to talk to her," Barbara said.

The woman nodded as if that was a perfectly okay reason. She typed in some commands on her computer, scrolled down, then said, "That would be Dr. Sally Krutchner. She was on call for emergency duty all of April. Her office is on Fifth Street. I'll write it down for you."

She made the note on an appointment card and handed it to Barbara, and before Barbara could say thanks, she picked up her iPod.

Barbara stifled a groan when she and Bailey entered the medical complex where Dr. Krutchner and three other doctors worked. There were seven or eight patients in the waiting room. Hoping most of them were for the other doctors, Barbara went to the receptionist's desk.

"I don't have an appointment, but is it possible that I could see Dr. Krutchner?"

"Are you a returning patient?"

"No." She handed the woman her card. "I'm an attorney and I need to have a few minutes of Dr. Krutchner's time."

The receptionist's eyes widened as she read the card. She stood and said to Barbara, "I'll ask her."

Barbara waited at the desk for a minute or two before the woman returned. "Please come with me," she said. Barbara turned to nod to Bailey. He stepped outside and she followed the receptionist through a short hall to an examination room. "Dr. Sally said for you to wait in here. She won't be long."

It was the same sterile, claustrophobic space as every other examination room, Barbara thought. Two people made a crowd, three would be a mob. She picked up an old *National Geographic*, prepared to wait, and had hardly opened the magazine before the door opened and the doctor entered. Sturdily built, sixty-something, with short gray hair, and suspicious brown eyes, she nodded coolly to Barbara.

"Ms. Holloway, are you sure you want to see me? Not my attorney?"

Barbara smiled. "No one's suing you, Doctor. At least not to my knowledge."

Smiling in return, Dr. Sally said, "Thank God for little favors. What is it that you want from me?"

"I want to ask about a woman who was brought to ER last April, the victim of a fatal fall from a cliff."

A stillness seemed to settle over the doctor and her expression changed from curiosity to one of guardedness. "May I ask why?" she said.

"I have reason to believe that the young woman might have been misidentified."

Dr. Sally did not move for several seconds, then she nodded. "Yes, I can tell you about that incident. But I have a patient getting her vitals taken and then I have to see her. She's my last patient for the day. We can talk afterward." She glanced around the small room and said, "I'll have to ask you to wait in here or else out in the general waiting room."

"This is fine," Barbara said.

The doctor nodded and left, and Barbara picked up the magazine and started reading about the Sargasso Sea.

When Dr. Sally returned, she said, "We can go to my office to talk, if you'd like. This way." She led Barbara through the back halls to her office. It was large with wide windows and a view of the parking lot. Dr. Sally adjusted blinds, letting in light but hiding the ugly view. She motioned toward a visitor's chair and went behind her desk to sit down. "What do you want to know?"

"Whatever you can tell me. I've talked to the couple who found her body and brought it to the hospital. Then what?"

"First, can you tell me why you are asking?"

"A mother is looking for her missing daughter, and that young woman fits her description."

"I see. I was on call for emergency duty. It was late in the afternoon on a Friday when I got the call. I examined her and determined that she had been dead for about three hours and her injuries were consistent with a fall. I ordered tests to see if drugs or alcohol had been involved. Neither was a factor. Then the sheriff called and said he was bringing in her mother and an interpreter and everything should be put on hold until they came to identify the body. I washed the girl's face. And I took a few pictures," she said. Her voice was monotone, flat, and her gaze was fixed on the wall behind Barbara as she spoke.

"What else did you find, Doctor?" Barbara asked. "Why did you take pictures? Had she been cut? Mutilated in any way?"

Dr. Sally looked closely at her. "How much do you know about her, what had been done to her?" she demanded with a new harshness in her voice.

"Nothing. That's what I'm trying to find out. What had been done to her?"

The doctor rubbed her eyes. "I've been practicing medicine all my adult life. I never saw anything like that before. She had been circumcised, a radical circumcision. It was well healed with minimum scarring. The clitoris, labia… "

"Oh my God," Barbara gasped. "Did you report it to anyone?"

"No. It was taken out of my hands, but that's why I took pictures, to have if I reported it, track down the doctor who did it, the monster who would do such a thing to a young girl."

"How was it taken out of your hands?"

"I told you the sheriff called and ordered us to put everything on hold. He came with a woman from the Chateau, Marion Thornby, the assistant to the manager, and a Hispanic woman. The Chateau is a big ranch that's been turned into a resort of some kind. The sheriff said Thornby had asked him to keep an eye out for a missing young woman who was insane and might be wandering about on the desert. Apparently someone from ER called him and told him about her. He said he notified the Chateau and met Thornby and a Mrs. Samos at the airport. They had come by helicopter from the Chateau. Mrs. Samos didn't speak English and Ms. Thornby acted as her interpreter."

Dr. Sally was speaking fast as she continued to describe that day. "Ms. Thornby asked questions, or relayed the sheriff's questions or mine to Mrs. Samos and told us what she said. She identified the body as her daughter, and told us, through Ms. Thornby, that her daughter had been kidnapped years before, that she had been scorned and mistreated by her neighbors, by everyone in their village because she was so pale, and little effort had been made to find her after she was taken. She said that last year her daughter escaped her tormenters and returned home. But she was insane, and she had been mutilated by those who had held her. When Mrs. Samos was offered a position at the Chateau, she had asked permission to bring her daughter with her, and it was granted."

"That girl was most definitely not a Chicana. North European descent."

"I brought that up and Ms. Thornby relayed the answer. Mrs. Samos had been raped by a gringo, a white man, resulting in her pale daughter. Mrs. Samos was weeping and wailing the whole time," she said. "It was hard to get anything out of her, but enough to satisfy the sheriff. There was paperwork to be done. Mrs. Samos had to sign various documents, under the guidance of Ms. Thornby, of course. I signed the death certificate, and the matter was concluded, out of my hands. The body was transferred to a mortuary where she was to be cremated, and her mother was to take her ashes back home to be buried next to other family members. The body was removed that evening."

"No autopsy! No investigation! Just sign here and it's over and done with! Who is that sheriff?"

"Joe Federer," Dr. Sally said quietly. "He's fairly new in these parts, ten years give or take a little, I think. He said he investigated it personally. She wandered away and fell off a cliff."

For several seconds neither of them spoke. Then Barbara said, "You said you took pictures. Do you still have them? I have a photograph I'd like you to see."

She showed the doctor the photograph of June Morgan and the doctor nodded. "She's younger in your photograph, but that's the girl. Yes, I have the pictures I took. I suppose I was hoping someone would bring up a real investigation, and I kept them." She rose and crossed the office to file cases against the wall, unlocked a drawer, and brought out a folder.

Barbara took the folder from the doctor. She made an inarticulate cry when she saw what had been done to June Morgan.

"The surgery was done by a professional," Dr. Sally said. "She was a virgin." She examined Barbara for a moment. "Are you going to be sick?"

Barbara shook her head. But she was more nauseated than she could remember ever feeling.

"Tell me this, Ms. Holloway, are you after the monster that did this to the girl? Is that your intent, to bring him to some kind of justice?" She had been coolly professional most of the time, but a new fierce intensity was in her voice, making it even harsher than the momentary lapse of a few minutes earlier.

"Yes. I have every intention of doing just that."

"I'm sixty-four years old," Dr. Sally said fiercely. "Three grown children, four grandchildren. If anyone ever did a thing like that to any of them, I'd kill him."

The doctor wrote out an account of that day in April. She signed and dated the photographs she had taken and added the current date, and she signed June Morgan's picture with a brief statement that it was the same girl who had arrived in ER.

When she was done and they both stood, Barbara asked, "Why were you so forthcoming with me? I wasn't expecting that."

"I lied to you about a patient," Dr. Sally said. "She was just in to have her blood pressure monitored. I spent the time looking you up on the Internet. I decided you were the one to tell, that you'd do something about it. That simple."

"I'm very grateful, Dr. Sally. And I have to say this, you could endanger yourself if you talk about this matter with anyone, anyone at all."

"I'd think you might be the one in danger," the doctor said. "As for me, I talk to patients for extended periods routinely."

They shook hands but, at the door, Barbara paused. "Just one more thing. I'm also looking for another young woman who disappeared in April at about the same time as the incident in ER. Her name might be Rosita. Any idea where to start a search without making a spectacle of myself?"

Dr. Sally looked surprised. "Rosita? Rosita Rodrigues. She ran off with a boy from Mexico, according to her mother. Rosita and her mother are my patients and her mother was out of her mind with worry for weeks when Rosita dropped out of sight. Then she got a postcard. So she might have been lost and then was found."

"Anyone can mail a postcard," Barbara said softly. "Has she been in touch directly?"

Dr. Sally took a step back, shaking her head. "I don't know. I haven't seen Maria Rodrigues all fall. She thought, we all thought, that since Rosita lost her job at the Chateau she saw a chance to get out of here and she took it." She walked to her desk and stood at the side of it, frowning. "Ms. Holloway, you seem to know a lot already about the situation here, and I assume you're not free to tell me any more than you have. Maria and Rosita are my patients and I can't discuss them with you beyond saying that Rosita worked at the Chateau as a companion to the young woman who fell to her death. You must talk to her mother if you have questions about the arrangement."

"Fair enough," Barbara said. "But will she talk to me, an outsider, a stranger?"

"I'll give her a call," Dr. Sally said. "She works nights for a company that cleans offices, so she's home at this time of day usually." She went around her desk and typed in computer commands, then wrote on a prescription pad, tore off the page and crossed the office again to Barbara. "This is her address. I think she'll talk to you."

Barbara thanked her and the doctor said, "Ms. Holloway, you warned me to be careful. Now I must do the same. It is not considered wise to ask too many questions about the Chateau and what takes place there."

"I know," Barbara said soberly. For a moment the two women regarded each other, then Barbara nodded. "Again, Dr. Sally, thank you very much."

There were several people in the waiting area when she left the doctor's office. Bailey was reading a magazine. He put it down and met her at the outer door.

"Now we hit the road?"

"Not yet. One more stop."

He groaned. Walking to the car he said, "It's getting colder and they expect fog, freezing fog, freezing rain, snow, whatever old man winter has to serve up, he'll dump on us going home."

They got inside the Lincoln and he asked, "Find out anything?"

"Not now," she said.

He gave her a quick look and asked for the address. She handed him the slip of paper, and he gave her another searching look. "You okay?"

"Fine," she said.

"Yeah. Right." He looked at the address and turned on the engine and neither of them said another word until he stopped before a small ranch house. "Do I come in with you?" he asked, turning off the engine.

"I don't think so. I'll make it as short as possible."

When she knocked on the door, it was opened instantly by a

heavyset Hispanic woman. "Ms. Holloway? Come in, come in. Dr. Sally said you would come."

The room they entered was small and cluttered. There was a television, a sofa with a coffee table, two more chairs, a wood stove, and a big basket of firewood. There were candles on tables and shelves emitting perfume scents. All the furniture had throws in bright primary colors, a bean bag in forest green was near the stove, and the walls were all decorated with many pictures: Virgin Mary and child, bullfighters, brilliant poppies… and several pictures of a young man and a young woman. In one of them the man was wearing a uniform. The young woman resembled Mrs. Rodrigues, and she was overweight.

"That's Miguel," Mrs. Rodrigues said, "and she's Rosita. My children. Please, take off your jacket."

Barbara took off her jacket. The room was very warm and there was a heavy odor of garlic, chilies, and spices in the air intermingled with the candle perfume. Her stomach knotted in reaction to the many odors.

"Dr. Sally said you want to know about the girl up at the Chateau," Mrs. Rodrigues said. "Come, let us sit at the table in the kitchen. Would you like tea or coffee? I just poured tea for myself, fresh made, in the pot."

"Actually that would be very nice," Barbara said. She sat at the table and Mrs. Rodrigues brought out a teacup with a saucer and poured tea. "Mrs. Rodrigues, as Dr. Sally mentioned, I am trying to learn as much as possible about the young woman at the Chateau. Your daughter must have known more about her than anyone else in town."

"She didn't know much," the other woman said. "They told Rosita not to ask her questions because she was sick in her head. She needed to be kept quiet and asking questions might make her have some kind of seizure, so Rosita didn't ask anything. She said Ruth was afraid of men and had to be kept all the way away from any man, she couldn't even stand to see a man." She lowered her voice and glanced about the small kitchen before she continued. "We thought maybe Ruth was raped or something like that happened to her and made her sick. It can do that, being raped can do that. And I told Rosita to never even mention such a thing. That might set her back."

"Did Rosita say how she was sick, besides not seeing men?"

"Little things, like wearing long dresses all the time, and sad. She was real sad and cried a lot. At first she wouldn't talk to Rosita and she said she was with the enemy, that she worked for the enemy, so I guess that was a little crazy. She had a little apartment, but no kitchen. They brought food to her, and Rosita too when she was there. Nice food, all kinds of good food. She had a television and they watched movies. There was a nurse, a psychiatrist kind of nurse, Rosita said. There was a little garden with a high wall. They were thinking they might plant some flowers."

"How long did Rosita work up there?"

"Maybe a year. After she graduated from high school last year, Ms. Thornby came to hire her. In July maybe. There's no work here for young people. That's why Miguel joined the army. So Rosita took the job, part-time, only four days a week, Monday to Thursday, but that was better than anything else she could get."

"It's so far away. So much of her time must have been spent just getting there and getting home again. Did she spend nights up there?"

"No. Never," Mrs. Rodrigues said emphatically. "We would not let her do that. A man picked her up and took her most of the way and she got in a van or truck or something and that took her the rest of the way. She sat in the back and couldn't see out, but she knew the road was very bad, very bumpy. An hour, about that long. That's all. She never got to see the swimming pool or the other house where rich people go sometimes. Just around the buildings to the other side and the nurse let her in."

Barbara sipped her tea and was glad she had accepted it. Her stomach had gone all queasy—first at Dr. Sally's office and again here with the miasma of too many scents in the house; the tea was helping settle it down again. Mrs. Rodrigues was watching her expectantly, as if waiting for more questions. "You said that at first the girl up there was not friendly with your daughter. Did that change? Did they become friends?"

Mrs. Rodrigues looked thoughtful, then shook her head. "Not friends, not like Rosita's other friends, always talking, laughing, trying on each other's clothes. Not like that. But better. When Miguel left, he gave Rosita his little computer, and she said it wasn't any good. It kept making mistakes or stopping or something. She didn't know how to fix it or how to make it work right. She said Ruth knew all about computers and she sneaked it in with her sometimes so Ruth could make it work better and teach Rosita about it."

"Did she say why she sneaked it in?" Barbara asked, hoping that nothing in her voice betrayed her interest in the computer.

"Yes. Ruth told her to. She said they would take it away from her if they saw it. I guess that was part of her madness, that she thought everyone was out to get her, or something. But Rosita believed her and she hid it under her poncho when she took it. And Ruth taught her how to use email, and she made it work better and didn't keep stopping all the time. She said Ruth told her the computer was obso… obso— She said it was too old and cranky and it had bugs. Rosita didn't know what that meant and neither do I." She spread her hands in a gesture of helplessness. "Before Rosita left she was able to email Miguel and that was good. We printed all his answers, just to have them. After she left I tried to use it, but it stopped working again. Now we just write letters."

Barbara ducked her head and sipped more of the tea. The computer was here, in this house! "You say Rosita left? Where did she go? Did she quit her job at the Chateau?"

Mrs. Rodrigues sighed deeply. "Last April Rosita didn't come home on a Saturday. We called everyone but no one knew where she was. We called the police and they said she was nineteen years old and free to come and go whenever she wanted to and we should wait a day or two and probably she'd be back. On Monday, Ms. Thornby came and she was mad. She said, where was she, did she run off with that Mexican boy she'd been flirting with. She said when Rosita came home to tell her, she was fired. Ruth was all upset because she didn't come on Monday and they couldn't have her getting upset again."

"Did you know anything about a Mexican boy?"

"They go to the Chateau and work for six months, maybe a year, and they go back to Mexico. They don't come to town. No one in town knows them. Ms. Thornby said in a loud voice that Rosita and one of the workers were meeting and he left on Saturday and she must have gone with him. She said Rosita would be good for him because she has Spanish and good English and he doesn't have any." She sighed again, more deeply than before. "Like the policeman said, she is nineteen. She sent a postcard. She's happy with Raul who is good to her, and she will write when they are settled."

Barbara knew Rosita would never write, but what was the point in breaking this woman's heart? Especially since there was no proof of what she knew was the truth. "Is Ruth still at the Chateau?" She asked. She knew the answer, but she wondered if Mrs. Rodrigues or anyone else in town had made the connection between the girl who fell or jumped off a cliff and the poor mad girl at the Chateau.

"I don't know," Mrs. Rodrigues said. "They didn't hire anyone to be a companion, not from town here, not that I heard."

Barbara finished her tea and refused a refill, thinking furiously about the computer that was still in this house. She said, "Mrs. Rodrigues, may I see the computer that Rosita took to the Chateau? I wonder if it's as old and obsolete as Ruth thought it was."

Looking puzzled, Mrs. Rodrigues stood. "Yes. I'll show you. My husband and me, no one here can use it. I don't even remember how to turn it on." She left and soon returned with a laptop that appeared to be at least ten years old, very much like one Barbara had once used.

She looked it over and said, "Yes, it's out of date. It can't run many programs available now, I'm afraid. Mrs. Rodrigues, I wonder if you might be interested in a deal I'd like to offer. If you let me take the computer, I'll call an electronics shop here in town and buy you a new one with all the latest programs, and I'll arrange with the shop owner for tutoring sessions for you and your husband. Then you'll be able to keep in touch with Miguel on a daily basis. I'm sure it's a worry not to hear from him more often than through written letters."

"Why would you do that?" Mrs. Rodrigues asked, with a new wariness erasing her former pleasant expression.

"Because you've been extremely helpful in my investigation concerning that girl at the Chateau. I'd like to do something for you in return. I can call the shop here, using your telephone, and you can speak to the shop manager or someone about when they can deliver it, get it set up, and when they can provide lessons convenient for you. There are plans that let you arrange for future help if you run into trouble. We can set it all up right now on my credit card."

"They would teach us how to use it? How to use email?"

"Absolutely," Barbara said. "And a great deal more."

Half an hour later Barbara walked out carrying the old laptop.

✦

CHAPTER 22

TWO BLOCKS FROM Mrs. Rodrigues's house the SUV passed the Lincoln and pulled to the curb in front of it. Alan, in the passenger seat of the SUV, was wearing a jacket that was very much like Barbara's, with a hood hiding his hair and most of his face. Bailey came to a stop and Barbara quickly got out and changed places with Alan. As the Lincoln drove off, Herbert shifted gears and said, "Reckon now we make tracks for home." He didn't start driving immediately. Then a block ahead of the SUV, a black car pulled away from the curb and fell in behind the Lincoln.

"There they go," Herbert said cheerfully. "Bailey will ditch them in Portland. Me and Alan already ate, but there's sandwiches, coffee, candy bars, other stuff in that there bag by your feet. Figured you'd want a bite on the way home."

The drive back was a nightmare as Bailey's weather forecast proved accurate. Snow flurries in Pendleton soon gave way to freezing rain, freezing fog, harder rain, more snow…

In the gorge, wind gusts rocked the SUV, and in places the road was icy.

It was two in the morning when they pulled into the driveway at Frank's house. He met them at the door and embraced Barbara, then drew back and examined her face.

"I'll just take Morgan out for a little talk," Herbert said.

"And you unwrap and go to bed," Frank said to Barbara, taking the laptop from her, then helping her off with her jacket. "Whatever you learned will keep until tomorrow. Bailey called, and he'll meet us in the office at ten in the morning."

The next morning Barbara felt as if she had been running all night. They were all gathered in Frank's office. Coffee was ready and a platter of blueberry muffins had been provided by Herbert.

"I'll just give the highlights," she said. She had the pictures that Dr. Sally had given her, but she had no intention of showing them. She hoped no one ever looked at them again. "The doctor on duty when they brought in June Morgan identified her positively… "

When she told them about the circumcision, Shelley turned pale and wiped her eyes, Bailey retreated behind a wall of ice, and Frank's expression became that of a stranger.

"God alone knows what that poor woman, Mrs. Samos, thought she was signing. I suspect she didn't survive long after claiming the ashes. So another Chapter closed. Mrs. Rodrigues believes her daughter ran away with a Mexican kid named Raul, but she probably was held at the Chateau from April until June on a starvation diet. She was a heavy young woman who had lost up to thirty pounds by the time Dr. Knowland signed her death certificate, citing pneumonia as the cause of death. I imagine they withheld food until she wrote her postcard. I have the computer with June's emails."

She recounted what all Herbert had told her on the long drive back. "From tidbits collected here and there, we know that a truck often takes a couple or three guys through town and onto the private road, that it returns in a day or two and heads to points west. That backs up what Paul O'Reilly said, that the guy in Medford takes one or two out for a few days in a truck. Mrs. Rodrigues said that her daughter went to the Chateau four times a week and that it took little more than an hour. We'll have to drag out those maps again. From what Mrs. Rodrigues said, and the fact that a truck seems to drive in and out, there must be a back door. I bet it's that track at the end of the runway. June never trusted Rosita and never confided in her, and she probably hid her own emails with a password, and as far as Rosita knew they didn't even exist. That explains their brevity, abruptly breaking off the way they did." She looked at Bailey. "When your computer guy goes to work on the laptop, try variations of Junebug and Stinkbug, with their ages, seventeen for her, twenty-three for him."

She paused, thinking of the captive girl trying desperately to get help, trusting no one, mutilated, afraid—*Stop that!* she ordered herself, then looked at her notes and continued.

"Alan and Herbert were able to find out that the sound of heavy artillery is heard sometimes. That the jet flies in and out often. That no one from town, with the exception of Rosita, worked at the Chateau. And that's about all we know about what's going on."

"And still not enough to take to the ATF," Bailey muttered.

"Right. Confirmation of what we suspected, and not enough."

With a difference, Frank thought. Barbara had bought that woman a computer, had used her credit card, and sooner or later *they* would know that. He poured himself more coffee, then rose and took the carafe to the door. “Time for a refill.”

“I need to know what else is in that envelope Morgan collects at the train station,” Barbara said. “And I want to dig deeper into Dr. Knowland. He could be the one who turns into Dr. Mengele on command.” Bailey’s notes on him were scant. He traveled a lot, possibly half the time, but nothing about where he went. He seemed to be well off, if not a millionaire.

Frank returned with the newly filled carafe and Barbara helped herself. “Two questions,” she said to Bailey. “First, is Morgan still going to the train station to collect those envelopes?” He nodded. “And is it still on the second Tuesday of each month?” He nodded again.

“That’s next Tuesday,” she said. “I think I know how to get that envelope. We’ll need both Sylvia and Wally Lederer.”

Bailey groaned and Frank gave Barbara a swift, penetrating look.

“She’ll demand a real agency, a desk, her own handcuffs, her own ID as a PI,” Bailey said gloomily.

“Deal with it. I’ll give Wally a call, and we’ll have to set up a time for a planning session. We have to move fast since next Tuesday is the second one this month.”

Wally had served time for pickpocketing, and reformed. He had become possibly the world’s best pickpocket. He could move through a packed Las Vegas room and clean out a dozen people on his way to the stage where, in his act, he returned watches, wallets, a belt or two, necklaces, earrings… He had made a video for a conference of law enforcement officers, teaching them what to look for. On his way to the podium where he lectured the group, he had collected guns, badges, wallets, the same way he did as a performer. Barbara had defended him when he was charged with murder, and he was grateful. He had said that if she ever wanted him to clean out Fort Knox, just give the word, he’d do it.

Barbara hadn’t realized how many people were traveling by train until she walked into the Portland station on Tuesday. People were lined up at the ticket windows and many of the seats were occupied, with other people milling about. Two teenaged girls were laughing, taking pictures of each other taking pictures. The mandatory crying baby was there, as were a few toddlers, young people loaded down with backpacks… She checked arrival and departure times. The train from Seattle was due in ten minutes.

Her hair was straight, long and blond, her fingernails long and hot pink, and she was wearing dangling earrings and a many-stranded gold bracelet. High-heel boots, a medium-long beige skirt, a white cashmere sweater, and a leather coat over her arm had made her a stranger to herself when she glanced at the mirror in Shelley's Portland hotel room. Shelley had giggled when she applied false eyelashes. From across the room Bailey had said, "You look like a high-priced hooker." Shelley had giggled harder. "You look wonderful! Gorgeous!" she had said through her laughter. Barbara felt ridiculous.

The train from Seattle was announced and she looked up from the paperback she had been pretending to read. People began to walk into the station from the train and others already there were rushing to greet many of them. She saw Morgan for the first time. He entered the station and moved toward the center, ignoring the arriving passengers until a man approached him. The man handed Morgan a manila envelope and moved out of sight. At the same moment Sylvia appeared and she looked like misplaced royalty. She had done something fantastic to her hair that poufed it up until it looked like a snowed-in beehive with a small fur hat perched on it. Her earrings were real diamonds reflecting light like a disco. She was wearing a long, blue oiled-silk coat. Searching the many travelers and those waiting, Sylvia ignored Morgan and raised her hand to wave to a young man who hurried toward her.

"Grandmother! Hello! Welcome to Portland!"

"Yes, yes," she said impatiently. "Here. This is the ticket for my bag."

He gave her a quick peck on the cheek, took the baggage claim ticket, and rushed away.

At that moment Barbara saw Wally. He entered the station, checked the board, and took a package of cigarettes from his pocket. He started to tap one out, looked around guiltily, and put the package in his pocket and turned back toward the entrance. He was carrying a newspaper under his arm and was wearing an unbuttoned raincoat. His path would intersect that of Morgan and Sylvia.

Sylvia was moving steadily toward Morgan, who had started to walk toward the entrance doors. She took a step in front of him, but then she staggered and threw out her hand as if to find a support. "Oh!" she cried faintly. She caught Morgan's arm and nearly collapsed and, even knowing what to expect, Barbara started to rise in alarm. Sylvia appeared to be having a heart attack.

Morgan caught Sylvia's arm and held her up. "Someone call 911," he said.

"No, no. I need my pill. Please, help me to a chair. My medicine. In my handbag."

She was clutching his arm and he was half supporting her when Wally paused. "Anything I can do?"

"My grandson. Jimmy. He knows. Medicine in my handbag," Sylvia managed to say. "I need to sit down."

"You'd better get her to a chair," Wally said. "I'll find Jimmy." He hurried away and seconds later Jimmy ran out of the baggage claim area to Sylvia and Morgan. Wally continued to the entrance, again taking the cigarettes from his pocket. He moved out of sight. The scenario called for him to move to the end of the covered area, light his cigarette, and pass the envelope to a man who would take it to a waiting van equipped with electronics that included a high-speed scanner. By the time Wally finished his cigarette, it was hoped that the envelope would be returned and Wally would reenter the station.

"My pillbox," Sylvia said faintly. Jimmy, searching her handbag frantically, dropped several items, a glass case, address book, handkerchief. He finally brought out a small gold pillbox. Sylvia continued to hold Morgan's arm, leaning on him as he helped her to a seat, then sat next to her as she kept leaning into him. Jimmy opened the pillbox and said, "Which one, Grandmother?"

A tall man approached them and said, "Let me see. I'm a doctor." He lifted Sylvia's free arm and felt her pulse.

"Shit!" Barbara said under her breath. "A doctor!"

"That one," the doctor said, pointing to the pillbox.

Jimmy picked up a pill and put it in Sylvia's mouth. She closed her eyes and rested her head against Morgan. The doctor continued to feel her pulse. After a time he placed her hand on her lap and drew away from her. Speaking to Morgan, he said, "She'll be all right. If you can let her rest for a few minutes, she should be fine."

Sylvia opened her eyes. "It just takes a minute or two," she said to Morgan. "I'm already feeling better and I'll lie down at the hotel." She neither looked nor sounded much better.

The doctor nodded. "Check in with your cardiologist at your first opportunity. Tell him about this little incident. He'll want to know." He nodded to them all and strode away.

This was where it could get tricky, Barbara had said at their meeting. Sylvia had to hold Morgan until Wally returned. Sylvia had laughed. "Don't be silly. Improvisation is at the heart of good theater. You never know when something will go wrong and you'd damn well better be able to improvise, or you're through."

Slowly she seemed to be regaining her strength, even going so far as to lift her sleeve to glance at her watch. It was studded with diamonds. Morgan's gaze was riveted to it, then up to her earrings, the alligator handbag.

"I'm keeping you," Sylvia said weakly. "Jimmy, get a taxi. I think I can make it out to a taxi."

"My good woman," Morgan said, "please, rest for a minute or two. I assure you this is not an imposition. I am at your service."

Undecided, Jimmy just stood there.

One of the girls with a camera drew closer. "Are you Reverend Morgan?" she asked, taking his picture.

He frowned, glanced at Sylvia, and stopped frowning. "Yes. No more pictures, if you don't mind. My friend here is not feeling well."

"A pastor?" Sylvia said weakly. "Thank goodness you were nearby. Someone who cares enough to stop for a stranger. Jimmy, give the pastor one of my cards. In the card case." She looked up at Morgan. "I must have your name and address. A donation. Your church does take donations, doesn't it?"

Wally approached the group then and asked, "Is everything all right? Are you feeling better?" He was still carrying the newspaper. "I believe you might have dropped something." He retrieved the dropped items and handed them to Jimmy, who was groping for the card case.

"Yes. This kind gentleman has been so helpful. Jimmy, haven't you found my card case yet?"

Barbara watched as closely as she thought was humanly possible, but she did not see Wally exchange an envelope from inside the newspaper with the one that Morgan had been holding on to. She knew it had happened because Wally walked away from them and sat down to read his newspaper. After that, Morgan gave Jimmy his card and accepted one. Jimmy left to get a taxi and quickly returned. If Morgan didn't already know who Sylvia was, he soon would, Barbara suspected. And no doubt Sylvia would send him a donation as promised. Ten dollars, Barbara hoped. Just ten dollars.

Barbara kept watching as Morgan and Jimmy helped Sylvia rise and totter out to the taxi. Morgan stepped back inside long enough to open the envelope, give it a quick look, and nod to someone behind Barbara. The whole charade had lasted thirteen minutes.

When her train was called, she went out, boarded and found her seat. A minute later Wally passed her on the way to his own seat. He didn't glance at her. She wanted to jump up and give him a hug. She didn't smile until the train had left the switching area, crossed the river, and was on its way to Eugene.

Barbara took a taxi to Frank's house where he met her with an incredulous expression.

"Good God, I wouldn't have recognized you!"

"Me neither," she said, tossing the leather coat onto a chair and whipping off the wig. Her head was hot and sweaty. "I have to get my real eyes back and get out of those damn heels." She headed for the upstairs bathroom.

When she returned she was wearing jeans, a sweatshirt, and sneakers. Her face was flushed from washing with soap and hot water. "Isn't it happy hour yet?"

"All right," he said, walking to the kitchen with her. "Tease a little if it pleases you. Sooner or later you'll probably get around to telling me how it went. I can wait."

Barbara laughed. "It was gorgeous, Dad. Just unbelievable. Sylvia is a terrific actor, and Wally still has the touch. That man's a magician, a real magician." She sat down and gave him a play-by-play account. "I nearly had a heart attack myself when a guy walked over and said he was a doctor. Sylvia must have thought of that. What if a real doctor had been on hand? She took care of it and provided her own. She's going to send Morgan's church a donation. Where's my laptop?"

"In the study. Sit still, I'll get it."

Bailey had said they would scan the papers and send a PDF. Frank brought the laptop and stood by her shoulder as she opened her e-mail and downloaded the PDF. There were five pages. As Barbara looked them over, her elation popped like a balloon. "Shit!" She was looking at pages of a sermon that at first glance appeared to be just about like the ones she already had.

✦

CHAPTER 23

BARBARA WAS STILL gazing at the sermon when her cell phone went off. "Darren," she said, her face lighting up after a glance at the caller ID. "Right back," she said to Frank as she stood and walked from the kitchen.

He continued to read the sermon for a minute or two, then muttered, "Drivel." It didn't make sense. It had to be the sermon itself that needed cover. Shaking his head he walked away from the computer. If there was a coded message, they would need an expert to decode it.

Barbara came back with a woebegone expression. "They made it as far as Chicago. Canceled flights all over the place again. He'll let me know when they can make the next leg. I advised a dog sled team."

Herbert walked into the kitchen at that moment, to Barbara's surprise. She had not seen him all day. "When did you get here?" she asked.

"While back. You know, I kept looking for you and looking for you, but you got away somehow and I decided to come on home. Never laid my eye on you most of the day."

"And I certainly did not see you."

His big smile broadened. "And now, if you two want to go set by the fire I can rustle us up some supper."

Frank bit back his automatic rejection of the proposal. He wanted to talk to Barbara. "Fine," he said. "For three. Darren and Todd are stranded in Chicago."

Herbert nodded. "That's how it is with them airplanes anymore. Just can't seem to get you to where you want to be when you want to be there."

They took cheese and wine to the living room, where Frank added a small log to the fire and gave it a poke. Sparks flared and settled again before he sat on the sofa.

Barbara was gazing moodily at the fire and appeared to be in no mood for chitchat as he regarded her soberly. "We have to face it," he said. "We may not be able to get enough to take to the ATF. There could be a coded message in that sermon, in all of them, but we don't have the expertise to ferret it out. It could take experts months to do so, assuming there is such a message. You have to put that on the back burner and concentrate from now on out on how to manage your case."

"I know. So close we can smell what's going on, but not close enough to bite. The feds would assume that we're just trying to pull chestnuts out of the fire, raise a smoke cloud to get Travis off the hook."

After a moment she said, "Even if the spotlight turns to Morgan and his sponsors, there's no real connection that can be proved. Kill one deliveryman, long live the new deliveryman. And no hard proof." She sipped wine and then said, "Assuming I could rouse their suspicions, one of two things would happen: They'd go in and ask a few questions and the operation would move to somewhere else; or they would start their own quiet investigation, and we all know that can take years."

"No one will make a move toward Polson without good cause," Frank said flatly. "Now that corporations are people, you could say he's what's known as a person with friends in high places. If pressed about the donations, he probably would not deny it, and point to a dozen charitable causes he donates to, some of them quite legitimate."

For a time neither spoke again. Thing One stepped onto Frank's lap and Thing Two landed on Barbara's. She stroked him absently. Hisses and faint random pops from burning wood, and the purring of two big cats were the only sounds.

"I wish I knew what Travis was so afraid of," Barbara said, breaking their silence. "What final straw drove him away. He can't talk about it, but the fear of his father is still there."

Frank considered it, then nodded. At the Thanksgiving dinner, alone with Minnick while they were preparing the feast, he had brought up Travis and his obvious hatred for and fear of his father. They had agreed that there was something being held back, something the young man wouldn't or couldn't talk about, something that still had the power to frighten him.

It was another bad night for Barbara. She kept trying to find a way to rationalize a plea bargain as the best option for Travis, when she herself hated the idea with all her soul. To plead guilty to a murder you didn't commit was the ultimate failure of the system, of your own integrity, of humanity itself. She tossed and turned.

There is no defense against two eyewitnesses and his fingerprints on the gun, she told herself over and over, before refuting it again and again: There has to be.

When she went down to breakfast the next morning, Frank gave her a searching look and did not say a word beyond, "Good morning."

"I have all those sermons at my office," she said, taking her chair, feeling slightly nauseated by the smell of bacon. "I'll print out this new one and spend one last day going over them and checking out every Bible reference. Then in the file they go."

"When you find out how Darren's doing with a flight home, let me know," Frank said. "If it's late, or even if it's not, let's have dinner here, and then the lot of you head for home. I'll cook," he added to Herbert, who had brought bacon and scrambled eggs to the table.

"Herbert," Barbara said then, keeping her gaze on her coffee cup, "I've been cooped up for what seems like a lifetime. I want to start taking walks again. How much of a problem is that going to be?"

She heard Frank's quick intake of breath and gave her coffee another unneeded stir.

"Not a problem. Me and Morgan's been thinking the same thing. That dumb dog's been telling me day after day that he wants to take a long walk, and I keep telling him to walk around the yard, but he has the brain of a flea and doesn't understand a word I say to him. You just don't want to set up no pattern. You know, one day at two o'clock and then maybe at noon, like that. And not the same place all the time."

"Good enough," she said. "You set the time. At least an hour. My brain goes numb with sitting around." She raised her head to give Frank a swift look. His deep frown said it all: he was not happy.

She had to do some Christmas shopping, Barbara thought that afternoon, but she refused to go from store to store with Herbert within arm's reach. She decided to shop on the Internet, token presents only, enough to show she had thought of them.

She put down the Bible she had been reading and frowned at it. The latest reference was from the second Book of Samuel, as meaningless in the context of the sermon as the others had been. She read it again: *And David said unto him, From whence comest thou? And he said unto him, Out of the camp of Israel am I escaped.* In the sermon the message had been doom and gloom about the coming collapse of the government.

"Okay," she said to the many stacks of papers spread across her desk, "off to the file case with the lot of you."

Maria buzzed then to say that Derek Peel was in the outer office.

"Two minutes and then send him in. Signal to Herbert that he's okay," Barbara said and began to close the folders that were opened. She was standing behind her desk when Derek Peel entered.

"Mr. Peel, please sit down," she said, motioning to the client chairs.

He shook his head slightly and crossed the office to look out the window, then stood there and surveyed the office as if he were a possible buyer of everything in it. That day he was dressed in jeans and a heavy sweater, carrying a jacket. "Nice," he said finally, and returned to the desk, tossed his jacket over one of the chairs and sat down. "Nicer than the restaurant. I have that date you asked for, but I want something in return."

She seated herself and nodded. "What do you want?"

"Information. Answers to a few questions."

"Mr. Peel, you know very well that I can't agree to answer questions that haven't been asked. Tell me what you want to know, and if I am free to answer, I will. However, you also know that my client and his case may make answering impossible. Your questions first."

He regarded her steadily for a short time, then nodded. "Do you know anything about a man named Daggart who was killed last spring?"

"Yes. Why do you ask?"

"When I asked my mother when Dad said he would quit, she turned pale. The middle of March, she said. She remembered because it was when Bob Daggart was killed. I looked him up and read the story in the newspaper. He had been beaten to death by street punks was the gist of it. If that's true why did it frighten her? Why did it make my father decide to quit his job? That's what I want to know."

"Did you ask her?"

"My mother has two ways of responding to any question. Either she will tell the absolute truth as she knows if, or she will clam up. She clammed up."

"What makes you think I know?"

"I have a friend who's a medic. I talked him into letting me look over the calls from last March and I know that Daggart was picked up in your father's office. I think you can tell me a lot."

"If you know that, you should also know that when the medics arrived they found him unconscious on the floor. He collapsed before he had a chance to say anything to my father. He was already dying when he dragged himself into the office. Dad immediately told his secretary to call 911. He helped Daggart to a chair and he collapsed before he had a chance to say anything. The ambulance arrived within a few minutes. We don't know what he wanted."

Derek studied her intently for a moment. "That would be on the police record?"

"Yes. He dropped a lot of papers that Dad handed over to the investigators, and later they were claimed by your father. They were membership lists for the church. Your father also identified the body and claimed it in the name of the church. Daggart was cremated and that was that." She met his steady gaze and asked, "What else has frightened your mother, Mr. Peel?"

"What makes you think something else has?"

"That incident with Daggart was many months ago, nothing more came of it, and your father continued his work for the church, yet you say she is frightened at this time. Why?"

He rose abruptly and returned to the window, where he stood with his back to her for several seconds. At last he turned and said, "She's scared out of her mind. And she won't say why. Last Friday Morgan came out to the farm. He came to offer his condolence, he said, and to offer her a trip to Hawaii. It was going to be hard to endure Christmas, he said. It always is after a recent bereavement, and with the trial coming up, it was too much for her to have to bear. To sit in court and see the man who killed my father, to hear medical reports about the fatal injury, to listen to false witnesses try to exonerate the guilty man. Even if it was his own son, he had to admit he was guilty, and he shared that guilt. He said he wanted to ease her suffering if he could. A free trip to Hawaii for Christmas and throughout January. All expenses to be borne by the church was his feeble attempt to ease the way for her to get through the next weeks. It was the least he could do."

"Wow," Barbara said softly. "What's he afraid of? Has the prosecution told her she would be a witness?"

"No. What do you mean, what's he afraid of?"

"You know what I mean. What did she tell him?"

"She turned it down. You think he's afraid of what she might say if she testifies?"

"Do you?"

He returned to the chair opposite her desk and sat down heavily. "Yes. And I don't have a clue about what her testimony could amount to, why it might damage him. Or why he thinks it might." He leaned forward and asked, "Do you intend to call her as a witness? A witness for the defense?"

"Mr. Peel, this gets quite complicated. But I can tell you this much, the state and the defense counsel are required to turn over their witness list before the trial begins. I can delay that a little, until just days before the trial. If I feel I have to call your mother, I'll subpoena her, make it abundantly clear that she is not taking the stand of her own volition. That's all I can tell you at this time. Is she afraid she'll be called?"

"What do you think?" he said bitterly. "Maybe I'll try to talk her into Hawaii."

"Or maybe just a week somewhere out of sight—California, Florida, even Arizona for a little while. A change of scene until the trial actually starts."

"Jesus!" he said. "I thought I was being paranoid before. You think she might be in danger?"

"I didn't say that," Barbara snapped. "I just have to wonder what Arlie Morgan is afraid of. Maybe she'll tell you what it is in the coming weeks. If she isn't a state witness, do you think she would talk to me?"

He jumped to his feet and snatched up his jacket. "This whole mess is a goddamn nightmare that just gets worse and worse. Do you believe for a second that she'd talk to the defense attorney for the man who killed her husband? I'll see you at the trial."

That afternoon Frank was sitting across the table from Travis Morgan. Frank had brought him another book, this one about some of the many ludicrous incidents that had occurred over the years in courts.

"Tell you one that didn't make it to the book," Frank said. "It could even be apocryphal, but it's one some of us relish. Happened a long time ago, back in the thirties maybe, or maybe not. Fellow was on trial for murder, and his attorney and the prosecutor had a big grudge that had been long-standing. Well, they were at each other's throats day after day, and on this day they got into it physically. Who threw the first punch no one seemed to know, but fists were flying, the judge was yelling his head off, the officers on duty were trying to separate the fellows who had mistaken the court for a boxing ring, and the prisoner got up and walked out. Just walked away and vanished. When the dust settled, the judge was fit to be tied, and he queried the jurors, demanded to know if they had seen the prisoner escape. Seems several of them did in fact watch him walk out and they admitted it. When asked why they hadn't called it to the attention of the police or the bailiff or someone, they said they'd decided the trial was a farce, that maybe the fellow was guilty and maybe he wasn't, but that particular trial wasn't going to settle it one way or the other."

Travis was grinning broadly and, watching his expression, Frank thought again how drastically it could change instantaneously. One second a kid having fun and then, in a flash, a frightened and angry young man who looked capable of committing murder.

After a moment he said, "There's a point to the story, Travis, a pretty good point, which is why some of us keep it in mind. You see, no matter what's going on in court, two lawyers slugging it out, or an elephant strolling down the aisle wouldn't matter, some of those jurors are watching the defendant. At all times, some are watching, and what they say in the deliberation room could have a lot of weight. What they would see in you is a young man who is very frightened. A trial is a frightening experience, to be sure, but you're not on trial in this room and your fear shows every time the name of your father comes up, whether it's Arlie Morgan or Benjamin Morgan. Like right now. What are you so afraid of, Travis? What did he do to you, or say to you, or threaten you with?"

"Nothing," Travis said through clenched lips.

"Something," Frank said, "and it shows. Your hands are trembling and your neck is as rigid as a pipe. Every muscle in your body has gone rigid. You're frightened now, just thinking of it, and it keeps coming back to you, doesn't it? Just hearing his name triggers it. You're going to hear his name repeatedly in court and your own reaction could make the difference in the outcome of the trial. Did he threaten you, a fifteen-year-old boy? Did he do something to you? Did he molest you?"

Travis had jerked his hands off the table when Frank pointed out that they were trembling. He clutched the tabletop then and cried, "Him? Molest me? Crap! That was the last thing on his mind. He was playing with a scalpel, you know, a doctor's scalpel, just playing with it and talking. Talking all the time. Just talking." He jumped up and looked around the room wildly and almost incoherently the words rushed out, ran together. "Eunuchs. He kept talking about eunuchs, how they were the only free men, how they were rational men, men without lust, without sin, blessed in the sight of God. Playing with that fucking scalpel. He cut his finger and held it up and said it wouldn't be any more painful than that, just a little cut and a lifetime of freedom. A man couldn't do more for his son than to free him from sin, from lust, that it was the duty of a father to set his son free! I ran to my room and put a chair under the doorknob. Scared he'd come after me with the scalpel."

He was shaking all over and as abruptly as he had leaped up, he sank into his chair. "That's what comes back to me. I'm that scared kid, hiding in the closet, afraid his father is on the way with a scalpel. I can see him holding up his finger with blood running down his hand. And light on the scalpel. I can't help it. I'm that kid again, scared shitless. He can't touch me now, but I'm that kid again and I can't help it! I can feel the closet wall, feel the door, and I'm afraid to breathe because he might hear me and know where I am. I keep listening for his footsteps in the hall and I can't breathe." Suddenly he burst into tears and mashed his face down on his arms on the table, shaking with sobs.

Silently, Frank stood and went around the table. He knelt by Travis and put his arm around his shoulders as he wept. When the convulsive shaking eased, he rose, took a handkerchief from his pocket, and placed it on the table, then went back to his chair. He waited several more minutes until Travis raised his head, groped for the handkerchief, and turned his back.

Finally facing him again, Travis said, "Crap! I want to go back to my cell!" His eyes were red rimmed and swollen.

"Wait, son," Frank said. "Did you cry then, when you were fifteen?"

"No. What difference does it make?"

"You were overdue, that's all. Travis, you were very brave when you came home and decided to confront your father, face him down. That took a great deal of courage and you were ready for it, but instead you landed in here. I imagine that when June said in her email that she had been cut, you plunged back in time to that night and your fifteen-year-old self who was terrified of his father with blood running down his hand, playing with a scalpel. Yet, you were prepared to face him down. You're not that kid any longer, and now that you've allowed yourself to cry over it, no doubt it will fade into the vast memory bank where all memories finally go, good and bad."

"I realized that night that he is really, truly insane," Travis said hoarsely. "That scared me as much as anything else. My father is crazy."

"I agree," Frank said. "But I'm not crazy, and neither is Barbara and together we make a pretty good team, and also together we intend to put your father out of circulation. One more thing before I leave you in peace. I want Dr. Minnick to come see you again. He's a crafty old man and he has tricks up his sleeves about how to manage memories. First, of course, you have to admit you have bad memories to manage, but now you've done that. Let him do his thing."

CHAPTER 24

"DID YOU HEAR a thing Todd was saying at dinner?" Darren asked softly, stroking her hair.

"Not a word. Did you like what you ate?"

"Did we eat?" He laughed, a low rumbling sound that shook his chest and hers.

She snuggled even closer. "I missed you so much."

"Yeah, me too. Let's not do that again."

Barbara didn't move until his breathing was deep and regular, until his arm around her relaxed enough for her to ease it away. Carefully, she got up and put on her robe. She had too much on her mind to lie in bed, where any minute she knew she would start turning and twisting.

Frank had told her about his talk with Travis and concluded by saying, "I think he'll be all right in court, especially after talking to Minnick a time or two."

She didn't recall a time she had dreaded a trial more than now, she thought on her way to the living room. Hope that Travis would not break when his father was mentioned, when he testified. Check. Discredit the two guys with him in that room that night. Check. Then what?

Back to the starting gate, she told herself. Reread everything. If there was a gap, a missing piece, something she had overlooked, it was now or never. The trial would start in three and a half weeks.

Both Darren and Todd were up early the next morning. "You should stay home and get in a few more hours just sleeping," she said.

"I've gotta tell Dr. Chu that it worked," Todd said, gulping down orange juice. "And I have to make up a lot of stuff, get makeup assignments, and like that."

"I'll take him to school and check in at the clinic, make sure the wheels are still turning," Darren said. "Bed at sundown tonight, promise."

"Right," she said. "I'll be in my office all day." She looked across the kitchen to where Herbert was doing something with a chicken. "What are you up to?"

"Been reading up on crock pots. Thought I'd try one out, see if it really does what they claim, like make a dinner while you're off to the movies or something. Don't put much stock in it but thought I'd give it a try."

Darren and Todd left together. She made the bed, gathered up her things, and by the time she was ready, Herbert said so was he. "That old crock pot is all we can count on for dinner, and I tell you this, I'll be doing a heap of praying that it works. I laid in some hot dogs just in case it don't work."

Minutes later, in her office, she started back at the beginning. She was reading Shelley's notes concerning Arlie Morgan when Maria tapped on the door.

"I'm going to lunch," she said. "Do you want me to bring you something?"

Barbara looked at her watch. It was one o'clock. "A sandwich, and ask Herbert what he wants, will you? Is there coffee?"

Herbert appeared behind Maria. "You want to help me exercise that good-for-nothing lazy dog around three?"

She did. She ate the sandwich Maria provided a short time later, and it seemed in no time at all that Herbert said it was almost three. They drove by the house to collect Morgan and then went out to walk the dog.

Reading everything was no help, she thought, walking on the trail by the river. The prosecution's case was simple and intact: Peel was working, DiPalma was looking for a book to read, Morgan and Dr. Knowland were in the upstairs study, Rostov answered the doorbell and walked Travis to Peel's office. A shot rang out. "Shit!" she said under her breath.

The river was winter high, grayed with meltwater, and very swift. It had a winter voice, and a summer voice. That day it was deep-throated, almost inaudible, more a vibration than a sound. In the summer it sang. An osprey swept in low as if it had spotted lunch, changed its mind, and soared again. It looked as if it had forgotten its long legs and feet, as if they were just dangling there, hitching a ride. A misty rain was in the air, not falling so much as simply hanging in space with gravity suspended, or else a cloud had descended to head level. That was it, she thought a second later, fog was forming and already the other side of the river was poorly defined; everything there had fuzzy outlines. Just the thought of fog was chilling. Abruptly she turned to head back to the car. Rain was okay, she was thinking; snow was okay. Hot weather a little less so, but still okay. Fog was not okay. It chilled her to the bone.

"Good timing," Herbert said when they returned to the car. "An hour almost to the minute."

She couldn't have recounted what her thoughts had been for a whole hour, and maybe that was what she needed, a time out from her disorganized thoughts, from the bits of conversations, bits of statements, faces, voices that were all running together and making no sense, offering no clue as to how she should proceed.

That day she called it quits at five thirty, but she took some files home with her to read after Darren went to bed. Herbert's experiment with the crock pot was a smashing success: chicken stew to which he added dumplings; salad, and apple pie for dessert completed the meal.

"Reckon that pot knows a thing or two about how to cook," he said complacently as they ate.

"Or you do," Darren said.

Todd helped himself to more of everything as Herbert beamed.

Late that night, the house quiet, Barbara looked in the folders she had brought home. Something Shelley had written, she was thinking, something she might follow up on. She found the folder and quickly scanned the pages until she found what she was looking for. Arlie Morgan had grown up in Jacksonville, where his father was a preacher and the family had a small farm.

She visualized the area in the mountainous southernmost part of the state. Now a minor tourist attraction, it was very isolated, but had once been a gold-mining town. Forty years ago it must have been backward, remote, with few amenities. She leaned back in her chair trying to see someone like Arlie Morgan in such a place. Talk to Ashley, she told herself and made a note.

Barbara was rereading Bailey's many reports the next day when Ashley Morgan arrived. Barbara glanced about her office and gave up at any attempt to create order out of the chaos around her. Every flat surface had files, papers, photographs, stuff.

"Try to ignore it," she said to Ashley. "That's how I can get through the day, by pretending everything's spick-and-span neat. How are you?"

Ashley looked wan and tired. She had aged during the past few months. "Okay," she said sinking down onto the sofa. "Winter blues, maybe."

"I'm sorry to drag you over here, but I'm pretty swamped."

"Please, don't. I want to do something, anything. And I want to tell you something. Travis mentioned Arlie this morning, by name. I haven't heard him say the name, 'Dad', 'my father,' none of that from the day he came home until now. Just once, and sort of stumbling over it, going stiff, but he said 'Arlie.'"

"That's good. It happens that Arlie is what I want to talk about, or rather to have you talk about while I listen. Growing up in Jacksonville, what his home life was like, things like that. Just whatever you can recall. That was rough country when he was a boy. Did he fit in? Were his parents kind to him, strict, what? That sort of thing."

Ashley thought for a moment, then said, "They were both good people, well meaning. I can't imagine that either of them ever said an unkind word about anyone or to anyone. She was not well. A heart problem, and she never got the kind of medical attention she needed.

It killed her a year after Arlie and I were married. His father was very hard working, both as a minister and as a small farmer, with a lot of nervous energy. He made Arlie work on the farm, milk the cow, gather eggs, help with planting, weeding, all those things that Arlie hated. And he taught him to hunt and fish. They got a deer every year to stock a freezer, and they went to the Rogue River to fish for steelhead. Arlie hated both. He was afraid of bears, afraid of the deep woods, but he learned to hunt and fish and if he had to, he could manage a small farm."

"He learned to shoot, then?"

"He was, according to him, an excellent shot. What spooked him was that sometimes the deer wasn't killed, and it took a shot to the head to finish it off." She thought for another moment or two. "When his father died, two years after his mother passed away, we went down there to close down the house, sell things, just wrap up that part of his history. Travis was a baby and it was up to Arlie to do most of it. He didn't want any of their junk, and I couldn't blame him. They didn't have anything. When he started burning things, I grabbed a shoebox of pictures and saved them, and he kept his father's guns and fishing gear. He sold the rods and reels later."

"What kind of guns?" Barbara asked.

"I really don't know. A couple of rifles, a shotgun, maybe some handguns. I wasn't paying a lot of attention. Travis was a toddler and I was afraid he'd get his hands on them and I kept him in the kitchen while Arlie boxed them up. He brought them back to Eugene with him. He might have sold them when he sold the fishing gear, but I don't know."

"What happened to the box of pictures?"

"When we separated, I kept the box. I thought that someday the children might want to see pictures of their grandparents, where Arlie came from. I took the box along with my own things."

"When are you going to Portland again? Could you bring that box back with you?"

Ashley nodded. "Why? But, yes I'll bring it. I'm going back up on Wednesday and not again until after Christmas. My sister and her husband are coming to stay with me for a few days over Christmas. They wanted me to go to Denver, be with some family at least, and I couldn't, so they're coming here. She will stay with me until after the trial. I'll spend as much time as possible with Travis. It must be hell for him, in jail for Christmas." She looked down at her hands. "Hell for him. Hell for me. Merry Christmas." She was near tears.

Barbara returned to Bailey's notes after Ashley left. The two girls who had been snapping pictures at the train station had taken pictures of Arlie Morgan accepting an envelope from a man, another of him supporting Sylvia, two or three of Wally picking up dropped articles and giving them to the man Sylvia called her grandson. There were three additional pictures: Morgan inside a bank, at the door to the safe deposit department, and at the teller's window. Bailey had taken them.

Neat, Barbara thought, it tells the story graphically. And it had nothing whatsoever to do with the murder of Peel. She started to put them in the stack of folders to be put away in a file, then drew back. Maybe they were useful, she thought, regarding the pictures for several minutes. She nodded, *absolutely* useful. She put them with the Peel material.

Packages were arriving at the office, and Maria squirreled them away in Shelley's office until they could take time to wrap things. Shelley went shopping several times and Darren and Todd went out on their own mysterious errands. Eugene had turned into a huge festival of lights. On Saturday they decorated a tree at home, and on Sunday they decorated Frank's tree. Night after night Herbert was doing things in the kitchen that made the house smell like a bakery.

"Not the park," Herbert said on Monday. "Let's pick something different."

The problem was that Barbara didn't want to spend her walking time just to get to a walking place. "Okay," she said. "Around the urban garden, the Eugene Garden. It's a couple of city blocks fenced off where organic vegetables are grown. It's probably pretty much deserted this time of year."

After they collected Morgan, she directed Herbert where to turn onto Washington, and then again onto a street with deep potholes filled with water. To her surprise there were men in dark rain gear working on the garden side of a high chain link fence. They were picking Brussels sprouts, she saw, and there were beds of cabbages and kale that appeared to be thriving. Drums as big as buses held compost and worms, and there were enormous piles of finished compost topped with pressed straw hats to keep the rain from washing everything away.

Herbert shook his head at her choice. The streets were deserted, that was true, but there was fog already.

"Just this end," she said, adjusting her hood. "Then up the side to the end and back, not all the way around."

The street was a muddy mess and she watched her feet as she walked along the fence. All that reading and what good had it done? She knew she had enough to instill a bit of doubt, but not enough to counter eyewitnesses and prints on a gun. She had talked to Travis and he really was making a great effort to overcome his reaction to a mention of his father, and he was getting much better. Minnick said he was doing great, but a watchful juror or two, and the inevitable one who decided on guilt with the charge, not with the trial, they were the ones Travis had to convince, and she didn't think he was there yet. Not quite.

She rounded the corner and saw two more workers approaching with their heads lowered against the cold fog. The street was not as gutted and potholed as the one she had left, but she was determined not to be the one to step off the narrow sidewalk onto it.

As the distance separating them narrowed, she edged in closer to the fence, and when they made no motion to veer to the side, she stopped walking to let them pass. They took another step or two when suddenly Morgan flashed past her and knocked one of the men down, and almost as fast Herbert dashed by and flung himself on the other man, knocking him backward to the sidewalk. Herbert flipped him over and had handcuffs on him with movements that were so fast that it was hard to see how he managed to do it.

Barbara heard Herbert say in an amiable way, "If I was you, I wouldn't try to move. That dumb dog might decide to tear out your windpipe or something. Not a thing I can do about it, neither."

Morgan was standing over the man, his jaws wide open, his teeth touching the skin of the man's neck.

The one with the handcuffs began to thrash about with his legs and Herbert kicked him in the thigh and then put his foot on the man's neck. "Reckon you don't want me to stand on you. Two-eighty last time I weighed." He glanced at Barbara and said, "You might want to call the police."

Not the police, she thought. Hogarth. She hit the speed button for him and waited a few seconds. "Two thugs, attempted assault. They're under control, but for God's sake no sirens, no publicity, no media. Four guys, plain clothes." She listened to his sputtering indignation and said, "Lieutenant, I'll fill you in, but right now two potential murderers are on the ground and I want them arrested." She told him where she was and disconnected.

"Five minutes," she said to Herbert. "Can you hold him that long? Can Morgan?"

"Morgan, I don't know. He might decide to chomp down, but I can sit on this one all day, all night. Don't make no difference to me." He looked at the terrified man with Morgan's teeth on his throat. "How you doing?" Morgan made a low growling sound. "If I was you I wouldn't try to move, and that there dog might hold like that for a spell. Never can tell about dogs, though. Sometimes they seem to think you're moving when all's you're doing is thinking about it. One drop of blood can make them get frenzied like."

The man being held down by the dog had been inching his hand lower. He stopped moving. The other one had not moved a muscle apparently after Herbert put his foot on his neck. Barbara was still holding her cell phone and realized that her hand was shaking hard, that she was shaking hard all over. She thrust her hands into her pockets and huddled down as much as she could into her jacket. She had been oblivious, she thought then. She had assumed they were just workers, like the others inside the fence. It would have worked. They would have grabbed her, killed her on the spot, dragged her away somewhere. Whatever their plan had been, it would have worked.

Hogarth arrived with four plainclothes men in two other cars. He came directly to her. "What the hell is going on?" he demanded.

"I'd be a mite careful with that one," Herbert said, jerking his thumb toward the man being guarded by Morgan. "Seems he might have a gun or something in that there pocket."

Two of the detectives headed toward him, then hesitated. Morgan backed away, growling at the man on the ground until the detectives hauled him to his feet, cuffed him, and patted him down. One of them withdrew a gun with a silencer from his pocket. Morgan trotted over to Barbara's side and sat down with his tongue lolling out, grinning a big dog grin. The other two detectives had taken control of Herbert's captive and one of them waved Hogarth over to look at his gloves. Hogarth cursed and spoke in a low voice to the detectives.

Hogarth turned back to Barbara. "Well?"

Her teeth were chattering. "They wanted to kill me," she said. "Can it wait? I want to go back to my office."

He examined her face, then nodded. "I'll follow you," he said.

They arrested the two men, Mirandized them, and started to put them in the cars when Herbert said, "That's their van up yonder. Least they came in it."

Barbara had not even seen it until then, a black van midway up the street.

"See," Herbert said, "I seen that there van come real slow around the corner and stop there, and I'm thinking that's funny. The gate's back that way. Nobody got out for a bit. Then they did, after Barbara went around the corner back there. And I seen those loaded gloves and I'm thinking that don't look good. And that one kept his hand in his pocket, a real deep pocket, and I'm thinking that don't look good, either. And Morgan here, he don't like it a bit when people stare at me and carry guns. Real protective, that there dog. Before I know it he goes into action and I just kind of followed his lead. And that's the story."

"Jesus Christ!" Hogarth said. He jerked out his cell phone, turned his back and talked.

After he disconnected, he waved his men away and said to Barbara, "I'll wait for the tow truck and come to your office as soon as they secure that van. Beat it."

She did not say a word after they got in the SUV. She shivered. The gun with the silencer had been for Herbert, she thought. The man with the loaded gloves had been for her. They knew about Herbert, had come prepared for him. Thank God they hadn't known about Morgan.

When they reached her parking spot, she reached over to touch Herbert's arm. "I don't know what to say. You were terrific. Thanks."

He looked deeply embarrassed. "We'd best be getting you inside with some hot coffee to warm you up."

Shelley wanted to hover. Maria wanted to hover. If either of them had been able to produce a blanket, she would have been swaddled, Barbara thought irritably. She wanted to say just leave me alone, but what she did say to Maria was, "Hogarth will be around any minute. Just send him in when he gets here."

"I'd best go out to introduce Morgan to him," Herbert said. "That there dog he wants to be introduced sort of formally. Sometimes he seems to think he's people." He left with Maria.

"Do you want anything?" Shelley asked as if pleading for there to be something she could do.

"Nothing. I was chilled, now I'm not. I'm fine." She held her coffee mug with both hands, welcoming its warmth.

"Maybe you could come out to our place to walk, climb the hills, you know, relax."

"Thanks. I may take you up on it." Her door opened and Frank strode into the office and straight to Barbara. She slammed her cup down and jumped to her feet. "Herbert called you? I'll throttle him!"

"I hired him and I pay him. He did what he was supposed to do." He held her shoulders and examined her face, then drew her close and held her. Herbert's call had filled him with ice that was only then beginning to thaw again. He drew in a long breath before releasing her; he kissed her cheek, and said, "Now I'd like coffee with a good shot of that Jack Daniels you keep for Bailey."

He barely had time to settle into a chair before the door opened again and Hogarth came in. His face was red with cold, or perhaps because he was furious. "I want to know what's going on. Why you said they wanted to kill you. Who they are. The works." He nodded curtly to Frank, pulled one of the visitors' chairs around and sat in it.

"I don't know who they are," Barbara said. "And I don't know why they want to kill me. I'm working on the Peel murder case, Travis Morgan's my client, and that's all I'm working on at this time."

"Did those guys threaten you?" He asked it harshly, bitingly.

"No."

"Did they say a word to you?"

"No!" she snapped.

"Did you see a gun?"

Suddenly she knew where he was going with his questions. She didn't have cause to file a complaint, to accuse them of anything. She shook her head. "I didn't see the gun until your guy lifted it from his pocket."

"Right. So we can hold them on an illegal weapons charge, and they can sue us for illegal search and seizure, and you know where the court will go with that one. They can sue your buddy for assault and battery, for intimidation by a dog. Thanks a lot, Holloway." He got to his feet glaring at her, turned and stomped toward the door.

Before he reached it, Frank said, "Milt, I suggest you charge them with suspicion of murder. Remember that fellow who was beaten to death back in March? The one who chose my office to start his death journey in? Robert Daggart's his name. If you still have his clothes in the unsolved-murder evidence drawer, there's a possibility that you can find fibers on those loaded gloves."

Hogarth wheeled about. "Fuck! What are you holding out on me?

"Take off that heavy jacket, sit down and have a cup of coffee, and let's talk," Frank said.

His voice was low keyed, but in his mind was the image of Daggart's agonizing last moments before he passed out, along with the words Hogarth had uttered: internal bleeding, broken bones, crushed kidneys… Not a roll of quarters wrapped in a fist, he was thinking, but loaded gloves, professional gloves designed to do one thing—protect the hands of a killer as he beat someone to death.

CHAPTER 25

"BARBARA, AS YOUR attorney, I advise you not to say another word," Frank said. "This is not your concern. It's mine." He turned to Hogarth. "Well, are you going to shed that jacket and have a talk or aren't you?"

Hogarth took off his jacket, moved a chair closer to the table and poured coffee for himself. "So, talk."

"Right. As you'll recall that fellow came to me, but he didn't have a chance to say what he wanted. We had to put it on the back burner, you and I both did. I didn't give it another thought until Peel himself was murdered, and I was willing to shrug it off as a coincidence until Barbara mentioned that Mrs. Peel had said that her husband had threatened to quit his job when Daggart was killed, that her husband had become very upset over that death, and possibly afraid after it. I began to poke around some. They both worked for the same church, Peel here in Eugene and Daggart in Portland, and on the surface it appeared that they never worked together, but I had to wonder. Daggart knew too much to be the simple day laborer he appeared to be.

Daggart could have been an assumed name, in which case someone must have turned up missing. I sicced Bailey onto it. Nothing came up in Portland, but there was someone who fit the description in Seattle. I followed through and it turned out that Daggart was undercover, writing a book about a militia being formed in the state here, and in all probability getting information from Peel. I regard Daggart as a client even if he didn't live long enough to finish signing the attorney-client agreement. I owed it to him to try to get to the bottom of what he came to tell me, and I owed him the confidentiality agreement that all clients have. I know enough now to know that he was right about the militia, but I don't have enough to take to the FBI, ATF, or Homeland Security. Since Barbara was investigating her own case, Peel's murder, our paths crossed several times, and I'm afraid the people I'm after think she's the primary meddling in their affairs. I got her into that, and by God I want her out of it. That's what I've been holding back."

Hogarth had a disbelieving expression and for once he seemed speechless. His face, down into his neck, flared with red, and his scalp, always pink, turned scarlet. He lifted his coffee, didn't taste it, and set it down hard. "Fuck! A one-man committee poking into a militia! Give me a little credit, for God's sake! If you have anything at all, you have enough to take to Homeland Security or the FBI. Let them have it, let them investigate."

"In time," Frank said. "Unfortunately the two men who did have hard information are both dead and one's cremated. I'm scratching around in the ashes. But it's not your bailiwick. You're homicide in Eugene, and I already told you the two you arrested today should be charged with suspicion of murder of the man who called himself Daggart. That's your department, none of this other business."

"Crap! It's all my department. I'll get in touch with the FBI if you don't!"

"And you'll blow the whole thing to hell," Frank said. "One whiff that an official investigation is under way and they'll evaporate. I've told you what I know and I'm done talking." He picked up the carafe, shook it. "It's empty," he said glancing at Barbara.

"I'll do it," she said hastily. "Right back." She took the carafe and went to the door.

"You'll damn well talk to the FBI," Hogarth was saying as she stepped into the outer office and closed the door after her.

She leaned against the door and breathed in deeply a time or two in an attempt to control her outrage. He was trying to shield her, making himself the target, turning Hogarth's wrath to him instead of her. He had wanted her out of there before she erupted.

"That bad?" Bailey asked from the far side of the room.

"He's grilling Dad," she said and handed the carafe to Maria.

"Jeez, can I watch?" Bailey said with a wicked grin. "Maria told me to cool it out here for a while, but it might be more fun in there."

"The lieutenant told me to stay out, too," Herbert said aggrievedly. He was standing in the doorway to Shelley's office with Morgan at his side.

"Forget it," Barbara said. "Who called you?" she asked Bailey.

"He did," he said, jerking his thumb toward Herbert, "but I would have dropped by anyway. I have a new flight to report."

"You're getting to be the town gossip," she said crossly to Herbert. He looked deeply hurt.

Bailey ignored that. "The Learjet took off today at six a.m. and came back at twelve, just in time to deliver two hit men maybe."

She closed her eyes. Drive down to Eugene, drive back to Portland to be flown out again as soon as the job was done. "Dad told Hogarth enough to get him interested in what we're up to," she said. "God alone knows what all he's telling him. Both of you stick around until Dad's through with Hogarth. Then we'll talk. Maria, is it coffee yet?" She realized she had reversed what was going on in the other office and bit her tongue.

"Almost," Maria said. "You want me to bring it in when it's ready?"

"Just knock on the door and I'll get it." She took another deep breath and returned to her own office in time to hear Frank say, "That's exactly what I'll do just as soon as I have anything hard and real. Until then we both keep mum."

Hogarth was still in his chair, leaning forward with a steady gaze on Frank. And he, for a man done talking, Barbara thought, seemed to have been putting on a one-man show. She sat down in her desk chair.

"Another minute or two," she said.

"Good," Frank said. "I think we've found a way to manage all this business."

Hogarth pulled out his cell phone and hit the speed dial. "It's me. Put those two guys in separate interrogation rooms, no phone calls, and hold them there until I get back." He listened and snapped, "Didn't you hear me? Just hold them, no questions, no anything." He rose and picked up his jacket, put it on, and went to the door where he paused. "I'm trusting you, Frank, to level with me on this one, and by God you'd better come through!"

"You have my word."

As soon as the door closed behind him, Frank said to Shelley, "You can move now."

She blushed. "I thought if I didn't move a muscle you'd both forget I was here. I didn't want to be chased out."

"I didn't intend to chase you out. Are Bailey and Herbert out there?" he asked Barbara. When she nodded, he said, "Well, haul them in and we'll talk things over."

"Dad," she said, going to the door, "this will work for a time, but not in the long run. He'll be sore all over again and think you lied to him. I really tried to separate the issues, my case and the militia, but after today I'm back in all the way."

"You're not," he said flatly. "You're out all the way. When we get enough, Hogarth's in, and he'll break it and get the glory."

"We'll see."

"Bobby, you're out! If you get an idea, a glimmer, you tell me and I tell him if it's hard evidence. You have a trial coming and that's all you have on your plate. Plus, you're running out of time."

For a long moment they stared at each other. He was praying that she would accept his pronouncement, and she was thinking that she couldn't accept it after that day's event.

She turned away and opened the door to beckon Bailey and Herbert. Morgan rose lazily and followed them in.

They all arranged themselves in the chairs and on the sofa by the round table. Maria tapped and Barbara went to the door and brought in the coffee carafe. "Tell him what you told me," she said to Bailey as she put the coffee down on the table.

"I haven't had time to write it up, but my guy in Portland said the Learjet left at six this morning, returned at noon," Bailey said. He had his notebook open.

"Give it to me and I'll add it to the other flight reports," Barbara said.

He ripped out the page and handed it to her. She glanced at it: *12-23 Dep 6am, Arr 12n*

She blinked a time or two. December 23! Tomorrow was Christmas Eve with dinner at Frank's, along with Shelley, Alex, and Dr. Minnick. Then Christmas Day at home. The following week two meetings with the judge and prosecutor. Get her witness list together and in the hands of the prosecution. Decide about Mrs. Peel. Prepare her case. New Year's Eve, New Year's Day, and then court. She could feel time pressing as if steel bands were being tightened inch by inch.

Frank had been talking. She rose to put the slip of paper on her desk and focused on his words.

"So he doesn't really know anything yet, just enough to interest him, and to take the pressure off Barbara. I want to keep it that way."

"What else did you tell him?" Barbara asked from behind her desk.

"I already told you," Frank said a bit sharply. "Nothing. He was asking the wrong questions. I didn't have to tell him anything else. Ask Shelley."

"Sorry," Barbara said, sinking down into her desk chair. "Wool gathering for a minute. Now what?" That's why he kept Shelley, she thought then. A witness to confirm that he had not sold the farm or something. She hated the idea that he had thought he needed a witness, but she had to admit, she might have doubted his word without it. His determination to protect her would override his natural impulse to stick to the truth.

"From here on out, no more walking around," Frank said. "And for God's sake, no argument about it."

She nodded. "No argument. I'll get a treadmill."

"Maybe a squirrel cage with one of those wheels to run on," Bailey said. "Mind?... "

He eyed the bar and she nodded. He rose and made his slouching way to the bar.

"Bailey," Frank said, "I think you should start reporting to me at my office, keep your visits here scarce. Just in case they're watching. They know about Herbert and nothing's to change where he's concerned."

"Dad, what will it take to go to the FBI and or Homeland Security, to say nothing about ATF?"

"One solid piece of evidence," he said. "Which is in short supply."

"Right," she said. "We want them in raid mode, not in asking-polite-questions mode. One whiff of an official investigation and I suspect all of Polson's McMansions will revert to playhouses for the rich and famous."

They talked about schedules for the coming days. Barbara's office would be closed from December 24 until January 2. "I'll work here, of course," she said, "but no official business."

Frank nodded. His office would be on much the same schedule.

"Bailey," Barbara said then, "I want you to provide Dad with a driver, someone to keep him company in those empty offices until this is over. On me," she added before Frank could shout an objection.

She met his indignant gaze with her own and it held for a moment, until he nodded very slightly and relaxed back in his chair. "*Touché*," he said under his breath.

Presents had been wrapped and some were on the round table, the rest in a festive shopping bag for Barbara to take home with her. The shoebox of pictures Ashley had given her was by the shopping bag. She had not opened it yet. Homework, she decided. She had chased Maria as soon as the wrapping was done, and Shelley minutes later. Now she sat at her desk putting papers in their proper folders. She glanced at Bailey's note from that day and opened the folder with the rest of his flight information and she stopped moving.

"My God!" she whispered. "It's been under my nose all this time!"

She pushed aside folders and loose papers, opened her pad to a clean sheet and began to note the dates that the Learjet had flown. After she had them all, she closed that folder and found the one she had made for the sermons, and her own compilation of the Bible verses that had been referenced. Minutes later she sat back and stared at her results: two columns of dates with lines crossing from one column to the other, matching numbers. Not all the dates had connecting lines, but many did have them. She rubbed her eyes and looked again to make sure, then she called Frank.

"Dad, I think I have something real," she said. "I'm coming over right now."

"Do you know what time it is?" he said sharply.

She looked at her watch. Ten minutes before six. "I'll eat a peanut butter sandwich there," she said, "and I'll call Darren and tell him he and Todd are on their own. See you in a few minutes." Without giving him time to argue she disconnected.

Twenty minutes later she was in Frank's kitchen taking off her jacket, and he looked as angry as she had ever seen him. "Cool down, Dad," she said. "I can't help it. Things keep falling into my lap. What am I supposed to do? Close my eyes and pretend I don't see them?"

"You folks want to go to the study and talk, I can put together some dinner," Herbert said.

"No way," Barbara said. "I think you're going to be involved in whatever we decide to do. We'll talk right here."

"I was getting ready to make lamb chops," Frank growled. "There's not enough for three."

"If it's all right with you, Mr. Holloway, I probably can rustle up something."

"Knock it off, both of you," Barbara snapped. "Herbert, do whatever you want. You can listen while you do it. And, Dad, please sit down and let me show you something."

She brought out the legal pad with her columns and sat at the table. With obvious reluctance Frank sat by her. "These are the dates that the Learjet has flown, sometimes with a bunch of guys, sometimes not. And the second column lists the references to the Bible that shows up in those sermons. Except they aren't references at all, they are dates. That's what we missed. Forget the chapter, just look at the numbers—10:15 for example, and think October fifteenth. The New Testament correlates with the times the jet flew without the militia guys, and the Old Testament corresponds with the times it took a gang out there and brought them back." She traced the crisscrossing lines as she spoke.

"Also," she said, "there's the matter of who puts those date in the sermons. Why would anyone at the Chateau have a copy of Morgan's sermons in the first place? I think they get them ahead of time, add the dates and the talking points, and send them back via personal messenger."

Frank made a noncommittal sound and she continued.

"Remember what Paul O'Reilly said, that sometimes Drake Wallenstein takes someone with him and is gone for three days. What if he goes because that jet brought in weapons, and they collect them for distribution to the other bullet-point men on those lists?" She paused while Frank studied her dates and the connecting lines. After a moment he leaned back in his chair frowning.

"Good speculation," he said at length, "but not good enough. Theoretical, hypothetical, suspicious, but not hard evidence."

"I know that," she said impatiently. "But we know they go somewhere for three or four days and it could be one day to drive to the Chateau, one or two days to load up, get orders or something, one day to return. They aren't out joyriding. What if we can intercept a truck on the way home and get hard evidence?" she said. "I think I know when that truck will make its next three-day trip."

"How do you know?"

"It's in that sermon we collected at the train station. Matthew 12:27. December twenty-seventh."

Silently Frank rose and crossed the kitchen to pick up a bottle of wine and glasses. He returned to his chair and poured wine, then said, "I'm going to call Bailey and get him over here after dinner." He looked at the dates and lines again. "We'll have to get Milt involved, let him make the bust, if one's to be made. What if that truck is empty, or loaded with potatoes?"

"Then Hogarth falls on us like a ton of bricks. But what if it's loaded with AK forty-sevens? Or explosives? Or automatic handguns?"

Frank lifted his glass as she raised hers. They touched glasses and drank.

At ten thirty that night Frank said, "Milt won't search that truck without probable cause. You heard him today. Illegal search and seizure makes whatever he finds inadmissible."

"Mind if I suggest something?" Herbert said.

"Please do," Barbara said.

"Takes Morgan," he said and twisted around in his chair.

They were at the kitchen table with a map spread out on it. Whatever signal he gave to Morgan was too quick and too subtle for Barbara to catch, but the dog was on his feet instantly, his hair bristling. He began to bark at the stove. The two cats that had been under the table rose and stalked from the room with their tails upright. Morgan didn't stop barking until Herbert signaled again.

"Way I figure it, a dog trained to bark at the first whiff of drugs might do the trick. Can't make him stop neither, until a door is opened and the drugs get found. Door, box, truck, don't make no difference to that there dog, he just keeps on a barking until he's satisfied."

Barbara looked at him in awe, then at the dog with the same kind of awe. "Wow, so they don't find drugs, but they find guns, but they had probable cause and the dog made a mistake. Happens all the time."

"And Hogarth calls in Homeland Security and ATF, maybe FBI, and the two guys in the truck are held incommunicado for quite a spell while they work it all out," Bailey said with a nod. "That should do it." He looked at the map. "Now for where it has to happen."

"Get the make of the truck, license plates, and make sure we have the right one, that it's Drake Wallenstein and not someone else," Barbara said. "That has to be the first step. We don't know for sure when he'll take off, or even if he'll take off on the twenty-seventh, maybe a day before, or the next after."

Bailey nodded. "I'll have that truck, any truck they use, under surveillance from the time it leaves home base until Hogarth steps into the picture."

There were details to be worked out and Bailey said he would tend to them. Good enough, Barbara thought, considering the smooth operation he had set up in the train station in Portland. "One more thing," she said. "Hogarth. How do we make sure he's on the scene without giving it away that the whole thing is a setup?"

"He'll know it was a setup after the fact," Frank said. "And that's how we have to keep it. After the fact won't matter. We have a day or two. I'll come up with something. He'll be there."

That was good enough, too, Barbara knew. Frank could manage Hogarth. She pushed her chair back. "Let's call it a day, unless there's more to be discussed."

"I'm ready to hit the hay," Bailey said. He folded the map. "I'll be in touch, but who do I get in touch with?"

Frank gave Barbara a long look, then shrugged. He never lingered over lost causes and didn't this time. "Whoever is available," he said. "It's all in the family."

Chapter 26

Christmas Eve dinner was beautiful: a leg of lamb, bundles of blanched asparagus wrapped in prosciutto that had been crisped in a hot oven, a tangy mint salsa with cranberries, shredded beet salad on Boston lettuce leaves... Festive, colorful, delicious, but what Barbara appreciated most was that Dr. Minnick had started Todd talking about his Washington trip, and Todd was more than willing to go on at length.

"Those senators just like to hear themselves talk," Todd said scornfully. "Ten minutes of a speech, a pretty meaningless question… " He rolled his eyes.

Darren laughed. "That was part of it, not all. Some of them were taking it seriously."

"Maybe," Todd said.

Frank began a story about a time he had testified about something or other, and Barbara was free to return to her inner ordering of the details of the case she was trying to put together.

Herbert brought out a tray of Christmas cookies. Shelley gasped and said, "It looks like you raided a French bakery! They're gorgeous!"

"My mom used to bake for weeks before Christmas," Herbert said. "She'd put a dime in about a dozen cookies and you never knew which ones, so you had to sort of keep eating. Maybe not real good mothering according to modern times, but, man oh man, could she bake cookies!"

"A thousand calories a bite," Barbara said before biting into one.

They lingered over dessert, Grand Marnier and coffee, but finally it was time to don the aprons Frank provided and clean up the dishes.

After Shelley and Alex left with Dr. Minnick, Barbara said, "Dad, I'd love to sit by the fire and just visit, but… "

"I know. You put on a pretty good show at being present most of the time, by the way. Now, off you go. Try to get some sleep."

It was late. No Santa yet, Barbara thought, standing and stretching. She had gone to bed with Darren and after a final kiss had left him there. Now, wearing a robe, she was going over the crime scene pictures again. Not the ideal way to spend Christmas Eve, she told herself on the way to the kitchen to nuke a cup of coffee.

She returned to her chair near the fireplace and picked up the last picture she had been studying. A shot of the office, taken from the desk area, showing the door standing open, the hallway beyond. Then a different angle that included Travis sprawled on the floor unconscious, blood under his head, a handgun several feet from him.

Something, Barbara thought, studying the picture. She searched for a different angle and this one showed much the same scene, taken from a point on the opposite side of the room near the windows, apparently. The bookshelves were in it, Travis on the floor, the door standing open.

She put it down with a sigh. That's what the jurors would see and there was nothing she could do about it. Gazing at the fire, she visualized that bookshelf in Peel's office. Five or six very dull-looking books, she remembered, but she could not recall any titles. She returned to the pictures and found the few that included the shelf of books. Why such heavy bookends for so few books? Using a magnifying glass she tried to read the titles, but she could make out only a few letters. She put that picture aside. Bailey work, or his photographer's work.

Something Frank had said about Hogarth came to mind. *He was asking the wrong questions.* She blinked hard, got up to go for a glass of water, and thought about the questions she had been asking of the photographs, the various statements she had read. "I've been asking the wrong questions," she whispered at the sink and forgot the water as she hurried back to the living room to start asking the right questions.

"Did you get any sleep at all?" Darren asked the next morning.

"A bit. I'll nap later on today. Herbert, this is wonderful!" she said, trying to avoid Darren's scrutiny of her face. Herbert had made waffles with pecans and a luscious blueberry topping. She smiled brightly at him and Darren both.

Darren patted her hand. "Sure you'll nap. That's going to be the day. I couldn't wait, or rather I should say Todd couldn't wait, so I gave him the Kindle. He's off downloading books."

"Good. As soon as he shows his face, I'll give him the gift card." It was for one hundred dollars at Amazon.

"And then off to his mother's for the next four days," Darren said. "I'll stop by the clinic for a few minutes on my way home."

"I'll be right here," she said.

They left together, with Todd carrying a red shopping bag filled with gifts for his mother and his other family. As soon as they were gone, Barbara went to the living room to start on the shoebox of pictures from Arlie's childhood and youth.

She had just opened it when Frank called. "Merry Christmas!" he said. "The birds left the nest and are on I-5 heading north. Thought you'd want to know."

"Drake Wallenstein and one other?"

"Yes indeed. And my nephew Alan is going to be a houseguest for the next few days, looks like."

Frank was an only child, there was no nephew, and Alan McCagno was Bailey's most trusted operative. Barbara breathed a sigh of relief. "Give him my regards."

"We'll be off to Sylvia's later on," Frank said, still in his jovial mood. "God, I hope she forgot presents this time."

Sylvia and Joe Fenton always had a few people, fifty or so, for cocktails on Christmas Day, and a few of them stayed for dinner, including Frank. One year she had given him a statuette of a voluptuous naked woman. "What on earth are you going to do with it?" Barbara had asked, staring at it in amazement. "Oh, I'll pack it up and stash it away in the basement with some other things," he had said. "The day you inherit everything it will become your problem, not mine."

She was smiling when she disconnected. God alone knew what all he had stashed away in his basement. She suspected that it would be wise to be alone when she began to unearth his treasures.

Her smile faded as she thought about what was happening. As soon as that truck got on I-5, a phone call had been made to two people in Portland who left instantly for Pendleton, to be there working as videographers long before the truck arrived. They would be at a location where they could get a video of the truck turning onto the private road to the Chateau and beyond, and they would be wrapped up and ready to leave as soon as that truck reappeared in town a day or two later. Ostensibly they were doing a documentary of the distress in many communities hard hit by the recession. They would stay with the truck until it reached the 105 exit, when a different car would pick it up and follow into Eugene.

If she had been right about the dates, the jet would fly to the Chateau the next day or the day after that and Drake Wallenstein and his companion would be on hand to do whatever they did. She followed that with sharp reminder, muttered under her breath, "That has nothing to do with the case I'm preparing."

She reached into the shoebox of old photographs.

Other people's pictures were so boring, she thought later, turning over another one of people she didn't know and had no interest in. Many of the pictures were out of focus, some faded, some with such poor lighting that faces were shadowed beyond recognition, or else in a glare of light that made their eyes glow strangely. A modest house, a church, a group of kids playing ball, Arlie as a tot, a boy about seven or eight, slightly older, his parents in various pictures. She drew in a breath and looked closely at the latest one she had picked up.

Written across the bottom were the words *Arlie's first deer, from start to finish*. He was on one side of a hanging deer, his father on the other. They were both holding rifles. His father was smiling, but Arlie looked sullen. The deer looked dead. Arlie's father was wearing a gun belt.

Using the magnifying glass she could make out a handgun in the holster. It looked like those she had seen in many westerns, or used by actors playing Russian roulette. An old-fashioned six-shooter, a Colt .45, the kind of gun that was used to shoot Joseph Peel to death.

She leaned back in her chair. Ashley said Arlie Morgan had taken guns and fishing gear. That gun? Those rifles? She put the photograph aside with the others for Bailey.

All afternoon she fumed over what she hadn't brought home with her, items locked away in her office that she could use now, and she alternated between telling Herbert that they had to go to her office, and telling herself that it was Christmas, a time to stay home, to let Herbert stay there and do whatever he was doing in the kitchen. She paced restlessly up and down stairs, down to the den, to the upstairs bedroom, back to the living room.

Every time that other scenario playing out entered her mind, she tried to banish it again, without any notable success. How far had the truck gotten? What if they were just going to dear old Aunt Maud's house to deliver a fruitcake? What if they lost the tail and headed for somewhere else, not the Chateau? She, Bailey, all of them could have messed up so easily, assuming they knew something they didn't.

Not my case! She wanted to scream. Forget it for now! She was in the living room when Darren entered with a tray. He put it on the coffee table. There was champagne in a cooler, a crock of pâté, Melba toast, and a bunch of red grapes.

Instantly contrite, Barbara put aside her legal pad. "God, Darren, I'm sorry. I've spoiled your Christmas." When she stood, he reached for her.

"Having you here, knowing you'll be here tomorrow, the next day, next year, you're the best present I ever had. And keep in mind I've seen you in this state more than once. And I know damn well that you were in something about like this state when you saved my ass." He kissed her deeply, then drew back and pointed to the tray. "But I also insist that for the next few hours, happy hour now and then dinner, you fold your wings and join me."

CHAPTER 27

BARBARA WAS IN her office early the next morning, and within minutes of her arrival there, Shelley tapped on the door and peeked in. "Hi," Barbara said, "you're supposed to be off this week."

Shelley looked embarrassed. "I have a few things—"

"Never mind," Barbara said, motioning her to come in. "I'm really glad you're here. There's something I'd like you to do."

"Great! Tell me."

"I want the name of the accounting firm Peel worked with for the church. It could be that the easiest way to find out is to call the church secretary and simply ask. If you hit a wall that way, I'm afraid you're in for a hell of a lot of phone calls. Can do?"

"Sure. You want me to talk to the accountant?"

"Yes. How good a bookkeeper was Peel, ever any problem with his bookkeeping, things like that. And I may want the accountant as a defense witness, depending on the answers to those questions. I'm assuming that Peel was very good, and hope I'm right about that."

Shelley looked so pleased that Barbara had to smile. "Bailey's coming around this morning, and I have to talk to Travis today. Tomorrow I'll be at the courthouse for the pretrial meeting. If I can get that name and add it to my witness list before that meeting, that would be good. I'll want a subpoena for Mrs. Peel. If the accountant needs a subpoena, we'll have to go that way there, too."

Shelley nodded. "I can take care of it. Anything else?"

"That's more than enough."

Bailey arrived a few minutes later.

"Are the travelers still on track?" she asked.

"Yep. They made a beeline to Pendleton and the private road. The jet took off this morning. Right on schedule, or off by a day. Who knows?"

"Right," she said. "Who knows? Meanwhile I have some pictures I want worked on." She spread them out on her desk. "This one, the deer's wounds. Where was it shot, and was a finishing shot put in its head. It looks like it might have been shot in the eye." Bailey examined it with a sour look. "Then this one," she said, pointing. It was one of Peel's desks, showing the computer and the closed keyboard shelf. "I want a close-up of it." She pointed to the next one, where Travis lay on the floor. "Is there a head wound visible? Another close-up. And this one. Can your guy embellish it enough to make out those book titles? I can get a few letters, not enough. Maybe he can." There were a few more, and Bailey's scowl deepened as she told him what she needed for each one.

"Jeez, Barbara, it's a holiday week. He could be off skiing for all I know."

"Or he could be home by the fire. There's someone out there who can do the job."

"Yeah, yeah. The whole world works right through the holidays." He didn't look happy, but he seldom looked happy about anything. He put the pictures in an envelope, closed his notebook, and ambled to the door. He paused there and, suddenly awkward and even embarrassed, he said, "Hannah said thanks for those croissants. They came in the mail a couple of days ago. They're good." He left swiftly as soon as he finished.

She was grinning when he left. *Good?* she thought. They were wonderful! A friend had given her a dozen frozen croissants years before. Thawed overnight, baked in the morning, they were the closest thing to breakfast in Paris she could imagine. Good? she thought again, shaking her head.

A little later, entering the jail conference room, she wished she could skip her own next task. She was dreading her talk with Travis. She couldn't let him go to trial without being fully informed of his right to a plea bargain, and it always implied a lack of faith in her case, but it had to be done.

He rejected it reflexively. "No! I won't say I did it! I didn't shoot Peel. They're lying!"

"I know they are," she said. "I hope I can break through that wall of lies. What I can do is try to raise a reasonable doubt, enough of a doubt to keep the jury from convicting you but, Travis, I can't guarantee it. That's what you have to know. I can't guarantee anything."

"I know that. Promise me something, Barbara," he said with a sidelong look at her. "Just promise you'll get my father. Just promise me that no matter how the verdict goes, you won't let up on him. That's all I'm asking."

He still stiffened when he mentioned his father or heard his name, but it was no longer a total change in his attitude, his posture. He no longer looked afraid, and no more miserable than any young man would be whose father testified for the prosecution against his son. Good enough, Barbara thought with satisfaction. He would do.

She held out her hand. He kept it for a few seconds as he said, "He's evil, Barbara. And he's dangerous, crazy and dangerous. Be careful. But take him down any way you can."

"We'll take him down, Travis. I promise."

When she drew back, she opened her legal pad. "One more thing," she said. "Did you ever see any guns in your father's house, either in Portland or down here?"

He shook his head. "What kind of guns?"

"Your mother said he boxed up a couple of rifles, a shotgun, and some handguns when your grandfather died. Did you ever see any of those guns? Or a box they could have been in?"

He spread his hands about three feet apart. "This long? That's not a regular cardboard carton. It wouldn't have been in the condo. Not enough storage space for a box like that without it getting in the way. I never saw such a box."

"Do something for me," she said. "Is there an attic in the residence here?" He nodded. "Okay. Take your time. Close your eyes and visualize the attic space and what's in it."

He looked skeptical, but closed his eyes for a moment, then shook his head again. "Nothing was up there. I used to sneak up there with a comic book. Just dust."

"Okay. Try it with the basement. What's down in the basement? Washer, dryer? What else? Sketch the whole area, appliances, furnace, whatever is there."

Again, he closed his eyes for several seconds, then reached for the legal pad. He drew a rectangle and began drawing boxes. "Washer and dryer, here. On this wall, a sink with counters on the sides. Ironing board. Back wall, shelves with some jars and pans no one ever used. Stairs. Furnace. On this wall there were cardboard boxes. I looked in some of them after Mother left. The books she couldn't read to us anymore. *Winnie the Pooh*, *Alice in Wonderland*, Dr. Seuss, like that. One box had her things in it: a little pillow she made for June, yarn, knitting needles. A hairbrush, a couple of dresses… " His voice trailed off and a faraway expression crossed his face. "I was embarrassed," he mumbled. "I stopped going through her things. I just closed the boxes up and never opened them again."

He started to put down the pencil, stopped, and frowned. "Wait a minute," he said in a strained voice. "There was a wooden box under the other boxes. They were stacked on top of it." He held up his hands about three feet apart. "I never moved the boxes on top of it, never opened it, but it was long enough, and it was wood."

"Did you see a lock on it?"

He shook his head. "I didn't look for one. I thought… I was afraid it was more of her personal stuff." Then he blurted out, "I was afraid I'd find her wedding dress, or nightgowns, stuff like that." Startled, he gave her a sharp look. "He had guns? All those years he had guns?"

"I don't know. I just know he took guns from your grandfather's house."

That afternoon Barbara got a piece of oversized poster board from her closet and drew a line down the center. On one side she printed *Morgan*, and on the other she printed *Militia*. She was not certain she could separate the two enough, but she started. At a quarter to six she called Frank.

"Don't run for cover," she said when he answered. "I'm not going to disturb your dinner again. I would like to come over later, though, and I want to bring Darren. I want to tell him what we're up to, and I have something to show you. Eight? Eight thirty? Will you even be home?"

"Make it seven and I'll feed the lot of you," he said. "But don't expect a feast."

"Deal, and thanks, Dad."

"You just can't help it," Barbara said at dinner. "Whenever you cook, it's a feast. This is wonderful."

He had made fettuccini with salmon and spinach, a huge salad, and bread from his favorite bakery. Mashed strawberries swirled into a creamy Greek yogurt was the perfect dessert for it all.

"If you guys want to start your conference, I volunteer for KP duty," Alan said. He was wearing a U of O sweatshirt, jeans and running shoes, and he looked like a perennial college student who never quite finished his courses and graduated.

"I'll help Alan," Herbert said. "Won't take us more then a couple of minutes."

"Join us when you're done," Barbara said. "You're both in the cast for tomorrow. I'll be filling Darren in about what's going on."

In the living room a minute later Barbara said to Darren, "You know I'm working on the case against Travis, and I told you there's more involved. It's a lot more. A whole militia more. Headquarters out near Pendleton, a big complex owned by the Polson Corporation, one of the farthest-right groups to be found on the face of the earth, with one of the world's richest men at the helm. We know or think we know they're outfitting militias in the northwest, outfitting and training, getting ready for Armageddon possibly. When I went to Pendleton to talk to the doctor who treated a suicide, she made a positive identification of June Morgan, who had been held a prisoner at the complex for two years."

Darren held up his hand, staring at her with a fixed gaze. "You went out there alone, knowing about them? For God's sake! You let me go off to Washington without a clue?" His voice was low and almost musical, the way it became when he was angry.

"That's why," she said. "I knew you'd worry. And I wasn't alone. Alan, Herbert, and Bailey were with me. It had to be done, and I did it."

"And ended up needing a bodyguard," he said.

"Well, it's done," she said reasonably. "Now, for what we're planning." She turned to Frank. "Is Hogarth on for tomorrow?"

"He'll be on hand," Frank said. He had seen the vein throbbing in Darren's temple and could admire his self-control, the way he had not raised his voice, but in fact lowered it. Not deliberately, Frank suspected, but unconsciously, possibly after an eruption or two in the distant past that had taught him not to let go again. But the strain was there, and Barbara could be enough to try Job's patience, he could personally admit. One time he had cautioned Darren that living with a defense attorney could be stressful. Darren had said living without her would be more stressful. And there it was, Frank told himself. For both of them, that summed it up.

While pondering his own thoughts, he was also watching Barbara prop a poster on an end table.

"My flow chart," she said. "What we learned about the militia and when, and how it corresponds to what I was uncovering for my own case. They really can't be entirely separated, Dad. If all goes well tomorrow and we find a cache of arms in that truck, Homeland Security, ATF, FBI, whoever covers it, will need a few reasons for our suspicions at the very least. I have to be there when explanations are given in whatever truncated form they take. Face it, Dad, I'm a better liar than you are."

"No lying," he snapped. "Federal offense."

"I misspoke. I won't lie at all, but neither will I reveal all I know. I have a client to protect and I can't reveal the complexity of my case before the trial. It's that simple."

"You're going to be there when they open a truck and find weapons?" Darren said in that strange, low tone.

"Nope. I'm going to be in Judge John Humphrey's chambers," she said. "But I have to be there when the dust settles and they come around for answers. I suggest you make it here, Dad. Invite them over here where we can all drink coffee or tea and have a civilized conversation."

Reluctantly he nodded. Whether a civilized conversation, time would tell.

"Okay," Barbara said. She stopped and waved Herbert and Alan on in. "Have a seat. Party's just starting. Herbert, it would be good if those two guys in the truck didn't get a glimpse of you tomorrow. They'll talk to a lawyer eventually, and if they describe you, it will be a giveaway that we're onto the whole scene, not just an isolated bust of a couple of gunrunners. Morgan's enough to make them a little suspicious, but a drug-sniffing dog isn't quite the same as identifying his master."

Herbert nodded. "Me and Bailey, we'll work something out. They won't see hide or hair of me."

"Good." Then, pointing to the chart she had drawn, she explained, "I put incidents in chronological order as much as I could—events, discoveries that relate only to my case, and what we've found out about the militias. The most interesting point is the first one on the left. The arrival of DiPalma and Rostov, weeks before John Varagosa was mutilated. Why arrive when they did?" There was no answer from her audience. "We know this whole thing has been going on for a number of years, long enough ago to establish Morgan as a screwball preacher that no sane person could take seriously. But his bodyguard and driver didn't come on the scene until nearly three years ago. Maybe a reliable pilot wasn't needed until then. Maybe heavy-duty weapons weren't being delivered and flown out to the Chateau until then. If that maybe becomes even a little more of a certainty, it could mean that we blundered into it during the end play. It could mean," she said slowly, "that they've been training militias for years, and that now they're supplying them with weaponry to carry out whatever they've been planning."

She paused a moment, than added, "That's something I have to tell ATF, Homeland Security, or the FBI agent tomorrow. Maybe they won't have a lot of years to work out a plan."

"And that makes it a lot hairier if you leave out very much," Frank said.

CHAPTER 28

AT TWO THE next day Barbara was admitted to Judge John Humphrey's chambers. Assistant District Attorney Jeffrey Wharton was already there. They had been on opposite sides in court before and while Jeff was a tough, smart opponent who fought hard for the prosecution, out of court he was charming and affable. They shook hands and she greeted the judge who was seated behind his desk. Humphrey was ready for retirement, had been ready for several years, but the shortage of judges and the backlog of pending cases made leaving a problem, a burden he reportedly was not ready to accept. He was an honorable man, he often said, deeply devoted to his duty as a judge, to the system of justice, and to the constitution. He kept hanging in there as a necessity, not a preference.

Heavyset with a double chin, wide blue eyes, white hair that was straight and a little too long, he used reading glasses and kept them on a gold chain, allowing them to dangle except when needed for close work. He fingered them, twirled them, polished them, or did something else with them whenever he wanted a little time to think before speaking. That day he eyed Barbara bleakly, nodding as she said good afternoon to him. "Make yourselves as comfortable as you can," he said motioning toward chairs facing his desk.

The room was almost as bleak as he was. When the new courthouse was completed, judges and staff members moved in, he had not brought his personal items: photographs of his wife of forty-four years, four grown children, many grandchildren. The furnishings, though, had been there for decades, first in the old courthouse, now in the new one, and they should have been discarded rather than moved. Very worn and somewhat faded, the upholstery might have been purple when new, but time had worked its magic, and the coverings had turned to a muddy brown. Springs with too little padding made sitting more than a few minutes an endurance test. The room was well lighted with wide high windows, but the day was overcast, with heavy cloud cover and a threat of snow or freezing rain by nightfall, and the light entering the room was dull and cold.

The judge began to inform the two attorneys of the kind of trial he intended to conduct. "There will be no theatrics, no tricks, no presentation of assumptions as if they were facts. Every statement must be verifiable by evidence or it will not be admitted… "

Barbara had heard this before, and her thoughts were with the developing action that would start just about at that time.

"What we should do," Frank said to Hogarth, "is find a place to park where we can keep an eye on that painter's truck. When he pulls out, follow him and keep close." They were in Hogarth's car on a side street not far from the entrance to Interstate 5. Herbert's truck with the dented right side and the sign *Quality Painting* was parked at the curb a short distance ahead of them.

"Frank, so help me God if this is a wild goose chase, one of your schemes that blow up in my face, I'll press charges this time. So help me God!" He pulled in at the curb.

"Now, Milt. We've both been around a long time and we know things don't always work out exactly as planned. We just do what we can and hope for the best." He glanced at Hogarth, who was already red-faced as if the blowup he feared had already occurred. "Milt, if this pans out, and if Homeland Security, FBI, ATF, whoever else gets involved, it might be a good idea to say you got a tip and decided to follow a truck until there was reason enough to pull it over. A reason always comes along. Speeding, rolling stop, no signal at a turn. You know how that goes. And when you pulled it over, to your surprise a DEA-trained dog set up a ruckus and you were compelled to open the truck. Not a bad story, considering that you did get a tip. From me. And there will be a dog, and so on."

Hogarth looked apoplectic. "It's a setup and you're dragging me into it! You've gone too fucking far this time. The deal's off—"

Frank touched his arm and pointed out the windshield. "He's moving. Showtime, Milt. Let's go."

Up and down the interstate, it seemed that at every entrance and exit ramp construction was being done. Bright-orange cones were closing off lanes, opening others, men with Slow signs, or Stop signs were on duty, and traffic was crawling. A worker in an orange vest and hardhat held up a Stop sign when Herbert's truck reached the on-ramp to the highway. Watching the highway, Frank saw a closed truck drive by, closely followed by a decrepit flatbed farm truck with many bales of hay. One more car passed before the worker with the sign motioned the paint truck forward. Hogarth was waved onward after it.

A blinking lighted sign advised that the right lane was closed ahead, and beyond the sign, cones were already in place. The closed truck was in the right lane, but the flatbed had already moved into the left lane, and when the closed truck tried to maneuver in, the flatbed sped up just enough to prevent that. Then the hay on the flatbed began to slide sideways, and the momentum brought it crashing on and in front of the closed truck, making the flatbed swerve wildly, straighten, then swerve again more wildly. It swung around in such a way that the rear of the flatbed was directly in front of the closed truck, and they both came to a halt.

The paint truck pulled into the right lane behind the closed truck and stopped there.

"You'd best use your flasher, don't you think?" Frank asked. "And you might want to get in front of that flatbed and call for backup. Not a good idea to get the staties involved. Maybe a couple of your own detectives, a few uniforms."

Hogarth was cursing in a steady, bitter stream as he pulled over in front of the flatbed. Alan, with a baseball cap on backward, and ear buds dangling, an iPod in his jacket pocket, had already jumped out of the flatbed and was yelling at the two men who had scrambled from the closed truck. They were screaming obscenities back at him.

Hogarth used the car phone to call for backup, then yanked his door open and got out to stomp over to the cursing men. He flashed his badge and demanded drivers' licenses, bellowing for everyone to shut up.

Trailing behind Hogarth Frank watched his old friend at work. Some of the construction men came running with more cones to keep traffic moving past the scene of the wreck. Within minutes, the first of Hogarth's backup appeared with sirens blaring, flashers on. The second car was there very soon afterward, then a third with uniforms. Now, a dozen police officers, the three involved in the wreck still yelling at one another, Frank, an interested bystander, and a couple of construction men all clustered near the two trucks and the scattered hay. Herbert and the shaggy dog Morgan got out of the painter's truck. Frank saw them, but apparently no one else did, as Alan continued to yell at the men from the other truck. They seemed to want to attack him and were being held back by uniformed policemen.

Herbert walked the dog to the closed truck, and was returning to his paint truck when Morgan began to bark.

"Goddamn it!" Hogarth shouted. "Shut that dog up!"

"He's acting like a DEA dog," Frank said. "Might be smelling drugs or something."

Hogarth snapped at one of uniformed officers, "Get back there and see what the goddamn dog's barking at and shut him up."

The uniformed man ran back to the truck, but Morgan didn't stop barking. Nor did the shouts of irate truck drivers stop. They were even louder, as if trying to be heard over the barking dog.

"You can't hold us! That idiot dumped a load of hay on us. I want that crap cleared away so we can go." The taller of the two men was in Hogarth's face.

Hogarth motioned two of his men over. "I want the keys to the truck, pat these two down and put them in two separate cars and keep them there."

"You can't do this! It's illegal! I'll have your ass for illegal search and seizure!"

A minute later they were in cars and Hogarth had the keys. Frank trailed along as Hogarth led the way to the rear of the truck, where Morgan was still barking at the door.

"I can't make that mutt stop," the officer said.

"Hold him back while we get those doors open," Hogarth snapped.

Gingerly the officer reached for Morgan, when suddenly the dog stopped barking, turned, and trotted away. Frank watched as he headed straight for the paint truck. The side door opened, and the dog jumped in. Frank nodded in appreciation. Of course Herbert would have a silent dog whistle. He turned his attention back to the truck as Hogarth unlocked the back doors and flung them open.

"Son of a bitch!" Hogarth said softly. Centered in the truck was a shoulder rocket launcher cradled on both sides by wooden boxes stacked nearly to the ceiling. He reached into the truck and lifted the top of one of the boxes to reveal AK-47 automatic rifles.

No one seemed to notice when the paint truck pulled around the wreck and joined the highway traffic. Frank suspected that Hogarth had noted it, but he had not interfered or said a word. The truck driver and his companion were taken away. Hogarth spent some time on his cell phone. When Frank suggested that since the rest was anticlimax, there was little reason for him to hang around in the cold, and maybe someone could give him a lift home, and swing by the courthouse on the way to collect Barbara. Hogarth nodded and gave one of his men orders to do that.

"Stay there," Hogarth said. "I'll come over and I don't know how many others will come with me. You and Barbara be there, and be ready to talk."

Barbara had been fuming in the law library for over an hour when her phone vibrated. She snatched it up when she saw that it was Frank.

"Dad? How did it go?"

"I'm fine," he said blandly. "I'm hitching a ride home with Detective Herb Jensen. We'll come by and give you a lift in ten minutes or so."

She felt her tension dissolve with his words. "Great! I'll be just inside the main entrance." She gathered up her things, checked her watch, then headed to the main lobby and the doors. Five minutes later the detective approached her and showed his identification.

"Ms. Holloway? Detective Jensen. I'm parked in an official-use-only reserved spot, so maybe we can hurry?"

"You bet, Detective Jensen." They hurried out and down the long flight of steps, to the parked car where Frank was seated in the front seat. After Jensen opened the back door for her, and as he hurried around to the driver's seat, Frank held up his index finger and thumb in the everything's-okay signal. He was smiling slightly.

At home again, Frank had built up a dying fire, and he had made a large pot of coffee. The fire felt good and the coffee was welcome. Detective Jensen had lingered in the kitchen until he received a phone call and left.

"Balanchine would have been proud," Frank said after he described the events on the interstate. "Choreography perfect. And now we wait for the proverbial shit to hit the fan and the questions start. It might take a while for them to get here. That's a real mess to clean up, and they might argue just a mite over who has jurisdiction. I suspect it's going to be Homeland Security and I hear that they can be tough to deal with. I'm going to call Martin and order dinner for all of us, whatever the specialty of the day is, to be delivered when I give the word after our guests leave. Why don't you tell Darren to come over here when he's ready?" At her nod he left the room to use his desk phone.

Herbert and Alan arrived together before anyone else showed up.

"Good work," Frank said to them both. "Alan, one day tell me how you managed to dump that hay at exactly the right time."

"Nothing to it," Alan said with a wide grin. "I had a switch to pull and the truck bed tilted just enough to send it sliding."

"Where's the wonderdog?" Barbara asked.

"Home," Herbert said. "He's plum worn out. We put the paint truck back in cold storage, and I'm using the SUV again and that's a good thing cause that rain's starting to freeze. I fed the cat."

When the doorbell sounded half an hour later, Frank said, "Make yourselves scarce until they're gone. I'll get the door."

"We'll be watching television in my room," Alan said.

Frank brought Hogarth and three other men back to the living room and introduced them to Barbara. "Philip Kyle from Homeland Security, Special Agent Roy Sunderland from the FBI, and Gary Strunk from the ATF. Gentlemen, my daughter, Barbara Holloway."

She shook hands with them and nodded to Hogarth, who was eyeing Thing One and Thing Two as if he expected them to attack without warning.

"Please, make yourselves comfortable," Frank said. "Would you like coffee? A soda? Wine?"

They all declined and took chairs grouped at the fireplace. Kyle was a middle-aged man with little hair and a worried, suspicious expression. He looked like a post office clerk handing out stamps or weighing packages, Barbara thought, someone who would be forgotten almost immediately after a meeting. Sunderland was what she had come to expect of FBI agents, fit looking, mid-forties, well dressed in shirt and tie, and sharp eyed. He had taken in at a glance the papers she had arranged on the coffee table. Strunk was tall and thin, a fidgety man with a body part in motion at all times apparently. When he sat down, his foot began to tap the carpet and he flexed his hands, relaxed, flexed them again.

"Gentlemen," she said when they were all seated, "I know that you have many questions for us, and I want to cooperate to the fullest extent possible, but I am also constrained by a pending case that could be jeopardized if I reveal certain details at this time."

"Ms. Holloway," Sunderland said smoothly, "you understand that our agency does not get involved in any way with local affairs, including murder cases. There is no need to withhold anything since we maintain strict confidentiality regarding the issues we take interest in."

"I do understand," she said, trying to be as smooth as he had been, "however, Lieutenant Hogarth is very much part of the local police department, and I fear that if his captain or the chief of police should demand a full account, he would be compelled to cooperate. Of course," she added, "that's as it should be, a well-maintained chain of command."

Hogarth's ruddy face color deepened to a brick red.

"I can tell you this much," Barbara said, "as soon as my case goes to trial and the trial is concluded, my father and I will share everything we know with you in detail. You do understand that he is my associate, don't you? Under the same constrictions that I am. And there is a condition that I insist we all agree to in advance. When we divulge everything we have learned, neither my father nor I will be acknowledged as whistle blowers, or informers, or referred to in any way as being connected to your operation, no matter what that future operation may be."

Kyle and Sunderland exchanged glances and Strunk examined his fingernails closely. Before one of them had a chance to speak, Barbara said, "I realize that you will have to consult others about the condition I'm imposing. That can wait for our next meeting. Tonight I am prepared to tell you as much as I can about what we have learned, and what we anticipate in the near future." It was easy to get their attention, she thought then, as they gazed at her with expressionless faces. Kyle's eyes had narrowed slightly, the only sign that he had any interest in what she had to say.

"First," she said, "we have a chronological listing of when a certain Learjet leaves the Ben Hadley Airport, a small airport that private planes often use, situated in Portland. And we know where the jet goes. It's a large compound south of Pendleton, owned by the Polson Corporation." The investigators, even Strunk, grew very still, perhaps held their breath, she thought, as she continued. "We have learned that at certain times when the jet flies out there, a truck also makes the trip to the complex and returns in three days, usually. At other times a group of men, ten to fourteen, we believe, are flown out there and they remain for up to two weeks, get flown back and return to their homes. We believe that a militia has been formed and training sessions occur on those longer stays, and arms are distributed on the short ones. Today settled our lingering doubts of the assumption we were making regarding the short trips. Until today all we had were suspicions and assumptions. Today we have verification."

"Who is your informant?" Sunderland demanded. "How did you gather this information?"

"No informant," she said. "We've been investigating my case for several months, and we have come up with some dates. I have a list of times the jet flew out, when it returned, when a truck unloaded a group of men, who departed on the plane, and when they came back. I have made copies of those times for you." She picked up papers from the table, glanced at them, and passed them around. "You can see the crossing lines, the double lines indicate the times the men were taken to the complex, and the other lines, as we verified today, are when arms were put in a truck to be taken somewhere else."

"What's this last date?" Strunk demanded. "One thirteen. There isn't a crossing line for it."

"I have reason to believe," she said, "that on or about January thirteenth, give or take a day or two, the militia men will be flown to the complex. If verified, the line will be a double line. It's an assumption, gentlemen, exactly as this day's events were informed by an assumption. I have no proof of what I'm telling you, only our assessment based on the intelligence we have gathered. Having the truck intercepted today could easily upset the schedule, especially if word leaks that more is involved than a case of two men working in the gun trade. If I were in your place, I would ask questions that make it clear that I believe they were running guns to a Mexican drug cartel for cold hard cash. Very likely they would repeat that to their attorney and he in turn would report it back to someone at the Polson compound."

The doorbell sounded and Frank stood. "If you'll excuse me a moment. That's probably our dinner guest. I'll show him to the study."

As he left, Sunderland said, "It could be that that's exactly what they're doing, running guns south of the border."

"So be it," she said. "Not my problem. If your men find a lot of guns and other weapons when you search those guys' premises, you might reexamine that assumption."

"What else do you have?" Kyle asked.

"The location of the Polson complex. And a few tidbits that we picked up here and there. They have a helicopter, a landing strip, probably other small planes, and it's been reported that they sometimes use heavy-duty artillery, for elephants no doubt. Their workers are imported from Mexico and they don't speak English. You may be interested in learning how we located the complex. It was through a computer program being developed by a Dr. Richard Chu at the University of Oregon, along with a senior high school student, whose idea it was, Todd Halvord. They had scant information, only weather reports for two days running, and a general description of a desert location. Also," she added forcefully, "they didn't have a clue about why we were interested in finding that place."

Finally Kyle had found something interesting enough to make a note about, she thought with satisfaction. A federal grant to continue the work would be good for Chu and for Todd, and it could prove useful in locating lost hikers, others lost in a wilderness, or even other sinister complexes.

Frank returned and nodded to Barbara. "He's in the study. And the report is that the roads are icing over pretty fast."

Barbara returned his nod and picked up the next set of papers. This was the map to the Polson complex. After handing out the maps, she pointed to hers, and said, "This looks like a rough track to nowhere, but actually it's passable, and it joins that private road to a ranch. It's how the truck gets in and out." She put the map down, and said, "One of the things that may prove interesting is the fact that Boris Rostov and Tony DiPalma, a bodyguard and a pilot, appeared on the scene not quite three years ago. It made us wonder if arms were starting to be distributed at that time. Again, pure speculation." She spread her hands. "And that, gentlemen, is all I'm prepared to confide in you at this time."

They objected, and she shook her head. "If the militia men actually keep that next date, I'll be busy with the upcoming trial, but it should conclude at about that same time. Then full disclosure."

"Ms. Holloway, please appreciate the fact that you have no right to withhold information in the investigation of what may be a matter of national security," Kyle said.

"Mr. Kyle, you and your associates have enough information in hand to initiate your investigation. No doubt, you'll have your people search the premises of the two men you apprehended today for additional weapons, and you'll track anyone who flies out to the complex, and keep them under surveillance. By that time I'll be done with my trial. Then we can talk again. I hope you'll inform us if our prediction proves true, but if you don't I'll understand."

There were more questions and objections to her answers and thinly veiled threats, until she finally said, "Gentlemen, I need little over ten days to see the conclusion of my trial. I've given you the basic information we have gathered, and after the trial I will be prepared to fill in the details, but the basic information won't change, and that information is enough for you to begin your own investigation."

After they were gone Frank said, "You damn near pushed them too far."

"Just to the edge, Dad. Just to the edge. I'll tell Darren it's safe to come out now. And maybe you can call Martin and tell him I'm starving and will settle for bologna sandwiches."

As they walked together to his study, he said, "Now, put all this out of mind and concentrate on your trial."

"Absolutely," she said. Forget hit men and two bodyguards, and a militia armed with a shoulder rocket launcher, unknown stocks of other weaponry, and a billionaire footing the bill.

✦

CHAPTER 29

SO IT ALWAYS began, Barbara thought that morning. Arriving in court dead tired, sleep-deprived, sluggish, as soon as the trial began, a surge of adrenaline rushed through her and she was refreshed to the point of hyper-awareness.

When Travis was brought in to take his place at the defense table she told him he looked spiffy in his nice gray suit. He attempted a smile. She gave the thumbs-up to Ashley, whom she had told to wear any color but black, and nothing flashy. Ashley was handsome and understated in a blue pantsuit.

Jury selection was relatively swift and as satisfactory as she could have expected, considering that the bookkeeper for a church had been the victim of homicide. Seven men, five women would decide the fate of Travis Morgan. Ranging in age from a twenty-four-year-old unemployed male to a seventy-one-year-old retired female librarian, the jurors included two Hispanics, two Blacks and eight Caucasians, a fair sampling of Eugene residents.

Jeff Wharton's opening statement was brief. Mr. Peel had been working at his desk when Travis Morgan arrived to visit his father… Nothing new was added, and from the expressions on various faces in the jury box, nothing more was needed.

Barbara's statement was even briefer. Travis had not killed anyone, had never fired a gun, and there were more questions to be asked and answered than the prosecution had indicated… The lunch break followed.

After lunch, Wharton's first witness was Detective Louis Grayling, in his forties, a ten-year veteran of the police department, eight years as a photographer in the homicide unit. If he was like all the other police officers who had ever testified, he hated being there.

"Just tell us in your own words exactly what you did when you arrived," Wharton instructed him.

"Yes sir. My partner and I arrived at seven thirty-eight. We found several people in the hall near the front door, and my partner escorted them to the living room to get their names and statements while I went into the room where the shooting had occurred. Two additional detectives arrived approximately one minute after we did and they secured the premises. Mr. Rostov was in that room standing guard over a man on the floor, and I asked him to join the others in the living room. We ascertained that Mr. Peel was dead and that the defendant was unconscious. I was engaged with taking crime scene photographs of the entire room, the hall, and the living room."

One by one Wharton introduced photographs and the detective said he had taken them.

Wharton finished with him soon after that and Barbara rose.

"Detective Grayling, when you took your photographs did you move anything to get a clearer picture?"

"No. I didn't touch a thing."

"Was Travis Morgan in your way, impeding your access to the room?" She showed him the photograph of Travis sprawled on the floor.

"No. I just stepped around him."

She introduced the enlargement of the desk. "Is this is the same desk, the same computer, the same everything?" she asked. Grayling said yes.

"To your knowledge was the computer turned on?"

"I don't know," he said.

"Was the keyboard shelf pushed all the way in, as it appears in the photograph?"

"Yes. That's how it was when I took the picture."

"Why did you take photographs of the hall and the living room?"

"There were some drops of blood in both areas," he said.

She nodded and said no further questions.

The lead forensics detective was next, and his statements were very brief. They had collected the gun as evidence. Only Mr. Peel's fingerprints were on the desk and chair, and the defendant's fingerprints were on the gun. He identified the handgun his unit had collected. It had been fired recently and there were still five bullets in the chamber. It was in a plastic evidence bag and was not passed on to the jury, but Wharton held it up to show them. He had the detective identify the bookend that had been used to subdue Travis. It was in its own plastic bag.

When Barbara rose to cross-examine the witness, she introduced three more photographs from the crime scene and then showed them to the detective. "Is this where you found the bookend?" she asked. It was on an end table, blood clearly visible on it, and on a drop on the floor near the table.

"Yes," he said.

"Where was it?"

He said in the living room, and when she asked about the drop of blood on the floor he said, "We collected a sample. It was the defendant's blood."

"And where was this drop of blood?" she asked showing him another photograph.

"In the living room, about five feet from the doorway. It was the defendant's blood."

There was another picture, this time in the hall, where drops of blood had been walked on and were not clearly visible.

"We got a scraping and it was the defendant's blood," the detective said.

"Did you find more drops anywhere? On the stairs, for example. Or in the study?"

"No."

"When you found fingerprints on the gun, did you also examine the bullets for fingerprints?"

"Yes."

"Did you find any on the bullets?"

"No."

She had no more questions.

It was going on four o'clock when Wharton called the medical examiner.

"The victim died at approximately seven thirty," Dr. Voorhees said, "from a single gunshot wound to his heart. The bullet grazed a rib, wobbled, and did extensive damage to the left ventricle, and it did not exit the body. I recovered it from the chest cavity. Death occurred within seconds. From the trajectory of the bullet and the nature of the wound, I determined that the shot had been fired from a distance between six and eight feet, without any significant upward or downward entrance."

Wharton had a few more questions such as how he had determined the time of death, and the general health of the victim. Voorhees said the stomach contents verified what the eyewitnesses had said, as did the temperature of the deceased. His general health had been very good. He had worn bifocal eyeglasses and had no other impairments.

Barbara wrote a hasty note: *B–find eye doctor*. She passed it to Shelley, who quickly rose and left the courtroom.

When Wharton nodded to her and sat down, she stood and approached the witness stand.

"Good afternoon, Dr. Voorhees," she said. "From your experience with gunshot wounds, how would you describe the impact on the human body from a gunshot wound produced by the Colt .45?"

"Objection," Wharton said.

"On what grounds?" Judge Humphrey asked.

"His opinion can't be verified and as such it can't be stated as factual."

"Dr. Voorhees has been a medical examiner for more than twenty years," Barbara said quickly. "He knows how a body reacts to trauma of many kinds, including gunshot wounds."

Judge Humphrey polished his eyeglasses, peered through the lenses, than said, "Overruled. You may answer the question, Doctor."

Barbara suspected a bit of ageism was in his decision. He and Voorhees were about the same age and their credentials were not to be questioned.

"I believe the first instant reaction would be a recoil," Voorhees said, "an autonomous jerk backward, followed by a larger forward thrust that could result in the victim falling."

"Dr. Voorhees, will you please inform the jurors on what you base your conclusion?"

"We have a database that details the reactions to various traumas, including the impact from different caliber gunshots. We have eyewitness accounts as well as videos of victims' reactions. I review those files often as I train assistants."

"So when you state he would fall forward, it is based on your knowledge, not simply an opinion?"

"I believe that most likely he would fall forward, based on my training and knowledge regarding the impact of a bullet."

"Would such a wound produce a copious amount of blood?"

"It certainly would."

"Would there be a spurt of blood?"

"Yes."

"Can you explain that, Doctor?"

He nodded and went on to describe the heart as a muscle, the chambers filled with blood under pressure. The sudden introduction of an outlet, such as one caused by a bullet wound, would release a quantity of blood almost instantly. It would spurt out.

"Was Mr. Peel wearing eyeglasses when you examined his body?"

"No."

"How did you determine that he wore bifocals?"

"I found them in his coat breast pocket," he said drily.

She smiled slightly, thanked him and said she had no more questions.

In his redirect Wharton went straight to the most telling part of the testimony. "Dr. Voorhees, you stated how the victim of a gunshot wound might react. Could there be other reactions than the one you have described?"

"Yes."

"Would a convulsive jerk to one side be a possible reaction?"

"It might be."

"Could you rule it out?"

"No."

"Might a victim simply fall backward?"

"He might."

"In other words there are a number of ways a victim of a gunshot wound might react. Is that correct?"

"The most likely way is the one I described. Other ways are possible if not likely."

"Your Honor, please inform the witness that a simple yes or no answer is required."

"Objection," Barbara said quickly. "The witness is trying to answer the question in a way that conforms to his long experience as a medical examiner."

Judge Humphrey fingered his eyeglasses, found a spot that needed cleaning, then put them on and peered at Wharton. "I believe the witness has answered your question, Counselor," he said. "Sustained." He looked at his watch, checked it against the wall clock, and nodded to Wharton. "You may continue."

Cue closing time for the day, Barbara thought as she resumed her seat.

As soon as Wharton finished with Voorhees, the judge said the court would be in recess until nine o'clock the next morning. He instructed the jury not to talk about the case, not to watch the TV news or read newspaper accounts of it, and not to use any electronic gadget to gather or receive any information concerning it. He had already warned them that anyone caught using an electronic gadget in court would have that gadget confiscated until the case was concluded. He frowned sternly at them, rose, and walked out. As the jury was being led out and before Barbara sat down again, she hurriedly scanned the observers. There weren't many, fifteen or twenty perhaps. She suspected that the FBI or Homeland Security or someone like that would be watching, and they could have been there without her spotting them. She did, however, see Derek Peel in the back row.

"Day one," she said to Travis. "How are you doing?"

He shrugged. "Your father said they would keep watching me, and they do. What do they think? That I might pull out a gun and start shooting, or jump over the table and slug the DA or the witness? They don't like me, and they already think I did it."

"Easy, Travis. They don't know what they think yet. We might have scored a point today and that's good this early in a trial. Hang in there, pal. I'm not done yet."

"Yeah, right."

As he was being led away Barbara turned to see Ashley watching him. There were tears in her eyes. At her side, with her arm around Ashley, was her sister. Barbara walked back to meet her and to reassure Ashley that nothing unexpected had occurred that day.

Mikaela Strong looked very much like her sister, and having seen pictures of June Morgan as a teenaged girl, Barbara knew this was how she would have looked in her middle years if she had lived.

"Mikey," Mikaela said as she shook hands. "They wanted a boy."

"Dad often calls me Bobby," Barbara said with a wry smile. "I know how that goes. Are you comfortable in the apartment?"

"It's lovely. And that's where we're headed. I stashed away a bottle of vodka, a gallon of orange juice, and another of bitter lemon. I'm teaching little sister how to drink."

"Good thinking. It's going exactly how I expected here," she added, gesturing toward the jury box. "But, Ashley, a little warning, it's going to look very bad tomorrow. It always does when the prosecution presents its case in the strongest possible way. That's Wharton's job and he's good at it. Don't let it get you down."

Ashley nodded and Mikey said heartily, "I hear a vodka sour calling. Come along, sis."

✦

At the defense table, Frank and Shelley were having a conversation when Barbara returned to pick up her purse and coat. "Arranging the coming days," Frank said. "It works pretty well to have lunch at my house or my office every day. I'll be around every evening if you need me for anything."

"Me too," Shelley said. "Or I can stay in town and go home later."

"No way," Barbara said. "After I have something to eat it's back to the office for me. I can't concentrate at home, it seems. Too set in my habits, I guess. Solitude, no noise, no one getting a snack from the fridge, or tiptoeing around me. Dad, anything from ATF or anyone?"

"No. And I don't expect anything. They'll play it close to the vest."

"Whoever sees Bailey first, pass the word that we'd like to know if a planeload of guys heads out on that jet on or around the thirteenth. Those bastards won't tell us."

Frank's lips tightened a little, but he nodded.

There had been a small article in the newspaper on New Year's Day about the arrest of two men allegedly in possession of illegal firearms. ATF was conducting an investigation. An anonymous source, one not authorized to speak, had let it leak that ATF suspected the men were transporting firearms to a Mexican drug cartel. Since then there had not been another word. Neither Homeland Security nor the FBI had been mentioned in the article.

"Barbara," Shelley said, "about Peel's eye doctor. I think I'll have that name for you tomorrow. Will we have to subpoena him?"

"How on earth did you manage that?"

"I don't know if it's too weird or something, but I saw Derek Peel out in the corridor and I asked him. He said he'd get it for us."

Barbara stared at her. "Weird or not, that's great. Anyway, I imagine a subpoena is in order. It could take a subpoena to get him in court."

She knew that few people wanted to testify in a murder trial, especially for the losing side, and most especially for a murder defendant who was convicted. Cover your ass, she thought derisively. They forced you to do it.

They made their way to the corridor where Herbert and Alan were waiting, and Barbara wished that she didn't have to go home and make nice for a couple of hours, wished she could go straight to her office and go to work, eat something later. She knew it was irrational, but there it was.

CHAPTER 30

WHEN TRAVIS WAS brought in the next morning, he looked drawn, as if he had slept little the previous night. Barbara patted his arm. "Keep your chin up," she said. "Today will be bad. It always is when the prosecution presents its case, but keep in mind that my turn is coming."

He nodded, drew the legal pad closer, and wrote in capital letters, *DAY 2*. "I'm okay," he said.

Wharton's first witness was Boris Rostov. He was a large man, six feet tall, powerful looking, with a thick neck, oversized hands and close-cropped pale hair. His face was broad and flat, his eyes so blue that the color was clear from a distance. Wharton had him inform the jury about his credentials to work as a bodyguard. He did so with concision. He had worked as a police officer in Dallas for seven years, then as a security guard for a private company in Iraq for four years, and finally for nearly three years as the personal bodyguard for Reverend Benjamin Morgan. He said he resided in the church residence when he was in Eugene, and in Reverend Morgan's condo when they were in Portland. He had one of the most expressionless faces that Barbara had ever seen, as if no muscles connected one part of his face to another. Only his lips moved as he spoke.

"Did Reverend Morgan tell you why he needed a bodyguard?" Wharton asked.

"Yes sir. He said he had been getting threats and he took them seriously."

"Did you take the threats seriously?"

"I sure did."

Barbara knew what Wharton was doing, the trap he had set for her. If she introduced the John Varagosa matter, it proved that a young man with a gun had tried to shoot Morgan in the past, and by implication reinforced the charge against Travis, that he could have been gunning for his father and got Peel instead. Wharton turned to the night of the murder, leaving the trap door open for her.

"What was the atmosphere in Reverend Morgan's residence on the night of the murder of Joseph Peel?"

"The reverend was happy and kind of excited. He said his son was returning to the fold and it made him thankful. That's all the reverend could talk about, how happy he was to have his son back."

"What transpired after dinner that night?"

"Me and Tony went to the kitchen to have a cup of coffee. When the doorbell rang I went to answer it and take the defendant to Mr. Peel's office so he could take him upstairs to the reverend. I walked down the hall with him and opened the door to Mr. Peel's office and he pulled a gun and shot him. Tony was by the side of the door and he hit the defendant in the head, and I ran around the desk to see if I could help Mr. Peel. But he was dead." Rostov was phlegmatic, his voice so emotionless he could have been reading from the telephone book.

"I ran back to where the defendant was on the floor and kicked his gun away from his hand and I called 911 and said there had been a shooting and the shooter was unconscious. I told Tony to tell Reverend Morgan and Dr. Knowland and they came down. I said just the doctor should come in, so Reverend Morgan and Tony stayed in the hall. The doctor looked at Mr. Peel to make sure he was dead. I told them all to stay back and wait for the police to get there, and I stayed by the defendant in case he might wake up and try to get the gun again. The detectives came and I went to the living room with the others."

"Did you see the defendant shoot Joseph Peel?" Wharton turned to look at Travis, and Rostov stared at him.

"Yes sir. He shot him."

Wharton nodded to Barbara and sat down. "Your witness, counselor."

She approached the witness stand slowly. "Mr. Rostov, why did you leave the police department?"

Wharton objected, and she said, "Your Honor, as part of Mr. Rostov's background we have learned where he worked. It is only fair to know why he left the various positions when he did in order to have a full account of his experience."

"Overruled," Judge Humphrey said. "You may answer the question."

"I was injured," Rostov said.

"I see," Barbara said, returning to her desk. She picked up and introduced a copy of the *Dallas Times* from July 19,1985. "According to this newspaper account, there was a street fight on July 18, 1985, in Dallas. Eyewitnesses," she read, "'testified that Boris Rostov, who was off duty, started the fight with the youths shooting basketballs. He was allegedly intoxicated at the time. He was identified as the one who hit—'" She stopped and said, "I'll omit the name mentioned here to protect his privacy." She continued to read, "'The youth was admitted in St. Joseph's Hospital in critical condition and remains in a coma.'"

Looking again at Rostov, she asked, "Were you suspended after that incident?"

"They got it all wrong," he said with no change in his expression or his demeanor.

"Were you suspended then?"

"I quit," he said.

"Does the record show that you were suspended, that your pension was forfeited, and then you resigned?"

"They got it all wrong," he said again. "I just quit."

She nodded, and had another newspaper clipping admitted. "A final newspaper account, this time a statement from William Conroy, Chief of Police of Dallas, Texas." She read it. "'Mr. Rostov has been suspended without pay, his pension has been forfeited, and our investigation is continuing. Mr. Rostov has turned in his resignation.'" She put the clipping down.

"Did you leave the area before the investigation was completed?" she asked.

"I quit and went to work for Silverstone," he said.

"Was the investigation ongoing when you left the area?"

"I don't know," he said with a shrug.

"And that brings us to Iraq," she said. "You stated that you were in Iraq for four years working as a security guard. She picked up and identified another newspaper clipping to have admitted. "In this *New York Times* account it states that on the night of April 3, 2004, a group of four Silverstone employees opened fire on unarmed civilians in their cars at an intersection in downtown Bagdad." She read,

"'Two people were killed, seven others injured. The four Silverstone employees were flown out of Iraq the following day on a Silverstone airplane. General Stone has ordered an investigation.' The newspaper gives the names of the four men who were flown out the next day. One of the names is Boris Rostov. Mr. Rostov, were you removed from Iraq within twenty-four hours of that incident?"

"My tour was up." He was watching her closely now, his eyes narrowed.

"Did you and your three companions fire on those unarmed civilians in their cars?"

"They were attacking us," he said. "It was self-defense. There was a war going on."

"Your Honor, I ask that the witness simply answer the question."

Judge Humphrey chose to examine his eyeglasses for a moment or two, then he nodded. "Answer the question," he said curtly.

"Yeah, we fired back," Rostov said.

"You were trained in the police academy in Texas, were you not?" He said yes and she went on. "And did you receive further training at Silverstone before you were sent to Iraq?"

"Yes. They always train their people."

"As a security guard were you trained in ways to spot a concealed weapon?"

"Sure."

"As a police officer were you trained in ways to spot a concealed weapon?"

"Yes," he snapped.

"Did you see a weapon when Travis Morgan entered the house that night?"

"He must have had it under his sweater or something. I didn't see any weapon."

"How was he dressed that night?"

"I don't remember." His answers were getting sharper and clipped although his expression remained almost blank.

"Let me refresh your memory," she said and called for the exhibit showing Travis lying on the floor. Taking it to the witness stand, she said, "It appears that he was wearing a close-fitting, light-colored sweater and blue jeans. Does that refresh your memory?" She handed the photograph to Rostov. He glanced at it and shook his head, then said no.

"Where would someone with a close-fitting sweater and close-fitting blue jeans hide a weapon, Mr. Rostov?"

"In his pocket or his waistband, or maybe strapped to his leg. His sweater wasn't that tight." He had returned to his earlier emotionless attitude.

She picked up the Colt .45 and walked back to the witness stand. "This is a sizeable object. If it had been in his pocket would it have created a noticeable bulge?"

"His jeans weren't that tight," he said.

"Oh," she said. "Then you do recall how he was dressed that night. As you walked to Mr. Peel's office were you at the right side of Mr. Morgan?"

"Some of the time," he said after a hesitation.

"When you reached the door were you at his side?"

"I was a little behind him so I could reach around him to open the door."

"When you were behind him did you see him reach back to draw a gun from his waistband?"

"No," he snapped.

"At any time did you see him bend over to retrieve a handgun from his leg?"

His no answer was more abrupt.

"Did you see him reach for a gun in his pocket?"

"No!"

"The doorbell rang and you opened the door that night," she said. "Following your extensive training in spotting concealed weapons, did you look over the young man who had arrived?"

"Yes."

"Did you see anything suspicious?

"No. Or I would have stopped him."

"As you walked down the hall with him to Mr. Peel's office, why did you leave his side to walk behind him?"

He shrugged. "I don't know. I didn't have a reason."

"When you reached the door, did you knock on it?"

"No."

"What did you do?"

"I reached around him so I could open the door."

"So you walked down the hall behind him, then opened the door with your left hand. Is that correct?"

"Yeah," he said.

"How wide is that hall, Mr. Rostov?"

He said he didn't know and Barbara produced a schematic of the front part of the house—the hall, a staircase, and several doors, with the doorway to Peel's office in a straight line with the front door. She introduced it and after it was accepted and shown to the jury, she referred to it as she continued to question Rostov.

"This shows that the hallway is twenty feet long and four feet, eight inches wide," she said. "In order to reach the doorknob to Mr. Peel's office, you had to be entirely behind Travis Morgan. Is that correct?"

He nodded, then said yes.

"Then you reached past him to open the door. Is that correct?"

"Yes. That's what I said before."

She regarded him for a long moment, then asked, "Wouldn't it have been more natural to stay by his side, to step in front of him to open the door, and then stand aside for him to enter?"

"I don't know."

"How close to the door was Travis Morgan when you reached past him to open the door?"

He said he didn't know.

"Well, did you have to extend your arm all the way?" He didn't remember. "Did you give the door a good shove when you opened it?"

"Not a hard push, just enough for him to go in."

"Could you see Mr. Peel?"

"I could see him."

"How could you see him if you were behind Travis Morgan?"

"I was sort of at his side, not right behind him."

"But you said you were behind him when you reached past him to open the door. Which is it?"

"I moved a little, enough to see him."

"All right. When you opened the door was Mr. Peel standing or sitting?"

"He was sitting down, then he stood up."

"Did he jump up?"

"He just stood up."

"Describe the chair he used."

"Just an office chair, wheels, with arm rests."

"When he stood up did he move his chair?"

"Yeah, he pushed it back out of the way."

"Was it a hard push, enough to send it back to the wall?"

"I didn't notice."

She nodded, returned to her table, and from there she asked, "Mr. Rostov, when you were behind Travis Morgan and reached past him to open the door, did you give him enough of a push to make him lose his balance momentarily?"

"No! I never touched him." He had his answer out almost before she finished the question.

"No further questions," she said and sat down.

Wharton didn't leave his table when he stood for his redirect examination. "Mr. Rostov, from where you were standing could you see the defendant shoot Joseph Peel?"

"Yes sir. I saw the gun in his hand."

"Could you see Joseph Peel's reaction to being shot?"

"Yes sir. He twisted around and fell down behind his desk."

"Did you inform the defendant that you were escorting him to Mr. Peel's office?"

"No sir."

The ball's in your court, Barbara thought, at Wharton, as he moved a paper on his table. The jurors would wonder why a preacher was threatened in the first place and why he felt threatened enough to hire private security. She did not breathe a sigh of relief when Wharton went there, but she felt it in her chest.

"You said that both you and the Reverend Morgan took threats against his life seriously. Can you explain why?"

"Sure. A kid tried to kill him before."

"Objection!" Barbara called. Standing, she asked, "Your Honor, may I approach?"

He beckoned her and Wharton and began to polish his glasses. "Your Honor," she said, "introducing a whole new element into the redirect is improper since I won't have a chance to cross-examine the testimony. I request that Mr. Wharton withdraw the question and that the answer be expunged."

"The jury has the right to know why the threats are serious," Wharton said sharply.

"Then you should have brought it up on your direct," Barbara snapped back.

"Both of you, quiet," Judge Humphrey said. He scowled at Wharton. "She's right, you know. You had your chance. Withdraw the question and just get on with it."

They returned to their tables and the judge said the objection was sustained.

"I withdraw the question," Wharton said. "No more questions."

Barbara rose instantly. "Your Honor, I request that the court advise the witness that he should hold himself in readiness to be recalled as a hostile witness for the defense."

"Objection!" Wharton cried.

Judge Humphrey beckoned them. "Chambers," he said. "Five minutes."

When they were both seated again, he announced that court would be in a short recess.

In the judge's cheerless chambers, Wharton said, "Your Honor, counselor is trying to confuse the jury, drawing out the trial unnecessarily, and insinuating alternative scenarios to what clearly happened. There's no earthly reason to bring back this witness."

Judge Humphrey unkinked the gold chain holding his glasses. "Well?" he said to Barbara. "Why do you want him recalled?"

"I believe he has a good deal of information pertinent to this case, and since none of it was introduced in direct, I could not bring it up. The bit about the attempt on Mr. Morgan's life in Portland is one example. I don't think we can leave it at that. The jury could be under the false impression that Travis Morgan tried to kill his father in the past."

"No, we can't just leave it," he said after a moment. "But, Ms. Holloway, if you purposely prolong this trial, I will bring you down to earth hard. Do you understand?"

"Yes, Your Honor. I have no wish to prolong the trial, and neither does my client."

Back in the courtroom the judge said, "The objection is overruled. Mr. Rostov, you will hold yourself in readiness to be recalled as a witness for the defense. The court will advise you of when that will occur. You may step down."

"I can't come back," Rostov said, getting to his feet. "I got a job to do."

"Mr. Rostov, you will come back or you will be arrested," Judge Humphrey said with a cold tone of finality.

Rostov cast a quick look at the jury, and it was impossible to tell if he was seeking sympathy or trying to grasp their reaction to the judge's harsh words. The faces of the jurors were almost as expressionless as his. He walked from the witness stand and kept his gaze on Barbara, and even though his face remained blank, she could feel his anger and hatred for her flaring from his blue eyes.

Wharton called his next witness, Anthony DiPalma.

DiPalma was a slender man, five feet ten inches, dressed in a handsome charcoal-gray suit with a pale-blue shirt and matching tie. His hair was jet black and wavy, his complexion olive. His most striking feature were his eyebrows, heavy, black and peaked. Barbara suspected that he plucked them to emphasize their shape and to frame his black eyes dramatically, as they did. She also suspected that he was a man who spent a good deal of time in front of a mirror.

Wharton had him describe his past employment that had led to becoming a driver for a preacher in Oregon.

"I drove a taxi in New York City, did a few runs as a delivery driver for a private packaging company, drove a candidate or two when they were running for office, drove a semi rig across the country a few times. I'm a pilot for a private company and made a few runs for them."

Wharton didn't linger over his past jobs, but got right to the night of the murder of Joseph Peel. "Tell us in your own words about that evening, starting with dinnertime."

"Sure," DiPalma said. "We ate in the dining room, me, Boris, Reverend Morgan, Dr. Knowland, and Mr. Peel. Mr. Peel said he had some work to do while we waited for the reverend's son. The reverend and Dr. Knowland went upstairs to the study and me and Boris went to get a cup of coffee in the kitchen. The doorbell rang and Boris went to answer it and I went to Mr. Peel's office to get a book to read. I was standing by the bookshelf when the door opened, the defendant took a step in and shot Mr. Peel. I hit him in the head with a bookend I was holding."

"Did you see the defendant shoot Joseph Peel?" Wharton turned to look at Travis and motioned for DiPalma to look at him.

"Sure, that's the one. He shot Mr. Peel."

Wharton asked for the photograph showing Travis on the floor and the bookshelf. He showed it to DiPalma. "Exactly where were you when the defendant stepped through the doorway?"

"Right there, in front of the books on the shelf. I was close enough that I could have touched him."

"Did you see the gun in his hand?"

"Sure, that's when I hit him. There was a shot, I saw the gun, and I slugged him with the bookend."

"How did it happen that you had the bookend in your hand?"

"The books were kind of wedged in tight and I moved it so I could take a book. I was just holding it while I looked over the books. I had it in my hand when he came in. And I turned to look at him. I wanted to get a closer look at him."

Wharton introduced into evidence the bookend in a plastic evidence bag. It still had dried blood on it. He showed it to the jury but did not pass it around. "Is this the bookend you used to hit him?" he asked.

DiPalma nodded vigorously. "That's it, all right."

"Then what did you do?"

"Nothing. Boris went to see Peel and said he was dead and I should go tell Reverend Morgan and Dr. Knowland and he called 911. I went upstairs to tell them and we came down and Dr. Knowland went in and said yes that Peel was dead and Boris said we should stay out of the room and not to touch nothing because the police were coming, and that's what we did. We stayed out in the hall. And the police came and took us to the living room and began asking what happened."

Wharton finished with him soon after that. He nodded to Barbara. "Your witness, counselor."

Judge Humphrey used his gavel then and said, "Court will be in recess for lunch until two o'clock."

CHAPTER 31

HERBERT DROVE THEM all to Frank's house in the SUV. A fine, cold rain was falling and they hurried inside when they got there. Barbara, without a word, went straight upstairs to the room Frank had turned into an office for her years before. Frank watched her go, then began to unload the bag of groceries he had asked Alan to pick up while they were in court.

"Do-it-yourself sandwiches," he said. "Ham, corned beef, cheeses, turkey, red balls passing themselves off as tomatoes, and a few other things. Wraps or bread."

After his offerings were put on plates, Mikey made a sandwich for Ashley and put it in her hand. Ashley stared at it as if it were an alien artifact. Frank made a generous sandwich for Barbara, wrapped it in plastic, and then made one for himself. He would give her half an hour before taking hers up, he decided. She wanted time alone for now to make her plans, line up her questions, mull over answers given already.

He was surprised when she came down in a few minutes.

"Herbert, let's go for a ride," she said, putting on her raincoat. "A day like this, how many people do you think will be out and about? Let's go to Skinner's Butte and let me hike up, then back to the homestead." Avoiding Frank's look, she said it almost defiantly, as if daring anyone to object.

Frank bit back his objection and handed her the wrapped sandwich. "Eat it on the way back. Coffee will be hot and you'll want it."

"Thanks," she said, thanking him more for not raising hell with her than for the sandwich.

After they were out of the house, Frank said to Shelley, "In a bit, we'll go over to her house and get her some dry shoes. She'll need them."

"It's not a good idea," Herbert complained, driving to the park. "You can't see a thing this kind of weather."

"That's the point. No one's likely to drive up since you can't see anything. Maybe a few other hikers, but they don't count."

He clamped his lips and kept watching out the rearview mirror and the windshield alternately. She ignored him, snapped her hood into place, and began to think of her afternoon strategy.

As she had predicted, there were no cars and only two other people trudging along the narrow road badly in need of resurfacing. It was a steep walk, not a real hike, but by the time she reached the summit, she was hot in spite of the rain.

Eugene was swathed in constantly shifting mist and rain. Spencer Butte, seven miles to the south was invisible, as were the Cascades to the east. Closer, fennel gone wild, was bent like oversized wickets waiting for the queen and her entourage to come play. With her hands in her pockets, Barbara leaned against a concrete guardrail at the lookout and took in deep breaths, visualizing DiPalma and his pretty hair and dramatic eyebrows. Vain, conceited, a bit arrogant, fancied himself God's gift to women, no doubt. She began sorting out her questions for him…

Then she was thinking of the city below her. In the valley sheltered by the Coast Range on one side, buttes on the north and south, Cascades to the east, it was like a giant protected nest. She smiled as she constructed the bird that would inhabit such a nest. Not a bird at all, she decided, and her smile broadened as she deconstructed her bird and created a magnificent dragon. Red, gold, blue, and silver with streaks of iridescent violet, vermilion green…

"Uh, Barbara, you know it's a quarter after one?" Herbert said, suddenly appearing at her side. "Ain't you getting a little cold?"

She laughed, thinking of the expression on his face if she told him she had been building a dragon. "Home, Herbert. Matter of fact, I'm cold to the bone, and didn't have sense enough to know it. I'm ready for that sandwich."

She ate the sandwich on the way and was thankful for the coffee Frank placed in her hand when they got there. She changed her shoes with a murmured thanks to Shelley, and they were ready to return to court.

"Sit here, Shelley," she said at the defense table, motioning to the chair near the aisle. DiPalma returned to the witness chair and was reminded that he was still under oath.

"Ms. Holloway, are you ready to proceed?" Judge Humphrey asked.

"Yes, Your Honor," she said, rising. Shelley had to stand and move out of the way as Barbara left the defense table. DiPalma kept his gaze on Shelley as she resumed her seat.

"Mr. DiPalma, how long have you been employed as a driver for Mr. Morgan?"

He blinked a time or two, and his eyebrows rose and fell as he did. "A couple, three years."

"Which is it, two or three?"

"Something like that."

"Mr. DiPalma, surely you know when you started to work for Mr. Morgan. Did you arrive at the same time that Mr. Rostov did?"

"About the same time."

"Mr. Rostov testified that it will be three years at the beginning of April when he started. Is that when you started?"

"About then."

"Did you and Mr. Rostov arrive at Mr. Morgan's Portland condo together to apply for the positions you were given?"

"Yeah, he was with me."

"Thank you," she said making little effort to hide her sarcasm. "Do you often have dinner with Mr. Morgan?"

He blinked, his eyebrows did their thing, and his pause before his answer was longer.

"No. I mean, yes. Sometimes."

"Mr. DiPalma, will you narrow that down to one answer, please."

"I mean sometimes I do."

"How often?"

"Not often, just now and then."

"Did you ever have dinner with him before the night of September 10, 2010?"

He had to think about it and finally said no. "But I've eaten with him a couple of times since then."

"Do you still have a valid pilot's license?"

It seemed as if his confusion contorted his face as he struggled to change gears. "Yeah," he said. "I keep it up."

"Do you still fly airplanes for the private company that had you on call in California?"

"Sometimes."

"Are you still on call for that company?"

"Yeah, that's how they operate."

"What does your position as Mr. Morgan's driver consist of?" When he seemed at a loss, she said, "Let me rephrase that. What exactly do you do for Mr. Morgan?"

"I drive him to where he wants to go."

"Do you drive him somewhere every day?"

"No. He doesn't go places every day. To church on Sundays, across town in Portland, down here to Eugene, to other churches where he preaches. He calls me and I go and drive him."

"Do you also fly him to places?"

"Sometimes."

"Are there days when your services are not needed?"

"Yeah. He doesn't go out every day."

"Are you on call for him the way you are for the company you fly for?"

"Yeah, something like that."

"Who is your primary employer?"

"What do you mean?"

"Well, if the airplane people call you, do you have to clear it with Mr. Morgan? Make sure he won't need you at the same time?"

"Yeah. He says it's okay. He knows I like to fly."

"How well did you know Joseph Peel?"

He had to blink several times again. "Peel? He was the bookkeeper. I didn't know him much."

"Did you two chat, have coffee together, lunch together, things of that sort?"

"No. He'd come in, did his work and left. He went out for lunch or brought it with him."

"Were you ever in his office?"

"No. I mean, yes. Sometimes Reverend Morgan said take this to Peel and I did."

"Did you know he had books in his office?"

"Yeah. I seen the books."

"Did you often borrow a book from his office?"

"No. I mean sometimes I did."

"Do you enjoy reading?"

"Sure. I read a lot of things."

"Do you live at the church residence here in Eugene?"

"No. I mean not really live there. I mean, when we come down here that's where I stay. I got my own place in Portland."

"So when Mr. Morgan calls you in Portland, you have to drive to his condo in order to take him where he wants to go? Is that correct?"

"Yeah, he calls first."

"When you take him to where he wants to go does Mr. Rostov go with you both?"

"Yeah, he's the bodyguard. I'm the driver."

"Did you and Mr. Rostov drive your car from California up to Portland to apply for your jobs?"

He had to think for several seconds, working his eyebrows while he did so. "Yeah, I drove us."

"Were you and Mr. Rostov friends in California?"

He hesitated before he said, "Sort of pals, not really, though."

"Well, did he tell you about the opening for a driver for Mr. Morgan?" It was a simple shot in the dark, she knew, but one worth taking.

"Objection," Wharton said. He sounded weary, or bored, or both. "Mr. DiPalma's history is not the issue. This line of questioning is irrelevant and a fishing expedition."

"Sustained," Judge Humphrey said. "Please move on, Ms. Holloway."

Barbara nodded. She feared that if he continued to polish his glasses so assiduously, he might wear them down to tissue-thin disks.

"Mr. DiPalma," she said, "do you usually have your own reading material with you when you drive to Eugene from Portland?"

"Yeah," he said quickly. "I forgot to bring something this time."

She glanced at the defense table and saw that Shelley was getting the second bookend out from a bag. DiPalma was watching also, and he continued to gaze at Shelley as Barbara walked toward the jury box. Pausing before it, she asked, "Mr. DiPalma, when did you decide to borrow a book from Mr. Peel's office?"

He jerked his head around to look at her, and he seemed to remember the jury and gave them a little smile. "You mean what time?"

"Yes, or approximately what time? For instance, was it before dinner?"

"I don't know. I just thought of it."

"All right," she said. "Let's assume you're still at the dining table. Who left first?"

He shook his head, blinked a time or two, then said, "Peel got up and left. Then me and Boris got up and went to the kitchen for coffee."

"Was the housekeeper still there?"

"No. I mean, yes. She was getting ready to leave and she left."

"And had you already decided to borrow a book at that time?"

"Yeah, or earlier."

Barbara turned to Judge Humphrey. "Your Honor, will you please ask the witness to stop turning his answers into a multiple-choice selection?"

The judge frowned at DiPalma. "Just answer the question to the best of your ability. If you need to think a moment or two, do so and then answer the question."

DiPalma nodded and ran his finger under the edge of his button-down shirt.

"My question was, when did you decide to borrow a book from Mr. Peel's office?"

"I don't know," he said. "Sometime that night."

"Had you looked over the books on previous occasions when you were in the office?"

"I seen them before."

"Do you recall what the titles were?"

"Just books. I thought I could read one of them."

"All right. When did you go to Mr. Peel's office to borrow a book?"

"That same night he got shot."

It took several questions and partial answers before Barbara established that when the doorbell rang, DiPalma and Rostov left the kitchen together. She produced the drawing of the house, and showed it to DiPalma.

"This is the hall from the kitchen," she said pointing. "From where it joins the front hall, the distance is six feet to the door to Mr. Peel's office. You turned to go there while Mr. Rostov went to open the door. Is that correct?"

He eyed it suspiciously and said, "If you say so."

"The measurements are clearly marked on the drawing, Mr. DiPalma. This is six feet from Mr. Peel's office door. Do you see those measurements? Is that six feet?"

"Yeah, it says six feet."

"When you reached Mr. Peel's door, did you knock?"

He didn't know and struggled between yes and no, glanced at Judge Humphrey, and finally said he didn't remember.

"You opened the door and entered the office. Did you speak to Mr. Peel?"

"I might have said something like I wanted a book."

"Did you say that or not?"

"Yeah. I said it."

"What was Mr. Peel doing?"

"I don't know. He was sitting down at his desk."

"Did he say anything to you?"

He had to think about it before he said, "He told me to help myself."

"Then what did you do?"

"I looked over the books."

"Did you look over the books before you picked up the bookend?"

"Yeah, sort of. Glanced at them and then picked it up. They were wedged in tight."

Barbara introduced the enlarged photograph of the shelf of books and had it admitted. She showed it to DiPalma. "It appears that the first book on the shelf is titled *Myths and Metaphors in the Old Testament*. The next one is *A Guide to Theology*. Then the *Old Testament*. She read the next titles, one on bookkeeping, one on simplifying spreadsheets, accountancy made easy, and a tutorial on electronic bookkeeping.

"Which one of them caught your eye, Mr. DiPalma?"

He was blinking rapidly and shook his head. "I don't know. I just wanted to get a closer look. I picked up the bookend so I could pull out a book for a closer look. They were wedged in tight."

"Why didn't you simply move the bookend away from the books? There is plenty of space on the shelf to do that."

He thought about it. "I just wanted to get a closer look at it," he said.

Barbara walked to the defense table and picked up the bookend. It was nine inches high, with a two-inch base. The eagle's wings were half opened, its head turned sideways. It was apparent that the base, the head, and the backs of the wings would be against the books. The wing tips were joined to the base to make a solid flat back side of the bookend. She introduced it, then said, "The bookend is made of brass and it weighs three pounds, nine-and-a-half ounces. It is identical to the one used to strike Travis Morgan in the head."

From his seat Wharton said, "Stipulated."

They had weighed it together in Judge Humphrey's chambers. It was admitted and Barbara took it to the jury box and handed it to the foreman, Harold Jameson, who took it in both hands, and passed it on. She watched as the eagle was passed to one juror after another. Most of them used both hands to hold it by the base, exactly the way she had carried it.

When she had it back, she took it to the witness stand and placed it on the rail in front of DiPalma. "This is exactly like the one you removed from the bookshelf," she said. "Will you please stand up and demonstrate to the court how you took it from the shelf and used it to strike Travis Morgan."

He looked puzzled and his eyebrows rose and fell as a frown creased his forehead. He stood and reached for the bookend with both hands. Then he attempted to hold it with his right hand by the base, but there was too little room that was graspable. The wingtips and the eagle's feet covered most of the base. He grasped it by one of the wings and nodded. "That's how I held it."

"You wanted a closer look and you held it by the wing," she said. "Is that correct?"

He nodded and said yes.

"All right," Barbara said. "You picked it up with both hands. You were facing the bookshelf at that moment. You shifted the bookend and held it by the wing. And you were at the end of the shelf that is within six inches of the doorway. Then what did you do?"

"I turned around when I heard the door open."

"Why?"

"I wanted to get a look at him."

"Why didn't you stay in the hall where you could see him from the front as he walked to the office?"

"I wanted a closer look," he said after a pause. He shifted the bookend to both hands again as he spoke.

"You stated that Travis Morgan was close enough to touch. When you turned around how close were you to him?"

"Right by his side."

"Please stand and pretend that you're hitting someone at your side with the bookend."

He seemed to remember that he had held it by the wing and shifted it again. Then he saw that he was too close and moved backward as far as the witness chair permitted. "I had to move back some," he said. He stretched out his arm and followed through with a swift forward motion as if hitting someone.

"And that's how you were holding the bookend?" Barbara asked.

"Yeah, by the wing."

She took it from him and placed it on the rail again. "Mr. DiPalma, from what you have told the court, you were facing the bookshelf, you picked up the eagle with both hands, then you shifted it to your right hand. When the door opened you turned to see Travis Morgan, and then you moved back a little in order to have a full swing at him. At what point in those actions was there a gunshot?"

"Right after the door opened. He came rushing in and shot Peel."

"Was he running?"

"I don't know. He looked like he was rushing in."

Barbara got the photograph of Travis on the floor. Showing it to DiPalma, she said, "His feet are barely inside the room. Is that correct?"

He looked at it and shook his head. "I thought he was in hurry."

"Did you see him draw a gun?"

"No. He just had it in his hand. And I hit him."

"I see," Barbara said. "Were you interested in the back of the eagle, Mr. DiPalma?"

"The back? Why? No."

"You said you wanted a closer look, and since the blood on the bookend you used was on the back, it means that you must have held the eagle in such a way that the back edge actually struck Travis Morgan. That would have been very difficult if you were holding the eagle in a way that permitted you to examine it from the front."

"I got it turned around again," he said after a long pause.

She picked up the bookend with both hands and took it to the evidence table. From there she asked, "What did you do with the bookend after you hit Travis Morgan?"

"Do? I put it down in the living room."

"Did Mr. Rostov tell you to advise Mr. Morgan and Dr. Knowland about what happened?"

"Yeah, he said to tell them. Up in the study," he added quickly.

"Did you stop by the living room first to put down the bookend?"

"Yeah. I mean, no. I went straight up to the study."

"Were you carrying the bookend?"

"Yeah. I was excited-like and forgot I had it."

"I see," she said, walking to the defense table. "You went upstairs carrying a three-and-a-half-pound bookend with blood on it, and did you carry it back down?"

"Yeah. I still had it."

"When the detectives arrived did you still have it in your hands?"

He had to think quite a long time before answering. "I must have put it in the living room before they got there."

"Don't you know if you did?"

"I mean that's where they found it. So I must have put it down before they got there."

"Mr. DiPalma, when did you put the bookend in the living room?"

"I don't remember," he said sullenly. "Before the cops got there. They would have seen it if I still had it."

"I imagine they would have," she said. "No further questions."

Wharton did what he had to do, she thought as she took her seat. He kept it simple.

"Were you at the bookshelf when the defendant entered the room?"

"Yeah."

"Did you see the defendant shoot Joseph Peel?"

"Yeah, sure I did."

"No more questions," Wharton said.

"Your Honor," Barbara said quickly, rising. "I request that the court advise Mr. DiPalma to hold himself in readiness to be recalled as a defense witness."

"Objection!" Wharton yelled. "May I approach?"

Judge Humphrey motioned them both to come forward. "Now what?" he demanded, glaring at Barbara.

"He has a lot of information that is pertinent to this trial. The only way to get at it is by direct examination."

"Haven't you confused and twisted him enough?" Wharton snapped.

"Not by half," she said hotly.

"Take your seats," Humphrey said. "Objection overruled. I'll advise him. Ms. Holloway, again I warn you, don't play games with this court."

"No, Your Honor. No games."

"I'm going to adjourn after this witness leaves," the judge said. "I've had quite enough for one day."

Walking back to their tables Wharton said bitterly in a near whisper, "No games! Shit! That's your style, games."

The judge told DiPalma that he was to be recalled and DiPalma looked around at the jury, at the observers, Wharton, everyone except Barbara. "Why?" he cried. "I answered all her questions. Why do I have to come back?"

"The defense counsel has the right to recall a witness," Judge Humphrey said. "You will be informed of when that will take place. Now step down." He banged his gavel. "The court is in recess until nine o'clock tomorrow morning."

In the SUV Frank turned to say to Barbara, "You led him in a merry chase. Good job." His eyes were twinkling.

"He's a stooge," she said. "Want to bet he won't show up for recall?"

Frank laughed heartily. "You're just like your mother. No bets unless you have the cards."

She wasn't at all sure that had been true of her mother, but she knew without a doubt that it described her father. "I have to go have a little talk with Travis in an hour or so," she said. "And between now and then, no thinking, no chitchat, nothing but a soft chair and a glass of wine. Deal?"

"You've got it," Frank said, turning to watch rain streak the windshield. He knew what Barbara had done that day, Judge Humphrey knew, as did Wharton, but Travis, his mother, others in the courtroom, probably not, he thought, and that was a shame. Maybe there was another book to be written on the ways and wiles of various attorneys.

CHAPTER 32

LATE THAT NIGHT Barbara regarded Herbert sleeping on her office sofa and felt regretful that she would have to awaken him to take her home. He looked peaceful where he was. For a few moments she sat still, wondering what the ATF people were doing, what Homeland Security was up to, what the FBI was pursuing. One day there would be an article in the newspaper about a massive raid, she thought with resignation, a number of people arrested and an ongoing investigation that was under way. She hoped there would not be another Waco fiasco.

She rose from her desk and instantly, it seemed Herbert was upright and to all appearances wide awake. "Time to go," she said. "Ready?"

"You betcha. Want help with anything?"

She didn't. They drove home and when she tried to get into bed without waking Darren, he turned, put his arm around her and drew her close. He was very warm.

Back in court the next morning Wharton's first witness of the day was Mrs. Abigail Pleasance, Morgan's housekeeper.

She was sturdily built with short gray hair, dressed in a navy pantsuit with a white shirt, no jewelry except for a wedding ring. Wharton led her through her history with Morgan quickly. She had been housekeeper for him for six years, had not known Travis, but she had known Ruth Morgan. She arrived five days a week at about noon, did some housecleaning, prepared dinner, and usually left a little before seven. When Morgan was not in town she cleaned the house once a week.

"Was the night of September tenth any different from other nights?" Wharton asked.

"Yes," she said. "Usually Boris and Tony ate in the kitchen, but they ate with Reverend Morgan and Dr. Knowland that night. And it was the first time Mr. Peel had dinner at the house."

"Did Reverend Morgan say why they were all having dinner together that night?"

"He said his son was coming home and he wanted everyone to celebrate with him. He wanted a big pot roast and apple pie for dessert. That's what I made."

"What was his attitude when he told you his son was coming home?"

"He was excited and seemed to be nervous. He said Dr. Knowland would have a little wine for dinner, and that was different, but he said it was a special occasion."

"What time did you serve dinner?"

"A few minutes after six."

"Do you know how long the dinner lasted?"

"I put the food in bowls and cut the roast in the kitchen so they could help themselves. When they finished that, Mr. Peel brought his plate and silverware out to the kitchen and said he would skip dessert. I cleared the rest of the dishes and took in apple pie. I cleaned up in the kitchen while they were having dessert. Then Boris and Tony came in to have coffee and said they were done in the dining room. I got the other things from the table and put them in the dishwasher, and I left. It was ten minutes after seven."

Wharton had little more to ask her and Barbara rose.

"Good morning, Mrs. Pleasance," she said. "I have just a few things I'd like to have clarified. When did Mr. Morgan tell you about the dinner?"

"As soon as I got there, almost. I was about to clean the refrigerator and he came down to the kitchen and told me. He said Dr. Knowland would bring a bottle of wine and I should put a wineglass at his place."

"Had he been up in his study when you got there?"

"Yes. They all were. I started to go up to do the bathrooms, but I heard their voices and decided to do the refrigerator first."

"When you say they all were in the study, who do you mean?"

"Tony, Boris, Dr. Knowland, and Reverend Morgan."

"What was the attitude of the others that day? Mr. Rostov, Mr. DiPalma, Mr. Peel, Dr. Knowland. Were they all as excited and happy as Mr. Morgan was?"

"No. But they didn't know his son, I guess, like I didn't know him."

"What about Mr. Peel?"

"He was just like always. Quiet and kept to himself the way he always did. When I asked him if he would be having wine, he seemed surprised."

"When did you ask him that?"

"In the late afternoon, about five, maybe, when I was thinking about setting the table. I went to his office and knocked and he said to come in. He was talking to his wife on his cell phone and I waited a minute for him to finish."

"Did you hear what he was saying?"

"Some of it. He was telling her that he didn't know what Reverend Morgan wanted, and she should go on alone. If he got through in time he would join her."

"Did he tell you that was his wife on the phone?"

"Yes. He said it was bingo night and he would save ten dollars by missing it."

"Was he working when you went in? Besides the phone call, I mean. Did he have his computer on, the keyboard out?"

"No. Everything was put away like he was done for the day."

"Was Mr. Peel friendly with you?"

"Objection," Wharton said. But Mrs. Pleasance had already answered the question with a quick nod.

"Sustained," Judge Humphrey promptly decided. He sounded annoyed. How could he tell the jurors to ignore a nod of the head?

"You stated that you knew Ruth Morgan. Was she introduced to you by that name?"

"Yes, she was, but she told me later that her name was really June. She'd come out to the kitchen to chat and watch me make piecrust or something. Of course, I didn't see her again after she left for a boarding school or something. So I don't know if she was going by Ruth or by June when she got older."

"Did you see her when she was sent home ill with pneumonia?"

"Objection!" Wharton called. "This is immaterial, irrelevant to this trial."

"Sustained," Humphrey said. "Move on, Ms. Holloway."

Barbara nodded. "Did Mr. DiPalma and Mr. Rostov usually have dinner by themselves in the kitchen?"

"Always, except that one night. Or sometimes they went out to get a pizza or something."

"On those occasions did they go out together?"

"Yes. They were real close friends, I guess, most always together."

"Thank you," Barbara said. "I have no more questions."

Wharton took Mrs. Pleasance back through her statements that Morgan had been excited and nervous and that the special dinner was to celebrate the return of his son. He then called Dr. Knowland.

To all appearances Knowland was the kind of old-fashioned doctor no one ever saw any longer outside of Rockwell art. He looked well fed, but not too heavy, with silvery hair, the start of jowls, and a few lines at his eyes and forehead. He had a benign smile for the jurors, and looked as if he felt comfortable in his skin and in his nice pinstriped suit with a discreet blue tie.

Wharton led him through his credentials as a physician, and his relationship to Morgan. He described himself as an old friend as well as being Morgan's physician, and said he was semiretired.

"Dr. Knowland, did you often have dinner with Reverend Morgan?" Wharton asked.

"Yes. I live here and he is back and forth a lot between Eugene and Portland, but when he's here in Eugene, we often dine together or sometimes have lunch together."

"Were you surprised when he asked you to dinner on the night of September tenth?"

"I was a little. He called me that morning and said his son had come home and wanted to see him. He invited me to dinner, and he asked if I could come to his house to discuss how he should treat his boy."

"Will you please explain what that means, how he should treat him?"

"I went to the house and he admitted to being a bit nervous, since he had not seen his son for seven years. He feared that Travis had succumbed to the many alluring activities that a city like San Francisco offers the young, that he might have left the straight and narrow, so to speak. He was also concerned that Travis might still be as rebellious as he was as a youth. He wasn't sure how to approach that."

"Had you known the defendant before he left his father's house seven years ago?"

"Oh yes. I was the family physician."

"Had he been rebellious?"

"Yes. He appeared to reject anything and everything that his father represented."

"During your talk with Reverend Morgan, were both Mr. Rostov and Mr. DiPalma present?"

"For a short time only. The reverend wanted to ask them if San Francisco was as sinful as he had been led to believe, if it was as permissive for young people as he had heard. They affirmed that it was, and they left us to continue our conversation."

"What was the outcome of that conversation?"

"We agreed that the best way to handle it would be to start fresh, not to refer to anything from the past, either when he still lived at home or during the years he had lived in San Francisco. He was very pleased with that decision."

"Please tell the court what happened after dinner that evening of the shooting."

Knowland nodded gravely and faced the jury as he spoke. "After we had dessert the reverend and I went upstairs to his study. It was after seven, but I wasn't noticing the clock, especially. We chatted as we waited. I didn't hear the doorbell, and I don't believe the reverend heard it, either. At least, he didn't react as if he had heard it. Then Mr. DiPalma ran in and said that Mr. Peel had been shot, and that the defendant had shot him. We were stunned and terribly shocked, and we hurried downstairs. Mr. Rostov said only I should enter to see to Mr. Peel. I did that, but there was nothing I could do. He was already dead. Mr. Rostov told me to wait with the others for the police to arrive, that he had already called them and called for an ambulance for the defendant. We stood in the hall waiting for the officers to arrive and they told us to go to the living room where one of them began to question us."

Wharton had little more to ask and soon nodded to Barbara. "Your witness, counselor."

She rose and stood at the defense table to ask, "Dr. Knowland, do you have a clinic where you see any patients?"

"No. Not any longer."

"Do you make house calls?"

"No, with the exception of Reverend Morgan."

"Is he your only patient?"

"Yes, he is."

"When Mr. DiPalma went upstairs to inform you and Mr. Morgan of the shooting, was he carrying the bookend?"

"I couldn't say," Knowland said with a rueful shake of his head. "I was too taken aback by his announcement to notice."

"When you entered Mr. Peel's office, did you have to step over Travis Morgan?"

"Yes. He was sprawled out on the floor. I saw the gun on the floor also, but I was mostly concerned with Mr. Peel."

"If Mr. Peel had still been alive would there have been actions you might have taken to try to save him?"

"A few. Stanch the blood flow, make certain his airway was clear, but there was no point in attempting anything. It was clear that he had died almost instantly."

"What did you do, after you ascertained that Mr. Peel was dead?"

"Mr. Rostov told me not to touch anything, and to go wait with the others for the police. I returned to the hall."

"Did you step over Travis Morgan as you left the office?"

"I had to," he said.

She had the photograph of Travis lying on the floor produced and showed it to Knowland. "Is that how he looked when you stepped over him going into and leaving the office?"

"Yes."

"Is his head wound visible in that photograph?"

"No."

"Can you see the massive amount of blood under his head?"

"There is blood under his head," he said coolly.

"Did you make any attempt to assess his condition? Did you check his pulse or try to stanch the blood flow? Did you attempt to evaluate the extent of his injury?"

Wharton was yelling objections and Judge Humphrey banged his gavel. "Multiple-part questions!" Wharton yelled.

"Sustained. Ms. Holloway, ask one question at a time," Humphrey said angrily.

"Yes, Your Honor," she said. She asked them one at a time and each question was answered with a curt No.

She returned the photograph and then asked, "How long have you known Mr. Morgan?"

"About ten or twelve years, maybe a little more."

"When did you become semiretired?"

"About thirteen years ago."

"Did you ever treat Travis Morgan for anything?"

"A few times. He was a very healthy boy and seldom needed medical attention."

"Did you ever treat Mr. Morgan's daughter June?"

"Yes"

"Did you treat her for pneumonia in June of last year?"

"I saw her and signed her death certificate listing the cause of death as pneumonia."

"Did you treat her for that illness?"

"By the time I saw her she was past treatment. She died within hours."

"Did you treat her in the hospital?"

"Objection!" Wharton called. "Dr. Knowland has testified that he treated the whole family. How he treated them is irrelevant to this trial."

"Sustained. Move on, Ms. Holloway."

"Dr. Knowland, can you splint a broken bone?"

Bored, he said, "Yes."

"Or stitch a simple cut?'

"Yes."

"Prescribe medications?"

"Of course."

"Have you done any of those procedures since you have been semiretired?"

"Yes, I have. I am a licensed physician."

"Have you ever performed a castration on a man?"

Wharton was on his feet yelling an objection, and there was a commotion in the courtroom behind Barbara. She kept her gaze on Knowland, and for the first time she knew she had cracked through his veneer enough to give him a jolt. His face stiffened and his eyes narrowed. He seemed to draw himself into his suit jacket in a defensive manner and at the same time to sit up almost rigidly straight.

Judge Humphrey sustained the objection more angrily than before.

"No further questions," Barbara said and took her seat. She put her hand on Travis's arm. He was shaking. "Easy," she said in a whisper. "Just relax. Try Dr. Minnick's trick."

She saw that on the legal pad she had provided he had scribbled a lot, with the word Lie underscored heavily. In a moment he did relax and she silently thanked Dr. Minnick.

Wharton started his redirect by going over what Knowland had stated before, how happy Morgan was that his son was coming back, how he had decided to let bygones be bygones and start fresh.

Then he asked, "When you stepped over the defendant as you left the office, did it occur to you to examine him, to determine the extent of his injuries?"

"It did not. Not at that time. I was too concerned with the state of shock that Reverend Morgan was in. I wanted to make certain he was all right. All I could think of at that time was that it had happened again, that a young man intended to shoot the reverend, and he happened to shoot the wrong person."

Thank you, Doctor, Barbara thought at him as she waited for Wharton to finish and take his seat. She was on her feet instantly when he did so, and again she requested that the judge inform the witness that he would be recalled as a defense witness. The same door had opened that opened before and Judge Humphrey did not hesitate to tell Knowland he would be recalled. He rose then and said court would be in recess for fifteen minutes.

As the jury was being led out, Frank touched Barbara's shoulder. "Do you want coffee?"

She shook her head. "I think I may have a date with the judge any minute now."

"I know damn well you do. I'll bring some for when you get booted out again."

A guard came to take Travis away, and in another minute the bailiff came to collect Barbara and Wharton. Neither spoke as they walked together to the judge's chambers.

He was at his desk and motioned for them to come close to it. He kept his icy glare on Barbara.

"Your Honor," Wharton said, "I'm doing my level best to move this trial forward in an expedient manner. I strenuously object to the defense counsel's obstructing that goal of finishing this quickly. She is on a fishing expedition for one thing, but, more seriously, I believe it is a deliberate attempt to confuse the jury."

"Your objections have been recorded," Judge Humphrey said coldly without shifting his gaze. "Ms. Holloway, I understand that Mr. Wharton's next witness, possibly his final witness, will be the Reverend Morgan. Do you intend to have him recalled as a defense witness?"

"If the scope of the cross-examination precludes certain questions that must be addressed, then I will have to recall him."

"He's a minister!" Wharton said furiously. "You'd impugn the testimony of a minister?"

"There are lies of commission and lies of omission," she said calmly. "Mr. Wharton has said repeatedly that this is a simple matter, and I say that it is not. It is complex and the prosecution witnesses all have information that must come out if we are to learn the whole truth."

"Enough," Humphrey said. "Ms. Holloway, you are exercising your rights as defense counsel to recall witnesses. If it turns out that your reasons are frivolous, if you make a mockery of these proceedings, I shall exercise my rights to punish you to the full extent of the law."

His voice was low and it was venomous, cold and deadly, his words like ice being chipped off a massive block. In spite of herself Barbara felt chilled.

Judge Humphrey looked at his watch. "Now leave, both of you. We will resume in fifteen minutes."

Walking away from his chambers Wharton said in an undertone, "Barbara, I hope you know how thin the ice is under your feet."

She glanced at him. "I know," she said. He had felt it, too, the ice in that warning, she realized. "Jeff, let me just say this. You were handed a rotten case, one that appeared so open and shut, so destined for a plea bargain that you simply accepted it as given. I started from a different stance. I believed my client and that perspective made me ask a lot of questions that I imagine you never even considered. If he was telling the truth, then who was lying, and why? And that brings us to today and a judge made of dry ice."

✦

CHAPTER 33

THE "BANALITY OF EVIL," Barbara thought when Arlie Morgan was being sworn in. He looked like the middle school teacher who always gave you a second chance, or the neighbor who never yelled if kids ran on his lawn to retrieve a ball, the guy who offered to help you with your flat tire. Everything about him was discreet, his nice gray suit, dark-blue tie, simple haircut exactly the right length. His face was rounder than it had appeared on television, his lips thinner, and he looked older.

The courtroom was crowded. It appeared that his parishioners had come to lend him support, his own cheering section.

Travis had stiffened at his father's appearance, but moments later his arm had relaxed again. "Good for you," Barbara murmured to him. "Just stay relaxed."

Wharton kept his examination in close and tight, establishing only that Morgan was a preacher with a church and a residence in Eugene, and another residence and church in Portland. Immediately after that he got to the day of the shooting.

"When did the defendant call you?"

"On the morning of September tenth, last year."

"When was the last time you talked to him before that call?"

"Seven, close to eight years ago, the day before he left home."

Wharton shook his head as if to say it was hard to believe. He was being deferential to his witness, sympathetic almost to the point of being obsequious. "Did he send you letters, call you, email, make any attempt to keep in touch during those years?"

Morgan sadly said, "No. Not even on Christmas or birthdays. Never a word."

Wharton looked down at papers on his table, cleared his throat, then asked, "When he called did he say what he wanted?"

"He said he had something to tell me, that he had to talk with me alone."

"Did he say anything more than that, that he had to talk to you alone?"

"No. He didn't ask about my health or how I was doing, nothing that you might expect. He was abrupt, almost rude, I have to admit."

"What did you tell him?"

"I started to ask him to come for dinner, but I changed my mind, afraid our first meeting after such a long time with no contact might be awkward for both of us. I asked if he could come at seven thirty and he said yes and hung up."

"Why did you ask Dr. Knowland to come to you that day?"

"I asked for his counsel about the meeting. We discussed the matter at some length and decided the best way for me to handle it was to forgive and forget the past, whatever he had done, why he left, everything, and to start anew with a father/son relationship of mutual trust and kinship, and in time restore the love we once had shared. I was overjoyed with his return. I had prayed every day for him to return, to have his faith restored, and it seemed as if my prayers had been answered. But I was nervous about it at the same time. I didn't know if he had outgrown his youthful rebellious nature, if he still harbored whatever ill feelings that he must have held in the past to make him leave home before he was sixteen. Forgive and forget seemed the best way to go forward and I prayed that afternoon that our meeting would result in harmony, that I could help him find the path of righteousness once again."

He had a very good voice and a good stage presence, Barbara thought, watching and listening. His timing was impeccable with pauses now and then for emphasis, rising and lowering tones expressing his happiness or his regret, and even choking up a little as he finished his lengthy answer.

Wharton had him describe the dinner and the aftermath. It was identical to what the others had said. "I was in a state of shock," Morgan said in a low voice. "I had very recently lost my beloved daughter, and now my only son a killer, my dear friend dead at his hand. I was afraid I was having a heart attack, the shock was so severe." He bowed his head and his lips moved as if he was praying.

And that covered Dr. Knowland, Barbara thought. His real patient might be having a heart attack, so of course he had no time to spare for the man bleeding out on the floor.

It would not have surprised her to see Wharton approach and lay a comforting hand on Morgan's shoulder, she thought derisively as the prosecutor made a hesitant step toward the witness stand. He didn't complete the action, to her disappointment. What was dismaying, however, was the fact that several of the jurors looked as if they would like to comfort the grieving man. She could hear a muffled sob from somewhere behind her, while at her side she could sense Travis stiffening again. She put her hand on his arm, gave it a little squeeze.

Leaning in close to his ear she whispered, "Write a dirty limerick, but for God's sake don't smile." Without waiting for a response she turned her attention back to Wharton.

"Reverend Morgan," Wharton said in a sepulchral tone, "was there any ill will on your part over your son's absence for so many years, any anger that he had left without a word?"

"Never," Morgan said, drawing himself up straighter. "I believe in forgiveness, in lending a hand to whomever has strayed from the path to purity, in accepting that all people are sinners at one time or another and that they can be redeemed. I wanted to help my son find his way, return to a life of righteousness, the path to redemption, regardless of what he had done or what he had been before. I prayed for the opportunity to counsel him, to guide him, pray with him, give him the chance to save his soul. That is still my prayer."

Judge Humphrey was swinging his eyeglasses by the chain with an almost hypnotic regularity. He was looking at her, Barbara realized, and possibly he was willing her to object to the self-aggrandizing lengthy answers. She had no intention of doing such a thing.

"Reverend Morgan, have you any doubt that the defendant committed the murder of Joseph Peel?"

"No. How can I? He was seen doing it. God is testing me, testing my faith, my belief, tempting me to deny the evidence in order to protect my only son. My faith in God, in justice, forbids me to deny my son the opportunity to find salvation through the confession of his deeds, and his acceptance of his fate." He looked as though he might start weeping and bowed his head again.

"Thank you, Reverend Morgan. No more questions," Wharton said.

Barbara rose leisurely and stood by her table, waiting for Morgan to raise his head to face her. He straightened, glanced at her, then looked out over the observers. He had not looked at her a single time since taking the stand until that one brief glance. Slowly she walked to the jury box where she stopped. Again he looked past her at the jury or possibly at one of them.

"Mr. Morgan, will you state your name, please?"

"Benjamin Morgan," he said to the juror his gaze was fixed on.

"Is that your official name, the one on your Social Security records, on your tax records?"

"No. It is a name I chose for myself when I had my calling."

"I see," she said, not moving from the jury box, fascinated at how he could concentrate so completely on the juror he kept looking at.

"What is your official name?"

"Arlie Morgan."

"In your testimony here today you did not refer to your son by name. Will you tell the court what his name is?"

"Isaac Morgan. I chose his name also when I received my calling."

"Did his school records reflect the change of his name?"

He hesitated for a moment, then said, "No. Public schools are too rigid, too bureaucratic, too secular to accept such a change inspired by religious belief."

"Will you tell the court what name is on his birth certificate and his school records?"

"It was Travis Morgan."

"Did your son accept that change of his name?"

"Yes. He was compliant as a child."

"Exactly when did he become rebellious?"

"When lust entered his heart as a teenager."

"Will you please inform the jury about the ways your son demonstrated a rebellious nature?"

"It was in everything he did and said."

"Well, did his grades suffer in school?"

"No, he knew better than to let that happen."

"Did he play truant?"

"Never."

"Did he stay out late at night?"

"No. He had a curfew. I enforced it."

"What did he do that was rebellious?"

"It was his attitude. He rejected good advice, good counsel."

Barbara regarded him coolly for a moment, wondering how many of the jurors had children who had gone through the turbulent hormone-driven storms of puberty, how many of them remembered their own teen years. Something to be talked about in the deliberation room she decided, and changed the subject.

"You stated that Mr. Peel was a dear friend. Did you exchange confidences with him?"

"No. He was quite reserved."

"Did he have dinner or lunch with you on occasion?"

"No. He preferred to eat alone."

"Did you ever visit him at home?"

"No."

"On what did you base your friendship?"

"He was a dedicated follower, a tireless worker for the good of the church, dependable and reliable in all ways. I considered that friendship."

"I see," she said, glancing at the jurors. One in particular, Susan Beale, seemed to be growing uncomfortable under Morgan's unwavering gaze on her. Susan Beale, she recalled, was forty-six, a homemaker, mother of three. Taking pity on her, Barbara walked past her to stand at the end of the jury box. Morgan's gaze shifted to the retired librarian.

"You say that Mr. Peel was a dedicated follower. Did he attend your services when you preached here in Eugene or in your church in Portland?" she asked.

"No. He and his wife lived out in the country and attended a church nearby."

"Can you explain what you mean by saying he was a dedicated follower?"

"He was a righteous man, a good man, a follower of truth."

Barbara nodded. "I see. When did you tell Mr. Peel that Travis was coming to see you the evening of September tenth?"

"Sometime that afternoon. I don't remember just when."

"Mr. Morgan," she said slowly, "the arrangement to have Travis admitted by Mr. Rostov, to be taken to Mr. Peel's office, and then escorted to your study by Mr. Peel seems very complicated. Why didn't you instruct Mr. Rostov to take him upstairs to your study directly?"

His answer was ready. "Joseph asked to have it done that way in order to have a moment with my son. He was quite fond of him as a boy and looked forward to seeing him that evening."

"By Joseph do you refer to Mr. Peel?"

"Yes, of course. As I said he was a dear friend, Joseph."

"Why didn't you have Mr. Peel join you and Dr. Knowland in the study to enjoy a reunion?"

"Joseph said he had some work to do and that he would get to it while waiting for my son to arrive, spend a few minutes with him, and then go on home before it got very late. He expressed a wish that I would have a pleasurable meeting alone with my son. He said it should be a private time to get reacquainted with him. I accepted that."

She moved away from the jury box and watched his gaze dart past her again to focus on the observers. Back at the defense table she asked, "When Mr. DiPalma came to inform you that Mr. Peel had been shot, was he carrying the bookend he used to strike down your son?"

"I don't know. I didn't notice. I was too shocked and stricken by grief."

"When you waited in the hall for Dr. Knowland's pronouncement of Mr. Peel's death did you make any attempt to go to your son to render possible aid, or even to pray?"

He shook his head. "I was in a state of shock, unable to think rationally. Joseph was dead, and they said my son had shot him. That's all I could think of."

"Did you consider that your son might be dying as he lay bleeding?"

"I didn't," he said. "If he was dying, it was God's will."

"As you and the others waited in the hall, did you see Mr. DiPalma carrying the bookend?"

"No. I wasn't paying attention to small details. I feared a heart attack onset. I could hardly breathe."

"Why didn't you go to the living room to sit down, or to lie down on the sofa there?"

"I don't know," he said. "I should have done that, but I didn't think of it."

"Did Dr. Knowland at any time suggest you should sit down or lie down?"

"I don't remember," he said.

"When your daughter arrived home ill, did you call Dr. Knowland immediately?"

"He was already at the house. I had alerted him that the school called to say she was sick and was being flown home to be cared for."

"During that call were you informed of the seriousness of your daughter's condition?"

"No. They said she was sick, that's all."

"What time did she arrive home?"

"Objection!" Wharton called, rising. "This is irrelevant, immaterial, and improper cross-examination."

"Sustained," Judged Humphrey said without a pause.

"Did Travis tell you he had been living in San Francisco?"

He said no and she asked, "How did you know it?"

"When he left home I hired a private detective to find him. He learned that my son had gone to San Francisco on a bus."

"Did you instruct the detective to locate him in San Francisco?"

"No. I knew there were gangs of young people hiding each other, covering for each other, eluding parents and authorities. It would have been pointless."

Barbara took her time to walk back to her table, turn and face him again. He was still looking at the jury. "Mr. Morgan," Barbara said then, "do you find it difficult to face a woman asking you questions?"

Wharton was on his feet instantly objecting, but Morgan ignored him and looked directly at Barbara with wrath writ large upon his face. "Yes!" he said in a booming voice. "Yes! It is offensive to allow an unrepentant sinner, a fornicator, a hell-bound woman to have the authority to question a man of faith, to have this court tolerate a libertine who mocks God—"

Whatever else he was saying was lost in the banging of Judge Humphrey's gavel and Wharton's bellowing voice calling objections. Others among the observers were crying out incoherently. The judge banged and yelled for the bailiff to clear the courtroom, that court was in recess, and he stalked out, walking like an automaton, inhumanly stiff and rigid.

Barbara sat down as soon as Judge Humphrey was out of sight. "Shit hits fan," she said in a low voice to Travis. "Chaos results." She gave him a swift glance and added, "Don't even think of smiling." The jury was being led out and some of the members looked shaken and disbelieving, but a few of them were still watchful of Travis and his reactions to whatever was being said. She felt Frank's hand on her shoulder and gave it a little pat. She knew he would not be smiling, but that inside he was laughing.

Beside her, Travis touched her arm. He looked stricken. "Can he get away with that, calling you names like that, attacking you? Can't you do something about it?"

"It's okay," she said quietly. "I wanted him to reveal that other side and now he has."

The guards came to take Travis to a waiting room. He tore off part of the sheet of paper he had been writing on and stuffed it in his pocket. His limerick, she thought. He probably had really written a dirty limerick. The rest of the courtroom had been cleared. She saw Wharton across the room talking on his cell phone, and her own phone vibrated. It was Derek Peel.

"Yes, Mr. Peel," she said, "what is it?"

"I want to see you."

She thought a moment, then said, "I'll go to Martin's restaurant as soon as I'm free to leave after court adjourns. Is that acceptable?"

"I'll be there," he said and disconnected.

Shelley and Frank were talking in low tones when she turned to them. "Shelley, will you call Martin and tell him to expect Derek Peel and me when we get out of here?"

"Did he say why?" Frank asked.

"Not a word."

"I thought you'd never get to lay a glove on him," Frank said gravely with a nod toward the witness stand. "And the jury was with him all the way, then pow! The librarian regards him with the same look she'd give a silverfish in her books."

"Do you suppose any of them knows the story of the sacrifice of Isaac?" she murmured.

Frank laughed. "Half of them know it by heart and they will be happy to share it with the others. The librarian may take the lead."

"I liked it when he compared himself to Job," Shelley said. "It's all about him, how he's being tested. Coffee, anyone?"

Barbara decided not to face what could be a crowd of Morgan's followers in the corridor outside the courtroom, and Frank said he'd stretch his legs and mosey along with Shelley. They left together and Barbara leaned back in her chair. It could be a lengthy recess. The judge might want to give Morgan time to get himself under control, or to have his private physician give him a fast-acting tranquilizer. It was still fifty-fifty if Humphrey would demand her presence in his chambers to raise hell with her again. She looked up with interest as Wharton approached.

"You know there's a saying to the effect that sometimes the best laid plans have a way of backfiring," he said sharply as he drew near.

"Have you read any of his sermons?" she asked. "You should. Interesting reading. Some of them are available on the Internet."

He had slowed his pace as he reached her table, then he quickened it again and continued to the door without another word.

✦

It was half an hour before court was reconvened. A subdued group of observers silently took their seats, Travis was brought back, the jury seated, Morgan returned to the witness stand, and Judge Humphrey walked in. He used his gavel lightly and said, "Anyone in the guest section of the courtroom who causes a disturbance of any kind will be escorted out and forbidden to return. Mr. Morgan, you must not answer any question if an objection has been raised, until the court renders a decision regarding the objection. Objection sustained, Mr. Wharton. The question and answer will be expunged from the transcript. Ms. Holloway, are you prepared to resume?"

"Yes, Your Honor," she said rising.

Before she could phrase a question, Morgan turned to the judge and asked, "May I have a word before we begin the proceedings?" He looked calm, and his voice was once again the well-modulated voice of a man used to public speaking.

"What is it?" Judge Humphrey asked irritably.

"I wish to apologize to the court, and to the jurors and any others I might have offended by my intemperate outburst. I do apologize most sincerely. I have been under a great deal of stress, but that does not excuse my behavior."

"It will be included in the transcript," Humphrey said. "Ms. Holloway, if you will."

"Mr. Morgan, when you are in Eugene, does Mr. DiPalma live in the church residence where you live?"

"Yes." He appeared to be making an effort to look at her, and even turned his head slightly in her direction, but his eyes were focused on someone to her right.

Deliberately she walked to the jury box before she asked her next question. His gaze followed and again focused on someone else, not on her. Fleetingly she wondered if it would cause another uproar if she waved her hand before his eyes.

"Does Mr. Rostov always live in your residence both here and in Portland?" she asked.

"Yes."

"Had you known either of them before you employed them?"

He hesitated momentarily, then said no.

"Did you do a background check on them before you employed them?"

"No. They came highly recommended by a friend of Dr. Knowland."

"Was that person also your friend?"

"No."

"Were you acquainted with that person?"

"No. I had absolute trust in Dr. Knowland."

"Did you interview any others for the two positions, a driver and a bodyguard?"

"No. There was no need since they were so highly recommended."

She nodded and returned to the defense table. "I have no further questions at this time," she said and sat down. He had already turned to look at Wharton.

"No further questions," Wharton said.

Barbara rose. "Your Honor, I request that the court advise Mr. Morgan that he will be recalled as a defense witness."

There was a gasp from behind her, quickly disguised as a cough.

"Mr. Morgan," Judge Humphrey said, "you will hold yourself in readiness to be recalled by the defense. The court will advise you of the time."

"Yes, Your Honor," Morgan said. "I'll be happy to answer more questions at the appropriate time."

The judge told him to step down and Morgan left the stand and walked from the courtroom. He bowed slightly to the observers but did not glance at Barbara or Travis.

Wharton stood then and said, "Your Honor, the state rests."

Humphrey nodded as if he had known that was to happen. He looked at Barbara. "Is the defense ready to present its case?"

"May I approach?" she asked.

He beckoned her and Wharton. At the bench she said, "I'd like to request a little time to advise my witnesses to prepare to attend these proceedings. May we have until tomorrow morning?"

Humphrey looked at his watch again and nodded. "Court will adjourn for the day and resume at nine in the morning."

When they left the courthouse, Herbert drove Frank home, where Alan was waiting for him, and he dropped off Shelley at Barbara's office. Then he took Barbara to Martin's Restaurant. Derek Peel was sitting in his car parked at the curb.

“I can wait out here,” Herbert said when he parked.

“Don’t be silly. Come on in and have a Coke or something, or pester Martin and Binnie in the kitchen, if they’ll put up with your nonsense.”

“Oh, Martin and me, we’re like this,” he said, crossing his fingers.

Derek Peel got out of his car and joined them on the walk to the door, which Martin opened almost instantly.

“Hey, Herbert. Looking good, man,” Martin said, ushering them all inside. “Coffee coming up,” he said to Barbara. “Mr. Peel, what can I get you?”

“Coffee,” Derek said.

“Right,” Martin said. Then he motioned to Herbert to come along and went back to the kitchen.

“Ms. Holloway,” Derek said as she took off her coat, “Travis didn’t do it, did he?”

“No.” She sat down and waited. He was regarding her with a steady look, somber and thoughtful, and troubled.

“I’ve been in court every day,” he said, seating himself opposite her. “They’re sleaze bags, both DiPalma and Rostov, but would they lie for Morgan? Kill for him? That’s where I stumble. Why would they? There’s something else going on, isn’t there?” When she remained silent, he held up his hand. “I know, sorry. Anyway, I talked to my mother last night.” He stopped when Martin appeared with the coffee carafe and cups.

After Martin returned to the kitchen and Barbara poured coffee for both of them, he finished what he had started to say. “I begged her to tell me what she had been so afraid of, and she did. She had met Daggart, under a different name, months before he started to work as handyman at the church. He came out to the farm and had a long talk with my father. She doesn’t remember what name he gave then. At the time she assumed it was about an order of grapes or something. Last summer, when they buried June, my father told my mother that when Daggart got killed, he had been working with him, that he was doing some kind of investigation. Mother doesn’t know what he was investigating, only that he was and my father was involved. That’s what upset him so much when Daggart got killed. That’s when he said he was going to quit in March last year. He was afraid they, whoever they are, knew he was working with Daggart and he might be next.”

"You realize that whatever you tell me now, if I can use it when she testifies, I'll ask about it," Barbara said slowly.

He nodded. "Of course I know that. She knows it, too." His level gaze did not falter. "That's the point, Ms. Holloway. Also, when Dad called her that Friday, he didn't have a clue about Travis's return, or his coming visit. Dad told her he didn't know why Morgan told him to stay. Morgan claimed that there was something wrong with the books, or that some money hadn't been accounted for, something like that, and Dad knew it was a lie, but that's all he knew."

"He told your mother that?" Barbara asked. The housekeeper had heard only the last part of their conversation then, not the important part.

"Yes. It was at about five when he called to say he'd be late. That's when Morgan told him to stay, a few minutes before five. He was ready to leave when Morgan stopped him. Mother had dinner in the oven and got a little hot about it, calling that late. They were both so ready for him to quit the job, just be done with it."

Barbara sipped coffee. "You know that Wharton will be rough on her, but does she know that?"

He nodded. "She knows. She's ready." He drank his coffee.

"I appreciate this very much," Barbara said. "Mr. Peel, why is your mother willing to help the defense, go through the ordeal of being a defense witness?"

He drained his coffee cup and rose. "Because she hates Arlie Morgan. It seems he suggested once that she had failed as a woman by having only one son. She couldn't have more children, and it was none of his damn business. She never told Dad because she knew he would quit on the spot and they needed the money." He headed for the door. "I'll see you in court tomorrow."

✦

CHAPTER 34

BARBARA PUT IN the afternoon hours in her office, had a quick dinner at home, and returned to the office. She thought she must have slept, since she woke up in bed the next morning, had something instantly forgettable for breakfast, then back in court, where the hours since the previous day seemed snipped out of time, and this was simply a continuation without a break.

Her first witness was Sandra Barilla, an accountant, a partner in the firm Barilla and Strum, CPA. She was sixty, a little overweight, with ash-colored hair that was streaked with gold highlights. She wore oversized gold-rimmed eyeglasses, dangling gold earrings, and a large ornate watch inlaid with gold and turquoise patterns.

"Ms. Barilla, were you acquainted with Joseph Peel?"

"Indeed. For more than twenty years." She nodded as she answered, and the earrings swung back and forth.

"Describe your relationship to him, please."

"I knew him when he was the bookkeeper for an automobile dealership years ago and I was the accountant for the company. Around the time that the company folded, Mr. Morgan asked me to recommend a bookkeeper. Joe came to mind. I recommended him and he became the bookkeeper for Mr. Morgan and his church. Over the years we became friends, had lunch together now and then, and we were in touch about taxes and other financial matters."

"How would you describe his work habits, his bookkeeping?"

"He was the best I ever worked with. Meticulous in every detail. Never had an adjustment to make. Just the best."

"What does that mean, an adjustment to make?"

"Well, you know how it is. Some people come up a little short when they try to reconcile an account, a few cents to quite a few dollars in some cases, and instead of trying to find the money, they make an adjustment. Sometimes in their favor, sometimes in the bank's favor. You know, add it in, or maybe subtract it from the balance. But Joe would hunt down every penny and not stop until he found the error. It was a pleasure to be the accountant with such a careful bookkeeper."

"Were you the accountant for Mr. Morgan and his church at the time you recommended Mr. Peel?"

"Yes, and his books were in terrible shape. He had come into a lot of donated money and couldn't handle it. That was about twelve or thirteen years ago now, and for the last eleven years Joe was his bookkeeper, and there hasn't been any problem since."

"Thank you, Ms. Barilla," Barbara said. "No further questions."

Wharton had no questions.

Barbara had Dr. Donald Whaite called.

He stated his credentials crisply. He was an ophthalmologist and Joseph Peel had been his patient for twenty years.

"I saw him every other year," he said. "I prescribed eyeglasses for him to correct distance viewing. About three years ago, he began to have trouble with close work and he used reading glasses. Two years ago he complained that it was a terrible nuisance to have to carry two pairs of glasses at all times and sometimes he pulled out the wrong ones. I prescribed bifocals. His only complaint was that if he had them on while walking, at meals, or while working at his farm, most intermediate distances, he was disoriented and he learned to wear them only when he was working at the computer or with bookkeeping ledgers, reading, any close work of that sort, or when he was driving. That solved his problem, and he was happy not to have to carry two pairs of glasses."

"Did he find them necessary when he was working with his computer?"

"Yes, he did."

She thanked him and said she had no more questions. Wharton had no questions.

Moving right along, she thought when her next witness was called.

Dr. James Tunney was middle aged. He had a receding hairline that made his forehead domelike and appear larger than normal. His eyes were keen, very dark blue, his eyebrows were thick and unruly, growing out in all directions.

"Dr. Tunney, were you on duty in the emergency room the night of September tenth of last year when Travis Morgan was brought in?"

"Yes, I was."

"Will you describe his condition and what you did that night?"

"He was bleeding from a head wound, and he was unconscious. I applied a pressure bandage to the head, and I ordered a MRI to determine if there was a skull fracture. There was already an IV started and I ordered monitors for blood pressure, heartbeat, oxygen level, and so on. I ordered a urine test and had blood drawn for lab work. I ordered a tetanus shot. Since there was no fracture, I had his head wound cleaned and the area shaved in order to suture the cut. When he regained consciousness, I asked him a few routine questions to determine his comprehension, to learn if he was disoriented. I sutured the wound, applied a bandage, and ordered acetaminophen and for him to be kept twenty-four hours for observation."

"Did your lab tests find any trace of alcohol or drugs?"

"No."

"Can you describe his wound in terms a layman can grasp?"

He smiled slightly and nodded. "Yes. It was a cut about two inches long and it was diagonally administered, not straight on. The skin was pushed upward and much of the adjacent skin was badly damaged, cut and shredded. Hair was embedded in the cut and had to be cleaned out."

"What do you mean when you say it was diagonally administered?"

He faced the jury when he answered. "A straight cut would have the skin on both sides of the injury equally damaged. A diagonal cut would show skin moved in the direction of the blow and it would be more damaged, cut and sometimes shredded, depending on the force applied and on the sharpness of the instrument. I determined that the instrument in this case was not a knife or something similar, but sharp enough to cut upward through to the skull, mashing hairs rather than cutting through them, and driving the hairs into the wound."

Barbara walked to the evidence table and retrieved the evidence bag with the bookend that had been used, and at the same time Shelley brought out the duplicate bookend. Together they walked to the witness stand and put both on the rail. Shelley returned to the defense table and Barbara picked up the bookend in the evidence bag to show to Dr. Tunney.

"This is the bookend that injured Travis Morgan," she said, handing it to him. "Can you clearly see the bloodstains on it?"

Holding it with both hands he examined it carefully, then said yes and handed it back to her. She put it on the rail and picked up the other one.

"This is an exact duplicate," she said. "Will you please mark on it where the bloodstains are on the other one." She handed him a marker.

She watched him mark the bookend, then motioned to Shelley, who immediately rose and picked up a life-sized mannequin's head. It was smooth and bone white, a hairless male head with closed eyes. Shelley brought the head to Barbara, picked up the stained bookend in the evidence bag and took it back to the evidence table.

"Dr. Tunney," Barbara said, "will you please mark on this head where the cut was on Travis Morgan's head."

"Objection," Wharton called out finally. "Your Honor, this is just theater. We all know that the defendant was injured when he was subdued after shooting Joseph Peel. His injury is not the issue before us."

Barbara said angrily, "Counsel is assigning guilt before the conclusion of this trial."

Judge Humphrey looked as if he wanted to toss them both out. "Rephrase your objection," he told Wharton.

"We concede that the defendant was injured when he was subdued, and we contend that it has nothing to do with the issue before this court, that it is theater, not relevant."

Barbara glanced at the jury, all of whom seemed entranced by the doctor on the stand and the plastic head he was holding. Judge Humphrey seemed equally fixated on the stand.

"Your Honor," she said, "it is very important to establish the nature of the injury Travis Morgan sustained and how it was administered."

"Overruled," Judge Humphrey said without a glance at Wharton. "Dr. Tunney, you may continue."

The doctor looked puzzled, his gaze going from the head and back to the bookend several times. He drew a line slightly off the horizontal about half an inch above the left ear to indicate the injury, then watched as Barbara took the head to the jury box to show them where he had marked it. She returned to the stand and placed the plastic head on the rail.

"Doctor, assuming you were going to hit someone in the head with that bookend, how would you do it in order to inflict the injury you have described? You may have to stand up in order to demonstrate this."

"Objection!"

"Yes, yes," Humphrey said irritably. "Overruled."

Barbara nodded to Dr. Tunney. He rose, then picked up the bookend in both hands. After a moment, looking from it to the plastic head, he turned the bookend so that he could hold it in one hand in such a way the back of it was facing him and he was holding it by the wing, the same way DiPalma said he had held it. The doctor picked up the plastic head and held it at arm's length, eyed the bookend, frowned, then turned the head around until it was almost facing him. After studying the bookend and the head another moment or two, he swung the bookend forward, but stopped short of touching the plastic head.

"It had to have been bent," he said, and it was not clear if he was talking to Barbara, the jury, or to himself. He tilted the head toward the floor, started to swing again, and stopped again. "Moving," he said. "That would work." This time when he swung the bookend, he also moved the head forward, and this time the bottom of the bookend connected to the head.

He looked at Barbara and nodded. "That's how it would work," he said.

She nodded. "You may sit down again," she said, taking the plastic head from him as he replaced the bookend on the rail. "Can you explain what you said, that it had to be bent?"

"Yes," he said. "It's how the cut could have been inflicted indicating an upward motion."

"Can you explain why it had to be moving?"

"Since only the bottom edge of the bookend made contact with the head, it indicates that the head was in motion away from the object. That also explains why the damage was less severe than it might have been if the entire back of the bookend had struck the head."

She motioned to Shelley once more and this time Shelley brought forth a ten-inch-tall flexible male doll. She removed the bookend, but left the plastic head.

"Using this doll, can you position it in such a way that it would account for the position of Travis Morgan when the blow was struck?" Barbara said, handing the doll to Dr. Tunney.

He looked at it with an ironic grimace, then began to manipulate it as if testing its flexibility. He turned the head toward the left, then tilted it to face downward. Slowly he bent the doll a little bit and it took on the appearance of a running man or, Barbara thought, a man who had been unbalanced momentarily. He studied it for another moment, shrugged, and said, "That position would account for the cut, especially if he was in motion, moving away from the weapon."

"Thank you," she said, taking the doll to the jury box, where she slowly walked until all the jurors had a chance to see it.

Done with the doll and the plastic head, she stood near the jury box and asked, "Doctor, you said you asked Travis routine questions to assess his state of mind when he regained consciousness. Please tell the court what kind of questions you asked."

"Did he know what year it was, who the president was, his own name, age?"

"Was he entirely rational, not confused?"

"Yes, he was completely aware, but in a great deal of pain. His first words were 'Who hit me?' That's when I asked him the questions."

"Was anyone in the room with you at that time?"

"Yes. There was a nurse, and a detective who had come in with him and stayed nearby."

"Did he speak to Travis?"

"Yes. He placed him under arrest for the murder of Joseph Peel. He read him his Miranda rights."

"How did Travis respond?"

"He expressed disbelief, bewilderment. He said he had been pushed and hit in the head, that he never killed anyone and didn't know what the detective was talking about. The detective said he was seen shooting Joseph Peel and it would be best if he just admitted it. Travis Morgan said he never shot a gun in his life. His blood pressure reading and his countenance both indicated that he was suffering from his wound. I told the detective that I had to tend to my patient and there could be no more questions or talk with him that night."

"Dr. Tunney, if Travis had not turned his head, or if his head had not been bent in the way you indicated, could a blow such as he received have been fatal?"

"Objection! Conjectural."

Judge Humphrey sustained the objection.

Barbara nodded. "Thank you, Doctor." She nodded to Wharton. "Your witness."

He looked murderously angry, she thought as she took her seat. At that moment Judge Humphrey tapped his gavel and said court would be in recess until one thirty. Barbara cursed under her breath.

Give Wharton time to come up with something to counter what he knew was damning evidence, she thought, furious with the judge.

Frank had made the base for fish stew the previous night, and when they returned to his house for lunch that day, he said, "Ten minutes, maybe fifteen, it will be edible." He busied himself at the counter, but he noticed that Barbara immediately headed for the stairs.

Five times up and down, he noted when Barbara came to stand at the sliding glass door, gazing out at a sad-looking sodden backyard. He doubted that she even saw it.

"It's ready," he said as they all took chairs and he began to ladle out the soup. "That doll business reminded me of a time I played with dolls during a trial," he said, smiling faintly. "Not as sturdy in those days as they are now, I guess. I had it just right and let the jury have it, and those idiots passed it around and twisted it this way and that, and first thing you knew, one arm got pulled off. Then a leg, and the head was hanging by a string. By the time I got it back I had a handful of doll parts and egg on my face." He chuckled and tore off a piece of dark bread.

Barbara smiled in the polite way of people who had not been paying a lot of attention, and a moment later she put down her spoon, mumbled something, and headed for the stairs again. This time she didn't return until Frank called up that it was time.

Dr. Tunney was back on the stand and Wharton stood at his table. "Dr. Tunney," he said briskly, "isn't it true that patients sometimes ask for a second opinion after receiving a diagnosis from a physician?"

"Yes."

"Are there times when that second opinion contradicts the first one?"

"Yes. It happens."

"Have you had patients ask for a second opinion?"

Again he answered yes.

"Can you say with complete confidence that you know what happened the night of September tenth?"

Dr. Tunney looked thoughtful, then said, "No."

"Are there possible other ways to explain the cut the defendant sustained?"

"There might be other ways."

"Can you state with absolute assurance that the way you described is the only way it could have happened?"

"No. Not absolute assurance."

"No more questions," Wharton said and sat down.

Good job, Barbara thought. He had pulled out the carpet of infallibility many people associated with doctors. She stood at the defense table to ask, "Dr. Tunney, in your opinion, is the scenario you described the most likely way the blow could have been administered?"

"Yes, it is."

"Did you consider other ways before you arrived at that conclusion?"

"Yes."

"Did you discard other explanations as being unlikely or not workable?"

"Yes," he said and looked as if he might go on, but she simply nodded and said no more questions.

Barbara called her next witness when he left.

Detective Gerald Eggleston was a twelve-year veteran in the homicide unit. Lean and sharp featured, with closely cropped dark hair and dark eyes, he looked as if he ran marathons or bicycled a lot.

"Detective Eggleston," Barbara asked after he had been sworn in and took his seat at the witness stand, "did you accompany Travis Morgan to the emergency room on the night of September tenth, last year?"

"Yes, I did."

"Did you read him his Miranda rights?"

He said yes. She asked him to read the rights to the court, and watched him pull a card from his pocket and proceed to read in a mechanical, nearly toneless voice.

"Did you make a note of everything he said when he regained consciousness?"

He said yes, and she asked what he did with those notes.

"I included them in my report and turned it in to my superior, Lieutenant Hellerman."

"Did Travis Morgan say he didn't know what you were talking about when you said he was under arrest?"

When he said yes, she asked about the other statements—that he had been pushed and hit in the head, that he had never shot a gun in his life. Each question was answered with the one word: yes.

"Did you advise Travis Morgan that it would be best for him to admit his guilt?"

Again he answered yes.

"Were all those statements included in your report?"

He said yes and she nodded to Wharton. "Your witness."

Wharton looked troubled when he stood and took a few steps toward the witness stand. "Detective Eggleston, over the years of service have you read the Miranda rights to many suspects you've placed under arrest?"

"Yes."

"Were you surprised when the defendant denied guilt on the night of September ten?"

"No. Most of them do."

"Why did you tell him it would be in his best interest to admit guilt?"

"It's true. It would have been in his best interest to avoid a trial, plead for leniency, express remorse. That always helps a defendant."

"No more questions," Wharton said.

Barbara said she had no more questions, and when Eggleston left the stand, she called her next witness.

Julius Straub was cherubic, with pink cheeks, bright-blue eyes, white curly hair, a potbelly, and a beaming smile. He stated his name and occupation. He was a gun appraiser. He had worked for the federal and local governments, for various auction houses, including Sotheby's in Britain, for gun shows, and for individuals. He was sixty-three years old.

"Mr. Straub," Barbara started, "have you had the opportunity to examine the gun used to shoot Mr. Joseph Peel?"

"Yes, of course. At the district attorney's office, where they keep evidence for a coming trial. You were there." He smiled happily at her.

She returned his smile and walked to the jury box, where she stood as she asked, "Will you please tell the court what you determined about that weapon?"

"Oh, it's a lovely handgun. A Colt single-action army handgun. They often just called it a Colt Six-Shooter. It was used by cowboys a lot. You see it in old western movies all the time, of course. Well, not originals but replicas. That particular model was produced in 1917 and 1918, and it's in excellent shape. No signs of any abuse, no dirt embedded in it. Someone took good care of it, probably kept it wrapped in a special cloth so it didn't get bumped against anything hard enough to damage it. The stock is metal, no inlays. It has a six-inch barrel, and an overall length of eleven inches. The six-inch barrel isn't quite as accurate as the eight inch, but it's considered very accurate. It weighs a little over two pounds. It's a collector's item."

"Mr. Straub," Barbara said as she walked back to the defense table, "you kindly provided photographs of this kind of weapon." She picked them up, ten-by-twelve photographs, and showed them to Wharton and the judge. "Are these the same photographs you gave me?" He said yes. "Using the first one, will you explain what you mean by single-action gun?"

He was happy to do so. Holding the photograph so that the jury and the judge could see it, he pointed as he described the parts of the gun. "The hammer, you can see, has this little spur to make it easier to cock the gun. You have to cock it before it will shoot. You pull back the hammer and it's ready to fire. When you pull the trigger, the hammer strikes the gunpowder in the bullet in the chamber and the explosion it creates propels the bullet forward. You have to cock it again to turn the chamber and bring another bullet in line before you can shoot it again, and so on. So it's a single-action weapon."

"How do you load it?" she asked.

He pointed to the bullet chamber as he showed the next picture. "That weapon has a side-loading action. See? It pulls out so you can put five bullets in the chamber."

"But you said it was a six-shooter," Barbara said. "Why only five bullets?"

His smile broadened. "It has no safety mechanism. Most often one chamber was left empty because once it's cocked, it's ready to fire. It may be only a story, but it's said that when duelists used this weapon, they rolled up a five-dollar bill to stuff into the empty chamber, and it paid the funeral expenses of the loser. Some of the guns had what they called a hair trigger, meaning that accidentally touching the trigger could fire it if a bullet was in the chamber when the hammer hit. It made it too easy for a man to shoot himself in the foot, or somewhere else even more distressing." He looked ready to laugh. "Hair trigger or not, after that gun is cocked, if there is a bullet in the chamber, it's ready to fire and it doesn't take much to fire it. A bump, if it's dropped, absently fingering the trigger, anything of that sort could fire it."

"How would such a weapon usually be carried?" Barbara asked.

"In a holster was the safest way. The spur on the hammer would be clear and not accidently cocked by drawing it out of a pocket, for example."

"Mr. Straub, will you please tell the court what is on the back of the photograph you're holding."

He turned it over and said, "My initials, JWS, and the numbers 27890. I wrote that myself."

"Thank you," she said, taking the two photographs. After having them admitted as evidence, she went to her table for another enlarged photograph. This was of the holstered gun that Arlie Morgan's father had worn the day Morgan bagged his first deer. Nothing but the holster and gun were in the photograph. After showing it to Wharton and the judge, she handed it to Straub. "Is that how you would expect such a gun to be carried?"

His expression was loving as he gazed at the photograph, and even traced the gun and holster with his finger. "Exactly," he said. "Together, the Colt and its own original holster would be a highly prized item for a collector. As you can see, the hammer is clear, the spur not likely to catch on anything."

Barbara passed the photograph to the jurors, some of who looked almost as interested as Straub, a few performing their duty without any show of real interest.

"You've said that this gun is a collector's item. How rare is it if it was an army-issue handgun, and widely used by cowboys?"

"Very rare in that fine condition," he said promptly. "Things vanish, they get sold off at a time when they have little value. Also, there was a finite number of them made. Double-action revolvers were coming out, and the single-action was considered old-fashioned and cumbersome. A collector might want to finish a collection of single-action guns from that period, or someone who wants all the Colts from one period to another, say 1890 to 1920, for example, or a museum looking to finish a collection. There are a lot of collectors and reasons they give for their dedication to collecting, and they often bid very high for an item. The owner of such a gun would probably advertise in one of the many gun magazines, or even online, and let the bidding start, with a floor of say five thousand to ten thousand dollars, sit back and wait. Then it's anyone's guess as to how high the bidding would go."

"Where would you, as an appraiser, set the floor?"

"Ten thousand," he said without hesitation.

"Will you please tell the court what is on the back of that photograph."

He nodded and glanced at the back, then repeated what he had said before. "JWS, 27890. I wrote it there, too," he added.

"Is the gun in that photograph like the one in the evidence bag, like the one you photographed?"

"Exactly like it," he said.

Got their interest, she thought, as she left the jury box and had the photograph entered as evidence. "Mr. Straub," she said then, "several times you've mentioned replicas. Are they very much like the original guns?"

"Almost exactly, except for the serial numbers," he said. "They are used extensively in movies, and they are available for sale to individuals. They turn up at gun shows."

"How much are the replicas worth?" she asked.

"Oh, new, from fifteen hundred to a couple thousand dollars. Used, a lot less than that, of course."

"If I went to a pawn shop, for example, to buy a gun would I be likely to find a Colt single-action army handgun?"

Wharton objected. "Irrelevant and conjectural," he said.

The objection was sustained.

"Your witness," Barbara said with a nod to Wharton.

He was on his feet instantly. "Mr. Straub, would someone unfamiliar with handguns, without your extensive knowledge of them, regard that weapon as anything other than an old gun?"

"Objection," Barbara said. "Conjectural."

"Sustained."

"No more questions," Wharton said and sat down.

But he had made his point, she knew. That lack of interest in some jurors until they realized the value of the gun had not been lost on Wharton. "Mr. Straub," she asked on redirect, "would a gun like this one be easily purchased through a regular gun outlet such as a store, a pawnshop, a gun show?"

"Oh my, no," he said with a huge smile. "People who deal in guns know enough to check the serial number, date of issue, things of that sort. It would not show up routinely. People who buy such guns don't want to use them, they want to have them."

✦

After a brief recess Barbara called Mary Ochmann. She was seventy-two years old, deeply wrinkled, and tiny. No more than five feet tall and about a hundred pounds, she carried herself like a model, stiff-backed, her head high, and she walked with a steady, easy stride. Her hair was silver, in a chignon with a tortoiseshell comb. She stated her name, spelled it, and took the witness stand, sitting bolt upright.

"What is your address?" Barbara asked.

She gave an address on Willamette, then added, "Right next to Benjamin Morgan's house."

Barbara asked if she was employed, and she drew herself up even straighter and said, "I do volunteer work for Meals On Wheels four days a week. I am a volunteer at Sacred Heart Hospital two days a week, and I am a volunteer worker for Friends of the Library. I do not have time for a regular job."

"Are you acquainted with Mr. Morgan?"

"I know him by sight. We've never spoken more than to say good day."

"On the night of June fifteenth, did you observe anything in particular happening at Mr. Morgan's house?"

"Yes. That's why I'm here, I assume."

Barbara smiled at her. "Indeed it is. Please tell the court in your own words what you saw that night."

"Objection," Wharton said, rising. "What happened in June has no bearing on the case at hand. Irrelevant."

"May I approach?" Barbara asked.

Judge Humphrey beckoned them both. "Well?" he snapped at Barbara. "Can you relate it to the case being tried?"

"Yes, Your Honor. Dr. Knowland either misspoke or else he perjured himself. In either event his credibility as a witness is under question."

He eyed her sourly. "I'll overrule for now," he said. "But if it turns out that this witness has nothing to substantiate your argument, I shall have the question and the answer stricken from the transcript. Now get on with it. It's getting late."

When they were back at their tables, the judge said to Mrs. Ochmann. "You may answer the question."

She nodded and faced Barbara again. "I usually have to go to the bathroom during the night, and I did that night. It was ten minutes past three when I returned to my bedroom. I never turn on lights when I get up. A bright light wakes me up too much and I use a small flashlight. On my way back to bed, I heard a car pull into the driveway at Mr. Morgan's house, and I looked out the window to see who was keeping such late hours. It was a hearse. I was surprised and a little alarmed, thinking that Mr. Morgan might have died, since I thought he had been looking poorly the last time or two that I saw him. No one went to the door of the house, however, and in a minute or two someone came out and went to the hearse. It wasn't Mr. Morgan or the two men who work for him. I had seen this person quite often before but I didn't know his name at that time. He got in the hearse through the rear door, and he stayed for twenty minutes. Then he went back inside the house and the hearse drove off. I went back to bed at three thirty, annoyed because by then I was so wide awake I was afraid I would be unable to return to sleep, which was the case as it turned out."

"Have you since that time learned his name?"

"Yes. His picture was in the newspaper after the shooting at the Morgan house. He was Dr. Knowland."

"Did you have a clear view of what was happening the night you saw the hearse?"

"Yes. I rent out the first floor of my house to a real estate company and I have the entire second floor. My bedroom is on the side of the house next to Mr. Morgan's house. I was at my bedroom window the entire time and I could see everything quite well. My room was dark, but house lights were on in the Morgan house, as well as in the hearse, and there was a streetlight."

"Are you certain that the vehicle you saw was a hearse? Not a van, or something else?"

"I know a hearse when I see one," Mrs. Ochmann said sharply. "It had double doors in the back, windows with curtains, and a company name on the side. I couldn't read it from above, as I was, but there was lettering and a scroll design. The curtains were closed, but there was light on inside and I could see it around the edges. It was a hearse."

Her words and the way she said them made it clear that she knew it was a hearse in exactly the same way she knew the sun would rise in the east.

Barbara thanked her and nodded to Wharton.

"Mrs. Ochmann," he said in a reasonable voice, "are you aware of the many different kinds of vans and other recreational vehicles that have windows with curtains and double doors?"

"It was a hearse," she said.

"Please answer the question," Wharton said in the manner of a nephew talking to an eccentric aunt.

She looked him over, up and down, her lips tightened, and she said, "I am not interested in recreational vehicles and I am not aware of how many there are and what they look like."

"If you get up in the middle of the night frequently, how can you be certain of the date of this incident? Might it have been a different date?"

"I know the date the same way most people do. I read the newspaper and listen to the news on the radio and watch it on television. I have a calendar on which I note any appointments as well as the days I do volunteer work. As I said, I was afraid I would not be able to return to sleep, and I couldn't. I rose at five thirty and read the newspaper when it arrived. When I went to the hospital later, I mentioned that I might be a bit disgruntled because of the carrying on of neighbors. That evening I had dinner with friends and mentioned it again to them. Then I saw the announcement in the newspaper that Ruth Morgan had died on that day. I know the date."

Wharton looked taken aback by her firm answer. She had become the aunt telling the nephew to go wash his hands again and try harder the next time.

"Mrs. Ochmann," Wharton said coolly, "isn't it possible that you did see some kind of recreational vehicle in that driveway, that you read that Ruth Morgan had died, and in your mind you connected the two incidents, reversed their order so that you would have an interesting story for your friends?"

"Objection!" Barbara called. "He's harassing the witness, badgering her."

"Sustained," Humphrey said.

Mrs. Ochmann was regarding Wharton with a cold look of her own and an even stiffer spine, if that had been possible.

"Young man," she said, "today's events will more than do for an interesting story to tell my friends."

"Objection!" he said. "I ask that the gratuitous remark be stricken."

"Sustained. The remark will be stricken," Judge Humphrey turned to Mrs. Ochmann, "Madam," he said, "you are required to answer proper questions and not to speak otherwise. Do you understand?"

"Of course I do," she said politely.

Wharton said no more questions and sat down.

Barbara rose. "Mrs. Ochmann, did you see a hearse in the driveway of Mr. Morgan's house on June fifteenth at approximately three-ten in the morning?"

"Yes. At exactly three ten in the morning."

"Did you see Dr. Knowland come from the house, get inside the hearse, and remain there for twenty minutes?"

"Yes."

"Did he then return to the house and the hearse leave?"

"Yes. At three thirty the hearse left and he went inside."

"Thank you," Barbara said. "No more questions."

When she turned toward the observers, she saw that Ashley Loven was weeping, with her sister's arm around her. At her table, Barbara touched Travis's arm. It was like steel.

"She was already dead," he said in a low, savage voice. "That fucking liar! She was already dead!"

"Keep calm," Barbara said fiercely. "Just don't lose it now!"

He bowed his head.

Judge Humphrey put on his glasses, consulted his watch, checked it against the wall clock, then said court would recess until nine o'clock the next morning. And not a minute too soon, Barbara thought, rising as the judge left. She watched the jurors as they rose to be led out. They were staring at Travis, at Ashley, at her and Wharton, and they looked completely confused.

CHAPTER 35

BARBARA TURNED TO speak to Frank only to realize he had already left.

"He said he'll see you in your office in a little while," Shelley said. "I think he might have gotten a buzz on his phone."

"Well, that's where I'll be."

An hour later, she was there when Frank walked in, closely followed by Shelley.

"Two things," Frank said, taking off his coat. "Bailey called. The plane left at eleven this morning, returned at five. The fellow he has keeping an eye out couldn't see who boarded. He's staying away from the various feds who are also keeping an eye out. It's too early, Bobby, if those Bible dates are right. They were due to fly out on Monday, if I recall properly."

"You do," she said. "What's the other thing?"

"What really dragged me out of court before you. Scuttlebutt has it that Judge Humphrey mentioned to his staff that he might want them in on Saturday. Seems he thinks you'll wrap up your part tomorrow, closing statements before lunch on Saturday and give it to the jury."

She stared at him for a moment. "He thinks it will be a guilty verdict, and that it won't take them long to come to that decision."

"God alone knows what he thinks, but I know what I think. He's sick and tired of sitting at that bench and his butt hurts. He's tired of the whole affair, of being a judge, of having to get up in the morning, maybe tired of living. But whatever is pushing him, it could mean you'll have to come up with your closing statement by Saturday."

She left her desk to go sit on the sofa. "It could all unravel," she said in a low voice. "The plane taking off too soon, a judge who's already made up his mind. ATF might decide those guys really were planning a gun sale in Mexico and let it go at that. A smart lawyer might even tell them to admit to it."

"Not totally unravel," Frank said. "The plane could be on a different mission altogether. Also, those two hit men Milt arrested are still on ice. He got a match from forensics, fibers from Daggart's coat were on the loaded gloves, and the other fellow with the silencer has an arrest warrant pending from New York, suspicion of assault with a deadly weapon. Enough to hold them without bail for now. He might be able to get something out of them."

"They won't talk," she said dully. "Humphrey has made it pretty damn clear that he won't allow me to bring up Morgan's theology, his rants about sex, anything to do with his church. He'll slam the door if I try to connect Peel's death with anything else." She looked at Frank with a bleak expression. "Well, if I have to have a closing statement by Saturday, and I have a full lineup for tomorrow, I'd better be getting at it. Oh, I'd better tell Darren not to wait dinner."

Frank put his coat on again. "Shelley, are you working late?"

She nodded.

"I'm going to call Martin and have him send over food for the lot of you," Frank said, going to the door. "Barbara, is there anything I can help with?"

"I wish," she said. "But no. You realize I don't have a clue about what to expect from Mrs. Peel? Never go in cold. You said that to me a long time ago, but tomorrow it looks like I'll be diving into ice water. See you in court, Dad."

When Dr. Knowland was recalled, the judge reminded him that he was still under oath and nodded to Barbara to proceed.

The good country doctor, she thought as she walked to the jury box, the doctor Robert Frost had in mind for that snowy evening. "Dr. Knowland," she said, "three years ago this April did you treat June Morgan in Portland for influenza?"

He looked startled. "I believe it might have been about that time," he said after a moment.

"Did you attend to her until the time she was sent away?"

"Objection! Irrelevant."

"Your Honor, I want to establish the last time prior to June of this year that Dr. Knowland saw June Morgan, and whether he had known her when she was ill at that time for comparison to his treatment of her this year. I believe he may have misspoken and I want the record cleared."

Judge Humphrey cleaned his glasses, put them on and peered at Knowland, then at Barbara, and finally said, "Overruled."

Barbara looked at Knowland. "Did you treat June Morgan through that period until she was flown out of Portland?"

"Yes. I was her physician. She made a good recovery and Reverend Morgan sent her to a boarding school. She was perfectly well by then."

"You stated that you attended June Morgan again in June of last year. Is that correct?"

He said yes and she asked, "Would you, as a physician, fly a desperately ill patient home from a boarding school?"

"No, but it might not have been clear how very ill she was when she boarded the plane," he said after a moment.

"Where was the boarding school she attended?"

"Objection! This is completely irrelevant!"

"It isn't," Barbara said quickly. "How long she was on a plane, what her condition was when she arrived in Eugene is very relevant."

"Overruled," Humphrey said.

"I don't know where the school is," Knowland said. "I didn't ask."

"You stated previously that she was dying when you saw her, and that she died within several hours. Is that correct?"

He hesitated a moment, then said yes.

"Is this the death certificate you signed, giving the cause of her death as pneumonia?"

She showed the copy to Wharton and the judge, then held it up for Knowland to see. After he said it was, she looked at it and slowly said, "On this certificate, you give the cause of death and you also give the time. Three a.m. Is that correct?" She held it up again and again he said yes.

She had it admitted as evidence. "Dr. Knowland, when did you learn that June Morgan was to be flown to Eugene?"

"Late that night, ten or later. I don't remember."

"What did you do when you found out?"

"I went straight over to Reverend Morgan's house to be on hand when she arrived."

"Did you prepare a bed for her, make certain any necessary medications were on hand, do anything to make treating her possible?"

"Not immediately," he said after a long pause. "I had no idea how ill she was, what would be needed."

"How and where did you assess her condition if she was not in a bed?"

"She was on a gurney when I saw her. In the house. I didn't have her moved to a bed. There was no point in doing that."

"How was she transported from the airport to the house?"

"By a medical van."

"Who made the arrangements for the medical van to transport her?"

"I don't know. I assumed the school did."

"Did Mr. Morgan see his daughter that night?"

He was losing his polish, Barbara thought, regarding him. The good doctor was starting to sweat a little.

"I told him to go to bed at about midnight," he said. "He needed his rest and there was no point in having both of us awake. When I saw how ill she was, that she was dying, there was nothing he could have done and I knew his grief would be overwhelming, that he would need his strength to get through the coming days. I didn't wake him up."

"Is Mr. Morgan suffering from a heart condition?"

"I can't discuss my patient's medical situation," he said stiffly.

"I withdraw the question," she said. Then she asked, "When you determined that June Morgan had died, what did you do?"

He moistened his lips and seemed to draw himself inward before he answered. "I signed her death certificate and told the ambulance personnel to take her body to the mortuary."

Without moving away from the jury box she asked, "On the morning of June fifteenth, did you walk from Mr. Morgan's house and enter a hearse in the driveway?"

"No," he said harshly.

"Did you see June Morgan on the morning of June fifteenth?"

"Yes. The morning she died."

"You signed and dated her death certificate, cause of death pneumonia, time of death three a.m., June fifteenth. Was June Morgan already dead when you saw her?"

"No! I told you, she was dying!"

"Did you lodge a complaint against the school for sending home a dying girl?"

"No. It wasn't my place to do so, and she could have been taken ill with pneumonia without their awareness."

She walked to the defense table and stood by it then. "Did you know Mr. DiPalma and Mr. Rostov before you recommended them to Mr. Morgan?"

He blinked at the change of subject. "I met them briefly to interview them," he said after a pause.

"Where did that take place?'

"In Los Angeles."

"Did you inquire about their past employment, or current employment at that time?"

"I hardly remember," he said after another pause. "I asked the usual questions and described the jobs we wanted to fill."

"You said the jobs 'we' wanted to fill. What did you mean by that?"

"I was acting on Reverend Morgan's behalf," he said, again hesitating before giving his answer. "Acting as his agent, you might say."

"Did you conduct a background check on either of them?"

"No. It wasn't necessary. A friend recommended them to me. He had known them for a long time."

"Who was that friend?"

"Objection!" Wharton said. "Immaterial. Irrelevant."

"It isn't," Barbara said hotly. "Those two men were placed in the household of a man who did not know either of them, and it appears that no one did even a cursory check on their backgrounds beforehand. It's relevant to ascertain the credibility of whoever it was who first recommended them."

Judge Humphrey said, "Overruled. Please answer the question."

"It was Robert J. McHenry," Knowland said. "We have been friends for many years and I trusted his judgment."

Barbara heard movement behind her but did not turn. She knew that Frank would be hurrying out with the name, and at his office two interns were standing by to do a quick Internet search.

"On the night of September tenth, the night Mr. Peel was shot to death, after you checked to make sure he was dead, exactly what did you do?"

"Objection. Prejudicial."

"Sustained. Rephrase the question, counselor."

"On that night, after you checked the condition of Mr. Peel, what did you do?"

"I stood in the hall with the others waiting for the police."

"Did you check Mr. Morgan's pulse?"

"No. I was keeping an eye on him, that's all."

"Did you advise him to go sit down, or to lie down?"

"No."

"The call was placed at seven thirty-one, and the first officers arrived at seven thirty-eight. Did you just stand in the hall for those seven minutes?"

"Yes. We were all stunned, shocked."

"While standing there, did Mr. Morgan exhibit any symptoms of a man on the verge of a heart attack?"

"He was pale and shaking. I was concerned."

"Why didn't you advise him to lie down to wait for the police?"

"He was too agitated to take advice."

"But you said you didn't advise him to lie down. Did you or didn't you so advise him?"

"I didn't because I knew he wouldn't do it."

"When you were in the study you said you didn't hear the gunshot. Was the door closed?"

"Yes, it was. And we were talking."

"Were you talking in loud voices?"

"Of course not."

She picked up a floor plan of the upper story of the house, and after having it admitted, she held it up before Knowland. "There are three bedrooms, two baths, and the study on the second floor of the house. They are marked. Mr. Morgan's bedroom, his study, Mr. DiPalma's room, and Mr. Rostov's. Where did you plan to put June Morgan when she arrived in the middle of the night?"

"I assumed a room was ready for her. I didn't ask about it."

"The study is across the hall from the stairs leading up. The door to Mr. Peel's room was open, the gun fired near the doorway. Yet, you say you didn't hear a gunshot. Did you hear any loud noise?"

"No, not that I remember."

She took the floor plan to the jury box and let them pass it around, playing for time, waiting for Frank to get back. After admitting the floor plan into evidence, she asked, "Were you and Mr. Peel friends?"

"No. I hardly knew him."

"His death was not a personal loss to you. Is that correct?"

"Death at the hands of a murderer is always a shock, but it was not a personal loss."

"You say you stood waiting for the police for seven minutes, shocked and stunned, that you were concerned that Mr. Morgan might have a heart attack, he was so shocked and stunned. You did not advise him to sit down or to lie down. You didn't even check his pulse rate. Were you so shocked and stunned that you completely forgot that you are trained as a doctor, so shocked and stunned that you forgot about the man lying unconscious and bleeding in the office behind you?"

"Objection!" Wharton yelled. "She's badgering the witness. Prejudicial!"

"Sustained," Humphrey said sharply. "Move on, Ms. Holloway."

She turned to her table for a sip of water and saw Frank returning. She waited. He put a slip of paper in her hand. *McH pres Aquapur Water distributor, on board Silverstone, and Epsilon, others.*

"Dr. Knowland," she said, turning again to him, "you stated that you advised Mr. Morgan to go to bed at twelve the night his daughter was flown home. You also stated that you were in attendance to her for several hours, and you listed her death at three a.m. Are those statements correct?"

"As nearly as I can remember. I wasn't checking the time minute by minute."

"When you ascertained that the patient had died, did you inform Mr. Morgan?"

"No. There was no point in doing so."

"Did you consult with him before you had the body removed to the mortuary?"

"No."

She regarded him silently for a moment, then asked, "Were you aware that Mr. McHenry was on the board of the Silverstone Corporation?"

"Objection," Wharton said. He sounded tired.

It was sustained.

"Were both Mr. DiPalma and Mr. Rostov still employed by the Silverstone Corporation when you interviewed them?"

He hesitated. "I believe so. I told them Eugene and Portland were laid back, not filled with the hectic activity of many major cities. They said that's what they wanted, something more peaceful than they'd had in the past."

Sometimes when a shot in the dark hits, it's wise to stop shooting, Frank had told her years before. She said, "Your witness, counselor."

Wharton rose, but did not leave his place at the prosecution's table. "Dr. Knowland, when you said you advised Reverend Morgan to go to bed, did you look at your watch, or any clock?"

"No. He was tired and I thought it best if he lay down to rest and sleep if possible. I didn't check the time."

"Did you check your watch or the clock when you determined that Ruth Morgan had passed away?"

He shook his head. "The last time I looked at my watch it was three in the morning. I don't remember how long after that the poor girl passed away."

"When you were waiting in the hall for the arrival of the police, can you explain why you and Reverend Morgan were in such a state of shock?"

"I can," the doctor said heavily. "My first thought was that it was happening again. I thought and still think that the defendant had come to the house in order to kill his own father, that he had entered that room expecting to see his father, and he shot before he could stop himself. That was shocking."

Judge Humphrey looked at Barbara, evidently expecting an objection. Instead, she said, "Your Honor, may I approach?"

When she and Wharton were at the sidebar, she said, "Your Honor, several different times now the reference has been made to an alleged attack on Mr. Morgan, resulting in a shooting death. Dr. Knowland has a right to explain his shock, but he has no direct knowledge of the incident in Portland. Anything he might say about it would be hearsay and I would have to object. Therefore, in advance, I request that Mr. Wharton not be allowed to pursue that line of inquiry further with this witness."

"You can't tell me what I can or can't ask of a witness!" Wharton said fiercely. "Leaving it where it is now would be irrational and do nothing but confuse the jury even more than you're attempting with your obfuscation!"

"Ms. Holloway, do you know that Dr. Knowland has no firsthand knowledge of the Portland incident?" Judge Humphrey motioned for Wharton to stop and he regarded Barbara with a cold look.

"I know that the police record says that he and Mr. Morgan left the scene minutes before it took place. Anything he knows is what others told him, if the police record is accurate."

"Do you intend to bring up the matter in a more suitable context, with someone who has firsthand knowledge of the incident?" Humphrey asked her.

"Yes, Your Honor. Boris Rostov shot the young man to death and I intend to question him about it to clear the air of that matter."

"Very well," Humphrey said after a moment. "Leave it alone," he said to Wharton. "Don't go there with this witness. Now, let's get on with it."

Wharton had a few more questions for Knowland, but nothing that changed what had already been said, and when it was Barbara's turn she simply said, "No more questions."

She called her next witness, Tony DiPalma. When he didn't come down the aisle, she glanced over the observers and at the rear doors, then sat down to wait. Judge Humphrey motioned the bailiff to the bench and had a whispered conversation with him. He beckoned Barbara and Wharton forward and asked her, "Will Rostov be the next witness after DiPalma?"

She said yes and he turned to the bailiff. "See if you can find either of them. We'll have a short recess while he rounds up the witnesses," he said to Barbara and Wharton with a deep scowl.

On the way back to their tables, she whispered to Wharton, "Want to bet that your two prizes have flown the coop?"

He snarled something back at her.

When she sat down again, Frank leaned forward and said, "They both skipped. I saw Derek Peel with a woman I assume was his mother, so she's available. And probably Morgan will be. Any game plan for how to proceed?"

"I'll have Peel first, save Morgan for after lunch," she said. "Humphrey will wait twenty-four hours, won't he, before he decides we have to wrap it up even if the witnesses don't show? That means closing statements on Monday, thank God. I'll have the lunch recess to put peanut butter in the rat trap for Morgan." She realized she was thinking out loud and stopped.

They were still talking a few minutes later when Humphrey's clerk came to tell her that the judge wanted her and Wharton in chambers. Wharton was already standing, watching her, and together they followed the clerk to the judge's chambers without a word being spoken.

Barbara was grateful that, for the moment, at least, the judge was directing his ire at Wharton, not her.

"Where the devil are your witnesses?" he demanded.

"I don't know," Wharton said. "They were notified that they had to appear today and why they didn't come in, I can't say."

"Do you have your people looking for them?"

"Yes, absolutely."

Judge Humphrey turned to Barbara, no less angry but with slightly less edginess to his voice. "Are you ready to proceed without them?"

"Yes. I'll call Mrs. Peel, and after lunch, it will be Mr. Morgan."

"This has turned into a goddamn mess," Humphrey said. "Tomorrow, if they haven't put in an appearance, I'll issue a bench warrant, and we'll have closing statements on Monday. Ms. Holloway, how do you intend to introduce evidence of the incident in Portland that keeps popping up if your eyewitness to it doesn't show?"

"I haven't had time to rethink my plan," she said honestly.

"Tell me what happened up there, just the basics, and I warn you not to introduce anything that can't be substantiated by evidence," he said, after vigorously polishing his glasses and putting them on in order to sharpen his glare, possibly.

She told it as briefly as possible. "It involves June Morgan and a young man, John Varagosa.... Morgan and Dr. Knowland were said to have left minutes before John Varagosa appeared. Shots were fired in the condo and Boris Rostov shot and killed John Varagosa. Rostov and DiPalma were the only eyewitnesses to what happened."

Wharton looked sick, and Judge Humphrey had closed his eyes as she related the story.

"Was the girl pregnant? Was there a child?" the judge asked harshly.

"She died a virgin," Barbara said. "I can prove that also, but that's a separate issue from the shooting in the condo."

Wharton seemed to rouse at her words. "Travis Morgan went there to kill his father, that's clear enough for anyone with a brain. Morgan said he'd been getting threats, and by God, he has been threatened twice now."

"Be quiet," Humphrey said. "Just can it. Ms. Holloway, Mr. Wharton, not a word of this is to be revealed outside these chambers. Do you understand? A complete gag order is in effect until I decide how to proceed. I want all the evidence you said you can produce regarding that shooting. Over the weekend, I'll make my decision about presenting any of this story to the jury. And meanwhile, if a word leaks out, I'll have your hides. Do you understand?" He scowled at them both as his voice rose.

They both nodded silently, and he said, "In a few minutes we'll resume with your next witness."

As they walked back to the courtroom Wharton said in a low voice, "I read the newspaper account. Not a word about the mutilation. Not a word."

"Read his sermons," she said coldly.

Wharton stopped walking and said in a savage voice, "Okay, so Morgan isn't a saint, but your client went to that house and shot a man to death. Wrong victim doesn't change anything. Let him do a plea bargain, and if those facts hold up, we'll go easy on him."

"I have a better proposal," she said even more coldly. "Withdraw the charges and reopen the investigation." She continued to walk.

"You're out of your fucking mind!" he yelled at her back as she kept walking.

✦

CHAPTER 36

FOR THE RECORD, Barbara called Boris Rostov as her next witness, and almost instantly Judge Humphrey tapped his gavel and said, "I have been informed that Mr. Rostov has not been located. Please call your next witness, counselor."

She called Margaret Peel. She was sixty but looked younger, despite streaks of gray in her dark hair. Her face was smooth, with a peach-tone complexion, and she had the body of someone who led an active life or worked out regularly, strong and muscular, lean rather than thin. Dressed in a navy-pant suit and a white shirt, with little makeup beyond pale lipstick, she appeared to be the kind of woman who could see what needed to be done and go about doing it efficiently.

"Mrs. Peel, please tell the court if you have ever met with me or talked to me," Barbara said.

"I never met you before now and I've never talked with you." Her voice, while low pitched, was clear and slightly lilting, not enough to think Irish, but close.

"Did you come today voluntarily?"

"No. I was served with a subpoena."

"Mrs. Peel, will you please describe your late husband's typical working day over the past few years."

"He got up early, six usually, and did some things around our farm, then left for work at about eight thirty. He was usually home again by four thirty or a little later some days. He worked on farm chores for an hour or longer after that."

"Was he satisfied with his position, working for Mr. Morgan and his church?"

Mrs. Peel shook her head. "He started off pleased that he had found a job after the one he had previously was lost when the company went out of business, but after a few years, it was just a job and he did it as quickly and as well as he could."

"Did he ever express dissatisfaction with his job?"

"There were several times."

"Please tell the court about those times."

"Objection," Wharton said, rising. "Hearsay."

"It's direct," Barbara said quickly. "Mrs. Peel heard exactly what her husband told her."

"Overruled. "

"Well, Joe didn't like having to go to Seattle every month. That started about eight or nine years ago, after he'd been working there for several years. He had to drive to Portland, take the train to Seattle and check into a hotel. The next morning he had to pick up a package at the front desk and take an early train back to Portland. Mr. Morgan met him at the train station and took the package and Joe drove home. He didn't like having to do that month after month."

"Did he say what was in the package?"

"Yes. He said it was money from an anonymous donor. He didn't like carrying that much cash on a train, and he didn't like staying in a hotel."

"All right. What were the other things about his work that he found unsatisfactory?"

"He didn't like it when that bodyguard shot and killed a boy in the condo. He almost quit at that time, he was so unhappy about it. He said the bodyguard was a violent man and he didn't like to be around him."

There was a rustle in the courtroom at another mention of the shooting and the jurors clearly were intrigued and listening intently.

"Anything else?" Barbara asked.

"Last spring." She was twisting her hands on the stand, seemed to become aware of it, and swiftly put them in her lap and drew in a long breath. "Last spring, a man who worked for the church was beaten to death here in Eugene. Joe was very upset, and he was frightened. I didn't know why he was afraid at that time. He wouldn't tell me. Later, after June Morgan died, he told me."

"What did he tell you, Mrs. Peel?"

"He reminded me that Mr. Daggart had come out to the farm almost a year before that, but he had a different name. Joe took him out to the barn and they talked for a long time. I had forgotten about him until Joe reminded me. He said Mr. Daggart was doing some kind of investigation and he had agreed to help him. He didn't say what the investigation was about, or what he had agreed to do, but when Mr. Daggart was killed, it frightened him enough that he decided to quit his job. He told Mr. Morgan that he planned to resign."

"Why didn't he quit at that time?"

"We talked about it," Mrs. Peel said softly. "I didn't know anything about an investigation then, I just knew that Joe wanted to quit and I talked him out of it." Her voice faltered and dropped lower as she continued. "We decided that if he could hold on through September, we could pay off the mortgage on the farm. We almost lost it before when he was out of work for nearly a year." She looked at the jurors, then at the observers, and finally at Barbara. "I talked him out of it," she said, her voice husky with regret and anguish. "And God knows how sorry I am."

Barbara waited a second or two before she asked, "Were those the only times Mr. Peel talked about quitting his job?"

"One more," Mrs. Peel said. "When June died and Mr. Morgan told Joe to arrange for her to be cremated and an empty casket put on display for the church funeral service and burial." Mrs. Peel paused a moment, then continued. "Joe was outraged, and very, very upset. He said it wasn't right to pretend like that. We began to mark off the days until the end of September. The rest of June, July, August, into September; we marked them off, day after day until he would be done. Every night after dinner we marked off another day. " Tears filled her eyes, and she bowed her head and found a tissue in her pocket to dab at her eyes.

"Mrs. Peel, did your husband ever tell you anything more about an investigation being conducted by Mr. Daggart?"

She shook her head. "No. He said he was sorry he even brought it up and that I should forget about it. He said that whatever it was, it was over and done with and none of our business."

Barbara walked to the jury box. "On the evening of September tenth, the night of the death of your husband, did you know he was going to have dinner with Mr. Morgan and others?

"Not until that evening. Joe called me at about five to tell me Mr. Morgan asked him to stay because there was a problem with the books. He didn't believe it. He never had a problem with the books, but he said Mr. Morgan was the boss, and he had to stay and find out what was on his mind. I was upset because I had dinner in the oven. We were planning to eat early and then go to play bingo, a money-raising event for the school. It just didn't seem right to tell him that late. They could have taken care of a problem during the day, if there had been one."

"Did he mention Travis Morgan? That he was coming to the house that evening?"

"Not a word. He just said a problem with the books. That's all. He said I should go on and play bingo and he'd join me when he got home."

"Did you and your husband ever socialize with Mr. Morgan? Have dinner, for example."

"No. It was a job. Mr. Morgan was his employer. Joe did his work and then came home."

"Did Mr. Morgan ever extend the hand of friendship in any way to you or your husband?"

Mrs. Peel hesitated, frowning. "Years ago he said that our son could live at the residence and attend the University of Oregon, here in Eugene. Derek already had decided to go to OSU and turned him down. I told Mr. Morgan that he wouldn't accept it and he became angry with me."

"How did he show that anger?"

"He said Derek, my son, would be corrupted if he wasn't already corrupted by lust. He wanted to act as his mentor and spiritual guide. It was my duty to see to it that Derek was saved. I told him it was Derek's decision to make, and he had made it. Then he said I was a failed woman because I had only one child and now I was failing that one child. I never spoke to him again after that incident, until he came to the farm before Christmas. He said the church would be willing to pay all expenses if I would go to a condominium in Honolulu for Christmas and all of January. I refused his offer."

"Why did you refuse such a generous offer?"

Mrs. Peel looked down at her hands, still in her lap, then said in a low voice, "I don't really know. I have too much to do at the farm, that's one thing, but I just felt it wasn't right to go away when the trial was going to be held."

"Did you ever tell your husband what Mr. Morgan said when your son rejected his offer?"

"No. I knew he would quit his job on the spot and we couldn't afford that."

"You called Mr. Morgan's daughter June. Were you aware that he had renamed her Ruth?"

"He called her that. But I heard her and Travis laughing and joking about their names. He called her Junebug, and she called him Stinkbug. They treated it like a joke back then when they were children. That was the day I told him Derek would not accept his offer."

Walking back to her table, Barbara asked, "Was your husband fond of Travis, have a friendly relationship with him?"

Mrs. Peel looked puzzled at the question. "No, not that I'm aware of. Travis was in Portland through the week and in Eugene some weekends. Joe never worked on the weekend, so they were hardly ever in the house at the same time. Now and then they came down from Portland before the weekend, but Joe was in his office doing his work and had no reason to see the boy."

Barbara hesitated momentarily, then asked, "Mrs. Peel, did it upset your husband when Travis ran away from home before he was sixteen?"

Her answer was swift. "Not at all. He said maybe it was the smartest thing he had ever done."

Barbara let out the breath she had been holding. "Thank you, Mrs. Peel. No more questions."

Wharton rose and looked at Mrs. Peel with a grave expression. "Mrs. Peel, do you dislike Reverend Morgan?"

"Objection! Prejudicial."

It was sustained.

"Well, let me put it this way," Wharton said. "Did you ever attend his church services?"

"Yes."

"Did you attend regularly?"

"No. Just once."

"Did you attend the funeral for his daughter?"

"No."

"Did Mr. Peel prefer to work on your farm rather than as bookkeeper for Reverend Morgan?"

"Yes. He loved the farm."

"You testified that your husband was home at around four thirty, yet that day he called at five. Can you explain that?"

"Fridays were always his longest days," she said. "He had to wait for the secretary in Portland to let him know if anything had come in late to be put on the books. He didn't want anything to be unaccounted for over the weekend."

"Was he resentful that he was forced to work for Reverend Morgan because of financial pressure?"

"No. He wasn't resentful, just bothered by some of the things going on."

"Besides the events and incidents you've mentioned already, did he complain about little things that might have occurred? Misplaced money, or wrong figures, things of that sort?"

"Once in a while he mentioned things like that, but he said everyone made mistakes now and then. It was to be expected."

"Your Honor, I ask that the comment following Mrs. Peel's answer be stricken.

"It will be stricken. Mrs. Peel, please simply answer the questions without adding an explanation unless it's asked for."

She looked at him and nodded, but her expression hardened a bit and her mouth tightened as she regarded Wharton again.

"Did your husband make an effort to see both sides of the various things he complained about?"

"I don't know which things you're asking about," she said.

Wharton started with the time Morgan offered to let Derek use his house while attending school.

"We never talked about why Mr. Morgan made the offer."

"Do you think the bodyguard should not have used force when an intruder entered shooting a gun?"

"Objection," Barbara said. "He's making assumptions about an incident that has not been properly introduced."

It was sustained.

"Did you or your husband try to find out why Reverend Morgan decided on cremation instead of a regular burial?"

"No."

"Did you consider that he might have had his own perfectly good reasons?"

"No."

"Mrs. Peel, did you yourself harbor a resentment that your husband felt forced to work for Reverend Morgan?"

"No."

"What did you feel about your situation in regard to Reverend Morgan and your late husband's employment with him?"

"A great sorrow," she said.

"Mrs. Peel, is it sorrow, or is it guilt that you feel because you talked your husband into remaining in a position he had grown to dislike for the sake of his paycheck?"

"It is both," she said in a faint voice.

"Are you trying to ease that guilt by casting Reverend Morgan in a bad light, shifting your own guilt onto him?"

"Objection!" Barbara cried furiously. "He is harassing this witness!"

"Sustained," Judge Humphrey said. "Move on, Mr. Wharton."

"No more questions."

Barbara rose and asked, "Mrs. Peel, why didn't you and your late husband attend the funeral for June Morgan?" Ice water or not, she had to ask.

"Joe said it wasn't right, people would be crying and mourning, and he would know the casket was empty. He said it was indecent to pretend like that and he couldn't do it. He didn't go, so I didn't go either."

"Why didn't either of you try to find out why that was done?"

She shook her head. "Joe stopped asking questions a long time ago," she said softly. "He said that as long as his work was legal that's what mattered to him, not what Mr. Morgan said or did."

Barbara nodded. "Thank you, Mrs. Peel. I have no more questions."

Judge Humphrey called for the luncheon recess as soon as Mrs. Peel left the witness stand.

While Barbara sorted the Varagosa file to deliver to Judge Humphrey, the others ate salads with grilled salmon, and it seemed that time did its trick by slipping away unnoticed until they were all back in court. She called Arlie Morgan.

He had brought his cheering section again that day. The courtroom was crowded and Judge Humphrey's expression was dour when he looked out over it, as if he anticipated another unruly outburst.

"Mr. Morgan," Barbara began, again standing by the jury box where his gaze instantly fastened on one of the jurors, "have Mr. DiPalma and Mr. Rostov taken a leave of absence?"

"Not that I'm aware of," he said easily.

"Have you dismissed either or both of them?"

"No, of course not."

"Do you know where they are?"

"Unfortunately, I don't. Something must have come up that demanded their attention."

"When you first hired them, did you know they were both employed by the Silverstone Corporation?"

"No."

"Are they still employees of that corporation while also working for you?"

Wharton objected and it was sustained.

"Did Robert Daggart also work for you and your church?"

"Not as a regular employee," he told the juror he was speaking to.

It was uncanny, Barbara thought, how his voice was so reasonable, low-pitched and friendly sounding, yet his eyes could not focus on her for a second. She wondered briefly if she should stand in front of Judge Humphrey's bench and see how Humphrey reacted when Morgan addressed him directly in response to her questions.

"What do you mean by that?"

"He was hanging around the church up in Portland, a pitiful man out of work, out of hope, and he needed a job. He took out trash, swept the walk, did some cleanup in the church kitchen. Just now and then, not regularly, and I paid him a few dollars for his effort. I helped him as much as I could, but he had no real skills or talent. Once in a while he ran an errand, picked up something from the grocery or put something in the mail."

"Were he and Mr. Peel friends?"

"I don't believe they ever met until one day when he stopped by to pick up our membership list, which he agreed to drop off in Medford for me."

"Please explain that incident to the court," she said, keeping her voice as polite as he was keeping his.

"I update our membership list several times a year. Usually we fax it to a fellow minister in Medford, but Joseph told me that the fax machine broke down that day, and Daggart had said he was going to California. I asked him to pick up the list from Joseph on his way and make a detour into Medford to deliver it. He agreed to do that. I paid him a few dollars for his trouble, of course."

"What happened to Mr. Daggart?" she asked.

He looked sorrowful and bowed his head slightly, but kept his focus on one of the jurors. "I never knew exactly. He picked up the list from Joseph, and the next thing we heard was that he had been brutally beaten by street thugs and he had died from his injuries. I asked Joseph to make the identification and to collect his things, since we had no record of his next of kin. Joseph claimed his body in the name of the church and we buried him."

"At that time, did Mr. Peel tell you he was planning to resign?"

"No. He talked about resigning from time to time, but it was always some future event, never with the intention of doing it immediately. He always said that when the time came he would find his replacement and train him. He never did that."

She moved a few feet along the rail of the jury box and watched his gaze shift. "The night your daughter was flown home ill, did you go to bed instead of waiting for her arrival?"

"Yes. I knew that when she got home, I'd be up with her the rest of the night, and decided to try to nap until she got there. Dr. Knowland told me the following morning why he didn't wake me up, that she was already dying and there was nothing I could have done."

"Wouldn't it have been of some consolation to you and to her to spend those few hours with your dying daughter?"

"It would have been," he said with heavy regret. "I chastised Dr. Knowland for not getting me up, even if he thought it in my best interest to rest."

"Where did she attend school during her last two years?"

"A small private girls' school outside of Moscow, Idaho," he said. "It's called Meadowlark Academy."

"Mr. Morgan, did you take any action against the school for not taking proper care of your daughter?"

"I talked to the headmistress," he said. "Ruth was recovering from the flu, but she expressed the desire to convalesce at home, and they made the arrangements. She walked to the plane and was seated when a mechanical problem arose. They called me from the airport to say they would be quite late, and that she was sleeping on board. No one realized how ill she would become in the next few hours, and at the time it seemed better to let her sleep than to send her back to the school. It was a mistake. A tragic mistake."

"You know that all calls are traceable, don't you?" she said coldly.

"Objection!" Wharton said. "Counsel is attempting to intimidate the witness."

"Sustained."

Morgan glared at her briefly, then swiftly refocused on someone behind her.

"Did part of Mr. Peel's position as bookkeeper involve a monthly trip to Seattle?" she asked. She moved to stand nearly in front of the prosecution table and watched Morgan's gaze shift again, she hoped to Wharton.

"Yes."

"Please tell the court about that arrangement, the reason Mr. Peel had to go to Seattle."

He described it and concluded by saying, "I had to honor the wishes of my anonymous benefactor, and that was how he wanted it done."

"Was Mr. Peel authorized to count the donation, make a note of it for his books?"

"No. He brought it to me sealed and I immediately took it to the bank to deposit the funds. Joseph was free to go home for the rest of the day as soon as he delivered the envelope. The following day he always checked the bank deposit on his computer."

"So he never knew how much cash he was carrying. Is that correct?"

"Yes."

"Since Mr. Peel's death how have those arrangements changed?"

"Now a delivery man comes by train and I meet him at the station to receive the donation."

"Has your anonymous donor ever asked for an accounting?"

"No! He believes in me and my message. He knows I'm doing God's work. He's doing God's work."

"Your Honor," she said, "I ask that his comments after his answer be stricken."

"They will be stricken," he said. "Mr. Morgan, simply answer the questions."

She walked to her table, where she picked up the photograph of Morgan receiving the envelope at the train station. After showing it to Wharton and Judge Humphrey, she handed it to Morgan.

"Can you identify this photograph, taken on Tuesday, December fourteen, last year?"

He stared at it as color flared in his cheeks. "How dare you have me followed and photographed! How dare you!" He looked directly at her and his voice rose to a shout.

"Can you identify it?" she snapped.

He flung it down and turned to the judge. "She has no right to follow me! It's illegal!"

Judge Humphrey banged his gavel. "Mr. Morgan, just answer the question!"

"Yes! It's me, receiving the donation our generous benefactor in the name of God bestows on my church!"

Barbara calmly picked up the photograph to show to the jurors. "The date and time of day are both automatically printed at the bottom of the photograph," she said, handing it to the foreman. When she had it back she had it admitted as evidence and walked to her table where Shelley handed her the next two pictures.

"Did you go straight to the bank after receiving that envelope?" she asked.

"Yes. I always deposited it immediately."

"Is this a picture of you entering your bank?" she asked after showing it to Wharton and the judge. Morgan's color had faded from the flush to a waxy lividity. His lips were tight and pale and only his eyes looked alive with rage.

"I'll sue you for this, intimidation, stalking and taking pictures without permission, harassing an innocent citizen—"

"Mr. Morgan, answer the question," Judge Humphrey said sharply.

"Yes, I'm going in the bank, just like I said I always do."

"Please note the time," Barbara said. "And this one." She handed him the final picture, where he was going through the gate to the safe deposit boxes. "Twelve seconds after you entered the bank, you were heading to the safe deposit box. Is that correct?"

"What are you accusing me of?" he cried. His face flared red, and he halfway rose from his chair. "I demand a stop to this inquisition! I've done nothing wrong! A man has a right to go to his bank and his safe. This is hateful anti-Christian persecution, an attempt to discredit God's word—"

"Answer the question!" Judge Humphrey demanded. "Just answer the question."

"Yes! I had business of my own to conduct, a personal matter, none of this woman's business, and—"

"Your Honor, I ask that Mr. Morgan's remarks after his affirmative answer be stricken," Barbara said over his voice.

"They will be stricken."

She handed the two photographs to the foreman and waited for them to be passed around. After she had them admitted, Humphrey beckoned her and Wharton to the sidebar.

"I'm calling a recess," he said in a grating tone. "Mr. Wharton, I advise you to speak to this witness and warn him that, preacher or not, he is in danger of a contempt of court charge."

"Judge, she's the one pushing his buttons," Wharton said angrily.

"He's your witness. You'd better get him under control, or so help me God, I will."

He waved them away and tapped his gavel to announce the recess, then stalked out rigid with anger.

As soon as he was out of sight, a loud buzz of conversations filled the room. The jurors were led out, and Wharton approached Morgan. He took him by the arm and led him away for their talk.

"To the woodshed," Frank said cheerfully. "Not that it will do much good."

Travis was taken out, but before he went with his guard, he said to Barbara, "He'll never forget this and he doesn't forgive. Be careful, watch your back."

"Good advice," Frank said at Barbara's side. "Want some coffee?"

"A shot of bourbon would be more like it," she said. "But I'll settle for coffee."

When they resumed, Barbara stood at the jury rail to ask, "Did you spend your childhood and youth in the Jacksonville area?"

"Yes," he said stiffly to the juror he was staring at.

"Did you hunt and fish?"

"Yes. Everyone did."

She walked to her table for the photograph of him and his father by the hanging deer. She showed it to Wharton and the judge, then to Morgan. "Will you please identify the people in this photograph."

He glanced at it, then took a longer look. "It's my father and me," he said.

"What does it say on the photograph?"

He looked at it again and his lips tightened. "Arlie's first deer, from start to finish," he said after a moment.

"Did your parents call you Arlie?"

"Yes."

"Was that the first deer you personally shot and killed?"

"Yes! That's what it says."

"Was your shot fatal? Did you fell it with one shot?"

He kept his eyes on the photograph as he said, "No. We had to track it down and finish it off. That's what you do, give it a merciful death if it's been wounded. It was food for our table."

"How do you finish it off?"

"With a close shot to the head," he said.

"How close do you have to get to do that?"

"Five feet, six, maybe closer."

"And did you fire that close shot to its head, hitting it in the eye?"

"Yes! Why do you keep asking me the same questions? I killed the deer! It was food for our table. We were poor, my father was a preacher doing God's work, providing game for our table."

"Did you use the rifle for that close shot to its head?" she asked coolly, ignoring his outburst.

"No! You use a handgun. That's what my father told me to do, use the handgun."

She nodded. "Is that gun in the holster that your father is wearing the same handgun you used to finish off the deer?"

He looked ready to fling down the photograph as he had done earlier, and his color was high again with a flush on his cheeks. It seemed a difficult effort for him to keep his eyes averted, not to give her the slightest of glances, but he kept his gazed fixed on the photograph.

"Yes! I used his gun."

"Please turn the photograph and read what is written on the back of it," she said.

He turned it over and read: "Two, seven, eight, nine, zero. It's just numbers, and some initials, nothing's written."

"Please read the initials."

"JWS. That's all."

She retrieved the photograph and went to the evidence table to ask for the enlarged photograph of the Colt .45. Taking it to Morgan, she identified the gun in the picture as being the one used to shoot Peel. Showing him the back of it, she asked him to read what was written there.

For a long time he remained silent.

"Mr. Morgan, what does it say on that photograph?" she asked sharply.

"Enlargement of two, seven, eight, nine, zero," he said in a rasping voice.

"What else?" she demanded.

"Initials," he said.

"What initials?"

"JWS," he said.

"Are they the same initials that are on the other photograph?"

"Yes! You know they are. You probably put them there!"

"Your Honor, I ask that the remarks following his answer be

stricken," she said. She took the two photographs to the jurors and waited while they were passed around.

Done with that, she asked, "Mr. Morgan, what happened to your father's Colt single-action army handgun?"

"I don't know," he said. "I haven't thought about it for years."

"Did you inherit your father's guns?"

"Yes."

"What did you do with the guns?"

"I don't remember," he said angrily.

"Well, were they in a box of some sort?"

"Yes. In an oak box. That's where he kept them."

"Is that oak box in your house?"

"I told you I don't remember!"

"Was the box locked?"

"Yes! And the key is in my desk drawer."

"Is that drawer locked?"

"Sometimes, not always."

"Where is the key to that drawer?"

She kept each question brisk and she didn't move as he fired off his answers. His gaze might not have been fastened on Wharton, but it was directed that way. Suddenly, his eyes shifted, and he seemed to be searching, then he locked in on someone else.

"Mr. Morgan, did you hear my question?" she asked.

"Ask her! Ask my so-called ex-wife! She took the gun. Make her tell you what she did with it!"

Barbara spun around to see Ashley sitting rigidly upright, staring back at Morgan. She was white but her gaze did not waver, nor did she back down.

"Mr. Morgan!" Judge Humphrey cried out furiously. "You must not comment beyond the question being asked! Where is the key to that drawer? That is the question before you. All other remarks will be stricken."

"I keep it on my key chain. That's how men keep their keys, on their own key chains, but that harlot could have taken it before she abandoned me, abandoned her family."

"Mr. Morgan, you are in contempt of court," Judge Humphrey said icily. "You will be informed of the penalty. I advise you, sir, do not make me add to that penalty. Just answer the questions put to you."

Morgan might have heard him, but he gave no sign of it as he continued to stare with hatred at Ashley.

Barbara looked at Wharton, who appeared almost as rigid as Ashley. A tic was jerking in his cheek. She turned back to Morgan.

"Mr. Morgan, is the holster for that Colt handgun still in the oak box?"

"Yes! It must be. I told you I haven't thought about it for years. The gun is there, too, as far as I know unless she took it."

"Mr. Morgan, when did you and your ex-wife file for divorce?"

Wharton objected and it was sustained.

"When did your secret benefactor start sending you monthly donations?"

Wharton objected again and once more it was sustained.

"If your benefactor stops the monthly payments, will you have to give up the church in Portland and the closed-circuit television screening of your services?"

Morgan's glare turned to her, and his eyes narrowed nearly to slits. Perspiration lined his upper lip and forehead. In what appeared to be an involuntary movement, he jerked forward, then clutched the rail before him as if he would have sprung if it had not been there.

"Objection!" Wharton called. "Counselor is fishing. This is irrelevant to the case at hand."

"Sustained. Move on, counselor," Judge Humphrey said sharply.

"Do you write your own sermons?" she asked. "Are you simply passing on a message from that benefactor?"

"Objection!" Wharton yelled. "May I approach?"

"Sustained," the judge said and waved them both forward.

"What the devil do you think you're doing?" Wharton demanded at the sidebar. "That man is clearly deranged and you're egging him on. Do you want him to have a fit of some kind? Foam at the mouth?"

"I want him to tell the truth," she said, equally angry. "He's nothing but a dim-witted tool being used by others. He's afraid he'll lose his benefactor, lose his nice church, his condo and his lovely house here, and be nothing more than he was before, a poor, sex-obsessed ranting maniac. You can smell his fear oozing out of his pores."

"Both of you, be quiet!" Humphrey said, scowling at them. "Ms. Holloway, I advise you to complete your questioning of this witness with all due haste. I want him off that stand as quickly as possible. And I want no more innuendo-laden questions from you."

Back at their tables, Barbara regarded Morgan for a second or two, then said, "I have no more questions for this witness."

Wharton stood and shuffled a paper or two on his table. "No questions," he said and sat down again.

"Mr. Morgan, you may step down," Judge Humphrey said.

Morgan rose, and now he was keeping his eyes focused on Barbara. He took a step or two away from the witness stand, then stopped walking and pointed at her. "You have called down the wrath of God!" he said in a loud voice. "You have disrespected the servant of God, and thereby you have disrespected God! By stone, by blade, or by fire will the wrath of God smite you down. Whore of Babylon! You will suffer the torments of hell all the rest of your life and throughout eternity… "

Judge Humphrey was banging his gavel and calling for the bailiff to escort the witness from the courtroom, and people behind Barbara were stifling cries, or crying out incoherently. She turned from Morgan's fierce glare to Shelley, who was wide-eyed and looked badly shaken. In an undertone Barbara said, "Knock, knock."

"Wh-who's there?" Shelley stammered, bewildered as, with an apparent effort, she turned her attention from Morgan to Barbara.

"Caesar."

"Caesar who?"

"Caesar by the horns, boys, and wrestle her to the ground."

Shelley's hand flew to her face to stifle a giggle, and Morgan's bellow became even louder. "Harlot, Jezebel, fornicator, God will strike you! You will suffer—" The bailiff had reached him and attempted to take him by the arm. Morgan wrenched away from him. At that moment Dr. Knowland rushed to him and grabbed his other arm. Morgan was still yelling, twisting around to scream curses at Barbara.

Barbara couldn't hear what he was saying as the bailiff and Dr. Knowland power-marched Morgan up the aisle and to the door.

When order was restored, Judge Humphrey said, "Court will adjourn at this time until nine o'clock Monday morning." He nodded to Barbara and Wharton. "I want you both in chambers in ten minutes."

✦

CHAPTER 37

"I DON'T KNOW," Herbert said, driving the SUV. "Your dad said to bring you to his office and I reckon I'd best do what he tells me, since he pays my freight, so to speak."

"Right," she said wearily. "To his office it is." She leaned back and closed her eyes for the rest of the trip.

To her surprise, Ashley and her sister were standing near the door when she entered Frank's office.

"What's up?"

"I want Alan to take them to their apartment, and to be on call if Ashley has to go anywhere, the jail, shopping, whatever," Frank said. "As I already told them, Alan can elude anyone who tries to follow them and pester them with a lot of questions. No point in submitting to anything like that over the weekend."

"Sounds good to me," Mikey said. "We don't need reporters."

As soon as Frank took them out to introduce Alan, and give him instructions, Barbara moved to sit on the sofa and put her feet up on the coffee table.

"Wiped out," she said when Frank returned.

"You have a right. What did you say to Shelley to crack her up?"

"You tell him," Barbara said, nodding to Shelley.

She grinned and repeated the Knock-Knock. Frank chuckled. "That really sent him over the edge," he said. "You two Jezebels refusing to pay attention when you're being damned to eternal torment."

"You think he might try to get at Ashley?"

"Who knows what a madman might decide to do?" Frank said. "I don't want to give him any opportunity."

"Just how crazy is he really?" Barbara said after a moment.

"You think all that screaming and yelling was an act?" Shelley asked.

"I think he really believes all his procreation nonsense. But I also think he can be crazy and still be shrewd enough to know that the gravy train probably has derailed, and he's preparing the groundwork for a stint in a rehab facility following a mental breakdown. Job rehabilitated and ready to march again."

Frank nodded. "What did Humphrey have to say?"

Barbara waved her hand. "No more tiger baiting. I gave him the Varagosa material and he'll review it over the weekend and speak to the jury Monday morning. If DiPalma and Rostov are found they will be detained. Bench warrants if they don't show up. I bet they were on that flight that took off ahead of schedule, and they're safely ensconced at the Chateau, or points beyond. When they don't show, and the defense rests, straight to closing statements. He's pretty pissed at the mess I've made of his neat little case."

"Barbara," Shelley asked hesitantly, "they won't find him guilty, will they?'

"It pretty much depends on what Judge Humphrey's instructions tell them they can or can't consider."

Frank agreed. A judge who no longer liked judging, a case that had spiraled out of control, a preacher using his courtroom to spout hell and damnation curses, witnesses gone AWOL… Judge Humphrey might well determine the outcome with his instructions to the jury.

By Sunday afternoon Barbara was ready to try out her closing statement with Frank. He had always tried out his with Barbara's mother and now it was his turn to be critic. He was merciless when it came to spotting a weak argument, or bringing up a point that had not been made, or not stressed sufficiently.

"Sorry, guys," she said to Darren and Todd. "You're on your own again for dinner. I'll be at Dad's, rehearsal time."

"Barbara," Herbert said, "you know what we might do, is let me mess around in your dad's kitchen while you two are doing whatever it is you do, and by and by these two can mosey over and we'll all have a sit-down dinner."

Darren nodded. "Better than pizza. And since you've given up on sleep, and never taste what you eat, it might even do you some good."

Minutes later, when Barbara and Herbert reached Frank's, house she told him the game plan. "Good. I would have opened a can of soup," Frank said with a straight face. "Herbert, when it's dinner, bang on the door. If we're not finished, we'll take a break and get back to it."

He took Barbara's arm and they went to his study.

Later, stopping Barbara in mid-sentence, Frank held up his hand.

"You're skirting pretty damn close to the edge where Humphrey tells them to disregard it, if Wharton doesn't object first."

"I know. You remember the story you told me a long time ago? The wayward son yells at his father that he's a dimwit, a fat, no-good slob with the manners of a goat. Then he says, 'But disregard my remarks when you write your will.'"

Frank chuckled. "Brain erasers are hard to come by, but don't get any closer."

"Watching my step," she said.

Herbert called them to dinner, which was one of his specialties they all loved: New Orleans gumbo. Afterward Barbara looked at Darren with a flash of guilt. "We're not done," she said.

"The house will be there, I'll be there when you are," he said and kissed her. "Come on, Todd. Homework's calling."

Back in the study, with Frank in his disreputable old chair with a legal pad on a clipboard, and Barbara moving around the room restlessly, they went back to the notes he had jotted down as she made her case.

"It's good, Bobby," he said when they finally finished. "Good and tight."

"I have a few places to fix. You're right. I can't just come out and accuse him of embezzlement or theft or anything else."

"I think they'll get the point," Frank said drily. "He certainly did in court. In fact, one could even say he made the point for you."

"Will they see him as the preacher being harassed by a wicked woman? That's the question?"

Frank laughed. "They saw a madman, and for some that's still a sign of religious fervor, I guess. All he needed were sandals and hot sand, blazing sun on his grizzled old head, and a prophecy or two."

"No burning bush?"

"His rants run to burning eyeballs," he said and rose. "Go on to your office and smooth out the wrinkles, but try to get a decent night's sleep. Try hard."

In court again the next morning, she called her two missing witnesses, who failed to show. Then she said, "The defense rests, Your Honor."

Judge Humphrey looked tired already. He had been snappish when Barbara and Wharton met in his chambers that morning. He informed them that he had told the jury the barest of details from the police report regarding the shooting of John Varagosa. And that meant no mention of June and no reason given for John's going to the condo with a gun. The police report concluded that gang activity was behind the mutilation and that Rostov had acted in self-defense. Period. Humphrey had given Barbara a cold look when he repeated what he had told the jury, and then said, "No speculation regarding that matter will be allowed. Do you understand?"

She understood all too well, she thought as Wharton got up to give his closing statement. She would not be allowed to refer to that mutilation, but would anyone on that jury remember that she had asked Knowland if he had ever castrated a man? That was all she could ask for at this point, that one or more them would remember and make the connection. She listened to Wharton.

"Ladies and gentlemen, the case you've just heard argued is really a simple one. There have been diversions, but they have no relevance to the plain facts that have been presented here. The defendant went to Reverend Morgan's house, was escorted to Mr. Peel's office and shot him as soon as he entered. That is the case before you. Two eyewitnesses testified under oath that they witnessed the shooting, and that the defendant was the shooter. If Mr. DiPalma kept up his other line of work as a pilot, that has no bearing on this case. Whatever occupation Mr. Rostov had before also has no bearing on this case. He was hired by Reverend Morgan as a bodyguard, and he fulfilled that duty."

Wharton replayed the scenario that had been described by DiPalma and Rostov: Rostov took Travis to the office, he entered, shot and killed Peel before DiPalma had a chance to subdue him. "The four people already in the house corroborated each other's story individually, and each one of them testified under oath as to the truth of their statements." He then turned his focus to Mrs. Margaret Peel. "… You must ask yourselves if easing her own guilt by shifting it to someone else is reasonable, something you've known others to do, possibly something you have done yourself at some time. It's a human trait. Guilt can be overwhelming and the impulse to shift it to another can be powerful. It can be unconsciously done and thus deniable….

"Mr. Peel was described as a conscientious man, one who minded his own business, kept to himself, and above all prided himself on work well done. Meticulous was the word used to describe his working habits. If he had decided to resign his position, wouldn't he have found his replacement and trained him in the method of bookkeeping he used?... "

Wharton referred to the donations Peel picked up in Seattle and again repeated that it had nothing to do with the case at hand. "We know that some people donate anonymously...

And so it goes, Barbara thought as Wharton explained away all the "diversions" that had been presented. He dismissed Mrs. Ochmann as an old woman who didn't turn on a light when she went to the bathroom in the middle of the night. Old, confused about what she saw and when she saw it, half asleep, she had conflated different times and different incidents. "And," he added, "besides that, it has nothing to do with the murder of Joseph Peel."

When it came to the gun, he was almost casual as he said, "Anyone who has tried to hide Christmas presents from children knows that it can't be done. They find anything and everything hidden away or locked away. Ask yourselves if a locked box would be too tempting for a child to leave alone. Then ask yourselves if a boy found a gun like the one that cowboys used, wouldn't that boy have been greatly tempted to play with it, possibly to hide it, and possibly to keep it."

He was good, Barbara thought as Wharton talked on, making his case. It took him over an hour and his final comments dealt with the big question of why kill Peel.

"Why would anyone want to kill him," he asked in a reflective manner. "He was a good man, and a harmless man. No one has mentioned enemies. The only answer is in the sworn testimony from Dr. Knowland when he explained the state of shock both he and Reverend Morgan were in on the night of the murder. Dr. Knowland said: 'I thought and I still think he came to kill his father.'" Wharton paused dramatically, then said, "He thought the defendant went to that house that night to kill his father, and expecting to be taken to him, he shot before he could stop himself. The question you must ask yourselves: Did the defendant expect to see his father behind that desk and shoot before he could stop himself? He went to that house with murder in his heart. He went armed with a gun, and he used that gun to shoot and kill a man. That, ladies and gentlemen, is murder."

Judge Humphrey called for a short recess when Wharton sat down. Barbara used the time to go to the restroom and give her hair a quick brush, and then, washing her hands, she looked at herself in the mirror and under her breath she said, "It's now or never."

When court reconvened, Judge Humphrey asked if she was ready to give her closing statement. "Yes, I am," she said, rising.

She walked to the jury box. "Ladies and gentlemen, Mr. Wharton described the case before you as a simple one, but it is not. The unexamined, simplest appearing structures and actions reveal complexity when that simplicity is questioned and closely examined. This case has many unanswered questions. Starting with Mr. DiPalma, I want to examine the actions of all the people present on the night of September ten, last year.

"According to Mr. DiPalma, he was in the kitchen with Mr. Rostov when the doorbell rang at seven thirty that night. Together they left the kitchen and they parted at the end of the of the hall where Mr. Rostov left to open the door, and Mr. DiPalma went to Mr. Peel's door and entered. He testified that he wanted to get a closer look at Travis Morgan, his reason for going to the office. He could have had a much better look at him from the hallway, where he would have seen him from in front. When asked if he knocked on the door, he didn't know. When asked if he spoke to Mr. Peel, again he was uncertain, then said that he might have said something like he wanted to borrow a book. "

She walked to the evidence table for the duplicate bookend and the enlarged photograph of the books. "These are the books on that shelf," she said, and read a title or two. "Just glancing at them, you might wonder if he really had an interest in borrowing a book. He said they were wedged in tight, and that's why he picked up the bookend." She hefted it, then set it down on the rail of the jury box. "You all handled that bookend," she said, eyeing it, then the jurors. "It's an awkward object to hold unless you use both hands, and most of you did use both hands when you passed it around. It is clear that the books were centered on the shelf, with a lot of space on both sides." She held up the photograph and walked along the rail for the jurors to see. "If you want to remove a book from a shelf and if there are bookends, think of the most natural way to take an individual book. Most people would simply move the bookend enough to leave room to pick up the desired book. Why pick up the bookend and hold it? If you want to look over a book, you really need two hands. One to hold it and one to open it and turn the pages. No, he was not interested in a book. He admitted it. He said he wanted a closer look at

Travis Morgan. So why did he go through the charade of looking at the books and picking up the bookend? When asked why he picked it up, he said he wanted a closer look at it." She picked it up with both hands and held it up as if examining it. "But curiously, he didn't seem interested in the eagle, but in the back side of the bookend. Then he had to go through a series of motions," she continued. "He had to turn it around in order to hold it in his right hand until the back of the bookend was the part he was looking at." She maneuvered the bookend until she had it positioned, held in her right hand by the wing. "This is the only way to hold it and account for the blood on the bottom of the back." Again she walked down the rail to let them see how she was holding it, where the blood had been indicated with the black marker.

Using the different pieces of evidence, she went through the motions DiPalma had said he did. "He had to have turned away from the bookshelf if he saw Travis Morgan enter the office. He testified that Travis came running in, but looking at this crime scene photograph, it is clear that he had not rushed or he would have been farther inside the room. One foot is where a single step would have taken it, and the other one has hardly cleared the threshold." She used the flexible doll, bent it the way Dr. Tunney had bent it, and then said, "Remember what Travis Morgan said in the emergency room, noted by Dr. Tunney and by Detective Eggleston, the arresting officer. Travis said someone pushed him, and he said someone hit him in the head. That figure is in the posture of someone who has been pushed and is catching his balance. The wound he suffered had an upward thrust that meant his head had to have been tilted, and the fact that only the bottom edge of the bookend contacted his head meant that he was moving forward, in a downward direction when he was hit. In other words he had been pushed and was off balance momentarily at the moment Mr. DiPalma struck him. He was in no position to have been able to aim a gun and fire a single fatal shot." She replaced the doll and picked up the bookend.

"But Mr. DiPalma had to have moved again before he hit Travis Morgan in the head." She held the bookend straight out and swung it to indicate hitting someone. "Mr. DiPalma was too close to swing it the way he said he did. He had to take a step or two back to get the room he needed. So, at some point, while he was getting a closer look at the back side of the bookend, he also moved a step or two away from the door. By then he was in position with the bookend in his hand the way it had to have been in order to hit Travis Morgan. If Travis had not had his head bent somewhat, that blow would have hit him broadside, and would have resulted in a much more severe injury. Mr. DiPalma said he heard the shot, and he saw the gun in Travis Morgan's hand. But could he have seen a gun in his right hand? He was on the left side of Travis, a step or two away from the door, and slightly behind him because Travis had taken a step into the room. His body would have blocked a view of his hand."

She paused, then said, "You heard Mr. DiPalma's various answers to questions. Yes, no, sometimes, maybe... He said Mr. Rostov told him to tell Mr. Morgan and Dr. Knowland what had happened, and he left the office to do so, still carrying the bloody bookend." Using the crime scene photographs, she pointed as she said, "There were several drops of blood here in the hall. One drop was at the doorway to the living room, another was five or six feet into the room, and another drop was by the table where the police officers found the bookend. The table had blood on it. But there were no drops of blood on the stairs, none in the upstairs study. It is inconceivable that the bookend with Travis Morgan's blood on it would drip on the hall floor and in the living room and be bloody when put on the table, and yet not a drop was on the stairs or in the upstairs study if the bookend had been carried up there. Does that mean that when he was told to inform Mr. Morgan and Dr. Knowland he went straight to the living room, entered and walked ten feet to the table to put down the bookend?"

She shook her head. "When asked if he and Rostov were friends in California, his answer was again of the pick-and-choose-your-answer variety. No, yes, but not really. Yet they were recommended to Dr. Knowland together and together when he interviewed them, they drove to Portland together and met Mr. Morgan together and got hired together. Mrs. Pleasance said they were close friends who often went out for pizza together. They both had worked for the same company. And now, although both were to be recalled to the witness stand, they are both gone."

She looked over the jurors as she spoke. Some were without any expression beyond impartial interest, a few nodded now and then, and one or two looked a little bored. One was regarding her with a distinctly cold look.

After she returned the various pieces of evidence to the table, she said. “Now I want to examine Boris Rostov’s testimony. She began to summarize the Texas beating and Wharton objected on the grounds that it had nothing to do with the case they were hearing.

“Your Honor,” Barbara said, “it is relevant if it establishes a pattern of actions. Mr. Rostov’s previous actions provide a pattern, and it is only fair for the jury to consider that pattern when they start their deliberations.”

Judge Humphrey nodded. “Overruled. You may continue.”

She finished the summary, first of the street fight he was accused of initiating in Texas, then the shooting of civilians in Iraq. “It appears that Mr. Rostov’s pattern is to leave the area before an official investigation is concluded. This trial is part of the official judgment of Travis Morgan, and Mr. Rostov has vanished before it is concluded, although he was warned of serious consequences if he failed to return for further questioning.

“On the night of September tenth, last year, he was in the kitchen with Mr. DiPalma when the housekeeper left at ten minutes after seven. They were still there, he stated, when they heard the doorbell at seven thirty. He went to open the door while Mr. DiPalma went to the office. He admitted Travis Morgan. Trained as a police officer, with more training as a contractor in security for Iraq, he looked Travis over when he admitted him to the house. He said he took the threats Mr. Morgan had reported seriously, and he was present when security was breeched in Portland and he himself shot and killed an intruder. But with that training, and that experience, he saw nothing suspicious, nothing that indicated Travis was carrying a gun.”

She retrieved the photograph of Travis lying unconscious on the floor. “You can see in this photograph,” she said, “the bulge made by his wallet. His clothes were closefitting and a gun, larger in every way than his wallet, would have been impossible to conceal.” Again she walked along the rail to let them all see the photograph.

“Mr. Rostov took Travis down the hall to the office, but he did not stay at his side during that short walk. He dropped back to walk behind him. Consider how many times you have been led to a doctor’s office with a nurse or an aide leading the way. Or in a theater with an usher leading the way. Or even in your own home when a repairman or a guest arrives and you lead the way. You don’t walk behind them. At the office door, he stated that he reached around Travis to open the door with his left hand. Again, compare that to the way you would first lead someone to a closed door and how you would then open it to permit a guest or a repairman to enter. If the room is occupied, you knock first, if only a light tap, to alert the person inside that you are entering. Then you open the door and step to one side to allow someone to enter. Mr. Rostov did not knock first. He reached around the back of Travis to open the door and give it a push.

"Did he also push Travis Morgan? They came to a closed door and stopped long enough for Mr. Rostov to reach around Travis to open and push it. Mr. DiPalma said Travis rushed in, but the position of his feet indicate that he barely got inside the room, instead of rushing in for even a few steps. In the emergency room some of Travis Morgan's first words on regaining consciousness were that someone had hit him, and that he was pushed. So the question for you to consider is whether he was pushed into the room or not. Did he stagger a little to regain his balance? Does that account for the way his head must have been tilted in order for the blow to have been administered with an upward slant?

"Mr. Rostov said he did not see Travis draw a gun, and since his hands must have been visible from the time he was admitted to the house, it is difficult to see when or how he could have drawn a gun without being seen. He was not wearing a holster, or a hidden strap of any kind that could have held a gun. His jeans were tight, and his sweater was close fitting. Yet, according to Mr. Rostov, he suddenly had a gun in his hand.

"After the shot was fired, and Travis was knocked to the floor, Mr. Rostov said he ran to see how Mr. Peel was, and to use his own words when he testified, and I quote, 'to make sure he was dead.' He told Mr. DiPalma to tell Mr. Morgan and Dr. Knowland what had happened. Then he kicked the gun away from Travis's hand. A question arises from that sequence. Wouldn't it have been wise to secure the gun first? He couldn't know yet how badly Travis had been wounded, whether he would start shooting again. Wouldn't it have been the first thing a security-trained guard would do automatically: secure the weapon, make it inaccessible to the shooter? It wasn't the first thing Mr. Rostov did."

She paused, then said, "And now on to the testimony of the third person present on that night of September tenth, Dr. Knowland. After finishing dinner, he said he and Mr. Morgan went up to Mr. Morgan's study, where they were chatting until Mr. DiPalma entered and told them of the shooting. He said they did not hear the doorbell or the gunshot." Using the house floor plan, she pointed to the study, the stairs, and indicated where the study was, across the hall from the top of the staircase. "Even with the door closed, a gunshot in that small space would be quite loud. The study is almost directly over where the gun was fired. How could they not have heard it?" She paused to let them consider it.

"Downstairs, Dr. Knowland examined Mr. Peel and pronounced him dead. Then he stood with the others in the hall waiting for the police to arrive. He did not examine Travis to see if he was alive or dead. He kept his eyes on Mr. Morgan, he said, because he feared that he might have a heart attack, that he was stunned and shocked to such a degree that he might collapse. He did not advise him to sit down, nor did he take him by the arm and lead him to a chair or to the sofa. He didn't even check his pulse rate. He stood there for seven minutes just keeping an eye on him while they waited for the police officers to arrive. That's a long time, ladies and gentlemen, especially if you fear that someone might have a heart attack."

She paused another moment, then said, "Let us examine another incident involving Dr. Knowland, one of the incidents that Mr. Wharton has labeled a diversion, and that I maintain is a defining one. It involves the night that June Morgan was taken to Mr. Morgan's residence."

"Objection," Wharton said. "That is a diversion and is not relevant to the case at hand."

"Your Honor, Mr. Wharton has already referred to it and dismissed it, but it is relevant in that it reveals a great deal about Dr. Knowland, who has played a major part in the tragedy of Mr. Peel's murder."

"Overruled," the judge said.

Barbara reminded the jurors of what Mrs. Ochmann had said about the night June Morgan was taken to the house and died that same night. "Keep in mind that she does volunteer work five days a week, and part of that volunteer work is at Sacred Heart Hospital. She knows what a hearse looks like. Seeing a hearse in her neighbor's driveway was extraordinary, and she was wide awake as she continued to watch to see what was happening next door.

"She looked at her clock and knew precisely what time it was, ten minutes after three, when Dr. Knowland entered the hearse. She knew him by sight and later learned his name. He admitted he was at the house all that night. She knew he left the hearse at three thirty and the hearse drove off at that time. She was peeved that she was too wide awake to go back to sleep, and she remarked on it to different people later that day.

"What Dr. Knowland has said about that night is quite different. He stated that they knew that June Morgan was being sent home ill, but he didn't know how ill she was until she arrived. He also stated that he tended her for several hours, and he signed her death certificate and gave her time of death at three a.m. Now, if he tended her for several hours, and she died at three, that means she had to have been in his care from around midnight until she died. Yet, he also stated that he told Mr. Morgan to go to bed at around midnight.

"If he was with her for three hours, what was he doing? How did he make his diagnosis? Why didn't he have her transferred to a hospital where they could have used a respirator, could have monitored her heart, her other body functions, could have infused antibiotics if necessary? Again I ask, was June Morgan already dead when the hearse drove into the driveway of Mr. Morgan's house? Would he have told her father to go to bed if he believed June would arrive ill?"

Barbara walked the length of the jury box as she said, "Those are two very different stories about what happened that night. They cannot both be true. If a witness is found to be less than truthful in one situation, then any other testimony given by that witness is questionable.

"Dr. Knowland's version of what happened that night is not credible, ladies and gentlemen. It doesn't make sense to send Mr. Morgan to bed at midnight and also to start ministering to June Morgan at about midnight. It doesn't make sense to expect a sick girl to be delivered late at night and not have a bed prepared for her. It doesn't make sense to tend to a dying girl for three hours when you're minutes away from one of the best hospitals in the valley. He said there was nothing he could have done for her, but there are procedures a medical team in a hospital could have done. He stated that he has performed medical procedures, minor operations, set bones, prescribed medications. He is not a faith healer, relying on prayer to heal the sick. But that night, it appears that he did little or nothing for June Morgan if his story of tending to her for several hours is truthful. In short, his testimony of what happened that night, and what he did, does not hold up to any real examination.

"You have the story Dr. Knowland related, and you have Mrs.

Ochmann's testimony about what she saw, and you have to decide which you believe. While you are deliberating this, you must keep in mind that it was Dr. Knowland who recommended that Mr. Morgan hire Mr. DiPalma and Mr. Rostov. He was instrumental in placing them both in Mr. Morgan's house."

Barbara walked to her table for a sip of water, and when she turned back to face the bench it was to see Judge Humphrey beckoning her and Wharton.

At the sidebar, the judge asked, "Are you at a convenient stopping point?"

"Yes."

"I'm going to recess for lunch, back at one thirty." He shooed them away and tapped his gavel, then made the announcement.

"Good," Barbara muttered as she watched him walk from the courtroom. As soon as he was out of sight, she looked over her shoulder at Frank. "How are they taking it?"

"Up and down," he said. "It's a cumulative process, as you well know. You're doing fine." His eyes twinkled then as he said, "For a better opinion, get a gander at Wharton."

She glanced at the prosecution table just in time to catch Wharton's expression before he picked up some papers and stuffed them into his briefcase. Wharton looked glum.

CHAPTER 38

BARBARA STOOD AT her old bedroom window, watching rain streak the glass. She was holding her Raggedy Ann doll. A gray sodden world lay out there, hostile for warm-blooded creatures, with the temperature hovering around freezing. "It's not enough without the bigger picture," she whispered to the crazily running water.

Forbidden territory, don't go there, she ordered herself sharply. She turned away from the window to see Frank in the doorway. She had not heard his footsteps.

"Bobby, come down and eat something," Frank said. "You have a tough afternoon facing you."

She put the doll down in its proper place on the window seat.

Strange, he was thinking, how gears shift even when you think you know exactly what you're doing and why. He had come up to tell her that Bailey had phoned in to say the bird had flown with twelve to fifteen nestlings aboard. When he saw her at the window and heard the sound of her whispering voice, not the words, just a whisper, he decided that Bailey's news could wait until later. For now, she needed to eat.

Back in the courtroom, she took front and center again and drew in a breath. "Let's consider Mr. Morgan's account of the afternoon and night of September tenth," she said.

"Mr. Morgan stated that he was nervous and excited by the coming visit of his son. He said he informed Mr. Peel some time during the day about the pending visit. However, Mrs. Peel stated that her husband called her at five to say he had only then been told he was to stay for dinner and a talk. He did not mention Travis Morgan. He said that Mr. Morgan wanted to discuss a problem with the books. It is not a minor difference in details. If Mr. Peel knew the reason for the dinner, according to Mr. Morgan's account, to celebrate the return of Travis Morgan, why didn't he mention it to his wife? Why make up a story about a problem with the books?

"Mr. Morgan stated that Mr. Peel was fond of Travis, had formed a friendship with him, and wished to have a minute or two with him. Mrs. Peel was puzzled when asked about a friendship between Mr. Peel and Travis Morgan and denied such a friendship had ever existed. Travis lived in Portland and was at the house on weekends and once in a while during the week. Mr. Peel never worked weekends. When was there an opportunity to become friends with Travis, and why would such a friendship develop between a middle-aged bookkeeper and a young boy?

"Mr. Morgan said he was nervous about the visit, and that he was overjoyed by it. Yet, he stated that he did not hear the doorbell and he did not hear a gunshot. You might think that he would have left the study door open, that he would have wanted to know when his son arrived. But according to his account, he and Dr. Knowland were chatting until Mr. DiPalma came to tell them the tragic news.

"Downstairs, after Dr. Knowland confirmed the death of Mr. Peel, the small group of men stood in the hallway for seven minutes waiting for the police to arrive. Mr. Morgan said that he was in shock because he had lost a dear friend."

She kept her voice and words crisp, one declarative sentence after another, just stating the facts that had been testified to the same way she might have said yesterday it rained, and today it is raining again.

"Mrs. Peel's account of the relationship between Mr. Morgan and her husband was the exact opposite. Mr. Peel considered their relationship to be that of employer and employee. It was a job to him, nothing more. There were no visits back and forth, no lunches or dinners together, nothing that indicates friendship.

"Turning now to the night that June Morgan was to be flown home, we have a third version about what happened. Mr. Morgan stated that he received a phone call from someone at the airport where the private plane was due to take off at about midnight, but was delayed because of a mechanical problem. He said he took a nap at around midnight, expecting his daughter to arrive hours later. According to Dr. Knowland's statement, she arrived home at about midnight. Why was no bed prepared for a sick girl expected to arrive in the middle of the night?"

The declarative manner of speaking was replaced now by a hesitant one. She spoke more slowly, frowned slightly as she invited the jurors to ponder with her the possible answers to the questions she was asking. "Why would a responsible school of any kind send a sick girl home in the middle of the night instead of waiting for a morning or afternoon flight? Had she been adequately treated at the school? He said he talked to the headmistress and was reassured that his daughter was recovering when she boarded the plane. He made no further effort to have an investigation of the treatment she had received. So there are three versions of what happened that night: Mrs. Ochmann's version, Dr. Knowland's, and Mr. Morgan's. Only one of them can be right." She shook her head slightly and repeated, "Only one of them can be right.

"There is the matter of the Colt forty-five, single-action murder weapon," she said. "It was inherited by Mr. Morgan with the passing of his father. Either that, or it was an exact duplicate of the gun he was bequeathed. Mr. Straub, who initialed the photographs of the gun, examined it and said it was in pristine condition, a fine collector's item, and that the gun had been carefully preserved for many years. Mr. Morgan said that it had been in a locked box made of oak.

He kept the key in a desk drawer that he said was locked sometimes. He keeps the key to the drawer on his key chain. Consider whether a collector's item of a gun that has been used as a plaything would have been in pristine condition. Consider whether a teenage boy in possession of such a gun would have held on to it for more than seven years and kept it carefully preserved all those years. Consider whether such a boy running away from home with no credit card and little cash would have sold such a gun or pawned it."

She stopped walking and looked over the jurors then as she said, "But most importantly, consider why there were no fingerprints on the bullets in the chambers. Travis Morgan's fingerprints were on the gun itself, but the bullets were clean of any prints. Did someone load that gun who did not want his fingerprints on the bullets?"

She paused and glanced at Wharton, then looked back at the jury. "Mr. Wharton dismissed the importance of the way money was transferred from an anonymous donor to Mr. Morgan's church. I insist that it is not a diversion, that it is, in fact, extremely important."

"Objection," Wharton said. "How Reverend Morgan's church receives donations has nothing to do with the murder of Joseph Peel."

Judge Humphrey polished his glasses and kept his gaze on them as he said, "Sustained."

Barbara walked to her table for a sip of water, and glanced at a note Frank placed there. He had written, *Many ways to skin a cat!* She nodded and took a drink of water.

"I want to remind you of what we know about Joseph Peel," she said, turning once more to the jury. "According to the accountant who worked with him, tracking down errors was a routine he followed rigorously, and it was one he had followed throughout all the years she had known him. It was not a cause for great discontent with his job, but a minor nuisance that he accepted. He also accepted the fact that he was required to go to Seattle to collect a donation every month. He didn't like doing it, but it was not a cause for resignation. It was just another annoying part of his job. For years he showed no real unhappiness with his position. But there were specific events that did cause him to become very upset and unhappy. They are not diversions, but rather turning points that were important to him, and to the matter before this court.

"The first such event was the shooting of an intruder in the Portland condo nearly three years ago. Two weeks after Mr. Morgan hired both Mr. DiPalma and Mr. Rostov, Mr. Rostov shot and killed an intruder. Mrs. Peel stated that her husband was very disturbed by this, and he told her he considered Mr. Rostov to be a violent man. On the night of that event, Mr. Morgan and Dr. Knowland had left the condo minutes before the intruder arrived, and they had left both the newly hired bodyguard and driver in the condo. Mr. DiPalma and Mr. Rostov were the only eyewitnesses to what happened that night.

"The next incident that was very disturbing and this time was also frightening to Mr. Peel, according to Mrs. Peel's testimony, was the fatal beating of Mr. Daggart, the handyman at the Portland church. Mrs. Peel stated that she had met Mr. Daggart briefly months before he was fatally beaten. At the time she met him he was using a different name, and he and her husband had a long talk. She said she had forgotten about that meeting until her husband reminded her, and he told her that Mr. Daggart had been conducting an investigation that Mr. Peel had agreed to assist. What it concerned she did not know. When Mr. Daggart was murdered, Mr. Peel became terribly upset and frightened, so much so that he decided to resign and informed Mr. Morgan of his decision. He didn't resign however, but stayed in his position for months, planning on leaving as soon as the mortgage was paid off on his farm. Mrs. Peel expressed sorrow over the fact that she had talked him out of resigning in March of last year, but at that time she didn't know about an investigation, and she did not know that her husband had agreed to cooperate with Mr. Daggart in carrying out that investigation.

"The last time Mr. Peel became very upset with his job was when Mr. Morgan had him arrange for the cremation of June Morgan, and for a funeral with an empty casket. Mr. Peel refused to attend the funeral, saying it was not decent to pretend that way when there would be mourners weeping and praying over an empty casket. He and Mrs. Peel began to count down the days until the end of September when he planned to quit his job. At that time he also explained his distress and fear when Mr. Daggart was killed.

"Mrs. Peel's statements concerned real events that might have upset anyone. A shooting death in the condo, the beating death of a handyman who worked for the church, and the church funeral and burial of an empty casket. She did not testify here voluntarily; she was subpoenaed and her statements were under oath."

Barbara paused and walked to her table where she stood when

she said, "When she was asked if she or her husband had considered Mr. Morgan's feelings about the funeral, if they had asked him about why it was being done that way, she said they had not. She said that her husband stopped asking any questions a long time ago. And she said that Mr. Peel also stated that as long as what he was doing was legal, he didn't care what Mr. Morgan did or said. Why would he have brought up the question of legality for the work he did? He was the bookkeeper who used the figures provided by his employer and made certain the books balanced. He did not count the collection, did not count the money from the anonymous donor. Mr. Morgan himself deposited that cash in the bank and Mr. Peel had to go to their Internet bank account to learn the exact amount. In fact, he handled no money whatsoever, and worked only with the figures given to him by others.

"Why then would he start to think about the legality of what he was doing? In April nearly three years ago, two new employees were added to the church expenses, and it raises the question of where enough money came from to pay their salaries. The cash flow through the church coffers had to be significant, and the expenses had to be significant: a condo and a church in Portland, a secretary and maintenance there, plus a bookkeeper and another church and residence here in Eugene. And suddenly two new employees. Mr. Peel knew better than anyone else what the finances of the church were.

"After Mr. Daggart talked to Mr. Peel and obtained his cooperation in an investigation, the question arises: What could Mr. Peel have known to assist in any investigation? He kept to himself, didn't chat with any of the others in the household, didn't exchange any confidences with Mr. Morgan, and was little more than a nodding acquaintance with Dr. Knowland. But he did know all about the financial situation, and that seems to be the only area where his cooperation with Mr. Daggart would have mattered."

Walking slowly back and forth before the jury box, Barbara said, "We come to the night of September tenth of last year. Mr. Peel told his wife there was nothing wrong with the books, but he had to wait and see what Mr. Morgan had on his mind. He had dinner with the others and, according to their various statements, he left them at the table to return to his office. But we have to ask what was he doing in his office?"

She went to the evidence table for the crime scene photographs.

"This photograph of his desk," she said holding it up for the jurors to see, "shows no papers, no ledgers open, just a desk that looks as if it has been tidied up after work. Nothing is out of place." She showed them a different photograph. "In this one we can see that the computer is black, and the keyboard drawer is pushed in all the way, indicating that he was not working at the computer. He needed his glasses for close work or work on the computer, yet his eyeglasses were in his coat pocket."

Holding a different photograph, she pointed to it saying, "Notice the position of his chair. It's a high-backed chair with armrests, five wheels, and a swivel seat. When you're sitting in such a chair, if you intend to rise and stand in place, you simply push the chair back a few inches to give you clearance from the desk. If you intend to leave your desk, it's a different maneuver. You might push the chair back slightly, but you also use the swivel feature to turn it sideways, permitting you to walk away. You've seen Mr. Wharton turning his chair in order to walk from it. You've seen me doing the same. And Judge Humphrey turns his chair when he leaves the bench. If you don't turn it, you have to move in an awkward sideways motion to get away from the desk. In this photograph, please note that Mr. Peel's chair has been turned sideways from his desk. The armrest is parallel to the desk. It's exactly the way you would expect it to be if he had pushed it back an inch or so, then turned it in order to stand and walk away." She handed the photograph to the foreman of the jury and waited as they passed it from one to another.

Barbara nodded to Shelley after she retrieved the last photograph. Shelley set up a tripod stand in such a way that the judge and the jurors could see it. Barbara placed on it an enlargement of the photograph of Peel's body in a pool of blood, and the back of his desk. She pointed to it as she said, "As you can see there is no blood anywhere on the desk, not on the top and not on the drawers. The medical examiner said that his wound would have resulted in a spurt of blood. If Mr. Peel had been rising from his desk when he was shot, there should be some blood on it. There is no sign of disarray on his desk that a convulsive reaction to a gunshot might cause. No papers scattered about, nothing disturbed whatsoever. All of the blood is on the floor behind the desk, where it would be if Mr. Peel had been shot after he stood, turned his chair, and faced the side of the room. Where it would be if he was moving away from his desk."

"Objection!" Wharton called out. "This is pure speculation."

"It isn't!" Barbara said hotly. "It's explaining the evidence of the photographs!"

Judge Humphrey took his time before he said, "I'm tabling your objection, Mr. Wharton, for the time being. I shall address it when I give instructions to the jury."

"Exception," Wharton said quickly.

"Noted," the judge said and nodded to Barbara. "Continue."

She nodded and removed the photograph, returned it to the table and brought out two more crime scene pictures. She placed them side by side on the tripod stand. "The first officers to arrive at the crime scene testified that they are trained to touch nothing until the forensics team has finished its work. The photographer is also trained to touch nothing. Mr. Rostov cautioned Dr. Knowland to touch nothing and stated that he touched nothing beyond moving the gun." She pointed to one of the photographs as she said, "This is a view of Travis Morgan and the doorway he had come through. The other picture is the same area from a different angle. I draw your attention to the position of the door." She pointed to it. It was slightly more than halfway open.

"Mr. Rostov testified that he reached around Travis to open the door and give it a shove," she said. "Mr. Rostov is a large and powerful man, six feet tall, and very strongly built. If he gave that door a shove, why did it stop there? Why didn't it open all the way back to the wall?"

She let them stare at the two photographs for a few seconds before she continued. "That brings us back to the question of what Mr. Peel was doing in his office from the time he left the dinner table until Travis Morgan was admitted to the house."

"Are we to believe that Mr. Peel sat at his desk looking at the door across his office for twenty minutes? He was ready to leave when Mr. Morgan told him to stay for dinner and said there was a problem. Mrs. Peel recounted that conversation with him, and Mrs. Pleasance, the housekeeper, confirmed it. She heard Mr. Peel speaking to his wife at about five. She stated that his desk was cleaned, that it appeared that he was through for the day. With Mr. Peel's work habits, it is most unlikely that he had left anything undone, or that there was a problem with the books. He told his wife he knew there was no problem. So what was he doing all that time? Both Mr. DiPalma and Mr. Rostov stated that he was at his desk facing the door when they entered. Was it because he had been talking to someone who had been standing in front of the door or a little to one side of it? Was there another person in that room that night? Does that account for the fact the door was shoved and stopped where it did because a person was there to stop it?"

Wharton was calling out an objection before she finished, but she got her final question out before she stopped.

"Sustained," Judge Humphrey snapped. "The jury will ignore the speculative scenario counsel has proposed." He beckoned Barbara and Wharton to the sidebar. There, he glared at her saying, "You are treading dangerously close to having me throw you off this case, and dangerously close to contempt of court. You know this is an improper closing statement. You are not to speculate again in such a manner! Do you understand?'

"Yes, Your Honor," she said as meekly as she could.

"Then get on with it," he ordered.

She walked to her table for a sip of water. Frank's face had a sober expression but his eyes were twinkling as she turned to face the jury again.

"Finally," she said, "let's get to Travis Morgan. Ladies and gentlemen, Travis does not have to prove his innocence. It is the state's burden to prove his guilt beyond a reasonable doubt. Travis is not required to testify and he could add nothing to the account already in the prosecutor's files. His first words on regaining consciousness in the emergency room were, 'Who hit me?' He said he was pushed into the room by the man behind him, then someone hit him in the head. He woke up in the hospital. That's all he could say about what happened in that office that night. He did say that and it is on record and was testified to by the arresting officer and the emergency room doctor. When advised to admit that he had shot and killed Mr. Peel he expressed bewilderment. He knew nothing about a shooting and he said he had never shot a gun in his life. He was in great pain. He was in no condition to make up and tell a lie. His answers and his bewilderment were as spontaneous as his answers to the routine questions the emergency room doctor asked.

"You heard Dr. Tunney's explanation of the wound Travis sustained that night. His head was tilted downward and he was moving away from the bookend that struck him. His position was exactly that of a man recovering his balance after being pushed. Ask yourselves if anyone in that position, staggering slightly, regaining balance could have fired a shot and hit a target.

"Detective Eggleston, the arresting officer, read Travis his Miranda rights. We're all familiar with that process. Miranda rights say you have the right to remain silent, that anything you say can and will be used against you, and you have the right to an attorney. Miranda rights do not say that the prosecution can and will use any exonerating statements you may make. Detective Eggleston passed his notes to his superior officer, and presumably the same notes were passed on to the district attorney's office, but the prosecution did not choose to reveal the exonerating details of Travis Morgan's statements. It is up to the jury to weigh those remarks as carefully as they would have weighed incriminating remarks if any had been made. Everything he said attested to his innocence."

"His clothing that night would not have allowed him to conceal a gun." She went to the evidence table to pick up the replica gun and held it up before the jurors as she continued. "This Colt single-action handgun weighs over two pounds, is eleven inches long and two inches wide at the chamber. He could not have concealed it on his person. He could not have drawn it from somewhere and cocked it without being seen."

She replaced the gun, then said, "There was no friendship between Travis and Mr. Peel and no reason for him to have been taken to Mr. Peel before seeing his father. Another question you must ask yourselves is why the strange arrangement was made to take Travis to Mr. Peel's office instead of directly to his father."

She looked over the jurors and stood before them as she continued. "Guilty beyond a reasonable doubt can be a high bar in reaching a decision. As you consider what happened in Joseph Peel's office on the night of September tenth, ask yourselves if you have any doubts about anything you have heard during this trial. Ask yourselves if all the questions you think important have been answered to your satisfaction. Why did Tony DiPalma enter the office and immediately pick up a bookend and position it and himself in the only way that accounts for the wound on Travis Morgan's head? Why did Boris Rostov walk behind Travis Morgan and open the door by reaching around him, then give the door a shove? Why did the door stop moving where it did?"

She paused between each question, letting it sink in and register before the next one. "Did Mr. Rostov give Travis Morgan a shove into the room? Can you account for the placement of the wound on Travis's head, the upward direction of the wound in any other way than that he was bent over, his head at a tilt, exactly the position of a man catching his balance? What was Mr. Peel doing after he left the dinner table and before Travis Morgan arrived? If Mr. Peel was facing the door when he was shot why was there no blood on the desk, no sign of disorder on the desk? Why was his chair turned sideways? Why did Mr. Morgan claim friendships that Mrs. Peel said did not exist? Why were there drops of blood in the hall and in the living room and none on the stairs or in the upstairs study? Why are there three very different versions of what happened the night Mr. Morgan's daughter was flown to Eugene?"

After a slightly longer pause, she said, "If you find that a witness has made a misstatement and maintained that misstatement on further questioning, you are free to judge that witness's statements to be less than credible in other testimony. When you are asked to determine which one of several versions of any event is more likely to be true than the others, one of the questions you must ask is whether any of the witnesses to that event has anything to gain or lose by it. Mrs. Ochmann had nothing to gain, nothing to lose when she testified. Mrs. Peel was an unwilling witness, she did not come forward voluntarily, and she had nothing to gain or lose by testifying."

She stopped walking back and forth as she said, "An important question to ask is why Mr. Peel was asked to stay late that night. And the most important question of all: Why was Travis Morgan taken to Mr. Peel's office instead of directly to his father when he arrived at that house that night?

It has been stated, repeated, and emphasized that Mr. Peel was a good man, a conscientious man, meticulous in his work. A good and harmless man who had no enemies. But was he perceived by someone as not harmless, but rather as a threat, a man with knowledge dangerous to someone? It has been suggested repeatedly that he was not the intended victim, but ask yourselves if perhaps he was the intended victim."

She moved away from the jury box then to stand near her own table where she glanced at Travis, who appeared transfixed. "The emergency room doctor testified that if the blow that injured Travis had been struck straight on with the full force of a body behind it, and the weight of the bookend considered, such a blow would have been far more severe. You might ask yourselves if it could have been fatal. If that had happened, ladies and gentlemen, we would not be here today. And this case would have been closed quickly as the case of a young man with a gun being struck down before he could kill more than one person. It would have resembled the incident in Portland at Mr. Morgan's condo nearly three years ago. The same two eyewitnesses would have given their statements.

"I remind you of what Travis Morgan said in the emergency room when he regained consciousness. He said, 'Who hit me?' And he said, 'Someone pushed me.' When advised to admit that he had shot and killed Mr. Peel, he said, 'I don't know what you're talking about. I never shot a gun in my life.' Those are the spontaneous statements from an innocent man, and they are true statements because Travis Morgan is an innocent man. He is the second victim of that fateful night, the victim who survived. Thank you for you attention, ladies and gentlemen."

Judge Humphrey called for a short recess as soon as Barbara sat down. She watched the jurors keep their eyes on Humphrey as he turned his chair, rose, and walked out. As soon as he was gone, before Travis was escorted out, he said, "You were terrific! Is it enough?" She could only pat his arm and hope it had been.

During the recess she sat numbly in her chair and was silently grateful for the coffee Shelley brought to her. "Great!" Shelley said. "That was great."

But was it enough? she kept wondering as she waited for Humphrey's return and his instructions to the jury. When they came, her numbness might have been attributed to ice water flowing through her veins. He sustained Wharton's last objection to her question of whether someone might have been in the room standing where the opening door came to a stop. He told the jurors they had to ignore all the speculations she had voiced and went down them one by one. They must examine the evidence and sworn statements, not theories, he said.

Then he turned the case over to the jury and there was nothing more to be done.

✦

CHAPTER 39

"WHAT THEY USUALLY do first is select a foreman, and have a straw vote to see how far apart they are, what bridges have to be built, what chasms have to be filled before they reach a consensus," Frank said, ushering Ashley and Mikey into the waiting room along with Shelley and Barbara. "We'll stay together because you never know when we'll be called back. Today we'll have to return to court at five thirty. Tomorrow, bring in books, music, films, whatever you like to pass the time. I have a collection of movies you might browse through. Or play cards, do needlework, watch television, do anything that helps keep your sanity while we wait. This could be the hardest part."

Frank made sure there was coffee at hand and cold drinks in the refrigerator, then motioned to Barbara. "We have a few things to do," he said. "Try to make yourselves as comfortable as you can."

"Barbara, before you leave, what do you think? Can you tell anything about how they were reacting?" Ashley was dead white and her fear was as palpable as a scarlet rash would have been.

"I think they were paying very close attention," Barbara said. "They have a lot to think about now and a lot of arguing to do, probably."

Frank made a grunting sound. "Nonsense! They were eating it up. Barbara had them by the scruff of the neck all the way." He nodded to Barbara. "Let's get to it."

They were silent as they walked to his office, but inside, with the door closed, she cried, "That bastard! That lousy stinking bastard! Humphrey wants them to hand over a guilty verdict! I knew it from day one. He tried to kill any case I was making. Forget the way money was passed, forget the safe deposit box, forget speculation about skimming off the top! Forget that two witnesses skipped town before I could get at them. They had given sworn testimony. Consider only the real evidence backed up with proof or sworn testimony! Sworn testimony of four different people. Bullshit!"

"Now, Bobby, remember, disregard my remarks when you write your will. They heard what you were saying, and God knows that once they close the door and start deliberating, no one can order what to remember and what to forget. Sit down and let me tell you what I heard from Bailey."

"The plane flew out! That's it? They kept the date and flew out?"

"They did. And that will bring up that other issue pretty damn fast. Patsy said I had a call from Philip Kyle, the Homeland Security fellow, this afternoon. Of course, since I was in court I was unavailable."

"Good God!" she cried and shook her head hard. "I can't deal with that now! They have to wait until there's a verdict. That was our agreement."

"I'm afraid they won't pay much attention to that agreement. I expect they were waiting to see if a planeload of men left as you predicted. Well, they did, and they will want everything you have, and want it now, not later."

"Not until there's a verdict. Probably tomorrow. After court tomorrow, if there's a verdict. Just tell them you don't have the information, I do, and if they want to haul me off to Gitmo or somewhere, that's what they'll have to do. After the verdict!"

She went to the door and turned to face him again. "Dad, if they bring in a guilty plea, I'm going to blow this goddamn case wide open! So help me God!"

"And then they'll drag you off to Gitmo," he snapped.

"So be it. I'm going to talk to Ashley."

Frank went to his desk and sat down heavily behind it. They wouldn't haul her to Gitmo, but they would make her life very uncomfortable. Obstruction, interfering with a federal investigation, threaten disbarment since as an officer of the court it was her duty to cooperate with an official request, seize her computer, telephone records, every scrap of paper in her office and home… After a few minutes he picked up his phone and dialed the number Kyle had left with Patsy.

In the waiting room Ashley jumped up from the sofa when Barbara entered. "Anything? Have they called us back?"

"No. Much too soon." Ashley sank down. "But I do want to tell you something I've been holding back and the reason for doing so. You kept hearing about that shooting in Portland nearly three years ago. You need to know the full details." She told them about John Varagosa and his castration and the big letter F that had been cut on his face. Both Ashley and Mikey turned milk white as she talked. Tears were running down Ashley's cheeks when Barbara finished.

"There was nothing more than one innocent kiss between them," Barbara said. "But Arlie Morgan with his filthy mind believed otherwise. That's when he sent June away and that's why he butchered that boy. I couldn't tell you, Ashley, and I especially couldn't tell Travis. The reason he ran away in the first place was that Arlie Morgan toyed with a scalpel and talked to him about how gloriously free from lust a eunuch was. He scared the kid to death and he ran."

"He told you that?" Ashley whispered.

"No. He told Dad, thank God. That's how he overcame that terrible fear you saw in him, that I saw in him. After all those years he finally got it off his chest. Think how he might have presented himself in court with that raw memory in his head, that fear still surfacing every time he saw his father or even heard his name. Think how his fear might have been magnified if he knew Arlie Morgan had that done to another boy. He would have reacted to his father with the fear of a fifteen-year-old boy. So I withheld it from both of you to protect him. You must not tell him until after a verdict has been reached. I'm telling you now because as soon as those jurors are done with their work, they will be free to talk about the case, about what they know, and this is part of what they know."

Mutely, Ashley nodded. She stood, touching her tear-streaked cheeks. "I need to wash my face," she mumbled.

Mikey jumped up. "Me too. Come on, let's do it together."

Watching them walk to the restroom, Barbara knew she would never tell Ashley what Arlie Morgan had done to her daughter.

As predicted, there was no call back before they returned to the courtroom at five thirty, where the foreman of the jury told the judge they had not reached a verdict, and he lectured them about not talking about the case, not reading about it, or watching anything about it on television… Court was recessed until eight thirty the following morning.

"Barbara," Travis said urgently, holding her arm as the jurors were being led out, "I thought you were building a case against that douche bag that gave me a shove, but it's really my father, isn't it? You think he shot Peel." He looked as if he had not slept, with deep shadows under his eyes, and his jailhouse pallor adding to his haggard appearance. His hand on her arm was shaking.

"Easy, Travis," she said. "First things first. And the first one is for the jury to reach a verdict, then on to the next."

"He was throwing me to the wolves," Travis whispered. "Isaac, on the rock with a knife at his throat. Only this time the knife was going to be used." He rubbed his hand over his face. "Can you prove he did it? Is there any way to prove it?"

"I'm working on it," she said as his guard approached. "Travis, take a sleeping pill if you need it, and don't go to pieces. Try to get some sleep tonight."

"I'm okay," he said and turned to leave. "Maybe tomorrow I'll know why he would do that."

She didn't move as she watched him out of sight. Frank's touch on her arm made her jerk startled.

"Sorry," he said.

"He's suffering," she said in a low voice. "Right now he should be worrying about nothing more than the verdict, but he's going over and over why his father hates him enough to see him sacrificed. He's been so screwed up by that man, it will take years for him to work through it all."

"But he'll work through it. That's the important thing."

"He'll have to get rid of the guilt first," she said, as if she had not heard Frank's reassuring words. "You can't live feeling so guilty because you think you did something that made your own father hate you."

"Bobby, come along now. I sent Alan to take Ashley and Mikey to their apartment and arranged for him to pick them up in the morning. Let's have Herbert take us to my place before you head for home."

She shook herself. "Did you call Kyle?"

"Yes, and I'll tell you about it at home."

In Frank's living room, where he had made a fire, Barbara stroked Thing One, or possibly Thing Two, and listened to Frank relate his telephone call to Philip Kyle of Homeland Security.

"So I mentioned that you're between a rock and a hard place. Judge Humphrey would raise hell if you failed to show if he called for a chat in chambers, or failed to be there for the verdict, and there are a few legalities that must be tended to after a verdict is brought in. I bought a little time, that's all. He wants everything on the table within twenty-four hours of the verdict. That's his bottom line. He's chafing at the bit, thinking you know things he doesn't know. Possibly afraid someone will blow up the Pentagon or something because you're sitting on information."

She nodded. "So they blow up the Pentagon. My fault. A shooting in Kansas City, my fault. He loses his sunglasses, my fault." She pulled out her cell phone and punched her speed dial. "Bailey," she said to Frank. Then, speaking to Bailey she asked, "Are you keeping tabs on Morgan?"

"Pretty much. You know it's dinnertime for some people?"

"So eat already. Keep him in sight tomorrow if he goes to his bank in Portland, and especially if he goes to the train station in time for the Seattle train."

"Me and a dozen feds," he said grumpily.

"Send someone," she snapped. "Come around to Dad's office around ten in the morning."

"Yeah, yeah. I'm going to finish eating."

Frank was scowling and his voice was sharp when she closed her cell phone. "Barbara, what are you up to? What are you planning?"

"Don't know yet," she said. "Get out, you useless lump," she said to Thing One and dumped him. He crossed the space to Frank and stepped up onto his lap. Thing Two pushed him off and he stalked from the room with his tail upright and stiff. "Right now I'm going home and eat whatever Herbert dishes out of that crock pot and after that I'm going to my office and find out what I'll do." She stood and eyed Frank steadily as she said, "I'm telling you this much, though. The feds can't have Arlie Morgan. You know how that would work out. They could take months or even years before making a move. He'd be on ice for an indefinite time, maybe make a deal with them, tell whatever he knows about the big picture in exchange for immunity for everything else. Or arrange for a suspended sentence. Or cut some other goddamn deal. And it isn't going to happen. Arlie Morgan is mine."

She paced the length of her office, through the doorway to the outer office wall and back again, and again, and again. Herbert sat on her sofa, reading a paperback book. When her thighs were afire she sat at her desk until the heat subsided. Then she paced some more.

"That's it," she muttered at last and went to her safe to extract some pictures. She used the scanner in the outer office, then replaced the photographs in her safe and locked it. Afterward, she sat at her desk, sometimes contemplating the scanned photographs, other times staring into space. At one o'clock, she stood and said, "Ready to go home?"

Although she thought Herbert had been snoring, he was on his feet so fast it seemed unlikely that, moments ago, he had been asleep.

"Yes, ma'am. Reckon bed will look pretty good tonight for both of us. Maybe I should carry you down?"

She laughed and shook her head. "I'll pay the price tomorrow, I'm afraid. I'm sorry to keep you up like this."

"Seems like I was down more than up," he said with a wide grin.

She turned off the lights and they left. It was bitter cold that night, in the teens with ice crystals on branches, on the pavement, overhead wires. They reflected streetlights, night-lights in windows, car lights, a plethora of impermanent diamonds. Glittering fairy treasure.

Then, at home, when she slipped into bed, Darren rolled over to hold her close. "You're like ice," he murmured sleepily. She welcomed his warmth and gradually felt it flow into her and she drifted off to a fairyland where Tinker Bell fairies gathered diamonds and put them in baskets festooned with flowers.

"I know it's a lot of nonsense," Frank said the next morning when he shepherded the crew back to his office waiting room. They had been to court, which immediately recessed until twelve thirty. "Thing is," Frank said, "the jurors can't talk about the case anywhere except in the deliberation room. So they have to be taken to lunch in a group, get hauled back to court, reminded of their duty, and pick up where they left off. And we have to be part of the process. If I ran things I'd streamline it, but until then, that's just how it is."

Neither Ashley nor Mikey had anything to say as they took off coats and scarves.

"I brought something," Shelley said. "See, I've had this puzzle for a couple of years and never had time to do anything with it, so now's my chance. A thousand-piece jigsaw puzzle of the Mona Lisa. And that card table looks like just the place to work it. Helpers wanted to get the pieces turned right-side up." She emptied the box of pieces on the table. "The thing about jigsaw puzzles is that you can work on it, walk away, come back for a few minutes, or whatever. Mindless enough but sort of distracting in a curious way… "

She chattered on and Barbara wandered over to help turn pieces. After a moment Mikey followed and Ashley tagged along.

Watching them for a few minutes, Frank knew how the day would go. He had seen Shelley do this more than once. They would work on the puzzle in a desultory sort of a way, with long pauses when they would just chat, and even laugh now and then. Occasionally one or the other would stroll away, pick up a magazine or a book, put it down, then return to the puzzle. He tried to get Barbara's attention without speaking, but she was avoiding him, and that was a worry. She had not met his look directly all morning. He knew she was planning something that she had no intention of talking about yet, and he knew there was not a thing he could do about it.

Abruptly he turned and left the waiting room to go to his office and have Patsy bring in his mail, which he did not want to read.

Barbara picked up a piece, studied it, than added it to a few other pieces that were starting to define a border. "Ashley," she said, "what kind of things did Arlie particularly hate about women's wear, appearance, fragrance, things like that?"

Ashley looked startled and puzzled. "Why? He hates everything about women."

"Curious," Barbara said. "Just curious. Did he object to women wearing pants, for example?"

"Absolutely. He preferred long dresses, but when I said no to that, he settled for just below the knee. Crazy. He liked long white dresses, but not white street wear. Never pants, jeans, shorts. He hates for women to wear perfume or jewelry. Red's a no-no. Dark blue, gray, black, maybe a white blouse with a dark suit, but mostly dark conservative colors."

"Gotcha," Barbara said. "He'd love this puzzle. Seems like it's mostly gray."

A few minutes before ten, her phone sounded. She glanced at it and said, "Something I have to take care of. See you later." Shelley and Mikey were exchanging stories about puppies, newspapers, chewed slippers when she left the table. Ashley was staring off into space.

She walked through the corridor to Frank's office, paused at the door to draw in a long breath, then entered. Bailey was on the sofa, Frank in one of the easy chairs, scowling.

"Did Morgan take off for Portland?" she asked on entering.

"Yep," Bailey said. "He's there by now. Knowland drove. Train's due at eleven or so."

"Good. I'll want to know if he comes back to Eugene later on." She took the other easy chair and said, "How well do you know Morgan's church here in town?"

"How much do you know about any church?" Bailey said with a shrug. "Seats about a hundred fifty when full, which it never is. There's a kitchen and an office. Old wooden building, 1940 vintage. On Twelfth between Polk and Chambers. Across from the Eugene Speech and Hearing clinic. They use the clinic's parking lot on Sundays, and Wednesday nights when they have Bible studies or something. What else?"

"Sounds ideal," she murmured. "Can you get inside and bug the hell out of it? All of it? Before Wednesday?"

"Barbara! Stop right there," Frank said sternly. "Just stop. What are you proposing to do?"

"I'm going to arrange a meeting with Morgan and Knowland, and I think it will happen in the church. We'll see what comes of it."

"You are not!" Frank leaned forward and jabbed the air with his forefinger. "One of them is bat crazy, and the other's a cold-blooded butcher! You're not to get anywhere near either one of them!"

"But I will," she said coldly. "You know as well as I do what's going to happen. Humphrey practically ordered the jury to bring in a guilty verdict. If they do, I'll appeal instantly. If they bring in not guilty, it's over for Travis. If they're hung, Travis is out of it, they won't bring new charges without their witnesses. But no matter how that goes, Morgan and Knowland will be off the hook, scot-free, and that isn't going to happen. I said I was going to bring Morgan down and, by God, that's what I'm going to do."

"That madman could shoot you on sight! Knowland would be his eyewitness that it was self-defense."

"No, he won't do that. I have something he'll want, and I'll make sure he knows you and others know about the meeting and have access to what I have." She faced Bailey again and snapped off the question, "Can you bug that church before Wednesday?"

He glanced at Frank, and she cried, "He isn't asking you to do this. I am! If you can't or won't, just say so and I'll find someone who can."

"Sure," Bailey said. "No sweat. Maybe I should know a little more about the game plan? Like why bug the whole place, why not wear a wire? Or use that briefcase I fixed for you back a couple of years?"

"They'll suspect a wire and I'll show the proof that it's not there. The briefcase is a good back up, and I'll take it, but I'm sure it will be the church, and I want their conversation after I leave."

The briefcase had a transmitter in the brass work of the clasp that was activated by opening the case. A good backup, she had already decided, but not enough.

"Why even include me in this talk?" Frank asked, his voice dripping ice, his face a frozen mask of disapproval.

"Because I want you to bring Hogarth along for the ride. He hates unsolved murders, and murderers who get away with it. I can't talk him into going along, but you can. We gave him Daggart's killers. Let's give him Peel's."

"He won't be part of it," Frank snapped. "Too chancy, too dangerous, too many ways it could backfire."

"He knows the feds will grab Morgan and Knowland as soon as they have enough to justify it. He knows that once the feds get them, he'll never see them again, and it makes him sore. Let him make the arrest before the feds pull in their fish. If he won't go for it, I'll move without him."

"Just what do you have that makes you think you can manipulate both Morgan and Knowland?" Frank demanded.

"The pictures of June Morgan's mutilated body. They both know if those pictures surface, the investigation moves to Pendleton and environs, and the Chateau's at risk, their bloody militia's at risk. Whatever it costs here, they can't take that chance."

Frank leaned back in his chair, shaking his head. "It's too damn risky. Too many unknowns."

Barbara glanced at her watch. "I told Travis I'd talk to him this morning, and I have to get the original photographs to my safe deposit box. Talk it over, fix the holes, patch up the loose ends, do whatever it takes to get Hogarth on board. I'm off to jail, and I'll see you in court at twelve thirty."

That day Travis was withdrawn, his forehead furrowed as he regarded Barbara. There was a bleakness in his expression, hopelessness and despair. "I know what the judge told them," he said without preamble. "I heard every word. He thinks I did it and he wants the jury to think I did it."

"That's not what I want to talk about," Barbara said. "It's something you said. You don't know what you did to make your father hate you enough to throw you to the wolves. Listen to me, Travis. Don't say a word. Just listen. The fisherman wants his son to take up his trade, the farmer expects his son to become a farmer, the businessman will leave the business to his son, and so on. It's a normal process, to pass on your knowledge, your expertise to your son, and as often as not it works out that way. But some sons become musicians, some become engineers, others find other paths to follow. They say no. That's what you did, Travis. You said no. I don't know why your father is so twisted, how it happened, what turned him onto his path, but whatever steered him to where it is now had nothing to do with you. You are not responsible for his becoming what he is. But there he is, a twisted, fearful man, a zealot, and that's what he would have molded you into, another twisted zealot. He has convinced himself that he is righteous, that his way is the right way, and by saying no you rejected his philosophy, his bigotry. Zealotry does not, cannot, bear any contradiction. He is right, you must be wrong. He is on the path to salvation, you must be damned. When Ashley rejected his zealotry, he very nearly destroyed her, but her rejection wasn't as powerful as having his son, his flesh and blood, reject him and his beliefs. If you couldn't be shaped, twisted, molded into his image, you had to be destroyed. You said no, that was what you did to him, Travis. That's all you did. Whether you articulated it doesn't matter. You knew instinctively, intuitively that he was wrong, and you said no. The day you ran away you made a choice to become your own person, to follow your own path. It was a courageous act, a gamble, there were terrible risks for one so young, but you chose not to become the mirror image of a zealot. You chose to reject his demented worldview, to become a normal, caring person in your own right. That's your crime, your terrible act, and he can never forgive you for it."

She stood and regarded him for a moment. As far as she could tell he had not moved a muscle while she spoke. He didn't move then. "As I said, I didn't want you to say a word, just listen. Now I have to go, a few things I have to do before court."

He rose and, still mute, held out his hand to her. She pressed it between her own hands before turning to knock on the door for the guard.

✦

CHAPTER 40

SHE ARRIVED IN court minutes before twelve thirty, and the process was repeated. The jury had not reached a decision and court was recessed until two o'clock. "I think Shelley should take Ashley and Mikey out to lunch," Frank said as the courtroom began to empty. He looked at Shelley, who nodded.

"Pappi's," she said, "and I'll bring an armload of goodies back to the office. Fat city, here we come." Turning to Ashley, she said, "It's a Greek restaurant. You'll like the change of scene and their deserts are heavenly."

Ashley was like a zombie, Barbara thought, watching her. She would have been unable to resist any suggestion, no matter how outrageous. Frank sent Alan out with them and motioned to Barbara. "Hogarth's coming around for a sandwich," he said.

When they reached the offices, Bailey was seated in the reception room. Barbara waved to him to come along and said to Herbert, "You too. Strength in numbers."

Inside Frank's office she asked Bailey, "Any news from Portland?"

"Our guy was stood up. He went to the train station and hung around awhile, then went to the condo. Hasn't left it yet."

"Great," she said. She took off her coat and tossed it onto one of the visitor's chairs, then went around the desk to sit in Frank's chair. He regarded her unhappily, and reached across the desk to buzz Patsy.

"We'll want six sandwiches," he said. "Two of them liverwurst on rye with onions. Ham and cheese for the rest. Beer, coffee, chips, the works. As soon as possible."

After that he crossed the office to sit in one of the easy chairs and motioned Bailey and Herbert to sit down. "Your show," he said to Barbara with more than a touch of sharpness in his voice.

"Yes, it is," she said. "As soon as Hogarth gets here, I'm going to call Morgan and make a date." She looked at Bailey, "Is your part done?"

"Last night," he said scowling. "Early this morning. Three, and it was like being in Antarctica. Froze my butt off."

"Good work," she said in satisfaction. She stopped when there was a buzz on Frank's phone.

He nodded toward it. "You might as well take over that, too," he said.

She picked up the phone and Patsy said *that* man was here. "Send him on in," Barbara said smiling slightly. Poor Patsy seemed to believe that every time Hogarth appeared, either Barbara or Frank was going to be arrested.

Hogarth was redder than usual, no doubt due to the cold. He was bundled up in a heavy jacket with a long wool scarf, and he was wearing a wool ski cap pulled down low over his ears. He came to a stop just inside the door and looked over Herbert and Bailey, then turned to snap at Barbara, "What are you pulling this time?"

"My team," she said cheerfully. "You've all met, of course. It's nice and warm in here, Lieutenant. Please make yourself comfortable while I make a phone call."

She opened her address book and dialed Morgan's number. Hogarth began to unwind his scarf. Knowland answered the phone. "Holloway. I want to speak to Morgan," she said crisply.

"He doesn't want to talk to you."

"The feeling is quite mutual, I assure you, but this concerns him. You also, I might add."

She could hear Morgan's voice protesting angrily that she had a nerve to call him, to hang up on her. She watched Hogarth take off the jacket to reveal an argyle sweater. He was taking no chances on the weather, she thought, waiting for Knowland to get back to her. Instead, it was Morgan's voice on the phone next.

"You filthy bitch," he said in a rasping voice. "I don't have to talk to you. I won't talk to you. You are a filthy whore, a Jezebel out to corrupt and destroy—"

He was still going on, but Knowland's voice was on the phone then. "As I said, he doesn't want to talk to you. Why did you call here? How did you get this number?"

"Listen, Knowland," she said. "I just turned on the speaker phone and there are several other people in the room with me. I have something that you and your stooge will desperately want because without it you are both in deep doo-doo. I will meet with you and Morgan to show you what I have and we can discuss details. There are several conditions, however. I won't meet you anywhere after dark. I won't go to the residence in Eugene. And the hours are between ten and twelve, or between two and four in the afternoon. I know you're in

Portland today, so we can make it tomorrow. My office is available, but possibly you feel about it the way I feel about your lair. I suggest a public place. The library or a restaurant, for instance."

"I won't be seen in public with that woman!" Morgan cried. "And I won't go to her office!"

"I heard you," she said. They were on a speakerphone, too, she thought. Good. Ignoring Morgan's continuing diatribe, she said, "Again the feeling is mutual. I don't want to be seen with that crazy creep, either. But not outside anywhere. It's too damn cold to have a rational conversation outside."

Hogarth was standing in the middle of the office, staring at her, holding his jacket and scarf, with the silly ski cap still on his head.

"We don't even know what you're talking about," Knowland said. "What do you have that you think we might be interested in?"

"Pictures that could put you and the nutcase away for a very long time."

"We could pick you up, talk in the car," Knowland said after a moment.

"No way. In a closed-in space with that lunatic? I want some distance between us. I don't want him close enough to breathe on me."

"The church," Morgan screeched. "It's a holy place. God will strike her down if she dares to blaspheme in His church—"

"Oh, for heaven's sake," Barbara snapped. "I have things to do. Is it a go or isn't it? I'd just as soon go the district attorney's office as haggle over this."

"The church," Knowland said. "We'll be there at eleven."

"So will I," she said and hung up. She looked at Bailey and winked. He grinned.

"Whatever it is, I don't want any part of it," Hogarth said.

"Okay," Barbara said. "But lunch is on the way, and you might as well stay long enough to eat your share." She turned toward Frank. "Dad, do you think that cloche you put over the lettuce is enough protection in this kind of weather?"

Hogarth snatched the ski cap off his head and tossed his things on top of hers on the chair.

"Not the lettuce," Frank said. "Endive, parsley, shallots, they might all freeze to the ground but they'll come back, and first day with a decent temperature I'll toss in some new lettuce seeds."

"You know, there's a peck of new materials for greenhouses,

cloches, stuff like that, guaranteed to be good all the way down to ten degrees," Herbert said. "I'd be right proud to make you a new house for your—"

"Cut the crap!" Hogarth muttered. "What are you up to this time?" He sat down in the remaining easy chair.

"I intend to hand over a murderer either to you, as a courtesy for all the cooperation you've given us in the past, or else directly to the DA," Barbara said. "Actually I don't much care who gets it, just so it's done."

"Way I heard it, the murderer is cooling his heels, waiting for the jury to clinch it," Hogarth said.

"Wrong guy. Anyway, no matter what the jury does, I still intend to nail the right guy."

Hogarth snorted and looked at his watch.

"Milt, have you been following the case?" Frank asked. He suspected that he had been, that he usually followed Barbara's cases.

"Enough. Open and shut from day one."

"Appearances can be deceiving," Frank said in a musing sort of way. "Fact is, young Travis Morgan was set up from day one, but then the house of cards began to tumble. I don't like what Barbara's up to, too dangerous, but it could be that she's right. If this isn't done now, it won't get done at all. Homeland Security will disappear a few people and the cloud of confusion about what happened to Peel will simply get denser."

"Also, the number of unsolved cases will increase by one," Barbara said. "What's the number today? Nineteen in the county? Make that twenty. At least you were able to nab Daggart's killer. Maybe that's enough for this year."

"Or," Frank said, "you can make this yours. Your operation, your plan, your killer in cuffs."

Barbara had thought that Hogarth couldn't get any redder when he entered the office flushed with cold. Wrong, she told herself. His scalp was cherry red, glowing brighter than before. He ran his hand over the fringe of fading hair that remained and deliberately turned away from her to face Frank. "So tell me what brilliant plan I've come up with this time," he said bitterly.

She leaned back in Frank's chair. Done. He was in. She let Frank fill in the blanks.

The sandwiches were delivered while Frank was talking. They

were passed around and Frank continued his narrative while they all ate.

Hogarth interrupted only once. "You're telling me Morgan tried to pin it on his own kid? A preacher framing his own son? It won't wash. No one's going to buy that." He reached for the second liverwurst on rye.

"They will buy it after tomorrow," Barbara said.

"Just what the hell do you have that will do the trick?" Hogarth demanded.

"I'll show you after lunch."

"Now let me wrap it up," Frank said impatiently. "As soon as the trial ends with a verdict, no matter what the verdict is, Homeland Security will move in and take over. They don't give a damn about a local shooting. They're after bigger fish. We'll give them everything we have, no holdouts, and they'll swear us to secrecy and deal us out of the game. Morgan and Knowland will be in their hands, off limits for any of us. Whether they get squirreled away instantly or, more likely, left in place for now, we won't be able to get near them. So we move first. It's that simple."

A long silence followed, broken by the sound Bailey made opening another can of beer, and Frank's movements when he stood and took the carafe to refill Barbara's cup. Hogarth finished his second sandwich and wiped his mouth on his napkin.

Bailey began to clear the table of paper plates and plastic wear, dumping the remains of lunch into the same box it had arrived in. Finally Hogarth stirred himself.

"If what you've come up with is smack on the button, if there's an arrest for murder, can Homeland Security still move in and take the guy?"

"I don't know," Frank said. "I haven't researched it yet, but I will. I tend to doubt that they would, especially if there's a confession or anything approaching a confession, or if it can be filed as just another local murder case, but it remains to be seen. So far we've been very careful to keep it local with no broader implications."

"Crap!" Hogarth growled. He glared at Barbara. "So what is the magic wand you have to bring them to heel?"

Silently Barbara rose and walked around the desk to pick up her briefcase. She drew out a folder and took it to the table where she placed the scanned pictures of June Morgan's crumpled body on the dirt road where she had been found. She put the other pictures of her mutilated body on the table. "June Morgan," she said.

Bailey took one quick look, then closed his eyes, his face frozen in a grimace. Herbert groaned and leaned forward with his hands covering his face.

"Jesus God!" Hogarth whispered hoarsely.

After a minute, during which no one spoke or moved, Barbara replaced the pictures in the folder and put it back in her briefcase. "It's nearly time to show up in court," she said. "I'll make sure Shelley has come back with the others and we'll head out. Dad, are you coming, or staying here to finish things?'

"I'll be along directly," he said. "We have things to talk about here. You go on."

She put on her coat and went to the door, paused there, and said, "Just keep in mind that I have an eleven o'clock date in the morning. Someone fill me in later."

In the waiting room Ashley was pacing and Mikey and Shelley were at the card table with the jigsaw puzzle. "Nearly time, kiddos," Barbara said, entering. "Potty break, wash hands, touch up lipstick, whatever. Now's the time to get to it."

Ashley studied her hands as if to reassure herself she had them, then, with an obvious effort, she walked to the door to the restroom. Mikey was at her heels.

"Shelley," Barbara said in a low voice, "there's something I want you to do for me if you can find the time."

Shelley's nod was emphatic. "You know I can. What is it?"

"I want the reddest sweater or blouse or some kind of top that you can find in my size, and I'll want it by morning. Can do?"

Shelley nodded soberly. "Bright, bright red. Right?"

"As bright and as red as they come." She added, "I'll fill you in after court adjourns for the day, my office, or maybe Dad's house. We'll figure out where."

Court convened, the jury had not yet reached a decision, and court recessed until five thirty. "I know this is hard," Barbara said to Ashley as they were leaving the courtroom. "Probably the hardest part of all, but there's nothing to be done except bear it. Do you need anything? Do you ever use tranquilizers?"

"Harder on Travis," Ashley said faintly. "I'm all right. There's

Mr. Holloway." She nodded toward a small group of men in conversation near the elevators.

Frank waved and came to join them. "I'm going to hang around for a time," he said. "I'll be back in an hour or so. How are you holding up, Ashley?"

"Fine," she said. "Keep pouring coffee into me and I keep moving." She attempted a smile that was not successful.

"Good enough," Frank said. "I'll see you all later."

As he strolled away, Barbara said, "He can get the walls to talk. He'll find out something about what's going on with the jurors. I'd bet on it, and I'm not a gambler."

Ashley smiled a real smile. It didn't last long, but it was genuine as she said, "You're not a gambler? You could have fooled me."

Everything ends, Barbara thought that afternoon in the waiting room. Bad headache, stiff muscles, nightmares... it didn't matter what it was, it ended sooner or later. Waiting for a jury verdict, the longest day, always ended. That day would end even if it seemed that time had come to a standstill.

Shelley had spread out an assortment of beautiful desserts: petit fours with multicolored glossy icing, golden deep-fried twists, baklava squares, saucer-sized honey cookies, jewel-like tarts with fruit fillings... "I got a lot," Shelley had said, "because whatever we don't eat, Travis will gobble down. Like Christmas candy after a long wait."

Frank returned to say that the jurors had been sending for various pieces of evidence, the gun, pictures of the crime scene, the layout of the residence...

"What does that mean?" Ashley asked.

"It means they're hassling about details," he said easily. "Earning their daily pay."

It meant, Barbara thought, they were concentrating on what Humphrey had called evidence based on facts.

No call came, and at five thirty they were back in the courtroom. No verdict had been reached, admonitions were given to the jurors about talking, and Humphrey beckoned Barbara and Wharton to the sidebar.

"Chambers in fifteen minutes," he said brusquely. "I'm going to talk to the jurors."

When Barbara, back at her table, told Frank she was due in chambers, he nodded and said, "Humphrey won't let them dither too much longer. He's too impatient to let this drag out."

And that was exactly right, she thought when once more she stood in front of Judge Humphrey's desk in his austere chambers.

"I told them to come to a decision in the morning," he said. "They've had more than enough time. If it's a hung jury, I expect you to have a response ready," he said curtly to Wharton.

"Let's talk," Wharton said to Barbara. "A plea bargain. We'll make it easy, a few years and probation."

"In your dreams," Barbara said coldly. "Your two star witnesses are long gone, probably in the Bahamas drinking rum and Cokes, and your other two witnesses are perjurers. You don't have a case."

"This isn't the place or the time," Humphrey said sharply. "Go make your deal somewhere else on your own time. Just be ready to respond if they're hung. There's to be no bickering in the courtroom over this matter. Get it settled."

Walking back to the corridor outside the courtroom, Wharton muttered, "Why doesn't he just resign?" He gave Barbara a sidelong look. "Want to talk about it?"

"Jeff, you know as well as I do that there's nothing to talk about. No deal. No plea bargain. And he won't resign, he'll be carted off one day kicking and screaming to an assisted-living facility where he'll make life such hell for the residents, they'll turn to the Death with Dignity option for relief."

She was not at all surprised when Herbert said cheerfully that his orders were to take her to her father's house. A fine misty rain had started to fall and the temperature had risen above freezing, but was expected to dip overnight, then up to forty the next day, with rain predicted, possibly mixed with freezing rain and snow. Back to normal, Barbara thought with relief.

Bailey was already at Frank's house, and Frank was preparing a tray of snacks when she arrived.

"It won't take long to outline the plan," Frank said. "But it never hurts to have a bite to eat while you're conspiring. Shelley said she'll be along in a little bit. She had shopping to do."

Bailey snorted. "She always has some shopping to do."

"What happened in Humphrey's chambers?" Frank asked.

"He practically said they're hung and he ordered Wharton to

have a new game plan ready if he announces a mistrial. What's up with the jurors?"

"That young computer fellow showed up today in tight jeans and a sweater under a sport coat. They wanted to see the gun, and no doubt wanted to see if he really could conceal it while dressed like that. A good sign, but there are two or three holdouts. Probably think that no one would give false testimony after swearing to God to tell the truth."

This time Barbara snorted.

Minutes later when Shelley arrived with a shopping bag, she nodded to Barbara, and said, "Done."

"Thanks. I'll check it out later," Barbara said. "Bailey's about ready to assign our roles in his game plan."

CHAPTER 41

COLD AND RAINING, Barbara thought with satisfaction the next morning. Her long black raincoat would be perfect, as would her black boots. Court, recess, and then showtime. When they once again went to the waiting room at the office, Ashley slumped down on the sofa, colorless, drained, and Mikey looked as if her vast resources of good cheer had finally dissipated, leaving her nearly as despairing as her sister.

"Coffee," Shelley said. "What a miserable morning. Anyone want to watch the Marx Brothers? *Duck Soup* is just the thing for a morning like this." No one responded. In a minute or two she went to the card table and picked up a puzzle piece. Soon afterward, Mikey joined her.

Barbara stayed with them until a few minutes before ten. "I have a few things to take care of," she said. She went down the corridor to Frank's office. He had already left. In the small bathroom off his office she changed her clothes. Black velvet pants, a bright red silk pullover top with a scoop neck. Two gold chains and gold hoop earrings. Shelley had included a lipstick exactly the same bright red as the pullover.

✦

At ten minutes before eleven a RideSource bus pulled into the parking lot of the Speech and Hearing clinic. Across the street, in the doorway of the Church of Purity and Redemption, Knowland watched with narrowed eyes. The driver of the bus jumped out with an umbrella, trotted to the side of the bus and opened a sliding door. He pulled out a walker, then reached in to give a hand to a young woman. She stepped out and opened another umbrella as he helped an old woman out of the bus, and made sure she was holding the walker handles. The young woman held the umbrella over her as they took a slow, halting walk to the clinic door. The driver, meanwhile, was helping someone else out, this time an elderly man in a shapeless khaki raincoat. He was using a cane. The driver walked at his side, holding his umbrella over him until they reached the door. After the old man entered, the driver ran back to the bus, shook the umbrella and tossed it inside, closed the sliding door and ran to the driver's side to get behind the wheel.

A woman with a child in hand came from the clinic and got in a Prius, drove away. A FedEx truck drove around the curving drive to stop at the clinic door, and again Knowland's eyes narrowed and he grew tense. The driver took a package inside the clinic, returned, left.

At two minutes before eleven Herbert drove up and parked the SUV at the curb and Barbara emerged, carrying an umbrella as well as her briefcase. Herbert got out and they walked together to the church door.

Knowland opened the door wider to admit them. "We came early," he said, "so we could turn on some heat in the kitchen. This way." He scanned the parking lot across the street, then up and down the street before he moved back inside and pulled the door closed.

"One more condition," Barbara said, not moving from the door. "Herbert's going to pat you down and if you have a weapon, he'll hold it until we're through, then he'll give it back to you."

"That's going too far," Knowland said. "Let's get on with it."

"If you don't allow this, we're through and I turn around and leave."

"Oh, for God's sake! Don't be so melodramatic. I have a gun, and I have a permit for it."

"So does he," Barbara said, nodding toward Herbert.

Knowland reached inside his coat, drew out a handgun and gave it to Herbert.

"Now the pat down," Barbara said. "Just in case you forgot one."

Knowland looked ready to erupt but he held out his arms and stood still as Herbert patted him down.

"Next, Morgan," Barbara said.

"Come on," Knowland said harshly. "You really think a minister comes to a meeting with a gun?"

He led the way down the center aisle toward the pulpit. It was a dismal church, cold and uninviting with faint light. There were no decorations, no ornamentation, just wooden pews, pale, plastered walls and high rectangular windows that looked nearly opaque with rain on the outside, fogged inside. Knowland turned when he reached the front of the pews. He went to a side door, opened it, and motioned for Barbara and Herbert to enter.

The kitchen was noticeably warmer, but as dimly lighted as the church hall. Barbara took it in quickly. An electric stove, a stained sink, counter space, a few cabinets, an old refrigerator, and a long table with a flowery plastic tablecloth, a potted plant, and an alarm clock. A few chairs were at the table. Morgan was standing by it.

"He wants to pat you down," Knowland said to Morgan. "Nonsense, but let him do it."

"What are you talking about? Let some heathen touch me? Pat me down? What for?"

"Morgan, just shut up and let's get on with this, or I'm out of here," Barbara said sharply. "I'm due back in court at twelve thirty and I don't have time for any of your bullshit. He pats you down, or I leave. It's that simple."

"Do it," Knowland snapped at Herbert.

Herbert was expressionless as he efficiently patted down Morgan, who stood quivering with outrage. Done with Morgan, Herbert picked up a raincoat draped over a chair and examined it, then tossed it back to the chair. Returning to Barbara's side, he said, "He's clean."

She handed him her umbrella and nodded toward the door. "Wait for me out there."

After he left, she crossed the kitchen to the table. "Now we're ready to talk."

"Not quite," Knowland said. "Let me have a look in the briefcase, and why don't you take off that coat."

She handed over the briefcase and took off her coat. Morgan's eyes bulged at the red top and gold chains. "Satan's handmaiden," he said hoarsely. "Scarlet woman, Whore of Babylon. Evil creature of hell… "

"Can't you shut him up?" Barbara demanded. "And, no, I'm not wired, if that's your next thought." She lifted the pullover top to reveal her midriff and turned to expose her back.

Morgan was muttering curses, or prayers, it was hard to tell. His voice was hoarse, the words inarticulate.

"Enough show and tell," Barbara said after Knowland returned her briefcase. She reached inside it and brought out the folder. She spread out the scanned pictures and stepped back. "That's what I have. I imagine you recognize your handiwork, Knowland. And you," she said furiously to Morgan, "did you stand by and watch him mutilate your child? Did you act as his surgical nurse, hand him the scalpel, the sutures, the bandages?"

"She was corrupted! Fornication is a mortal sin!" Morgan cried. "I purified her. By the blade, the stone, by fire, shall they be purified. It was my duty to purify her, to save her soul!'

"Your daughter died a virgin! You had that done to a virgin girl."

"You lie! God acted! He judged her! It was His will that she die by stone! He threw her off a cliff to purify her."

"She jumped, Morgan! She knew what her future would have been, and she chose to jump." She turned to Knowland. "I have the original photographs in my safe deposit box, along with an account of everything I know about her, her death, her virginity. That's what I have. And it's enough to destroy both of you. There will be questions about the woman he tried to pass off as his daughter. Was she starved to death? Where is the school where June Morgan was said to have been for two years? Why was her body found on that dirt road in April? There will be questions and they will reopen the whole damn case surrounding Peel's death. My questions during the trial will take on new meaning and demand real answers. Did he split the rake-off money with you? Is it all stashed away in his safe deposit box? In a Cayman Island account? What was your share? Who was Peel talking to that night? You? Or him?'

"What do you want?" Knowland demanded harshly.

"I want one hundred thousand dollars. In return you get the originals and my notes."

"You're out of your mind. We don't have that kind of money laying around."

"He's been skimming the cream for years! Don't tell me you don't have it."

"That's a lie," Morgan cried. "They told me to put some aside for later, for when I retire. They said I should!"

"You're a fool!" Barbara said contemptuously. "A tool to be used until you outlived your usefulness. They set you up from day one. Sure, put money aside for you golden years, until the IRS got a tip, or your own bookkeeper found out. They didn't care how crazy you are, how insane your rants are. The crazier the better because no one will pay any attention to you. Just another crazy voice in the wilderness, howling to the jackals and owls. That's what you've been to them. Serving their cause, passing along their message, as disposable as a used Kleenex as soon as you blundered too much. And you've blundered too much. You're been cut off, the spigot's gone dry. You're on your own to howl in the wind. You pitiful little worm, framing your own son, mutilating your own daughter, killing your handyman, and finally killing your faithful bookkeeper, Joseph Peel. Your lies caught up with you and you're finished. I want mine before you clean out your safe deposit box and run."

She raked him up and down with a merciless look and said icily, "That's it, isn't it? You knew Peel was a good man, a man with a conscience, and one day his conscience would make him finish what he started with Daggart. He would have exposed you as a common thief, stealing from your own church."

"He wouldn't listen," Morgan whispered. "I asked him to pray with me, to understand. The devil was in him." His voice rose and he shouted, "The devil was in him! He succumbed to Satan. He would have ruined me! Satan wants to destroy me and my church. That's Satan's plan, to destroy me and my church! And now he's sent you to do his will!"

"Why don't you put a cork in him?" Barbara said to Knowland. She stepped to the table, picked up the pictures, and took them to the sink where she pulled a lighter from her pocket and set them on fire and let the flaming paper and ash fall into the sink.

She looked at her watch, put her raincoat on, and started to walk to the door. "You have until Friday morning to come up with the money. If I haven't heard that you have it in cash by noon Friday, I'll go to the district attorney with what I have. Knowland, understand this, I can prove every word I've said here. You know as well as I do that the nutcase here is finished. He's on his own. No more monthly donations. No more cash for his own tidy pot. The stooge is done. Lead him by the hand to the safe deposit box, or else hit your own savings account. I don't care where it comes from."

She gave him the same kind of contemptuous look she had cast on Morgan. "Maybe you can salvage something for yourself. Give them Morgan. You were dedicated, and you lied about being with him when Travis was admitted to the house. Maybe you can make a deal if you give them enough. And I don't give a shit how that works out. Just get my one hundred thousand by Friday morning."

"No!" Morgan yelled. "No!" He ran to the counter by the sink and yanked open a drawer, pulled out a Colt .45. "Stop right there!" he cried. "Don't take another step."

Knowland rushed to him before he had time to cock the gun. He tried to wrench it from Morgan's hand. "You goddamn fool!"

"Let go of me! I'll take care of her! I took care of Peel and I can take care of her! She doesn't know everything. She didn't know there were two of them. She doesn't know anything. I can finish this right now. She came here to burn down my church! You heard her. There are the ashes of the fire she started. She was going to burn down my church. You saw her! She hates the church, everything I stand for, she threatened me, and I had to do it! God wants me to give His message to the world and she—"

Barbara backed up two steps closer to the door. Knowland was holding Morgan's arm, trying to take the gun away with the other, and Morgan was screeching, the gun pointing one way then another. She took another step backward and the door flew open and hit the wall with a thunderous bang. Herbert stood in the doorway holding his own gun.

"Better put the gun down, or I might get a mite nervous and start shooting before I can stop myself," Herbert said.

The struggle at the sink came to a dead stop. Morgan's gaze was riveted on the gun Herbert was holding. Knowland wrested the gun away from him and put it on the counter by the sink.

"Put Knowland's gun on the counter nearest the door," Barbara said, "and then let's get the hell out of here!"

In the RideSource bus across the street, Frank felt Hogarth's touch on his arm and heard him say, "She's out of there. Relax." He felt as if he might pass out and sucked in one long breath after another. "I'm okay," he mumbled after a moment. "It's okay."

"Yeah," Hogarth said. "Sure it is. Let's listen."

The bus was crowded. Bailey was at a computer, another man wearing earphones at another one, two plainclothes detectives nearby, Hogarth and Frank on stools. A speaker was on, a green light blinking steadily, and from inside the church kitchen everyone in the bus could hear Morgan's shrill voice.

"You should have shot them both when they came in. She brought a killer with her, an armed man with a gun, threatening you. You shouldn't have let him take your gun. That's why I hid mine, so he wouldn't take it. You should have ended it right there and then."

"For God's sake, just shut up and let me think."

"What are you doing? What's that?"

"It's a tape recorder. I got every word. Now be quiet."

"She can't have the money! I won't let that whore enrich herself with my money! I earned it and I won't let her have it."

"Shut the fuck up and go sit down! She isn't going to get a penny."

"She'll go to the police. Even if she gives us the pictures, she'll go to the police. You can't trust her!"

"If you don't shut your mouth I'm going to shut it for you! Just sit down and let me think!"

There was a scuffling sound, a chair being dragged on a wooden floor, then a grunt. "Stay down and don't say another word!" Knowland said in a rasping voice. "She isn't going to get your money. We'll swap what she has for my tape. A little editing and it's clear she came here to shake you down. She'd be disbarred if that came to light. Just an even swap."

"That's not enough! She knows things! She's like Peel, she'll tell others, an investigation. Like she said, questions. Too many questions. We have to kill her. You should have let me do it. What are you doing?"

There was the sound of running water. "I'm washing ashes down the drain. We don't want anyone wondering what went on here. And I'm turning the heat off again. What time does your thing start tonight? Who gets here first, when?"

"Seven thirty. What difference does it make?"

There was silence, the sound of footsteps. Then Morgan was

speaking again, almost whining. "You know we have to get rid of her. We can't risk it. You should have let me do it. We could have made it look good this time. You said it would work before, but it didn't. This time we'll be careful, take our time. No questions."

"It would have worked if that moron hadn't screwed up. Tony blew it."

"But we can fix things this time. Tell her to come back and talk. We can fix it this time."

"I'll get rid of her," Knowland said harshly. "But no more shooting, no more beatings. An accident. Hit and run, or she'll lose control of her car on a coast road. An accident, but not too soon. Too much suspicion already. We can't have more suspicions raised. We can't have anyone poking around in Pendleton."

There was another prolonged silence, then the sound of something breaking.

"What are you doing? Why did you do that?"

"The clock was a little slow," Knowland said. "I had to reset the time. It's now one forty-five. Forever one forty-five. It slipped and broke, unfortunately."

There was the sound of paper rustling.

"What's that?" Morgan asked.

"You remember a few years ago, one of your flock was crying, admitted to using birth control pills? Remember? You told her she had to confess in front of the congregation, confess her sin and plead for mercy. Remember?'

"She did sin! She said so. She was taking pills. She was trying to find salvation. She was repentant, begging for mercy. She wanted me to tell her what to say, how to get in God's good graces again."

"This is what you told her to say in front of everyone. You wrote it out for her to read. *'I'm sorry. I sinned and I beg God to forgive me.'*"

"You have that? Why? It was years ago."

"Yes. And I've carefully preserved it in its own little padded envelope for the day it would come in handy, as I knew it would. After Daggart came to light, I began to carry it with me. I'm afraid Holloway nailed it. You're washed up, disposable. You've become a liability. We knew it was coming, just not when. This closes things. No more questions, no more prying, just closure." He laughed, a startling sound, quickly cut off. "You know the biggest irony of all? You never got around to writing a will, and your son, Travis Morgan, will be your heir."

"What are you talking about? I'm leaving! Get your hand off me!"

"Sit still. My story is that we came here to meet Holloway and she tried to talk you into helping your son, and you refused. After she left, you were filled with remorse and began to cry and pray, and at that time you confessed to me that you pulled the trigger, you killed Peel. I was stunned and left you here crying and praying to God to forgive you. I left at five minutes before twelve, and went to a café for coffee. I should get there by twelve, I think."

Hogarth yelled, "Get in there, now!" The two detectives in the bus were out almost instantly. Pulling on his jacket, Hogarth ran after them. Two more detectives emerged from parked cars and they all ran to the church. Before any of them reached the door, there was a gunshot.

Frank closed his eyes and waited, listening. The sound of the church door flying open, banging against the wall, running footsteps, another door banging open, a shout, "Drop it and put your hands on your head!"

Slowly Frank rose and put on his overcoat.

CHAPTER 42

BARBARA BARELY HAD time to change back into her court suit, toss her scarlet-woman clothes onto Frank's sofa, and hurry to the waiting room.

"Time to go," she said. Shelley was examining her anxiously and she nodded and held up her thumb and forefinger in the okay sign. "Hang in there, Ashley," she said. "Just a little while longer."

The rain had eased considerably and was little more than a mist when they went out to the SUV. In the courthouse corridor, as they made their way to the courtroom, Barbara saw Wharton talking with two other men, one of them the district attorney.

Travis was brought in, the jury seated, and seconds before Judge Humphrey appeared, Wharton slipped into place at his table.

The judge addressed the foreman of the jury. "Have you reached a decision?"

Before the foreman spoke, Wharton rose and said, "Your Honor, the state has a statement to make."

Humphrey looked furious when he turned to face Wharton. "What is it, counselor?"

"The state withdraws all charges against Travis Morgan at this time."

Barbara felt a jolt, and she heard Travis gasp. From behind her, she heard Ashley make a soft moaning sound. Travis clutched her arm. "Wait," she said. Judge Humphrey was glaring at Wharton and beckoned him and her to the sidebar.

"What is the meaning of this? Are you out of your mind? Explain yourself."

"Your Honor, minutes ago I learned that Mr. Morgan confessed to the murder of Joseph Peel, and that Dr. Knowland shot him dead. I don't have any more details, just those two basic facts, which have been verified. We withdraw our charges based on that information."

Barbara felt a second jolt with his words. When Judge Humphrey turned his glare to her and said, "Did you know about this?" she could only shake her head.

"You've turned this entire proceeding into a fiasco," Humphrey said to Wharton angrily. "You've wasted this court's time, the jurors' time. This trial is over. Take your seats."

When they were back at their tables, Judge Humphrey rapped his gavel and turned to the jury. "Ladies and gentlemen, thank you for your participation in this trial. Since the state has withdrawn all charges against Travis Morgan, you are now relieved of your duties and you are free to leave." He turned to Travis then. "Mr. Morgan, you are free to leave." He banged his gavel and announced, "This case is dismissed. Court is adjourned."

He wasn't even out of sight when the courtroom erupted. Two reporters rushed to Barbara, and she said, "Ask Wharton. I don't know anything."

"Barbara, what happened? Why is it over?" Travis asked hoarsely as Ashley ran to him and threw her arms around him. Keeping her voice low, Barbara said, "Wharton said that Arlie Morgan confessed that he killed Peel, and he said that Knowland shot Morgan and killed him. That's all I know."

"Oh, my God!" Ashley gasped. "He's dead?"

Frank came to the group. "I want you folks to go with Alan, back to the apartment. Travis is going to want a bath and a change of clothes, some decent food to eat. As soon as we know more, we'll come around. Go now, before you're swamped with reporters."

He looked at Barbara. "I'll see that they get out and come back for you and Shelley. No one has a comment, no one. It's the DA's game now."

She nodded and watched him take Ashley's arm with one hand and Travis's with the other and propel them and Mikey from the courtroom.

"Barbara, what happened?" Shelley asked, wide eyed with disbelief.

"You heard what I told them? Knowland killed Morgan and he confessed to shooting Peel. It happened after I left them. I don't know what was said after I took off. And, Shelley, I don't care. I won't celebrate anyone's death but, God, I am glad he's gone."

The reporters had left Wharton to hurry out after Frank, and now Wharton came to her table. "I hope with every cell in my body that I never have to try a case in his court again. You work a good case, Barbara. For your sake I hope you never have to go up before him again, either." He held out his hand and they shook.

"Is that really all you know about what happened?" she asked.

"Right now it is. Why do I suspect that you know something about it that I don't know?"

"You have the mind of a prosecutor. That's why."

"I'm out of here before the jurors come demanding answers," he said. "Any and all statements will come from the office. I think I'm due a few days off." He walked away swiftly.

"Let's go out to the corridor to wait," Barbara said to Shelley. "He's right, the jurors will want to know what happened and my lips are sealed."

In the broad corridor, Shelley touched her arm and said, "Look."

The reporters evidently had been given the bum's rush by Frank, and they were talking to several of the jurors. Barbara and Shelley hurried in the opposite direction and met Frank on his way to them.

Frank had Herbert take them to the Electric Station where he had a reservation for lunch. "You too," he told Herbert when they arrived. They were led to a booth, left alone to study the menu, and then ordered with little or no talk. Only after drinks had been brought did Frank tell them what had happened after Barbara and Herbert left the church. "Bailey will bring a tape around for you to listen to," he said, "but here it is in a nutshell. He was still holding the gun, a mate to the Colt Morgan used on Peel. Knowland was wiping off his prints when they burst in on him. The important thing is that you, Bobby, set it all up so that only money will be considered as motive. Good work, but let's not do anything like that ever again."

"Amen," she said fervently.

They became silent as their waiter brought lunches. After he was gone again, Shelley asked, "Do you think they will suspect how much more you uncovered?"

"I don't think so. I made it pretty clear that I was only interested in sharing Morgan's stolen money."

"Speaking of which," Frank said, "it appears that Travis is his one and only heir. There's no way on earth to prove how money got into Morgan's safe deposit box, not unless his benefactor comes forward, and in my considered opinion, I tend to doubt that anyone will do that."

"He probably won't take it," Barbara said.

"I'll talk him into it," Frank said. "The young man needs an education and it's going to be costly. Let the leader of the militia pay for it, and who knows, Travis might turn out to be their number one enemy in due time."

"Maybe he'll want to be a lawyer," Herbert said. "Seeing as how much he owes you two, I mean."

"He won't be a corporate attorney," Frank said complacently.

Looking at him, listening, Barbara thought, *Good heavens, he has himself a protégé*! She speared another shrimp from her salad and hoped she was right about that. Her father was a great teacher. "Dad," she asked then, "how split was the jury?"

"Two holdouts," he said. "Hung, mistrial, but this is better. They wouldn't have charged him again, but Travis would have had a cloud hanging over him the rest of his life."

Barbara agreed, better this way.

"I guess you folks won't be needing me much longer," Herbert said with a woebegone expression.

"Just another day or two," Frank admitted. "Long enough for Knowland to talk to his attorney and get the word passed that all Barbara knows is the money angle, that she's no threat to anyone."

After a moment, Barbara said, "So Kyle and others gather around and we give them all we have, convince them that Knowland thinks all we have is the money angle, and hope they don't screw things up down the line."

"That's it," Frank said. "Milt's coming over to lay it out for them, the charges against Knowland, how limited the investigation was, is, and will be. And they go away, and we never hear from them again until there's a splash of news on a late Friday night." He eyed Barbara soberly and said, "It could become a little hairy, dealing with them, defending not coming forward sooner with that list of bullet-marked individuals, things like that."

She waved her hand. "Anyone who can go to trial in Humphrey's court can deal with the likes of Kyle and company. I have to talk to Ashley and Travis. I'll give them the money version, too, of course. Not a word about June, militias, hit men, just greed and skimming cream off the top of the milk." She looked at her watch. "What time do you expect the grilling to start?"

Frank said, "If you mean by Kyle and his crew, four, at the office."

"That gives me time to see Ashley and Travis. I'm going to urge them to get back up to Portland as soon as they can gather up their stuff. Time for Travis to start building a new life, and for Mikey to go back to Denver. Ashley's going to need a little time before she's ready to return to work, I imagine, but she should do it as soon as she can."

Travis, his mother, and his aunt were all incoherent in their relief and gratitude, with tears and sudden laughter, many hugs and kisses, promises to keep in touch, to visit…

Barbara arrived at her office minutes after leaving them and hurriedly gathered all the material to be delivered to Homeland Security. She did not go to her bank to get the photographs of June Morgan's mutilated body. The pictures of her crumpled body on the side of the road and her schoolgirl pictures were enough. The others would stay buried forever. At fifteen minutes before four she entered Frank's office. He was on the sofa with his feet on the coffee table.

"You're a sight," she said. "Tired?"

"Thinking. There's a lot of cleanup work to do. Nina Atkinson. I'll take the train up to Seattle later this week and give her copies of everything we took away, along with the personal things. I suppose we'll talk about how she should handle the Homeland Security people when they come knocking on her door."

"And I have to see Wanda Haviland in Portland, and have a little talk with Derek Peel. All anyone's to know, besides Nina, is the money angle. It's enough."

"More than enough," he said.

When Patsy tapped on the door to say *that* man was there, Frank said bring him on in. He didn't shift from his place on the sofa with his feet on the table. At the opposite end of the sofa Barbara sat with her feet on the table also.

"Have a seat, Milt," Frank said when Hogarth entered. "Plenty of room on the table for a couple more feet."

"Knowland hasn't said a word, tighter than a spoiled clam," Hogarth said, taking off his heavy jacket. "He'll lawyer up and we'll go on from there. Good thinking to bug the whole damn church," he said to Barbara. "What they said after you left is icing on the cake." He looked hesitant then. "Frank, more than likely they'll invite me to go away after we talk about the Knowland business. You know, the need-to-know bullshit."

"One of these cold evenings when you're free, why don't you drop in for dinner with me. Just two old friends having a little chat."

Hogarth grunted and sat in an easy chair.

"I just don't get it," Barbara said. "Even if they have a couple hundred guys armed to the teeth, do they really think they can take down the government?"

Hogarth shifted in his chair and found that his fingernails needed close inspection. "Word is," he said without looking up, "that if you have enough coordinated attacks, a bridge or two, a railroad, maybe a shopping center, hits on the Internet, a trucking company, cuts in supply lines, stuff like that, panic sets in. Martial law follows."

Barbara caught in her breath. "A police state!" she whispered.

Patsy tapped on the door at that moment to announce that they had arrived. It was four o'clock.

Kyle and Sunderland had brought two or three others with them. Barbara paused at the door to the conference room, drew in a breath, then entered. Now it begins, she thought.

It was ten minutes after seven when Kyle stood and one of his aides closed a tape recorder. Sunderland pocketed his own tape recorder and his aide began packing up all the material Barbara had collected over the past months. Everyone seemed satisfied. They shook hands all around and the government men put on overcoats and left.

Back in Frank's office Barbara said, "We won't hear another word from them, will we?"

"Probably not. And that suits me just fine."

"Me too. I'm totally wiped out, and I know you must be, too. Come home with me. Herbert put on chili this morning in the slow cooker thing of his. Come have chili with us."

They put on coats, she linked her arm with his and they walked down the long corridor to the elevator, where Herbert was waiting to take them home.

About The Author

Kate Wilhelm's first short story, "The Pint-Sized Genie," was published in *Fantastic Stories* in 1956. Her first novel, *More Bitter Than Death*, a mystery, was published in 1963. Over the span of her career, her writing has crossed over the genres of science fiction, speculative fiction, fantasy and magical realism, psychological suspense, mimetic, comic, family sagas, a multimedia stage production, and radio plays. Her works have been adapted for television, theater, and movies in the United States, England, and Germany. Wilhelm's novels and stories have been translated to more than a dozen languages. She has contributed to *Redbook*, *Quark*, *Orbit*, *The Magazine of Fantasy & Science Fiction*, *Locus*, *Amazing*, *Asimov's Science Fiction*, *Ellery Queen's Mysteries*, *Fantastic Stories*, *Omni* and many others.

Kate and her husband, Damon Knight (1922-2002), also provided invaluable assistance to numerous other writers over the years. Their teaching careers covered a span of several decades, and hundreds of students. Kate and Damon helped to establish the Clarion Writer's Workshop and the Milford Writer's Conference.

Kate Wilhelm lives in Eugene, Oregon.

CPSIA information can be obtained at www.ICGtesting.com
Printed in the USA
BVOW05*1750090214

344406BV00002B/12/P